THE SALES PIT

PROFESSIONAL SPORTS SALES:

THE ULTIMATE DREAM JOB - UNTIL IT WASN'T....

A NOVEL BY

CHRIS MUSTAKAS

CONTENT WARNING:

This book discusses topics related to men's mental health, including depression, anxiety, dark thoughts, and suicidal ideation. Some readers may find these themes distressing or triggering. If you are struggling, please consider seeking support from a trusted friend, family member, or mental health professional. You are not alone—help is available. For immediate assistance, please reach out to a local crisis helpline or support service. In Canada, you can contact Talk Suicide Canada at 1-833-456-4566. In the U.S., the Suicide & Crisis Lifeline is available at 988.

Dedications

To my children, Kallianna and Theodore. I hope it shows you the importance of persistence and staying committed to your dreams, even when the journey becomes challenging. Life will present obstacles that may test your resolve, break your spirit, or lead you down unexpected paths. Remember that every step you take—no matter how small—brings you closer to your goals. Embrace setbacks as learning opportunities that can fuel your determination. Keep pushing forward with your hearts full of passion and your minds focused on your aspirations, and you'll get there. Always believe in yourselves and never underestimate the power of perseverance. I believe in you both, and I know you will accomplish amazing things.

Love always, Daddy

Author Acknowledgements

The stories in this book began as scripts—scenes scribbled in the margins of memory starting in 2012. The Office meets Workaholics meets Entourage meets...Hockey Night in Canada. Eight episodes were written. Then they sat, waiting. For years, I didn't have the energy or clarity to return to them. But during the quiet and chaos of the COVID-19 pandemic, while the world slowed down, I opened the folder originally labeled *The Pit* and found something still alive. I rewrote some of it. Then I lost my spark again. But on January 7th, 2025, I found my spark. I was visiting a former client whose Undifferentiated Pleomorphic Sarcoma (UPS), a rare and aggressive form of cancer, had returned, and gave him months to live.

At one point, I shared that I had been writing a book for years but hadn't touched it since 2021. What he said next stayed with me: "Chris, I wish I had written more when I had the chance. My story's going to die with me. Your story needs to be shared, otherwise it will be buried with you."

That conversation changed me. It gave me the push I needed to start writing again. From that day until February 13th, I poured myself into completing The Sales Pit. This time, not as a sitcom, but as a story of redefining strength in men's mental health. I gave him updates via Facebook Messenger and he even asked to read it when it was finished. I sent him snippets throughout the process.

"You should be proud of what you've written. Knowing you, it will be a great read. Keep up the good work, my friend."

I would never hear from him again. Jacques passed away on March 5th at the age of 61 after a courageous battle with cancer. Thank you for your encouragement, Jacques. May your memory be eternal.

To my original beta readers

To friends and family who said they'd read it back in 2021 but never quite got around to it—thank you. Your good intentions and ghosted PDFs were surprisingly motivating. That silence became fuel. It pushed me to dig deeper, write harder, and create something even better than I had imagined—something I *knew* you'd want to read... eventually. Here's your chance!

To those who *did* read *The Sales Pit* in 2025

Your feedback, insight, and support made this book what it is. Thank you for putting up with horrendous formatting, late-night text rants, and endless "can I run a passage by you?" messages. Jen, Maria, Darren, Chris, Dustin and Leesa, you encouraged me through bouts of imposter syndrome and helped me push past creative blocks. I am so grateful.

To my partner, Jennifer Daley

You allowed me the privilege of practicing narration aloud as we drifted to sleep. You were my soundboard, my safe space, and my greatest cheerleader. Thank you for letting me be vulnerable, process trauma, and break down when I needed to—without ever making me feel judged. Your love, patience, and quiet strength made all the difference. This book may be my story on paper, but so much of it was your reality. All my love. xoxpxox

To my sister, Maria Mustakas

Your strength and perseverance continue to inspire me. I can't fully express how much I admire you, but I'll keep trying.

To my friend, Darren Wiebe

Your journey—and the honest conversations we've had—have shaped me more than you know. You were the first to read this cover to cover, and so much of the character growth in this book came from our chats. Thank you for always keeping me accountable to honest, open communication.

To my former Sales Manager and friend, Chris Atack

You were the mentor I needed. You gave me the freedom to succeed—and the space to fail fast and learn. We pitched ideas that were often too ahead of their time, but you always listened. From work to life to music, our conversations evolved, and your support never wavered. I was proud to share the final draft with you first. Thank you, Chris.

To Dustin SanVido

You were always pushing the envelope—whether it was at work, in the gym, or in the mosh pit at a Queens of the Stone Age show. You've inspired me to keep leveling up, and your energy is in every part of this.

To Leesa Kelly

Thank you for your insight, your honesty, and for sharing a woman's perspective on some of the difficult themes in this book. It made a difference.

To my colleagues, far and wide

Some of you are still in the game. Some, like me, have found new paths. We all remember the grind, the victories, and the sacrifices. We carried a weight few others could see. I'm thankful for those who bore it with me—because only we know what it meant to stand together. This book is for you:

CA, WillyStyles, Churchy, Army, BD, DJU, CZ, Choy, Harding, GB, Bear, Dash, Weirsy, MC, MM, ScottyMac, Matt B, Boothy, Murph, KM, EK, KMac, MAP, TB, KR, DL & CN, JO, JK, CL, SV, TR, Cy, JL, CH, CM, CD, MB and others.

Specifically,

To WillyStyles

Arguably the most passionate Account Manager I ever met. You taught me the ropes, gave me the arena tour, and helped me find my feet. A lot of your advice lives in these pages.

To Churchy

You were a brother when I needed one most. We shared laughs, long talks, and tough times—especially when we lived together during those rough patches. I love you, man. Let's catch up more often.

To Army

You were the wise, battle-tested veteran—the heartbeat of the sales pit. Thank you for the stories, the sarcasm, the support, and the quiet leadership. I'll always respect and admire you.

To BD

You taught me confidence. You taught me sales. You taught me how to tie a proper double Windsor. You also made me buy the first round of drinks... as an unpaid intern the night before Good Friday my first season. And you paid your share too. You're still one of the best assets the team has.

To Matt Corluka

In 2012, we started writing *The Pit*. Those characters and stories helped us laugh—and helped us heal. The project sat dormant while I worked through PTSD and burnout. But you always encouraged me to write, especially when we reconnected in LA in 2022. Thank you for believing in this.

To my favourite clients

You allowed me to build authentic relationships between the team and our season ticket holders.

Brighton, Lisa & Danny C, Jeff and Joann B, Ian S, Nathan and Ange K, Jim B, Greg and David S, Dave R, Jonathan R,

Borden H, Bill K, Kent and Eva B, Earl D, Suzanne & Jacques B—it was an honour. Thank you.

To my parents

You've always stood by me. Supported me without question. Showed me what unconditional love and family truly mean. I didn't ask you to be beta readers, mostly because I need you to buy *a lot* of copies and help me hit the bestseller list. (Thanks in advance!) I know there are dark moments, colourful language, and maybe a few... embellished adventures. Please rest assured—some of those stories are fictional. Probably. Maybe. Who's to say?

To my medical and support team

You saved my life in more ways than one. You saw me at my lowest, believed in my ability to heal, and never gave up on me.

Dr. Bill M., Dr. Luis O., Dr. Bruno N., Debra-Lynn M.—thank you for your guidance, your compassion, and your refusal to let me go numb. I'm still here. This book is, in part, because of you.

To Katie

You lived through much of this in real time with me. You saw the weight of it all before it became words on a page. You experienced the burnout, the frustration, the jaded sarcasm, and the version of me that struggled to be present. I'm sorry for how that affected you.

To Robaire Nadeau:

Thank you for the impromptu legal advice and for inspiring me with your own drive and determination. It's been a pleasure working with you on your own passion project, State of Mind, Magic for the Intelligent Mind. You are North America's premier Mentalist! Onwards and upwards!

To J. Paul Nadeau, Cierra Campeau, and Jackie Mustakas:

Thank you for sharing your creative processes and writing experiences as authors and international bestsellers. I appreciate the helpful tips and encouragement. Thank you for connecting me with my formatter, Paul!

To my production team, Paige Lawson and Oprah Milan:

Thank you for your expertise and guidance in bringing the pages of The Sales Pit to life. Having never worked with an editor or formatter before, you were always available and played a crucial role in producing this amazing book.

And finally—

Please, if you have questions about the nature of this book, I would genuinely appreciate if you asked me directly. This story is personal. While inspired by real experiences, it is *not* an exposé. It wouldn't be fair—or accurate—to assume that every outrageous story, workplace failure, or HR nightmare ties back to one employer or person. Please do not assume anything. Please do not ask current or former employees for comments; this is not their story.

If you've ever worked in sports, in sales, or really, in any office environment—you'll know what I mean when you read this book.

My time in the industry came long before we began holding toxic workplaces to account. Before *#MeToo*. Before the *Do It For Daron (DIFD)* movement. Before mental health was part of the conversation. The world is different now—and in most ways, for the better.

We can't rewrite the past. But we can learn from it, grow from it, and yes—playfully laugh at the absurdity of what we endured together. Because as CZ once said, *"You really can't make this shit up."*

Another Disclaimer

This book is based on my personal experiences, observations, and real events. However, certain details, characters, and events have been altered, reimagined, or combined for storytelling purposes. Creative liberties have been taken to enhance the narrative, and some characters and situations are fictionalized and exaggerated for entertainment.

Any similarities to actual persons, living or deceased, or real places are purely coincidental and should not be interpreted as fact. The views and opinions expressed in this book are my own and do not necessarily reflect those of any individuals, organizations, or entities.

This is an example of multiple sales cultures all over the world and in pretty much any discipline. This book is not intended to be viewed as a definitive account of any event or person, and readers should approach it as a work of creative nonfiction rather than a documentary record.

Table of Contents

Macho Man Randy Savage
on 'Macho Men'

"It's ok for macho men to show every emotion available. I've cried a thousand times. I'm going to some more. But – but I've soared with the eagles, and I've slithered with the snakes, and I've been everywhere in between. I'm gonna tell you something right now: there's one guarantee in life and that there are no guarantees. Yeah, and understand this. Nobody likes a quitter, nobody said life was easy. So if you get knocked down, you take the standing eight count, you get back up, and you fight again. That's the Macho Mania, dig it!"

~ Macho Man Randy Savage, on The Arsenio Hall Show, 1992

CHAPTER 1

"The Pandemic and Virtual Pit Beers"

It was 7:58 p.m. on April 21, 2021, and Jay Laroque was sitting at his kitchen table, nervously watching the seconds tick by. He was anticipating the first guests to join the video call he had arranged. At 28, Jay had mastered the art of living his best life: conquering NHL 2021 on his PS5 and indulging in his fair share of weed while meticulously avoiding adulting.

This was his eighth season with the team—a solid entry on a résumé where he'd already achieved what many only dreamed of. He had landed a spot on the inside sales team while his college diploma in business management was still warm from the printer. After demonstrating some serious hustle in those initial months, he'd been promoted to account manager.

Jay was soft-spoken, kind, and painfully shy, traits he masked well with his "suit of armour" that consisted of V-neck T-shirts that flirted with the concept of professionalism, a blazer that screamed, "I promise I own real pants," and skinny dress pants that made him feel more stylish than functional.

Back in the day, he was the go-to guy whenever one of his female friends decided to move. "Hey, Jay! Can you help lift this sofa?" Yes, for the longest time he was the Friendzone king, especially he thought when it came to Kelly, the fiery receptionist. He once had a secret crush on her that was so massive it could have had its own postal code. While he'd never confess his feelings to anyone, the mere mention of Kelly, even in passing or in the break room, could set off a cascade of crimson waves across his neck and ears. It was as if someone had installed a built-in thermometer for his romantic despair, and everyone seemed to enjoy taking note of it. With each blush, Jay's dating history—or the distinct lack thereof—became a painfully obvious topic of office gossip.

"Alright, time to impress," he muttered, adjusting his blazer one last time as if it held all the secrets to women.

Everyone in the office had been rooting for Jay, especially his closest friend and former housemate, Shane Sanders. Shane, a sharply dressed and quick-witted thirty-two-year-old, had two missions in life: to see his "baby boy" Jay finally get lucky and, to make as much money as possible. Known for his charm and cheekiness, Shane would have been cancelled had cancel culture existed back then, as Shane was a notorious womanizer. He once kept a meticulously organized journal of his exploits, ranking and summarizing each of his sexual conquests in explicit detail. At the back lay a cheeky "hot or not" scribbled list featuring every woman aged 20 to 48 he'd ever slept with, which he dubbed his "wheelhouse."

Strangely, this sacred volume was stashed haphazardly in the middle drawer of his cubicle desk, buried beneath a mountain of expense reports. To Shane, it was a map of his conquests. The cover of his locked journal had a photo of Kevin Garnett of the Boston Celtics the year they won the NBA title. While many people resonated with a poster of a cat hanging from a wire with the words 'Hang in there, baby', the photo of Kevin Garnett acted like Shane's secret motivational poster and a constant reminder that "anything is possible."

If Shane were to be evaluated by a psychologist, he'd learn that the lenses for which he saw his world through, or, his primary schema, was that he had unreasonably high expectations—of himself and everyone around him. It meant he often operated under a deeply ingrained belief that stressed achievement, near-impossible perfectionism, and meeting exceptionally high expectations. While he rarely spoke about his past, Shane's critical inner voice was likely the result of the conditional love or praise tied to achievement from his parents. Most of his childhood was in an environment where mistakes were criticized, and there was little time for anything but the best. Unfortunately, there was also little time for Shane and his brother from their self-absorbed parents.

Not surprisingly, Shane felt like he always had to be on and in control. His feelings of inadequacy only fuelled the hidden fear and anxiety within because he could rarely allow himself to be vulnerable, slow down, or even feel satisfied with himself. It was a wonder how Shane hadn't already burnt himself out maintaining such high standards, given how emotionally and physically exhausting it was on him. At least nobody knew if he was burnt out because he never would admit it.

Nevertheless, Shane had a knack for sidestepping anyone or anything that threatened his financial success, making him the quintessential sales team alpha male. He was in his twelfth season with the crew, only taking a shocking but brief hiatus of four months back in 2015 to become a territory manager for a quirky, robotics start-up. The now-defunct company, which touted itself as the worldwide leader in commercial robots, had no manufacturing facility or a single robot sale. During Shane's interview, he was fed bold statements like 'Take a look at that parking lot, every one of those cars represents a robot you are going to sell this year, Shane.' Success was a sure thing to the CEO, and that was enough to lure Shane. He lasted a week. It was a learning experience for Shane, to say the least. Not surprisingly, the company collapsed in 2016, about a year after burning through all of their investments chasing shiny object after shiny object.

While he never admitted a mistake, Shane humbly pleaded for his old position. Thankfully his track record of sales was his legacy and it was an easy management decision to welcome him back. Since then, he had led the sales team in new sales every season, basking in the spotlight and regularly employing shock-and-awe tactics to keep everyone entertained—even if it often made them squirm in discomfort. His blend of controversial opinions and self-deprecation was a recipe for laughter if not mild existential crises.

It was now 8:04 p.m., and the Zoom call was filling up with a familiar cast of characters. Friends and colleagues logged in from their living rooms, home offices, kitchens, and even basements—some propped up on laptops, others on phones, and a few comfortably settled on their couches.

While some attendees hadn't crossed paths in the real world, a peculiar camaraderie filled the virtual air. They were all linked by one critical thread—they had all worked for the same hockey team at some point in their careers. The strong bond was due not only to shared experiences but to the countless tales—part hilarity, part heartache, part post-traumatic stress—that had been passed down and lived out.

The tales of road trips in this sports world were legendary, often marked by chaos: ejections from games, stern warnings from sober teammates or worse, spouses. There were missing teeth and the occasional bout of projectile vomiting. Drunken escapades were woven into so many of these narratives like a thread through a worn tapestry. Perhaps alcohol was a way of coping. Nevertheless, alcohol was also woven into the fabric of the Sales Pit's culture. No one was immune to the prompting of shared stories about romantic conquests, and the cardinal rule loosely echoed among all: "Never dip your pen in company ink." The key phrase? "Whenever possible." But let's be honest—life had a way of throwing that out the window, or rather, face down, ass up and on all fours in a gallery level suite.

Countless anecdotes circulated about clients who really should have been fired from their roles as season ticket holders. "If only we had a waiting list, we could replace these bozos," Jay once said. "Yeah, replaced with even bigger bozos," Shane would correct. Many clients had an aura of entitlement. Their outrageous demands, persistent payment issues, and perpetual dissatisfaction with the team's performance—on and off the ice—became the stuff of office legend. Prop bets were often placed on the total number of requests to come in over any given weekend or the number of last-minute ticket exchanges within 24 hours of game time. Angry emails about failed promotional giveaways, parking lot egress times and the price of anything and everything.

Yet, amidst the madness, those remarkable clients evolved into genuine friends, surprising their account managers with heartfelt appreciation and, in some cases, lavish gifts. It was rare, but some of those stories lingered. Like the time one account manager received three signed football helmets—Aaron Rodgers, John Elway, and Dan Marino—from a particularly grateful client.

But not every account manager was so fortunate. Many bright-eyed FNGs (Fucking New Guys) entered the sales team with dreams of making it in the professional sports arena. Yet, the crushing weight of the job soon dimmed their enthusiasm, twisting their idealism into cynicism as they faced relentless pressures, shattered promises, and, eventually, their own broken hopes.

What originally united this spirited group was the undeniable reality of their shared passion—hockey, their team, or simply the allure of professional sports. Yet, that initial fire couldn't disguise the emotional bankruptcy that took over most of them. So many were mere shadows of their former selves, drained and defeated. And while they all recognized the toxic environment they inhabited— thankless, cutthroat, and exhaustingly relentless—the truth was that, for many, this was their life, and it made them who they were.

But this Zoom meeting wasn't to look back in anger. Jay organized it as an opportunity to check in with those colleagues who became friends and those friends who became family.

"Alright, looks like we're mostly all here now," Jay said, addressing everyone. "The only notable no-shows so far are...Kristina and Frank. Let's give them and some others a few more minutes, and then someone should text them."

"Krissy is going to be a few minutes late. She's on her way home," Dan updated as video tiles shifted focus with the new speaker.

"Whoa, whoa! Look who's joining us now, boys!" Shane exclaimed, excitement bubbling as he pointed at his screen (which nobody could see). The empty Zoom window populated, and a choppy, pixelated video filled the space.

Almost in unison, the other fourteen participants shouted, "FRANK!"... while staring at the top of Frank's zoomed-in forehead.

"Fellas? I can't hear or see anyone," Frank mumbled, leaning closer to the camera. "How do you work this fucking thing? One second, let me ask my daughter."

"And there you have it, ladies and gentlemen—the one and only Frank Washburn, former sales mutt extraordinaire, now living the drrrrrrrrrrrrreeeeeeeeeeeeeeeeeaam, doing whatever the hell it is he's doing these days!" Shane announced. "We could see and hear you, Frankyboy!"

Frank Washburn was a seasoned and sarcastic veteran with twenty-two seasons under his belt. He had been through it all with the team—on team charters, entertaining clients, driving players to events, and even getting into altercations with opposing team fans, sometimes right in the arena. Frank was one of the heroes of everyone in the pit. He was known for his humour, incredible stories, and impressive—borderline ungodly—alcohol tolerance. He had a knack for speaking his mind without a filter, and those fortunate enough to work alongside him cherished his softer side along with his ability to tease those he cared about most.

"Fellas? Amber's here trying to help me see everyone. Can anyone hear me?" Frank's voice, now strained and frustrated, echoed through the virtual room as his camera flickered off and back on.

"Again, we can see you AND hear you, Frank! You're good to go!" Jay reassured him. "Don't sweat it; it's only 2021. Technology just hasn't caught up with you yet, man." He leaned back in his chair, adding, "It looks like almost everyone is finally here. It's April 2021, and we're still stuck in this shithole of a pandemic. Who would have thought these lockdowns would drag on for so long?"

"How's everyone doing? You all are taking care of each other, right?"

"Of course, Frank," Shane affirmed. "Be kind, always."

"That's good to hear, boys... I remember when the first lockdowns were announced—just a few weeks after what's-his-name made all those cuts to the department," Frank said, now back online with a crisp image and clear sound. "What a piece of work he was. But hey, right time, right place for me, am I right, boys?"

"No, Frank, that was four years ago," Shane replied. "It's called COVID-19 because someone ate bat soup in China and sneezed on a bus in 2019."

"I don't think that's exactly how it happened, but you are right. It started in 2019, a good two years after Garry fucking Breckenridge," Dan explained.

"Remember when he tweeted about how lousy our working situation was—stuck working in the arena's basement, hardly ever seeing the light of day? Then he tried to screw us over with that insane compensation plan, which he presented MID-RENEWAL?" Frank recalled, shaking his head.

"Yeah, that was totally illegal," chimed in Steve, a former employee who had also been let go during the same round of cuts as Frank and Rusty. "Rusty fought for all of us."

Frank closed his eyes and bowed his head.

Rusty was a passionate advocate for his colleagues. He'd dedicated years to the company, pouring his heart and soul into every project. When he, Frank, and six others received the news of their termination, it wasn't just a shock—it felt like a betrayal, especially for Rusty. The severance package they were all handed seemed more like an afterthought than a gesture of goodwill.

As he quickly reviewed the numbers, Rusty felt that something was off. He discovered that the termination process violated employment standards, amongst other legalities. Fuelled by a sense of justice—not just for himself but for those who had stood beside him in the trenches—Rusty acted.

"He definitely took one for the team, man," Jay said. "We all respected that. No way you guys should have been treated like that—or any of us—but we appreciated him going to bat for us. They never implemented that new compensation plan, even after he was sacked."

"That's because nobody signed it. By law, we all would have needed to sign the new compensation plan to implement it. But we were never formally presented with it before they tried to set it up, making it seem like they had no choice. We never got the chance to even consider signing it. Nor should we have signed it. So, our old compensation plan, by law, remained in force. I'll let you in on a little secret a client once told me: always start your argument with 'I've been advised that...' and then go from there. Most management doesn't know the actual laws," Frank explained. "Most management is so far in over their heads that the mere thought of someone questioning their position or decisions gives them serious bouts of heartburn."

Rusty had once shared a cubicle pod with Shane and Jay. Eccentric was a mild term for him; he had a flair for fashion that included bold Robert Graham shirts and John Fluevog shoes. Boldness was his signature—bold tie patterns, eye-catching shoes, and always novelty socks. While few appreciated his style, those who did really valued his uniqueness, and Rusty naturally gravitated toward them.

Rusty—whose full name was Richard Geare—was known as one of the most loyal and trustworthy colleagues Jay, Shane, and others had ever worked with. A bit older, yet still in his mid-thirties, he played a primary role in season ticket holder retention, much like Jay and about ten others on the call that night. But with a Master's in Sports and Recreation Administration and an MBA, he craved more than just selling tickets. He was one of the creative minds on the sales team, often researching other teams in various sports—hockey, baseball, basketball, football—looking for proven strategies to engage fans, enhance their experiences, and, of course, sell tickets.

Unfortunately, everyone on the call knew Rusty's ideas were deemed "too aggressive" or "too modern" for a relatively conservative executive team still entrenched in the late '90s—maybe early 2000s. Much of his hard work and research were frequently shelved for "next season" or, worse, never considered at all.

At one point, like everyone else on the call, working for a professional sports team had felt like a dream to him. However, as time passed, he and others realized that professional sports were not the end all and be-all for their identities. Initially, he had been the guy who bought jerseys, purchased tickets for the experience and sought out games whenever he travelled to other cities. However, within a few months of starting, the politics of working in sports began to wear on him, dulling his once passionate enthusiasm.

Like Frank, Shane, Jay, and several of their colleagues, Rusty demonstrated a remarkable ability to cultivate positive relationships with his season ticket holders. This was especially impressive given that when he first started—like so many others when they first started too—he inherited clients that others had abandoned, either because they were unwilling to engage with them or, worse, had never even communicated with them. Still, the pressure of a base salary of $30,000 was daunting, especially with a growing family on the horizon. Rusty was perpetually looking for new job opportunities—inside or outside of sports, he didn't really care—because he understood there was more to life than the glitz and glamour of game days and meeting the players.

So when he, Frank, and a handful of others were unceremoniously let go, it was a shock and a major blow to his ego. His termination also came at arguably the lowest point of his life, which only further exacerbated things.

"I remember when they handed me my severance package and said, 'We believe this is more than fair for your years of service and the results from this renewal campaign,'" Frank recounted, his voice deep and slightly slurred. "I didn't know what to think. But I know Rusty took one look at it and thought, 'Uh, nope. Those numbers are all wrong. Fix the numbers and present me with a better offer.'"

In Rusty's Master's program, he had taken contract law, which helped him understand that the compensation numbers were drawn from the percentages the team was advocating for that year. However, as he had explained to his teammates just minutes earlier, those figures were not legally binding; the organization had never formally presented an updated compensation plan. Therefore, the previous compensation structure still applied, and the figures needed adjustment for accuracy.

Steve and Frank's tales of misrepresented compensation plans were all too common. Commission cheques were notorious for their inaccuracies. Claw backs were frequent, leaving employees with pay stubs showing negative balances. The organization showed little incentive to implement changes that could lead to higher commission payouts. When George, another colleague of theirs, left to work with one of his clients, the team continued to pay him for three months. It was only after he brought it to their attention that they demanded he write them a cheque for their mistake.

Poor contract signings involving players past their prime, those who had been waived but were still on the books, or even those stuck in the minors on NHL-level, one-way contracts—these were accepted parts of the business. Yet fair treatment of hardworking employees was a rarity. At staff Christmas parties, employees had to pay for their ticket out of pocket if they wanted to bring a spouse or significant other. Meanwhile, players freely invited their wives and girlfriends as part of the perks.

"Alright, let's switch gears here, boys," Brad said, pouring himself another glass of Pinot Grigio. "We're not here to whine; we're here to drink wine!"

"Fuck you, Brad. While I appreciate your clever pun, I thought complaining was the whole point of this call," Frank replied with sarcasm, now finishing his second beer and popping open another. He let out a great belch, then squinted at his screen.

"No, Frank. That wasn't really the point," Jay corrected.

"Then what the hell am I doing here with all these unfamiliar faces here?" he added. "Like you," he pointed at the younger guy in the middle row, two from the left on his screen. "Speak!"

Unfortunately, no one could see who Frank was pointing at.

"Uh, Frank? Me?" one said as two others pointed at their selves as well.

"Impossible," Frank scoffed, shaking his head. "I would have remembered you. I remember everyone I've ever worked with." He paused, then added with a dramatic flair, "Although I was mostly talking about the quiet blonde lady. Yeah, I don't remember yooooouuuu either!"

"Jay, Frank... my... my name is Jay? We worked together for like... six seasons... no, more than that," Jay interjected, slightly flustered (it didn't take much to rattle him). "Wait, blonde lady?" he continued, his confusion growing. "I invited you to this Zoom call, for Christ's sake."

"Ah yes, Fraggle Laroque, just messing with you," Frank chuckled. "I didn't recognize you with your long surfer COVID hair. Although you look more like Boober than ever!"

"Boober?"

"Fraggle Laroque?" chirped Shane, clearly too young to understand the Fraggle Rock reference. "What the fuck does Fraggle Laroque mean? What the fuck is a Fraggle?"

"Have you never heard of Fraggle Rock, Shane?" Dan, the team's former sales manager, asked.

"No. Why? Should I have?" Shane replied, puzzled.

Here we go, thought Dan.

"Fraggle Rock is only one of the best children's television series EVER created," Frank explained enthusiastically. His eyes lit up as he dove into his favourite topic. "Created by Jim Henson—the genius behind The Muppets, like Kermit the Frog and Miss Piggy, as well as Sesame Street characters like Bert, Ernie, Big Bird, and Mr. Snuffleupagus...amongst others. You babies are from the Tickle Me Elmo era, also a Henson creation."

He paused, a dreamy smile creeping across his face as he made elaborate gestures with his hands on the screen.

"Fraggles were these small, adorable creatures—playful little things, really. They lived in a vast network of tunnels underground. There was Boober, Red, Gobo, Wembley, Mokey, and Uncle Travelling Matt. They came in a variety of colours and led a generally carefree lifestyle. But those pesky Gorgs would have none of it! Oh! And the little green Doozers—those guys just worked all the time."

Frank chuckled, reminiscing. "All the Fraggles wanted to do was dance their cares away, let the music play, and save their worries for another day... and eat radishes and Doozer sticks, which were ironically...made from ground-up radishes!"

He suddenly became serious.

"And just like you, Shane, Fraggles only worked for thirty minutes a week!"

Dan laughed out loud, spitting beer. "How old are you again, Shane?"

Frank chuckled, shaking his head. "Come on, Shane, you seriously missed out. It was classic stuff! You must have been living under a rock."

Shane felt his cheeks flush, mocking tones and laughter from Frank, Dan, and others ringing in his ears.

"Yeah, well... I was busy with other things," he protested.

"Things that mattered. Not everyone had the privilege of wasting time on cartoons."

Dan's laughter quickly faded, replaced by an awkward silence as he noted the growing tension.

"Hey man, it's all in good fun. No shame in missing some childhood nostalgia."

"Right," Shane snapped. "Because who doesn't want to look back and be reminded of how normal everyone else's childhood was? Great. Just great."

He forced a smile that didn't reach his eyes, the shame creeping in like dark clouds on a sunny day.

After all, for Shane, normal might as well have been the elusive title of a children's book he never got to read.

"Anyway, I've never heard of Fraggle Rock and don't understand the reference. Thank you for explaining it. I'll have to Google it."

"What about Fred Penner?" Dan asked, hopeful.

"Nope, never heard of him either," Shane stated dismissively.

"Sharon, Lois, and Bram?" added Frank, his eyebrow raised in disbelief.

"Nope. Who are they?"

"How dare you question Sharon, Lois, and Bram in all their Skinamarinkeedo-ness!" Frank exclaimed, bewildered, as though Shane had insulted a national treasure, which he had.

"How about Iggy, Gloria, and Jacob from Under the Umbrella Tree?" Dan inquired. "And then there was Holly... wow, Holly. Am I right, Frank?"

"You magnificent son of a bitch, Dan. Holly was an absolute gem!"

"You're not helping, Dan!" Jay groaned. "Stop encouraging Frank!"

"And no, I've never heard of Under the Umbrella Tree or whatever you just said," Shane added. "Some of us were born in the late '80s, but most likely in the mid-'90s."

Rattled, Frank paused briefly to gather his thoughts.

"Mister... Dressup? Tell me what you know about Mister Dressup."

"Yeah, Mister Dressup. Wasn't he a clown?" Jay chimed in as Frank's eyes widened with disbelief as he searched the screen for Jay.

"Jay! If you're going to say idiotic things like Mister Dressup being a clown, then I have no time for you! I think it's time you leave. I'm going to ask you to leave now."

"But I am the host!" Jay whimpered.

"Very well," Frank continued, sighing. "You may stay."

"To be honest, Frank, I thought Mister Dressup was a clown, too," Shane admitted. "I mean, isn't that what clowns do? They dress up?"

An awkward silence engulfed the Zoom call as the others watched in playful horror, witnessing Frank's growing frustration. If this were a cartoon, thick smoke would be billowing from his ears. No one truly understood Frank's passion for 1980s children's TV, but they all leaned in, eager to glimpse Frank Washburn's world. With his fiery personality, it was anyone's guess which direction he would take next.

"I have no words. Both of you are clowns—CLOWNS!"

"Well, with that, let's change the subject again, shall we?" Dan interjected again, swooping in like a lifeguard to save Jay and Shane from Frank's wrath.

"Hey Shane, do you remember when you and Jay tried to plan that road trip with Rusty?"

"Which one? There were several of them," asked Shane before taking a sip of his drink. "So many back in the day, back when we could at least go on road trips instead of being quarantined in these prisons," he added, looking around his lavish condo.

"Right. I've never seen a prison with 70-inch televisions... or that casting couch you're sitting on, Shane," Dan quipped.

"Casting couch," Shane repeated softly with a grin and a quiet chuckle.

"Yeah, I miss those old days," added Jay, completely unaware of what a casting couch was.

CHAPTER 2

"San Francisco via Las Vegas"

Back when it was socially acceptable to hang out in local establishments, Jay and Shane enjoyed each other's company most weekends. When they weren't in a larger group of five or six, they were practically inseparable. Planning an improbable road trip was never out of the question—even after Shane moved in briefly with his recently separated brother to help him float the house. With Shane now back on his own in a condo downtown, there were never enough excuses not to go out. Jay considered himself Shane's wingman, although Shane didn't really need one—he did all the damage himself. Their idea of a good time was going out, spending too much money, getting blackout drunk, and then regretting their choices, at least until the next outing.

Jay and Shane frequently hit the local clubs dressed to impress. Jay's go-to attire was a shiny grey suit, probably from Le Château, paired with his plain white V-neck shirt. Shane sometimes donned not one but two polo shirts with their collars popped—yes, he was that guy long before it became uncool.

The double university town also had several smaller colleges, ensuring a steady supply of eligible young women by the bar for this dynamic duo to feast upon. Whether they were 2s, 4s, or the rare 8s, 9s, or elusive 10s, Shane never had a shortage of bachelorettes. Sometimes, he would consider two 3s "for a respectable 6," but the only thing lower than his standards was the poor attendance numbers when the team played badly—which was often.

Jay typically pounded vodka sodas or vodka cranberries, while Shane opted for gin and tonics. He hated the piney taste of gin but thought it made him sound appealing to women, especially when he ordered it for himself and any girl who paid him a brief bit of attention. Gin and tonics also fuelled Shane's infamous "gincidents." The first time he coined the term, it received modest fanfare from colleagues, so he kept it as part of his vocabulary.

A few 'gincidents' in, Shane often found success by chirping the 'weakest link' in a group. "If I chirp her, like, for example, make fun of her jean jacket or canvas handbag, then she'll be forced to seek my approval and want to sleep with me." You didn't need to understand psychology to know that the world of Tucker Max also applied to Shane—unfortunately, more often than it should have.

For Shane, the pursuit of validation—both in himself and how he interacted with others—had become an essential part of who he was, particularly in his relationships with women. Unfortunately for him, most of his connections often felt shallow, fuelled by an urgent desire to be accepted in the moment, with little outlook on the future.

"You know, nurses—better yet, slutty nurses—are the wild ones," he once mused, grinning into his half-full rocks glass as he dispensed his unsolicited advice to Jay. "They think they can save you. Always looking to care for someone, you know? But let me tell you a little something about me, Jay. They can't save me."

"Is that because you are too far gone?" Jay asked.

"What? No! That's not it. I just can't be saved because... uh...I'm a free-roam horse. The ones allowed to roam free in the wild."

"I'm not sure if you mean you can't be tamed," Jay tried to correct his friend as he played with an ice cube from his drink now on his tongue. "Wild horses cannot be tamed. But I am not sure how you are to save a wild horse...unless there's, like, a forest fire or something. I also don't know how a wild horse relates to a nurse, slutty or otherwise."

"You're missing my point, Jay," Shane said, completely missing Jay's point. "All I am saying is that slutty nurses can get a little intense and very unstable. I had to get a restraining order against one I dated for a bit... wow."

Unbeknownst to him, Shane had just revealed more about himself than he realized. His so-called high standards stemmed from a deep-seated fear of inadequacy, manifesting in his desperate, superficial pursuits for connection. Behind the bravado lay something else pain. The instability he claimed to avoid. He was drawn to it, mirroring his relentless cycle of seeking approval while never feeling worthy enough to receive it.

"And then there are the hairdressers! They're just so eager for recognition," he continued, his tone shifting slightly. "If you don't compliment their work, it's like throwing gasoline on a hot mess of a dumpster fire. They crave that approval even more."

He leaned back, reminiscing. "Hey, remember how, as kids, we'd always get to choose a treat after a haircut? For me, it was usually a lollipop," he chuckled. "And to be honest, I still get a kick out of it—especially when the hairdresser enjoys sucking on a lollipop as much as I do. It's all about the experience! Be sure to tip your hairdresser, Jay!"

Jay groaned. "Just the tip?"

Shane cast a disappointed look. He paused, moved past it, and continued like Jay hadn't said a word. "Oh, speaking of horses! Don't even get me started with girls that ride wild horses," Shane added with a wink. "Wild things!"

Shane was practically a walking public service announcement for reasons to practice abstinence.

He also wanted things—and his women—to be as easy as possible. One time, he proudly announced in the sales pit, "Have you ever had sex with a fat girl? It's like a Krispy Kreme donut; you know they're bad for you, but when you only have them occasionally, they're delicious."

The comment was not well received—especially by his numerous female colleagues.

Much like Shane's vulgarity, Jay's shyness with women and inability to control his drinking were constants. Shane's trouble with steady dating—and what he believed was an impressive alcohol tolerance—were likely what made the two click so well. No matter who you asked, their memories— and subsequent broken stories—were never in sync and always a bit fuzzy.

Mondays typically started with Shane asking, "What happened to you Saturday night?"

This question almost always occurred as Jay stood, mindlessly staring at the ticket printer as it spat out tickets. The way the BOCA printer spat out tickets was eerily similar to the way Jay often threw up vodka cranberries into the general direction of a toilet or a poor, unsuspecting bush.

His response was usually, "I don't want to talk about it."

This Monday morning was no different.

"I'm not talking about it...mostly because I can't remember what happened," Jay admitted, rubbing the back of his head, still in a bit of a daze.

Sadly, Jay's memory was noticeably short even at his relatively young age. He frequently had trouble piecing together the bits and pieces of his evenings, which arguably made the stories better—and even funnier. Sometimes, he would lose his train of thought altogether or have what he called 'popcorn thoughts', where ideas would just pop into his head. Shane was the king of popcorn thoughts.

"I think we hit our usual haunt," he began. "I was downing vodka crans like they were water and chatting up some total stunners. But there's a big black hole where the rest of the night went. I woke up on my bathroom floor Sunday afternoon with no clue how I got there. Still fully clothed. Totally missed setting my fantasy football lineups and my parlay—which would have cashed me a cool gino if I'd put a hundred bucks down. And, for some reason, my shower curtain was wrapped around me like a cozy, drunken blanket."

He frowned. "There was water everywhere. At least...oh God, I hope it was water."

Shane burst out laughing. "Ah, classic. Totally epic night, man. We shouldn't have ordered that second bottle."

Jay rubbed his temples again and winced. "Absolutely not. No."

"To our credit, though..." Shane acknowledged, wagging his pointer finger at Jay, "Those babies said they were coming back!"

"Wait, was that before or after I decorated the bathroom floor with vodka cranberry?" Jay asked, now as more of his Saturday night was popping into focus.

"Uh, I think before. No— that was definitely after."

Those who knew Jay could assume he preferred lying on his bathroom floor post-bender rather than on his bed or couch. If there were a VIP membership at a bathroom concession stand, he'd have it. In fact, if a bathroom attendant dispensed pillows and blankets instead of just mints and towels, Jay would easily be their number one client. After another long night out, he'd stroll into a lavishly appointed restroom, where plush pillows awaited his weary head and soft blankets draped over the stall doors like a welcoming embrace. He'd settle onto the cool tiles, cocooned in comfort, his sanctuary amid the chaos of life. After all, why should comfort be confined to the bedroom when the best escape was merely a vanity away? At least he kept it relatively spotless—probably out of necessity and due to his sometimes crippling, undiagnosed obsessive-compulsive disorder.

Nevertheless, he hid his OCD well...most of the time.

"There's something oddly soothing about a cold floor after a hot night out..." Jay muttered, staring off into the distance. "But let's be real. I need to change my life. I'm swearing off drinking right now...forever."

Shane scoffed. "Come on, Jay. Look at the anatomy here!"

Jay frowned. "What are you talking about?"

"Compare the size of your liver to your heart!" Shane touched the top of Jay's head before moving his hand down to his chest as Jay stood and watched uncomfortably. "We were literally made to drink more and give fewer and fewer shits. I'm pretty sure that's scientific. Just Google it."

Unfortunately, Jay's resolve to quit drinking had become a weekly ritual—like Sunday brunch or watching reruns of Trailer Park Boys, Futurama or SpongeBob Squarepants while high. He was the boy who cried 'never again,' far too often, and no one believed him anymore.

"So, anyway," Jay muttered, squinting at a ridiculous email demanding three signed jerseys from a whimsically named charity, "what happened to you that fateful Saturday night?"

"Remember that girl in the jean jacket?" Shane replied, stretching his arms behind his head.

Jay frowned. "I'm going to go with a solid no."

"Right, well," Shane continued, undeterred, "I took her home, we made out for a bit, and then, uh... let's just say my expensive Italian leather couch saw some action."

Jay shook his head. "So, just to clarify—you're telling me that belittling women is the secret art of seduction?"

"Maybe," Shane said without hesitation. "You gotta mess with their self-esteem a little," as he rolled his hands while explaining. "The more you push them away, the more they want you."

Jay stared at him deadpan. "That is a horrible and outdated take on life. You should be ashamed of yourself."

"Look it up, man. I'm pretty sure that's also scientific," Shane insisted before pointing to a computer keyboard. "Just Google it."

Jay sighed. "Got it...remind me never to Google that. Ok, you insulted her... and boom, she ended up on your lap?"

Shane grinned. "Correct! She ended up...in my lap, err...on my lap, and on my expensive Italian leather couch! Spoiler alert: it doesn't matter if it's sauce, sweat or semen, expensive Italian leather cleans up pretty good."

Jay groaned. "You're disgusting! Remind me to never take your dating advice again... or sit on that couch again." He exhaled.

Shane smirked. "Expensive Italian leather," he corrected. "What can I say? Expensive Italian leather was a genius move!"

Jay nodded. "And you? Were you a 'genius' on this typical Saturday night?"

"Well," Shane admitted, rubbing his face, "I may have bitten off a bit more than I could chew. Afterward, she wasn't leaving, so I pretended to be asleep, just waiting for her to finally get bored and leave. Or, worst case scenario, nod off."

"Uh-huh."

"Jesus, it felt like an eternity. So then I opened my eyes, and—bam!—she was staring at me. Like one of those creepy-ass porcelain dolls your grandmother collects with the wonky eye!"

Jay winced. "That's...very unsettling."

"You're telling me?" Shane said, shaking his head. "I thought I was about to be murdered in my own goddamn bed."

"Hey, at least you got the attention, right," Jay pointed out. "Last girl I dated came over after work, gushed over your old dog like he was a celebrity or king, and completely ignored me."

"Wait, seriously?"

"Dead serious. I was sitting right next to the dog, and she was just like, 'Oh, who's the cutest wittle guy?' Meanwhile, I might as well have been a potted plant."

"Ah yes, Jason, I remember that experiment," Shane said, rolling his eyes while making an exaggerated hand gesture to suggest she was flat-chested. "Good riddance. Didn't you tell me she refused to share your queen-sized fuzzy blanket because she claimed she was the queen, and therefore, the blanket was already at max capacity?"

"Sadly, yes," Jay muttered. "There's a reason it only lasted four days."

"That's beyond embarrassing, even for you, Jay," Shane laughed, shaking his head. "Speaking of embarrassing, my ex once tried to humiliate me in front of her friends by claiming I was terrible in bed. You should've seen her face when they all disagreed."

Jay raised an eyebrow. "You slept with her friends too?"

"Most of them."

Jay exhaled, rubbing his temples again.

"Hey, do you remember those 4 a.m. text marathons you had with that girl who ultimately ghosted you? Where is she now, Jay?"

"Probably settled down with a kid...maybe two."

Shane leaned back with a smirk. "She probably re-read those texts the next morning, realized you were too much of a nice guy—a walking red flag she didn't need—then ran off to shack up with some bad boy to restore the balance of the universe."

"Well said, philosopher," Jay quipped before sighing. "I'm not ashamed of the number of girls I've dated—just the quality."

Shane's face lit up as if he had just solved a puzzle. "You've dated, what... one girl?" He held up a single finger. "I could make a similar comment about my 'quality' score when it comes to the number of girls I've slept with." He paused dramatically. "But hey, if I could snag us tickets to the Raiders game next Sunday, would you be in?"

Jay frowned. "I have no idea how you connected those two points, but... are you talking about the Raiders or the Riders?"

Shane groaned. "Da Rrrrrraiders!" he exclaimed, rolling the R like a wrestling announcer.

Jay squinted. "As in the Oakland Raiders?"

"Yes!" Shane nodded. "Why would I ever want to go to a Canadian Football League game!? That's not even real football!"

"That's fair. So, the Raiders...as in, Oakland, California's Raiders?"

"Exactly! Oakland...California—soon to be Las Vegas, Nevada."

"Are you insane?"

"Aw, come on! Don't dismiss the idea before I even lay out my master plan," Shane pleaded. "This could be the ultimate epic road trip."

"Epic, maybe. But it's hardly a 'road' trip. A road trip implies we drive somewhere—a place like, I don't know, five hours away, MAX. But we'd have to fly unless you've found a way to drive to Oakland or Vegas in a few short hours. Plus, jumping on a trip like this in the middle of our homestand would be career suicide. We'd come back to an even larger dumpster fire of trade requests and a tsunami of lost tickets."

Shane's impulse-driven ideas often lacked consideration for the consequences, financial or practical—thanks in part to his undiagnosed adult ADHD. His mind raced with random thoughts, but time management and organization were foreign concepts to him. Yet, these wild ideas fuelled him. He also relied heavily on Jay—or anyone, really—to keep him grounded, out of trouble, and most importantly, share expenses. Despite making very good money, Shane was notoriously cheap in some ways. He would have no issue spending $30 dollars on designer socks or $300 on designer dress shoes, but somehow, Winners scrutinized spending $20 dollars on a pair of boxes. Nevertheless, he would often justify to himself, and sometimes Jay, that his next idea could be the big one.

"Look, all I am saying is we take a flight into San Francisco, Uber across the Bay…ooh, maybe we can stop over in Vegas! Vegas, baby, Vegas!"

Jay simply blinked. "How did Vegas come into this?"

Even as Jay questioned the logistics of an impromptu trip to Oakland that now could include a stopover in Las Vegas, Jay's response was perhaps why he and Shane fed off each other's ideas so well and why they somehow always entertained how they could bring their ideas, however dreamy to life. This was easier for them because most of their colleagues had families—wives and girlfriends who would never allow a last-minute boys' weekend. Especially not one to Oakland with a detour to Sin City. Hell, even a last-minute road trip two hours out of town would likely be off the table. No matter how often they tried to persuade their significant others, "Can I go?" was usually met with a resounding, "Not a (fucking) chance," followed by a laundry list of reasons why they weren't allowed—prior responsibilities, plans, or just making up lost time because they were at the arena forty nights a year.

"Also, why does everything we do have to be epic?" Jay asked, exasperated. "Jesus, man, you use that word way too often. Whatever happened to low-key weekends? Just hanging out? Why can't we get together, watch the game, maybe order some Wild Wings or Hot 'N Ready pies, and drink some pints?"

Shane abruptly cut him off. "Because I am epic and will never apologize for being awesome!" He punched the air triumphantly. "A low-key weekend? That's not me, man. It's never going to be me, and I know for damn sure it's not you, Jay." He pointed dramatically. "Everything has to be ballsout because we're young and have nothing holding us back—no wife, no kids, no ball and chain in the way of our bad decisions."

"I am a bad decision," Jay muttered, hanging his head.

"No, Jay. Marian Hossa made a bad decision."

"What the hell are you talking about now?"

"Never forget the 2007-08 and 2008-09 seasons," Shane began, his tone shifting to that of a historian recounting a great tragedy. "Remember when Marian Hossa, while playing for Pittsburgh, lost to Detroit in the Cup Finals? Then he signed a one-year deal with Detroit the following season only to lose to Pittsburgh in the Cup Finals the year after?"

Jay frowned. "Yeah... but didn't Hossa go on to win three Cups with Chicago after that? Didn't he go to the Cup Finals in 2010, then again in 2013 and 2015? Now, that move was a great decision. Hossa is a Hall of Famer, man."

Shane grinned and pointed at Jay. "See? There you go!"

Jay blinked. "There I go? What? Where did I go?"

Shane leaned in, eyes gleaming. "Hossa made a bad decision, but then he made a great decision again and again. He learned. And the great decision... was going on this epic roadie!"

Jay groaned.

Shane continued, undeterred. "Besides, low-key weekends are for pussies like Rusty and guys who used to be us—who traded in their man cards for weekends spent in the garden centre at Home Depot with their old ladies. Also, Rusty."

Sitting within earshot, Rusty finally interjected at the circus that had started to transform their sales pod. "Keep it down...and also go fuck yourself, Shane."

Rusty didn't appreciate being called out.

Shane flailed his arms animatedly like a Muppet having a meltdown. "Whoa, whoa, whoa! Get a load of this guy!" He turned to face Rusty. "I was just using you as an example, bud. No need to get offended, Rrrrrichard" Shane said rolling his R.

"Why am I always the example?" Rusty shot back. "You always use me as an example. Not cool, asshole."

Shane smirked. "Look, Rusty, if I thought shopping for Gerbera daisies at the garden centre was fun, I'd have settled down years ago. Besides, I think you like my attention."

Rusty exhaled. "Shane, you're what...27? 28 years old? This isn't the 1940s. Nobody settles down that early. And no, I do not like that kind of attention."

Despite Rusty's objections, deep down, he liked being included in these conversations. No matter how ridiculous the activity sounded, a simple invite would have been nice. He often wished he could join one of these "epic roadies," but he knew his wife Amy would never let him go.

"Dude, I have a guy..." Shane started.

"You mean a scalper client," Jay interrupted.

Shane huffed. "Err, a guy who builds ticket consortiums and happens to have Raiders season tickets right on the 50-yard line. He told me I should call him if I ever wanted tickets—said he'd give me a good price."

Rusty gave him a deadpan stare. "Okay, so...he's definitely a scalper."

"Yes, fine! For argument's sake, let's say he's a 'scalper,' a 'ticket broker,' a consortium builder," Shane said, using exaggerated air quotes. "I've helped him get playoff tickets a few times without buying the entire strip. That was also a great decision."

Jay squinted. "Is he the guy who gave you all those signed football helmets?"

Shane crossed his arms. "Those were gifts...but maybe... and by maybe, I mean yes. Yes, he did," he said, beaming with pride.

Rusty smirked. "What about that 'gift basket' of single malt Scotches that mysteriously showed up at your desk one day? Same guy?"

Shane waved a dismissive hand. "That's irrelevant. Besides, if you let me finish... Oakland and Vegas wouldn't be that expensive."

The truth was, Vegas was always expensive. It wasn't dubbed Sin City for nothing—temptation lurked around every corner, especially at the craps tables, where Shane and Jay often found themselves at the local casino. Add in two aimless twenty-somethings with no fear of financial consequences, and you had a recipe for disaster.

Humouring Shane, Rusty engaged, "Alright, so what are we talking about?"

Shane perked up instantly, pivoting in his chair and typing rapidly on his laptop. "Alright, check this out: We fly to Oakland with a stopover in Vegas. We leave Friday night, land in Vegas by dinnertime, crash at a budget hotel off the Strip, and spend a night and a day soaking it all in."

Rusty leaned back, unimpressed. "With all that cocaine and Red Bulls, I don't even think you'd need a hotel."

Shane's eyes grew to the size of toonies as Rusty's comment about mixing uppers flew as high over Shane's head as the potential flight to San Francisco via Las Vegas. "Exactly! And by the time we catch our flight Sunday morning, we'll have won enough to cover the entire trip! We land just in time for kickoff, and we finally sleep as we take the redeye, we we we we we all the way home. I'd say with all that sleep flying back, we'd wake up refreshed Monday morning." He grinned wildly. "Fuck, Rusty, your wife wouldn't even know you were gone."

Rusty exhaled sharply. "That sounds complicated and, frankly, downright ridiculous. It's like a bad mashup of Swingers and Little Giants."

Shane waved him off. "You're out to lunch, Rusty. It's not complicated at all. I'm saying no more than three hundred for the tickets."

Jay arched an eyebrow. "Three hundred each?"

"YES, Jay, per ticket!" Shane emphasized. "Is this your first professional sporting event?"

"Three hundred American?" Jay pressed.

"Yes, let's go with USD. And just in case," Shane continued, flipping to an Excel spreadsheet, "we budget for a 'Cleveland Steamer'-style hotel somewhere off the Strip near the airport— split between us, of course. Plus, booze, meals, and some hastily acquired souvenirs. It's a hot grand." He leaned back, pleased with himself. "Jay, we've burnt more than that on a weekend here!"

Rusty frowned. "Why stay off the Strip at all? That's like paying for a hooker and falling asleep before anything happens, only to wake up and realize she's stolen your wallet."

Jay pondered quietly, "What about the one with the flamingos... that's Tropicana, right? I heard that's cheap. Or what about that Egyptian pyramid-looking place?"

"Excalibur," Rusty deadpanned, knowing full well Jay meant Luxor.

"Yeah, that's it!" Jay affirmed.

"But yes, those are just as affordable and way closer to the action. You do know how far 'off the Strip' actually is, right?"

Shane, unfazed, gestured broadly. "Look, everything is so close! Everything is within walking distance. Every casino is right next to each other...minus a fountain here, a parking lot there...super close."

Rusty scoffed. "Let's get real for a second. In Las Vegas, 'walking distance' is a fantasy. Sure, you might see one hotel from another, but the reality? The Strip itself stretches over four miles."

Jay and Shane merely blinked. "That's like six and a half kilometres...so when you say something is 'just a block away,' it could easily mean a 20-minute walk over hot asphalt, dodging traffic, homeless people, pedestrian bridges, an endless sea of slot machines, and avoiding those showgirls who insist on taking pictures with you. You might as well be hiking the Grand Canyon."

Shane leaned back, grinning. "Wow, now that's a memory from the spank bank I haven't thought of in years." He sighed dreamily. "Give me a second, I'm just...making a movie, err, a sex tape in my head...with Elizabeth Berkley."

Rusty softly slapped Shane across the face. "Stop."

"Arguably one of the worst movies ever made," Rusty continued, shaking his head. "But I do see how someone trying to claw their way to the top through sex and seduction would resonate with you, Shane."

Shane smiled and blinked rapidly.

Rusty got back to his point. "And another thing— 'off the Strip' doesn't just mean a different hotel; it often means edge-of-town sketchiness, where you're at risk of crossing a multi-lane highway just to grab a late-night snack from 7-Eleven."

Shane waved him off. "Exactly! It really can't be that bad."

Rusty groaned. "Shane, the Strip is designed to keep you inside. They count on you getting lost in the lights and crowds. If you want to enjoy the city without feeling like you've just run a triathlon, staying on the Strip is worth every penny."

Shane opened his mouth, but Jay cut him off. "Forget the prices for a second. It's about convenience. Whatever savings you think you're getting by staying somewhere cheap will evaporate once you factor in the cost of getting to where you want to be—like a nice dinner, a show, or even a decent bar. Plus, let's not forget the time wasted just wandering around."

Shane crossed his arms, considering their points. "Alright, alright," he finally conceded. "Fair enough. Maybe we can revisit the hotel discussion later. But what do we do about everything else?"

Rusty closed his laptop. "Let's not kid ourselves that we're, I mean, you are saving any money here. In Vegas, you either pay upfront or through the nose in inconvenient trips and missed opportunities."

Shane turned back to Jay, grinning. "It sounds like there's a legitimate shot at Rusty joining us." Rusty shot him a flat look. "That's not what I'm saying at all."

But Shane wasn't listening.

And with that, as memories of their previous misadventures in Sin City swirled in their minds, the trio knew they faced a weekend of decisions that would cost them—one way or another.

"Also," Jay continued, "you haven't even mentioned flights aside from the fact that we'd be flying to Vegas."

Shane waved him off. "Flights are on you, man! I'm using points."

Jay narrowed his eyes. "Well, I don't have points, Shane," he said. "I have no idea how much a flight would cost. If you're saying this trip is going to be a grand, I know you haven't factored in our own stupidity. So, your 'hot grand' could easily turn into two grand—if not more. I just wish I had more time to plan my finances."

"That's the smartest thing either of you have said this entire conversation," Rusty chimed in. "I fully support you taking the necessary time to plan your finances to make your trip safe and affordable. Besides, you don't want to end up in some sketchy back alley when you could be rolling a different kind of dice instead."

Just then, a memory flashed through Jay's mind—the time he and Shane went to Atlantic City with their buddy Kyle. Nothing good ever happened on Martin Luther King Blvd after 1 a.m.., especially when you were three Canadians in cheap blazers.

On that trip, they had ended up down some dimly lit alleyway, figuratively and literally rolling the dice at a gentleman's club.

<< Flashback <<

Shane had waved over one of the dancers. "Excuse me, miss! My friend 'Randall' would like to ask you a few questions." He smirked.

The dancer flashed a sultry smile. "Sure, baby! You can ask me anything. Wanna come with me?"

"Oh, you know he does! Go get 'em, Rrrrrandy!" Shane laughed, giving Jay a playful smack on the ass as he stumbled forward. "It's okay, we play sports!"

As they moved to a quieter corner, the dancer laid out her terms, starting at $100 and up. Visibly flustered and intoxicated, he pulled out his faded black and orange Baltimore Orioles nylon wallet and yanked it open with a loud rip, which announced to the strip club that shit was going to get real — or that he was about to make a financial decision with monumental consequences. As he rummaged through the worn pockets, he briefly paused. His eyes landed on a single red thread stubbornly caught in the web of the Velcro teeth. Shaking off his existential lint crisis, Jay looked back towards Shane, who gave him an encouraging thumbs up from 'Perverts Row.' He continued fumbling with receipts and slot machine vouchers as he tried to sort through the mess of Canadian and American bills.

"How about I give you fifty, and we see what you can do with that?" he slurred.

The stripper rolled her eyes and walked away without a word, leaving Jay standing there, clutching his very thin wallet. When he turned back to find Shane and Kyle, they were already lying on the stage, two other dancers crawling above them on all fours.

>> Flash Forward >>

"Back to reality," Rusty's voice cut in.

"Yeah," Rusty continued, shaking his head. "Using the Shane multiplier, if he says this trip will be a Gino, you know it's gonna be three. Minimum. Who the hell has that kind of money to burn?"

Shane scoffed. "Look, take a loan, live a little! When are we ever gonna be this young again? I think this one has legs, man. Really sexy, Elizabeth Berkley legs."

And, without even realizing it, Shane gave himself a firm squeeze. Like Jay, who unknowingly developed a rash whenever someone mentioned Kelly, Shane had a physical tic whenever he got too excited—whether it was about a hot sale, a hot inbound call, a hot night out, or a hot idea that had hot sexy Elizabeth Berkley legs. There was a lot of crotch honking.

Rusty pinched the bridge of his nose. "Must you do that in my presence?"

"Do what exactly?" Shane blinked innocently.

Rusty exhaled, shaking his head. "Forget it."

Unfazed, Shane continued, "Take a loan so Future Shane and Jay can pay for Present Shane and Jay's fun."

Rusty tilted his head. "Ring ring ring. Hello?" He mocked as he held an invisible phone to his ear. "Oh hey, Future Shane and Jay! You're calling to say you missed the bus and had to walk to work because you couldn't afford your car payments?"

Shane rolled his eyes. "Shut up, Rusty. Nobody cares for your opinions." He turned back to Jay. "Look, let me do some more number crunching, and I'll get back to you shortly. Stay frosty." With that, he strutted out of the cubicle pod and down the hall.

Jay and Rusty exchanged a knowing look.

Jay knew exactly what was coming— Shane would return with some brilliant idea to bring a third person along to cut down costs. However, there was zero chance Rusty's wife was going to let him go. Hell, she barely let him go out for lunch, let alone out of the country for a boys' weekend.

CHAPTER 3

"Peter, Baby Bjorn and John"

Practically every account manager—past or present—on the virtual pit beers call or not—had at least one epic story. Even Rusty. Unlike most, his didn't involve blacking out. A few years back, when the team was actually good, Frank, Rusty, and two carloads of sales mutts road-tripped to New York City for Game three of the second round of the playoffs. Rusty, Frank, Shane, Jay and a few others managed to get themselves escorted out of Madison Square Garden after the game. It was entirely predictable, given their antics and the fact they were all wearing jerseys—when the final buzzer sounded, and their team secured a 2-1 overtime victory, those visiting fans took their celebration a little too far. The MSG crowd, less than thrilled, responded by launching empty bottles, popcorn bags, plastic beer cups, and a handful of half-eaten pretzels at them.

"You're on your own, boys. Goodnight, and good luck," a security guard said dryly, leading them through a side exit onto Madison Avenue.

Technically, they were not kicked out of the arena, and the security guard helped avoid disaster. The real disaster unfolded later that night.

After hours of barhopping, Rusty took a solo walk around Lower Manhattan. It was the kind of thing a man does when he wants to soak in the energy of the city or at least pretend he's in a cinematic montage. By the time he got back to the hotel, it was well past 3 a.m. — and Frank was smack in the middle of his bed.

Wearing nothing but his tighty-whities, Frank was passed out spread eagle. His considerable beer belly rose and fell with each deep, rumbling snore that echoed through the room and now the hallways of the Double Tree.

Rusty stood in the doorway for a long moment, contemplating his life choices as the scene unfolded in real-time, especially after noticing a frayed hole in Frank's underwear near the man's taint. Then Rusty heard the elevator door open as a man walked towards him. "Good evening, sir," a hotel security guard greeted him in the hallway. "We've had complaints of marijuana on this floor. Do you know anything about that?"

Still processing the situation in front of him in his hotel room, Rusty blinked. "Me? No. I just got here. But..." He gestured toward the barely conscious mass of Frank sprawled across the bed as he and the security guard leaned inside the room. "I can't speak for him."

The security guard took one look and let out a long, weary sigh. "Oh my."

"It's...it's like jiggling...custard," Rusty joked, directing the security guard's gaze with his head.

"Do you mind if I come in?"

Rusty stepped aside.

"Why is there a towel near the door?" the security guard asked.

Rusty frowned. "That's... an excellent question."

"The window is open."

"Yes, it appears to be."

"There are rolling papers on the dresser."

Rusty exhaled. "I don't know how to accurately respond to that, sir," knowing the game was up. "But I don't think we have to worry about any more shenanigans from this guy."

The guard studied the scene for a moment, looked back at Frank and then shook his head. "Alright. Just keep it down." And with that, he left, probably deciding this particular mess wasn't worth the paperwork.

Rusty, meanwhile, vowed then and there: Never again. That was the first and last time he ever shared a room with Frank—or anyone—on a road trip. He valued his sleep too much. And, more importantly, he wasn't about to get kicked out of a damn hotel for something he didn't even do.

Still, he had a sinking suspicion Shane had something to do with all this. Because, really, who else would it have been? His gut feeling was confirmed moments later when he texted Shane for an update. To his credit, Shane took full responsibility—for pushing everyone a little too hard, for buying the first round at every establishment, and, of course, supplying Frank with the weed he got from Jay.

>> Flash Forward >>

Moments later, Shane returned, already launching into a new type of sales pitch. "Alright, hear me out, Jay... I heard from my guy, and he only has three tickets left. We'll need a third guy to make this work."

Jay glanced over at Rusty. "What about Frank?"

Rusty, who now had his back turned, didn't even flinch.

Shane shook his head. "No chance. Frank's been banned from all travel for the foreseeable future." Jay frowned.

"Why?"

"Remember the Boston incident? Or was it Long Island? No, Denver—the team charter incident. Regardless, he's done. Plus, we need someone to keep us out of prison."

Shane was right. Frank's wife had indefinitely banned him from travelling. He didn't realize that his wife had banned Frank from travelling with Shane after multiple past indiscretions.

"How about Speedy Pete from Ticket Operations? Isn't he a big Raider's fan?"

"He bleeds silver and black, but...remember when he punched a fan during a charter with key sponsors? Normally, I'd say he's worth a shot, but road trips had nearly cost him his job—twice! If he was that reckless on team-sanctioned trips, I don't even want to think about what he'd get up to with us."

Jay snorted. "Fair point. What about John?"

"Absolutely not!" Shane yelled. "Don't you remember Johnny's own gincident three seasons ago in North Carolina?

"Uh, how it involved getting drunk on a playoff road trip, wandering off, and getting lost? Didn't he end up losing a tooth and..."

"It was two teeth and, temporarily, his passport. But right before good old John turned into Goofy, he hailed a cab and asked the driver, 'Where can I go for a blowjob?' to which the cabbie replied, 'To give, or to get?'"

"Is that even true?" Jay asked.

"Why the hell would he make that shit up? Besides, it's because of incidents like this he was banned from future excursions. He sobered up quickly after that."

Suddenly, something shiny caught Shane's glance, and he quickly pivoted. Now locking eyes on the back of Rusty's head, he walked quietly across the pod towards Rusty. "Hey Rusty, are you—"

"Nope," Rusty said, still typing on his computer.

Shane groaned. "Wow. I was going to say something you would absolutely like, but now I don't even want to tell you."

Unknowingly, Rusty and Jay rolled their eyes.

Undeterred, Shane continued pacing around the pod. "J-Rock, my boy, we need a third guy to cut costs. You wanted smart and frugal? Rusty is the smart and frugal play."

"Agreed. I am the only frugal thing about this plan," Rusty muttered. "And it's still not gonna work."

"Well, Rusty, if you must know—"

"No, Shane, I must not."

"Per our previous conversation just minutes ago, it now seems appropriate to ask if you are in for a little football roadie next weekend. A little football, some tailgating, a couple of gentleman's clubs..." He grinned devilishly. "Tits in your face, Rusty. Tits in your face."

Rusty spun around in his chair.

"Can't do it, Shane," he said, shaking his head. "I've got an epic weekend of my own with the wife for a Dave Matthews Band concert back in New York City." He leaned back. "No shot she lets me go two out of three weekends—especially not with you two assholes."

Shane clutched his chest in mock heartbreak. "Wow. Just wow."

Jay smirked, already settling in for another round of Shane's increasingly desperate attempts to recruit Rusty into his latest bad idea.

Shane exhaled dramatically. "You know, this is gonna be the first year I'm not going to a Dave Matthews Band concert because they're not touring in our area." He shook his head in mock disappointment.

"I guess you didn't renew your Warehouse membership?" Rusty deadpanned.

"Normally, I don't go because, well, DMB sucks," Shane continued. "Secondly, I wasn't aware of your little trip. A simple invite would have been nice, that's all." He threw up his hands. "This really is a one-sided friendship, wow. I could have shown you some sights, introduced you to some places, little hole-in-the-wall bodegas, some vintage shops in Chelsea...black-and-white cookies—"

Rusty pinched the bridge of his nose again. "Where is this going?"

"Thirdly, a football road trip next weekend with Jay and me would be much better, AND—" Shane leaned in. "You might actually get laid on that trip."

Rusty swivelled in his chair. "Firstly, Amy is never going to let me go two out of three weekends. Secondly, notwithstanding the cost of flying to Vegas, Oakland, or even Australia, plus the football tickets and all the expenses, I don't want to afford it." He folded his arms. "And thirdly—" He paused for dramatic effect. "We're having a baby."

Silence.

Jay coughed on his coffee. "Wait... what? Another one?"

"Yeah, I traded future considerations and whatever goodwill I had in my marriage for a guitar player named Dave Matthews and a weekend away in NYC," Rusty said, completely ignoring their reactions. "You weren't invited because we don't want to go with you." He smirked. "And our sex life is...just fine, thanks." He turned back to his monitor. "Also, I'm not having sex with either of you two."

Jay coughed again, harder this time. Shane squinted. "Wait... you're having another kid?"

Rusty nodded as Shane looked at Jay, then back at Rusty. "Wow." He leaned back in his chair. "I honestly don't know how to respond to that."

Jay exhaled. "I do." He pointed at Shane. "There goes our road trip."

"You guys aren't pregnant!" Rusty shot back.

Shane crossed his arms. "I feel like a trade deadline deal just blindsided me."

Rusty scoffed. "Suck it up, buttercup."

Jay was still processing. "So... wait. When did this happen?"

Shane rolled his eyes. "Oh yeah, Jay, as if we want to pinpoint the exact time and position. HOWEVER, if there's a sex tape, Rusty...please advise!" he said violently, wiggling his eyebrows.

"Go fuck yourself, Shane!"

Undeterred, Shane suddenly gasped. "Oh my God."

Rusty and Jay turned. "What now?" Rusty asked cautiously.

Shane pointed at Rusty, eyes wide. "This is huge. This is era-defining." He turned to Jay. "Our boy Rusty is gonna be a dad."

Jay scratched his head. "Yeah, Shane, we just established that it's kid number two."

Shane ignored him, still staring at Rusty like a lab experiment. "Holy shit," he whispered.

Rusty sighed. "Are you done?"

"Done?" Shane scoffed. "Oh, buddy, we're just getting started." Shane rubbed his hands together. "Alright, boys, let's talk godparent applications."

Rusty groaned, rolling his eyes. "Oh, for fuck's sake—enough!"

"I'm just saying," Shane interrupted, "it would be irresponsible of you not to consider me for the role. Who else are you gonna pick? Someone boring like Dan?"

Rusty snorted. "It's tradition to ask the oldest sibling. And they must be baptized themselves. I don't think there is any denomination that would overlook all your sins, Shane."

"Plus, they'd absolutely pick Dan over you" Jay laughed and grinned. "Yeah, Shane, I feel like you'd be the guy who shows up drunk to the baptism and hands the kid a flask instead of a pacifier."

Shane pointed at him. "I would never do that." He paused. "But if your kid turns eighteen and doesn't know how to shotgun a beer, have I really done my job as an uncle?"

Rusty shook his head. "You aren't the uncle."

"Not yet," Shane corrected. "But hear me out—maybe I marry your sister, and..."

"No."

"—what if we compromise and I co-Godparent with Jay?"

"Still no," Rusty said, typing aggressively at his keyboard.

Shane turned to Jay. "Dude, how awesome would we be as a godparent tag team?"

Jay thought for a moment. "Yeah, except I'm the responsible one, and that doesn't leave any room for error. We'd be teaching the kid bad life choices before they can even crawl."

Shane opened his mouth, reconsidered, then shrugged. "Alright, fair point."

Jay chuckled. "Look, Rusty, if it makes you feel better, I definitely wouldn't let Shane be my kid's godparent either."

Rusty finally turned to them, exasperated. "Neither of you have kids...that you know of!"

Shane smirked. "Exactly! So, we've got plenty of time to practice on yours."

Rusty covered his face with both hands. "I hate you."

"See...this is great news! We have to plan the baby shower bachelor party."

Rusty stared at him. "We absolutely do not. Please stop."

Shane leaned in. "Theme idea: Vegas."

Rusty turned back to his computer. "If I could block you from this pod I would, you know that, right?"

"I love you too, man," Shane dismissed. "Jay will start planning the fiesta!"

"As long as you are not involved..." Rusty replied briskly. "You remember the last time you came to my place for a road game viewing party, don't you?"

"Oh, the Doritos incident," Jay solemnly said, bowing his head in shame.

"Up to this point, no, I hadn't remembered that," Shane said. "But thank you for the reminder now."

The first time—arguably the last time—Amy had let Rusty invite his colleagues over to watch a game on their brand-new 100" high-definition projection screen, Shane quickly made his mark. Specifically, on their pristine, newly installed Berber carpet. He had opened an already half-empty bag of Doritos, sending an avalanche of neon-orange crumbs onto the floor. To this day, Amy was convinced remnants of that disaster were still embedded deep within the fibres, a permanent tribute to his lack of coordination.

"You are such a bitch, Rusty. You never forget anything," Shane huffed. "I'll say it again—this is a one-sided friendship. I invite you to all these events and trips, and you don't even consider me? Wow… shocked… disappointed." He turned to Jay, arms outstretched for dramatic effect. "Can you believe this guy? Besides, I paid for the carpet cleaning."

"No, you didn't," Rusty deadpanned.

"Well, I thought about it!"

"No, you didn't," Jay added, shaking his head.

Before Shane could argue any further, Frank strolled in from the adjacent cubicle pod, clearly entertained by their back-and-forth. "Hey, Franky, Jay and I are thinking about catching the Raiders-Niners game next week. Divisional championships, baby!"

"Yeah, no. That's idiotic. Crazy. Utterly ludicrous," Frank scoffed. "It's the middle of a homestand, and neither of you even like the Raiders or the 49ers. In fact, I don't even know what team you do cheer for, Shane, and don't you like the Canadian Football League, Jay?"

"Yeah, exactly," Rusty chimed in, nodding.

"Nobody asked you, Rusty," Frank shot back. "Also, Shane's right—Dave Matthews Band sucks."

Rusty's jaw tightened. "You know what, Frank? I'm going to make you an iTunes playlist, and it's going to change your life."

Frank squinted. "What's an iTunes, Rusty?"

Rusty let out an exasperated sigh. "Fine. I'll dig through my box of abandoned electronics under the stairs, find my old laptop with a CD burner, and burn you a CD." He crossed his arms. "And that will change your life."

Frank pointed a warning finger at Rusty. "Deep tracks only, Rusty. None of that Crash Into Me bullshit." Rusty's eyes narrowed. "How did you know about—?"

But Frank was bored and had already started walking away. "You ladies can finish this conversation without me— I've already lost interest." He made it halfway back to his desk before stopping in his tracks. His phone buzzed. He glanced at the screen, then turned back with a wicked grin.

"Boys," he announced, "just got a text from Ben from the group leader bus trip."

In the context of professional sports, a group leader is an individual who represents a community organization, such as a local nonprofit, business, or civic group. The group leader is responsible for coordinating group outings to attend hockey games where members of their organization can come together to enjoy a game, enhancing community engagement and fostering relationships among group members.

Group ticket leaders often have established connections within their communities and are skilled at rallying support for events. They play a crucial role in filling seats at games while also promoting the team in their networks. These leaders may arrange for group discounts, special seating, and other perks, making attending the events more attractive for their organizations.

As a way to recognize and reward the efforts of these group leaders, the team offered incentives, such as an annual road trip. This road trip typically involved taking the group leaders to see the team play in another city, providing a unique experience that acknowledges their hard work and dedication.

Frank held up his phone like it contained the gospel. "Shit allegedly went down."

Rusty raised an eyebrow. "What kind of shit?"

Frank's grin widened. "Inter-office sex...allegedly. But there's no context on whether it involved one of ours or one of the group leaders...or both."

"I bet it was Leanne. Ben's always had a thing for her," Jay mused.

Frank let out a nostalgic sigh. "Remember that skiing trip when drunk Leanne was walking around in just her bra and panties? Great ass. Majestic tits... like the Guns of Navarone."

Rusty smirked. "I heard that was accidental."

"How did I miss that?" Jay asked, frowning.

"You may have been the only one to miss that, Jay," Frank chuckled.

Shane let out an exaggerated yawn, stretching his arms above his head. "Inter-office sex? Are you kidding me? Please, wake me up when you've got some interesting news." He leaned back in his chair. "Take it from me—dipping your pen in company ink happens a lot more than you'd think. Highly overrated, especially with the farm team we have here!" He gestured around the pit. "But then again, a freaky six is way hotter than a nine who only does missionary."

The room fell silent. Everyone glanced at Shane, secretly hoping he'd elaborate on who the freaky six was in the office.

Frank broke the silence first. "Yeah? Well, sex is great and all, but have you ever farted so beautifully that your crippling stomach-ache just magically disappeared?"

Rusty sighed. "Why are you asking that now?"

Frank grinned. "No reason at all. Just wanted to foreshadow that in our conversation." He then let out an unapologetic, stomach-ache-relieving fart as he crop-dusted his way back to his cubicle.

Rusty buried his face in his hands. "Jesus Christ."

Frank shared his pod with Salty and Brad, and as he settled in, the waft of his stench had now impregnated their pod.

"Holy Christ!" Brad bellowed, recoiling with a look of disgust.

"Yep," Frank grinned. "Had leftover Chile Rellenos when I got home from the game."

Salty shook his head in disgust. "You are vile."

Brad, however, took a different approach. He took a thoughtful sniff, then nodded. "Ah, yes. I recognize the spiciness in the air." He took another sniff. "It's quite powerful, Frank. Was that with Poblano peppers or Hatch peppers?"

Frank looked at him, genuinely confused. "I really don't know if there's much of a difference. I think you can use Hatch, Poblano... even Anaheim peppers would work."

Brad clicked his tongue. "Ah, touché. But... were they made with Oaxaca cheese?"

Frank blinked. "Why the hell are you asking me that? It is a known fact and written in the bible somewhere that without Oaxaca cheese, there are no Chile Rellenos." Then, turning to Salty, he changed the subject. "Hey, Salty, why didn't you respond to my text last night?"

Salvatore (Sal) DiRienzo—Salty, as his colleagues affectionately called him—barely looked up from his monitor. "I didn't feel the need to respond."

"Excuse me?"

"I don't want to trade with you, Frank." Salty didn't even look at him. "In fact, nobody wants to trade with you. Now if you'll excuse me, I need to call this client back."

Frank leaned in and put his finger on the phone hook, preventing Salty from dialling out. He bent down, getting on Salty's level, their faces inches apart.

"I was offering you the players you need to make your team better," he murmured.

Salty sighed, pinching the bridge of Frank's nose and guiding him back. "Let's look at the four players you were offering me. Last week, they combined for seventeen PPR fantasy points—seventeen, Frank. One of those guys is probably getting suspended for illegal gambling and dogfighting."

Frank let go of the phone and stepped back. "Right, yeah. I suppose his dismal performance was God getting back at him."

Salty frowned. "What?"

"I mean, obviously, God and Noah were tight," Frank explained. "And there were a lot of dogs on the Ark, so, you know... the Big Guy upstairs wasn't too thrilled about the whole dogfighting thing."

Brad, who had been half-listening, suddenly perked up. "Wait, weren't there only two dogs on the Ark?"

Frank shook his head. "Not at all. Noah needed extra dogs to herd the other animals. Minimum nine or ten. Probably more."

Brad nodded. "Huh. Makes sense."

Salty groaned. "I hate you all."

Though pushing fifty, Salty still carried a quiet authority in the pit. He wasn't the loudest, nor the flashiest, but his presence was steady, his words carried weight, and his ability to keep a level head made him the kind of guy rookies gravitated toward. New hires and veterans sought his advice, not because he was their boss, but because he was the closest thing to a mentor this chaotic sales floor had.

But not everyone was in awe of Salty. Frank, for example, had a more complicated relationship with him. Where others saw wisdom, Frank saw a constant reminder of his own shortcomings. He admired Salty, sure, but that admiration was laced with resentment—an unspoken rivalry that only existed in Frank's own mind.

Despite his role as one of the team's unspoken guides, Salty carried his own baggage. His relentless work ethic, which had earned him respect, had also cost him plenty. Missed birthdays, cancelled vacations, a marriage that barely had a pulse—all casualties of his all-consuming commitment to the team. At one point, he'd dreamed of running the show, of being the guy who made the big decisions, who shaped the organization. But that dream got buried beneath renewal targets and spreadsheets somewhere along the way. Now, with more than twenty seasons under his belt, he found himself at a crossroads: keep sacrificing for the team, or finally put himself first?

That inner battle only intensified when Rusty was hired—a younger version of himself with fresh ideas, an MBA, and just enough charisma to make people listen. Salty saw both promise and a threat in Rusty. Did he help shape him into a leader or keep him in check to protect his own place in the hierarchy? It was an uncomfortable question that forced him to confront not just his insecurities, but what kind of legacy he wanted to leave behind.

More and more, Salty found himself mending fences rather than building walls. His once-unshakeable confidence had cracks now, and instead of pretending they weren't there, he was starting to patch them up. He worked on rebuilding his strained relationships, especially with Rusty and, to some extent, Frank—though the latter was more of a side project than a priority.

Still, there were days when even Salty's patience was tested.

Meanwhile, over in the other cubicle pod, Shane and Jay were still working their angle on Rusty.

"What if you told Amy this was a work thing?" Shane suggested, adjusting his testicles yet again.

Rusty grimaced. "Why do you always do that?"

"Do what?"

"That." He gestured vaguely at Shane's crotch region.

Ignoring him, Shane plowed ahead. "Yeah, tell her Dan picked you, me, and Jay for a special fan development project."

Jay nodded. "Through our LinkedIn contacts, we got invited—"

"By the Raiders front office," Shane jumped in, "to tour their new stadium."

Jay pointed. "In Vegas first, obviously, to assess the concourse experience."

Shane snapped his fingers. "Exactly! Then in Oakland, we'd be doing, uh... some guest experience shit."

Rusty crossed his arms. "Guest experience shit. I'm sure Amy'll believe that. At an NFL stadium. Us. Three Canadian ticket sales mutts."

"Uh, yeah."

Rusty stared at them. "Do you even hear yourselves right now?"

Shane wasn't deterred. "Rusty, you have to go."

"You pretty much have to go," Jay echoed, throwing up a high-five that Shane immediately returned.

Rusty turned his chair around. "Okay, let's walk through this. Why the fuck would the Oakland Raiders invite three complete nobodies from Canada to tour their new stadium?" He threw up air quotes. "To get our perspective on concourse design?" He scoffed. "Our concourse is not the envy of other teams. It's a fucking dumpster fire. You guys are insane."

Jay and Shane exchanged a glance.

"Well..." Shane started.

"And even if, somehow, you idiots got me on board with this bullshit," Rusty continued, "how do I explain the plane tickets, hotel bookings, and food expenses to my wife? We have a joint bank account."

"That's where gambling comes in," Shane said. "By the time she sees the withdrawals, we'll already have won back the expenses at the tables."

Rusty laughed dryly. "You do realize how gambling works, right?"

"With confidence, am I right, Jay?"

"You can't keep living like this, boys. At some point, it will catch up with you."

He exhaled. "And this is the same logic you two use with women, by the way."

Shane looked offended. "How dare you."

Rusty continued, pointing at Jay. "Despite Shane having a rotating cast of drive-thru fuckfriends, and despite both of you outdoing yourselves every weekend, how is that good for your soul?"

Jay opened his mouth.

"Shut up, Jay."

Jay closed his mouth.

"If you really want to meet women, go to a Starbucks or an outlet mall food court. The ratio is 10 to 1, and they're already looking for things they don't need."

"Or," Frank reappeared suddenly, "you can just search Facebook Marketplace for 'slightly used' wedding dresses." He winked at Shane. "Instant candidates. You can even filter by size."

Rusty stared at him, eyes wide. "You do realize you're married, right?"

Frank scoffed. "Why is this suddenly all about me?"

Salty clapped his hands. "Alright. Enough. Jay, Shane, this whole plan is stupid."

Jay pointed at Frank. "Isn't that his biography?"

Frank put a finger to Jay's lips. "Dut-dut-dut-dut."

Salty sighed. "Don't you idiots have work to do?"

CHAPTER 4

"Chasing Amy"

As the virtual pit beers continued, a few more familiar faces had joined the call—including Kristina Lee. Kristina was a rising star in sales, one of only three women in the male-dominated office, and the only one who could truly keep up.

With a Portuguese mother and an Asian father, she had a striking, athletic presence. Picture Katie Nolan mixed with Erin Andrews and Meghan Markle—a blend of elegance, confidence, and fierce determination. Her skin glowed under any light, her almond-shaped eyes sparkled with ambition, and her impressive height—made even more commanding by a good pair of heels—gave her an effortlessly powerful aura. Especially when she wore her 'power suit.'

A soccer scholarship had taken her to Rice University in Houston, Texas, where she pursued a degree in sports management with a minor in communications. But in her final year, a torn MCL and ACL ended her playing career and crushed her dreams of going pro. Devastated but never one to quit, she channelled her competitive drive into her education. Graduating with honours, she returned home and quickly landed her current role. Management had been immediately sold on her razor-sharp wit, quirky sense of humour, and compelling personal stories of overcoming adversity. She was authentic, approachable, and had the confidence to back it up. It didn't hurt that she carried herself like an athlete—because she was one.

Kristina always felt she was on a different path than most colleagues. She had ambition. She didn't see this job as just working for a sports team; it was her stepping stone to something bigger.

Unlike many women who frequented the arena, she had zero interest in being a 'puck bunny.' She wasn't a blonde looking for a meal ticket, unlike so many of the players' wives and girlfriends— women who, in her mind, had no real understanding of professional sports beyond the lavish lifestyle their athlete husbands provided. Maybe it was an unfair generalization, but it came from experience.

She had fought for every opportunity in this industry, while others seemed to glide through on connections and relationships.

For her, this job was more than a fancy business card. And at the end of the day, she understood one simple truth: there was only so much lipstick you could put on a pig.

"Hey! Sorry, everyone. I got caught in the rain walking Higgins and had to change," Kristina announced as she sat down, a damp towel draped over her shoulders.

Kristina had an effortless charm. She brought an infectious energy to every conversation, making people feel like they were chatting with an old friend, even if they'd only just met her.

"What did I miss? Anything notable?" she asked, cracking open a Mike's Hard Lemonade.

"Jay, Shane, and Dan were just talking about one of their many failed road trips," Frank said.

Kristina smirked. "Right. Which trip was that again? Cleveland for the Rock and Roll Hall of Fame induction? Game seven of the NBA Finals? Or was it one of Rusty's many Dave Matthews Band concerts?"

"Those were some of the failed attempts, yes," Dan admitted. "Well, one of them was. I mean—no, help me out here. Wasn't this the trip Jay and Shane were trying to plan to Oakland, California?" He fumbled, growing flustered.

Kristina smirked. "Right, to see two teams they had zero affinity for. Just another 'epic' boys' weekend, 6,000 miles away. Totally doable on our base salaries, riiiight?" She sipped her drink and raised an eyebrow. "Wait... that trip never actually happened, right? Tell me that never happened."

"Well, it almost did!" Shane declared, recalling how close they'd come before the plan crashed harder than so many marriages in the pit. "Maybe if Rusty knew how to talk to his wife, we could've made it happen."

"Hey, the guy who's never been married and never will be should probably show some respect," Frank interjected.

As Shane's words hung in the air, a collective pause settled over the group. Still, he and Jay pushed forward, continuing their retelling of the ill-fated Oakland trip pitch.

"Guys, I seriously can't even consider a trip to Vegas and Oakland," Rusty had explained an hour later, frustration creeping into his voice.

"We're just trying to include you because we think you'd have a good time," Jay reasoned. "We'd all have a good time."

"Beyond the DMB show in a few weeks, Amy and I already planned to go shopping for the baby next weekend. We find out if it's a boy or a girl this Thursday, and she'll definitely want to start shopping. And I refuse to buy gender-neutral outfits."

Jay and Shane exchanged a glance, silently evaluating whether this was really the guy they wanted on their so-called epic trip.

"You know," Shane said, arms crossed, "I never understood the need to shop for a baby five months before it's born. Makes zero sense."

Rusty let out a deep sigh. "Life changes the moment you find out you're having a kid, man. The married guy with a pregnant wife can't drop everything to go on these kinds of trips with two single dudes whenever he feels like it."

"Honestly, Rusty," Shane drawled, shaking his head dramatically, "your dedication to the life of Mr. Better Homes and Gardens is... well, it's admirable, really." His voice dripped with sarcasm. "But let me be stupid for a second and point out that this opportunity might never come around again."

Rusty leaned back in his chair, arms crossed. "Look, I've had my wild days. I've slayed my share of dragons and survived more late-night road trips than I can count. Been to countless events and concerts. My tinnitus is basically a badge of honour." He paused, rubbing his temple as if recalling every ringing note in his ears. "I used to think chasing the next big thrill was what I needed. But then I grew up and realized... I don't have to keep chasing it. A wise man once said, 'What I want is what I've not got. But what I need is all around me.' And I think that applies to both of you, too."

Rusty placed a hand on each of their shoulders and gave them a firm look. "Sometimes, if nothing can be done, you just have to make the best of what's around."

A head popped up from the adjacent cubicle like a whack-a-mole. "Am I hearing a reference to DMB's Best of What's

Around in that motivational speech, Rusty?" Frank asked. "You know what? I take back what I said earlier."

Rusty arched an eyebrow. "Oh really? What exactly are you taking back, Frank?"

Frank hesitated, then smirked. "Actually, no, never mind." He leaned back in his chair. "Dave Matthews Band still sucks."

Rusty muttered something inaudible before regaining his composure, returning his attention to Jay and Shane.

"Would you at least send Ashley an email?" Jay suggested, completely forgetting Rusty's wife's name was Amy. "Just pitch her the idea. As discussed, mention it's work-related— you're only responsible for your own ticket. Fly down with points like Shane did, and we'll cover the hotel for now. You can pay us back later. Just tell her you have to go."

Rusty crossed and uncrossed his arms, clearly conflicted. "Isn't the whole point of me going with you two idiots to split the costs evenly? If you're covering my hotel, what difference does it make if I go?"

Jay and Shane exchanged a knowing look before Shane thumped Jay on the back of the head.

"Let me get this straight," Rusty continued, brow furrowed. "We've been invited as special guests of the Oakland Raiders, for whatever reason... and we still have to pay for our own tickets?"

"Yes!" Jay and Shane shouted.

Rusty exhaled sharply, slumping against the cubicle wall. "Alright," he muttered. "If I email her, can this be the end of it?"

"For now, yes," Shane said with a nod.

"Thank Christ! And when she asks why I'm going with you two, what do I say then?" Rusty waved his hand between them. "Remember, she doesn't exactly think highly of you, Shane. Do I need to remind you of that little escapade in that strip club?"

Shane leaned back, grinning like a man reliving his glory days. "You mean when I treated you to four consecutive songs of private dances?" He smirked. "Classic Shane moves."

Rusty chuckled, rolling his eyes. "I wasn't even thinking of that—and I had totally blocked it out. Thank you for the reminder." He shook his head, sighing. "Hey, you know, it was wild—what was I thinking?" He smirked again before sobering. "Anyway, let's skip that trip down memory lane and focus on the task at hand." He fixed them both with a pointed look. "Seriously—why are the three of us involved in this 'project'?"

"Come on, Rusty," Shane coaxed. "You and Jay won the sales contest, and well, I'm the top dog with all the West Coast connections. What more do you want?"

Rusty exhaled sharply. "Well, Amy probably remembers that I've won three sales contests over the past two seasons, but the rewards? We've never actually seen a dime. Need I remind you of that other trip that turned into a peaceful yellow school bus ride to the Best Western? What happened to that promised round-trip train, dinner, Westin hotel stay, and $100 spending money? We basically got paid in vouchers for our own game." His voice rose with indignation.

Jay, who had been quietly pondering his own standing, finally spoke up. "Okay, backtracking a bit—yeah, we all know what Amy thinks of Shane. But what about me? What's her take on me?"

Rusty smirked, barely suppressing his amusement. "Honestly, Jay? Not much, really. But it's nothing personal. I think she confuses you with Brad. Might be safer if it stays that way."

Jay threw up his hands in mock offence. "Great. Just great."

"Yeah, Jay. Real nice." Shane clapped him on the back before turning to Rusty. "Open your Outlook, and we'll draft this message together." Without waiting, Shane reached for Rusty's mouse and opened a blank email.

"I can do it," Rusty said, rolling his eyes and yanking the mouse back from Shane's grip. "But don't expect miracles. I give it a 3% chance of success."

He stared at the blank screen, his fingers hovering over the keyboard.

"Hey, how about this?" he muttered, typing slowly. "'Hi, babe...'"

"I'm overwhelmed already," Jay interjected, shaking his head.

Rusty shot him an annoyed grin. "Find a girlfriend, Jay!" He continued typing. There's an opportunity for me to go to Oakland by way of Vegas with Jay and Shane the weekend before NYC. Jay and I won a sales contest. I think I told you about it earlier this month, didn't I?

"Wow, I never pictured you as a control freak, Rusty," Shane said, leaning over Rusty's shoulder. "Keep going."

"Can you not breathe down my neck?" Rusty muttered, opening his desk drawer and handing Shane a piece of gum.

He continued typing: As it turns out, we get to choose where we go this time, and the boys want to go to Oakland for the Raiders game. Since they're moving to Vegas in 2020, we also get to tour their new stadium during our stopover in Vegas.

"It's for work, Rusty! For work!" Jay reminded, making air quotes.

Rusty sighed, adding, I mean, it's more than just a football game... it's also for work, right? The Raiders have invited us to tour their new stadium and discuss their guest experience program.

"You already told her about the stadium tour, idiot! She's going to think something is up!" Shane scolded before reaching over and aggressively pressing the backspace key six times.

Rusty glared at him. "Personal space!" he said, somehow keeping his cool. You know how I was working on that suite project during the last strike? Remember how marketing told me to 'stay in my lane,' then stole all my ideas and passed them off as their own? Well, apparently, Dan wants me to gather as much info as I can on the Raiders' suite program to see if we can 'secretly implement' anything back here.

"I like where this is going," Shane said, grinning as he honked his crotch in excitement. "Throw in something else—tell her we're also representing the team at the league meetings on Friday and that we'll watch a Golden Knights game while we're there, too."

"Jesus, Shane. This is already a very slippery slope. I'm not about to dig myself into a deeper hole," Rusty snapped.

He continued typing: What are your thoughts on this? I know it's the weekend before NYC and DMB, but can you please let me know before you leave work today?

"I don't even think you should mention DMB weekend," Jay advised. "Just act cool. Nonchalant."

"Yes! Why remind her of the other weekend, Rusty?" Shane added. "Just let sleeping dogs lie." Then, without warning, Shane reached over Rusty's shoulder, snatched the keyboard, and resumed typing. "I need to let Shane know," he muttered aloud as he typed each word carefully. "Now you say, 'I'm sorry for such short notice, love. This is one of those trips I've been waiting for with the job, and who knows if this will ever come again.' Right? There. Send it." Shane leaned back triumphantly.

"Wait, wait!" Rusty yanked the keyboard back, adding a final touch.

He typed: Thanks, my love. Love you. Richard xoxpxox

Disgusted, Jay turned away and muttered, "I'm proud to say that I have never used an emoticon in any setting."

"When was the last time you got laid, Jay?" Rusty asked, leaning back in his chair. "Actually, let me rephrase—when was the last time you even spoke to a woman... present colleagues and your mother not included?"

Jay looked down in shame. "...Uh..."

Shane squinted at Rusty's email draft, his face contorting in confusion. "Wait a second... You also added a 'p' in your hugs and kisses."

"Take it out, you amateur!" Shane exclaimed, scandalized.

"The extra 'p' is for a tongue, you amateur," Rusty smirked and explained as he flicked his tongue and blew Shane and Jay kisses.

Shane and Jay's minds practically short-circuited.

"Eww, gross!" Jay recoiled.

"Actually...I kind of respect it," Shane admitted, nodding reluctantly.

Before Rusty could react, Shane lunged over his shoulder, snatched the mouse, and clicked Send with reckless abandon.

"This is good enough! Click send! CLICK SEND!" Shane howled, grinning like a madman.

Rusty let out a heavy sigh, slumping back in his chair. Deep in his soul, he knew that nothing good would come from this.

CHAPTER 5

"Bennettfits"

Around the same time, Salty and Frank had moved past their earlier fantasy trade dispute and were now debriefing the team's disastrous West Coast road trip. Five losses in six games had pushed them eight points out of a playoff spot with just over a quarter of the season left to play.

"You know, this road trip just fucked our renewal prospects, eh?" Salty said matter-of-factly.

It was no secret that the entire city became an ally when the team was winning. Tickets were impossible to find, and fans were willing to pay a premium. But the moment they started losing, interest evaporated faster than a puddle on a July afternoon.

"Hey Franky, why didn't you go with the group leaders to Long Island and Boston this time?" Salty asked.

"I've been advised not to talk about it," Frank replied.

"They're still holding that against you?" Salty smirked.

"They probably should."

"Dude, what happened again?"

"I may have punched a few fans. Maybe one or two from our group, too."

"Jesus."

"And by maybe, I mean yes. Thankfully, no charges were laid. Plus, I may have also encouraged some... illicit behaviour," Frank said as his bit his lip.

Salty shook his head and shifted in his seat. "What illicit behaviour did you encourage?"

Frank sighed. "Well, there were a few gincidents, of course. But...mostly Jägerbombs. Many, many Jägerbombs." He shook his head as if still trying to process his poor decisions.

"I thought one of your cardinal rules was 'Blondes, not Bombs'? Since when do you even drink Jägermeister?" Salty asked. "You realize you're over fifty, right? How do you still have a job? Or a liver? Stick to lagers or IPAs, for Christ's sake."

"I know, I know!" Frank pleaded. "I was just following orders, like a good soldier."

"Orders from who, Frank?"

"Dan and Kent. You and I both know they're ten times worse than me. And they know I've seen them act worse...far worse." Frank leaned in conspiratorially. "I've seen things, Salty. Things only Ray Donovan has seen or could fix."

Salty chuckled. "Give me an example."

"Ever seen Dan throw ice at people when he's hammered?"

Salty nodded. "Oh yeah, he calls it the 'hailstorm.'"

"Right! Just random people getting pelted in the head with ice cubes from five to fifteen feet away. It's disgusting. But his aim—even in that drunken state—it's impressive as fuck."

Salty laughed. "That's not nearly as controversial as when Darryl threw mushrooms off his pizza at a little person and told him to 'grow like Super Mario.'"

Frank winced. "Darryl's lucky HR wasn't faster on that one."

"Well, he doesn't work here anymore, so there's that."

"True." Frank nodded before his expression darkened. "Have you ever been kicked out of a Cracker Barrel?"

Salty's eyes narrowed. "Wait... what?"

Frank leaned in. "Next time you see Jimmy Bennett, ask him how Kent got us all kicked out of a goddamn Cracker Barrel."

Salty laughed. "Jesus, I need that story."

Frank smirked. "Jimmy tells it better."

Frank was referring to Dan Christianson, the Sales Manager; Kent O'Neil, the Director of Sales; and Jimmy Bennett, an account manager who had narrowly avoided being fired multiple times for questionable ticketing practices.

Dan had been with the team for twelve seasons, serving as Sales Manager for the past seven. His career in professional sports started in his early twenties when he landed a junior sales position. Like many industry newcomers, he was fuelled by a genuine love for the game and threw himself into the job, quickly earning a reputation around the league for his innovation. His ability to read people—identifying their strengths, weaknesses, and motivations—set him apart.

Management took notice, and before long, he was climbing the ranks.

However, the relentless pressure of the role came at a cost. Like so many in his position, Dan had never financially recovered from a messy divorce. His high alcohol tolerance, a byproduct of years in the cutthroat world of professional sports, often masked deeper emotional scars. While he managed to keep things together during work hours, he wasn't always as composed after hours. Under the influence—whether it was booze or the occasional recreational substance—his behaviour could turn juvenile, even reckless. Thankfully, those moments rarely bled into office hours, but he couldn't hide it if he was out with some of his team. Beneath his often crude, sarcastic exterior, which had hardened into a defence mechanism over the years, lay the heart of a passionate and empathetic professional who still cared—perhaps too much.

Dan's rapid ascent in the organization was built on his sharp instincts and infectious enthusiasm. He spearheaded creative promotions, pushed for more personalized fan engagement, and consistently fought for improvements in the sales department. But his leadership style was a double-edged sword. He believed that a balance of fear and freedom was the key to performance—demanding excellence while allowing his staff the space to be creative, as long as it served the team's goals. If you followed the rules, Dan had your back.

At his core, though, Dan still aspired for more. He felt like he was a middleman caught in the perpetual crossfire between ownership's profit-driven agenda and upper management's ever-shifting priorities. The "What have you done for me lately?" mentality made it nearly impossible to motivate a sales team. Promised bonuses and incentives dangled like carrots, yet they were rarely delivered when goals were met. This inconsistency chipped away at his and his team's morale, making it hard to foster growth. Dan often fought battles he knew he couldn't win, wedged between the expectations of those above him and the frustrations of those below.

But the problem wasn't entirely his own. Dan was simply forced to carry orders from his superiors, including Kent O'Neil. Time and again, Dan was forced to push directives that contradicted his own views on leadership and team building, creating a cycle of frustration. The sales team knew Dan wasn't the root of the problem, but they also saw that the results were almost always the same no matter how many times he tried to shake things up.

Dan was trapped, and he knew it. The question was—how much longer could he keep playing this game?

Kent O'Neil, the Director of Sales, was a master of corporate survival. To upper management, he appeared to have everything under control, but he was merely coasting, relying entirely on Dan's dedication and the team's endurance. Kent sidestepped accountability while reaping the rewards of Dan's hard work.

His leadership style was infamous. He often vanished when his team needed him, indulging in long lunches, weekend getaways, or conveniently timed "phone troubles." During crises—such as failed bonuses or a lack of strategic direction—Kent was notably absent, leaving Dan and the overwhelmed team to shoulder the burden.

Promises of bonuses, once a motivational beacon, became meaningless. Each unfulfilled promise deepened discontent, fuelling resentment among team members who whispered their frustrations and exchanged glances that revealed their diminishing faith in a leader preoccupied with other priorities.

Dan and the team sought guidance, especially during high-stakes moments, but faced relentless stress from unmet expectations instead. Conversations shifted from innovative strategies to uncertainty and fear. As tensions escalated, colleagues became vigilant, anticipating the next miscommunication that could spiral the team into further disarray. What was once a collaborative environment devolved into isolated roles, each weighed down by disappointment and distrust. Kent's and upper management's silence exacerbated the situation, causing a fracture in team cohesion and a loss of enthusiasm.

The damage was profound; it would take more than empty promises to restore motivation among a team that had learned the consequences of faltering leadership. Team members recognized that their morale would continue to plummet without Kent's active support, and growth would remain a distant dream.

To the younger staff, Kent's name became synonymous with the Polkaroo, a TV character known for disappearing before important events. Shane and Jay, though too young to appreciate the '80s reference, quickly realized Kent was rarely present during critical moments.

Despite his detached approach, Kent excelled at selective involvement. He would enter meetings, reword someone else's idea, and then retreat to play games on his outdated BlackBerry, maintaining just enough visibility to appear engaged while contributing little.

Unfortunately, the culture Kent fostered and upper management overlooked was toxic. He prioritized appearances over results, quarterly numbers over morale, and personal leisure over professional responsibility, yet somehow remained untouchable. A living embodiment of bureaucratic inertia. Almost equally problematic was Jimmy Bennett, a relic of the old-school sales world. In his late 50s, he sported slicked back, greasy and thinning hair, a husky voice seasoned by decades of menthol cigarettes and whiskey, and a wardrobe that hadn't been updated since the late '80s. His double-breasted polyester suits, or three-button suits—likely sourced from the deepest bins of Value Village—were as outdated as his sales tactics. He was twice divorced, lived with his son Chad, and carried himself with the smugness of a man who'd closed more deals than he could count.

Jimmy was the definition of a Willy Loman-type salesman, and like Loman himself, he wasn't exactly well-liked in the office. He did what he wanted when he wanted—a trait that didn't go unnoticed by the younger, hungrier employees in the pit. Some called him arrogant, others labelled him old-fashioned, but everyone agreed on one thing: Jimmy didn't care. He knew who he was, and he was unapologetic about it.

He was also unapologetic about bending the rules.

Last season, Dan had finally lost patience and attempted to fire him, only for Kent to intervene, urging Dan to "reconsider." Dan had scheduled a surprise one-on-one meeting—often a prelude to termination. Kent was supposed to attend but, in typical fashion, requested a later time for a "prior engagement" that conveniently wasn't on his calendar.

By 11:29 AM, Dan entered the boardroom, prepared to address Jimmy's long history of questionable practices. Lena, the team's HR assistant manager, was already there, a stack of papers and an envelope in hand. By 11:45, with Kent still missing, Dan's foot impatiently tapping was too much, and he and Lena decided to proceed without him.

Dan sat across from Jimmy, sharply dressed in a pinstripe suit, contrasting to Jimmy's rumpled Harris Tweed. He exhaled deeply before sliding a report across the table.

"Jimmy, I'm tired," Dan began. "Tired of looking the other way, hoping things would change, while you keep letting me down."

The report detailed Jimmy's accounts, many highlighted or circled, with notes scrawled in both Dan's and Kent's handwriting. Jimmy barely glanced at it. He had been around long enough to know what this was about—and was honestly surprised it had taken this long.

Dan let out a slow exhale. "We can't keep tolerating this. You've been discounting tickets without authorization just to pad your group sales numbers. You didn't renew top accounts but somehow managed to sell their seats to their own family members—just so you could collect the new sales commission?"

"A sale is a sale," Jimmy said smugly with a lopsided grin. "Plus, there was a change in ownership. What did you expect me to do, Dan?"

"Bullshit." Dan winced, and his voice rose. "Bull. Shit."

Lena flinched. The top of her knee hit the bottom of the boardroom table.

"You've been giving away free parking to close deals. Breaking up pairs to sell individual seats. Screwing up our inventory system by hijacking management holds. And let's not forget the Bennettfits."

Jimmy cocked an eyebrow. "The what?"

"The 'Bennettfits,'" Dan repeated. "The little Jimmy Bennett perks you throw in to sweeten deals. The clients love them, but they're a goddamn nightmare for our financials."

Jimmy smirked. "I like that name."

Dan ignored him. "Every time I walk past your desk, you're either gone or on your cell. You've been a terrible influence on the new guys, and honestly? The team's done with you."

Jimmy leaned back, unfazed. "You always tell us to treat this job like our own business, Dan. I've been running mine successfully for twenty-two years. Before you were even here.

When we were hitting our targets, nobody gave a damn how we did it. But now, suddenly, we can't turn a blind eye?" He sarcastically laughed and shoved the report back toward Dan. "When sales are good, we're told to 'do whatever it takes.' It's only when things go bad that everyone pretends they don't know how the sausage gets made. Shouldn't it be the other way around?"

Dan clenched his jaw. "Doing whatever it takes? There's a difference between taking care of business and selling out, Jimmy. And I don't need to tell you which one describes you. You're a snake."

Jimmy smirked; his lips parted as he was about to speak. But before he could respond, the boardroom doors burst open as Kent crashed into the room like the Kool-Aid Man. He was twenty-seven minutes late for the meeting he had requested. He was still talking into his phone with a cup of non-sponsor-friendly coffee in hand, and yet, almost completely oblivious to the weight of the discussion, he simply waved a dismissive gesture to Dan, Lena and Jimmy, as well as his caller. "I'll call you back. Yep. Yep. Okay, thanks," he muttered before hanging up.

Without acknowledging the time or apologizing to anyone, he plopped into the head seat, perpendicular to Dan and Jimmy.

Dan blinked, momentarily thrown off. "Uh. Hello, Kent."

Kent adjusted his tie, finally addressing Jimmy directly. "You were comfortable. And you were a whore for making money."

Jimmy snorted. "Always dramatic, eh, Kent?" as Kent leaned in closer.

"Excuse me?"

Dan exhaled sharply. He knew this conversation had just taken a very different turn.

"Nice to see you, Kent. Thank you for gracing us with your presence," Jimmy said smoothly before turning back to Dan, disregarding Kent. "I stayed because of my clients. I take care of them, and they take care of me—it's the circle of life in professional sports. You build a relationship, not just sell them tickets. Do you think half our business clients even need tickets? Of course not. But if you treat them like family, they stick around—no matter how bad the product on the ice is," he snapped.

"But you know what, Dan?" Jimmy leaned forward, his voice laced with bitterness. "This team can't even do something as simple as sell tickets right. This team finds a way to screw it up every single time. Wrong tickets sent out. Season ticket packages delivered to the wrong addresses or in flowerpots. Meet-the-player events where the player doesn't even care enough to show up.... We throw every freebie imaginable at casual fans just to get them in the door, but when Mr. and Mrs. Season Ticket Holder—the ones who've been loyal for years—ask for something, we ignore them. We overpromise and underdeliver. Constantly."

Dan hesitated before answering. "You're not wrong, Jim. Regardless of the many mistakes, what you have done is unacceptable."

"Unacceptable? Who do you think has to clean up those unacceptable messes? The sales guys. Me. That's how you get ahead in this game. You make good on broken promises, leading to referrals, renewals, and long-term loyalty."

Dan and Kent sat quietly for a moment, letting Jimmy's words settle. Dan knew the organization had a long history of screwing over its own customers. Dan sighed, trying to regain control of the conversation. "That might have been how it worked before, Jimmy, but it can't be that way anymore. I need to show my guys how to succeed legitimately and with integrity. No quid pro quo, no back pocket favours. We need to keep some integrity because we can't always rely on bending the rules."

Jimmy scoffed and looked around the room before locking eyes with Kent, who was still casually sipping his coffee. "Integrity?" Jimmy repeated, his voice laced with disbelief. "Look around, Dan. Nobody has integrity here. This is the culture this organization has created—the culture you've cultivated. You're firing me like I'm the problem? Like I'm the only one doing this?"

Jimmy leaned forward, his expression unwavering. "What do you expect, huh? That I'm going to be tossed to the wolves so the rest of the sales pit magically starts playing by the rules? You're delusional, Kent. Sales guys get paid a shit base salary for the chance to chase a championship and maybe—maybe—get a ring out of it. But we know we won't. Not with this owner. We live off our commission. That's our bread and butter. And when the team is as dogshit as they are right now, those guys will do whatever it takes to close a deal. That's the plain and simple truth, Dan."

"The plain and simple truth, Jimmy, is that this is what—strike five? Strike six?" Kent said, finally leaning forward, startling Dan. He hadn't expected Kent to be this involved in the firing, but here he was, taking the lead.

"How many chances did you need to get it right?" Kent continued. "You still didn't give a shit. You still didn't make it a priority to change. Dan gave you another shot last season. I told him to make you go away. And now..." Kent paused for effect. "I—we—have decided to let you go. Effective immediately."

Jimmy exhaled sharply, his eyes narrowing. "You're making a big mistake here, Kent."

Kent raised an eyebrow.

"You let me go, and you lose every relationship I've built over the past two decades. Those clients aren't going to stick around for whatever poor bastards take over my accounts. You're setting them up for failure—and when they can't hit your bullshit numbers, you'll be left scratching your head, wondering why."

Kent didn't flinch. "Your services are no longer required, and those accounts will be reassigned like always." He waved a dismissive hand. "And those fresh kids in the pit? They need to see that this behaviour doesn't fly anymore. That selfishness and shortcuts don't cut it here."

Jimmy shook his head, scoffing a laugh. "It's too little, too late, Kent. Plus, Dan and I already covered that fifteen minutes before you waltzed in here late with your Starbucks in hand," Jimmy muttered. "Let me clue you in, Kent—firing me won't change a damn thing in that pit. Those kids never learned what I know in their bullshit sports management degrees. You really think they're going to play it straight? Please. As you always say, 'take a look at yourself in the mirror.'"

Lena, who had been nervously silent the entire time, finally spoke.

"Here are the details of your severance, James," she said, sliding an envelope toward him.

Jimmy didn't even glance at it.

"We're giving you one week's pay for every year you've been with us," she continued. "Your health benefits will continue for one year. And you'll receive a commission on any sales made through the end of the month."

"Legitimate sales, once illegitimate commissions are clawed back," Kent corrected.

Jimmy let out a slow breath. He knew it was over.

Dan took a deep breath. "I'm sorry, Jim. This is how it must be. Take a week to review the terms—seek legal advice if you need to. Then, once you sign your release, you'll be cut a cheque. I'm—"

"I'm sure you'll agree that this is more than fair given the circumstances of your termination," Kent cut in, not even letting Dan finish. His tone was clipped, impatient, and his interest was fading.

Lena, ever the professional, followed up smoothly. "I'll escort you back to your desk so you can pack your immediate belongings. The rest will be packed and returned to you when you pick up your cheque," she added, tilting her head slightly. "Assuming you collect your cheque."

The tension in the room settled like a heavy fog.

Dan stood up first, extending his hand.

For a brief moment, Jimmy just sat there, staring at it. Then, composing himself, he slowly stood, mirroring the gesture. Their hands met in a firm, brief shake.

"Feel free to use Kent as a reference," Dan said.

Jimmy smirked. "Oh, I definitely won't be doing that."

Dan turned slightly, glancing at his boss—only to see Kent completely disengaged, hunched over his phone, furiously typing a text.

Of course he was. Classic Kent.

Jimmy exhaled sharply and shook his head. "Unbelievable," he muttered as he turned to follow Lena out the door.

CHAPTER 6

"An Unrequited Reply"

About thirty minutes later, Rusty was at his desk wrapping up a project when his inbox pinged with an email reply from his wife, Amy. He read it quickly. Then printed it out. With the warm paper in hand, he walked over to Shane's desk, tapping Jay on the shoulder as he passed.

"Here you go, boys."

"Oh, a quick reply! This is good...no, this is great news," Shane said excitedly, snatching the page from Rusty's grip. Clearing his throat, he dramatically began to read aloud.

"'Hi baby...'" He immediately stopped, gagging in disgust. "You two disgust me," he groaned.

Jay and Rusty smirked.

"'So... is this a work thing? Will you be paid for it—you know—by work? How will you be travelling? If it's something you have to pay for, then I'm sorry, I have to say no.'"

His face contorted. "No, no, no... this is bad—this is really bad."

Rusty fought back a smile. Shane's voice turned serious as he read on, "'With everything going on these days, we really…'" He suddenly stuttered, his excitement draining. "'Well, we don't have… the extra money…'"

Deflated, he handed the page to Jay. "I can't read this," he muttered.

Jay held up his hands, refusing to take it.

"Fine," Rusty said, reclaiming the page. Clearing his throat, he continued, "'It's one thing if it's for work, but… it's not really for work, is it? You need to think about what's best for you, me, and our family before asking me these things. Pick your battles, sweetheart.'"

Jay and Shane slumped in their chairs.

Rusty, however, remained serious until he turned to Shane, his eyes gleaming with amusement. "Let me guess, did Shane put you up to this? We can talk about it later, but I think I know the answer already. You know what I think of him… and—which one is Jay again? Is he the little Scottish guy with the nice hair? Or the chef?"

Jay's jaw dropped.

"What the hell?" he stammered. "Who's the little Scottish guy? My hair is nice, isn't it?"

Rusty, still grinning, continued to read. "'Besides, why would a team from Oakland invite the three of you to 'tour their stadium?' No offence, but you need to give me a bit of credit here. This is a spur-of-the-moment trip by two guys who don't have family commitments or responsibilities and need a third guy to lower their overall costs, right? Didn't you say they tried to pull this shit on someone else before?'" Rusty lowered the paper, raising an eyebrow at Shane and Jay. Rattled, Shane blurted out, "Why would you even tell Amy that?"

Rusty shrugged.

"Well," he said, folding the email, "this went about as well as I thought it would. Maybe even better."

He finished reading, "'Again, I'm sorry, but it will be a hard no for me on this one, babe. I hope you're having a good day; I'm about to leave work and pick up some groceries on my way home. Love you to the moon and back. Amy xoxoxp. P.S., what do you want for dinner tonight?'"

Shane recoiled.

"Jesus, Rusty. You didn't need to read that last part," he grumbled, rubbing his temples.

Still reeling from the "little Scottish guy" comment, Jay shook his head in disbelief.

"What else have you told your wife?" he asked, narrowing his eyes.

Rusty didn't answer right away.

Because the truth was... he had told Amy everything.

His hopes. His fears. His ambitions.

Being vulnerable with her was the one thing he had never second-guessed.

And maybe that was the difference between him and Shane. Between him and Jay.

They lived in the moment. He planned for the future.

Amy deserved better.

But this trip? "A work trip?" This could very well be the straw that broke the camel's back, or at least the first domino to fall, because this wasn't just about Vegas or Oakland.

This was about the gap between the man he wanted to be for Amy... and the man he was trying to be with Shane and Jay.

"Rusty?"

Kristina's soft yet stern voice pulled him back. She had just walked into the pod looking for Shane.

He blinked, looking up.

"You good over there?" she asked, eyeing him curiously. Rusty took a deep breath and straightened in his chair.

"Yeah," he said, forcing a small smile. "Just thinking about how crucial communication is—especially right now. Every word matters. Whether we're talking to clients, our team, or our spouse."

Jay turned in his chair and raised an eyebrow.

Just as Rusty remained with his thoughts in the flashback, Dan also found himself staring at his screen but back on the virtual call. He remained grounded in the moment as he leaned back on his couch. His focus on the meeting wavered, and he found himself in a distant corner of his memory, back in that stadium, sitting three rows up from the ice. He'd had a conversation with Kristina years ago about glass ceilings, outdated mindsets, and the reality of unrealized potential. He could almost feel the cold air, hear the faint echoes of pucks hitting the boards, smell the stale popcorn concessions, and taste the burnt coffee he poured in the kitchen before the meeting.

Dan and Kristina had a strong professional rapport. He admired her work ethic and saw her potential to surpass her peers in the pit. He knew the cards were stacked against her— it was nearly impossible to meet such high expectations. But she was authentic and never went against the grain for personal gain.

They often walked down a long, narrow corridor underneath the stands, past the ticket operations office and the team's gym, until they reached one of the exclusive club sections. Their weekly one-on-one sales meetings frequently occurred in Captain's Club, one of Dan's finest projects. What was once a converted storage closet was now an intimate, high-value season ticket-holder-exclusive section adorned with large paintings of the team's captains by a local artist. Entrance required club seats, arguably the best seats in the house. Captain's Club was the place to be seen with leather couches, a private bar, unlimited snacks, and private restrooms. Despite its hefty price, it offered arguably the best value in the arena, especially with complimentary valet parking and the section's exclusive cache.

At this point, Kristina had been with the team for three seasons. She worked hard to follow standard operating procedures for tagging leads in the Customer Relationship Management system (CRM) and had to fight for accurate commission cheques on multiple occasions due to someone switching sales codes. She had faced those unnecessary setbacks too many times for it to be considered accidental. Jimmy Bennett was responsible for three lost sales, and Dan was determined to claw that back from Jimmy to make things right for Kristina.

"Have you ever thought about working elsewhere, Dan?" Kristina asked, staring ahead at the action on the ice as Dan reclined in his stiff but padded chair, pondering her question.

"All the time, Krissy," he said confidently. "Professional sports may appear glamorous, but it's not as enticing as people think. It's easy to assume we get to attend every game, meet players, and do all the fun things, but there's a lot they don't see. So much bullshit. Bullshit that kills spirits. Why do you ask?"

Kristina turned to him. "I guess I've struggled with where I am and where I'm headed. I like it here, don't get me wrong, and I think I'm good at what I do..."

"Krissy," Dan politely interrupted. "You don't have to preface anything like, 'I like it here.' Say whatever you need to say. You've earned that right, and you've been here long enough to understand the dynamics of the sales pit. Let's set aside the team and the league standings and just focus on the pit for a moment. What is the sales pit?" he asked rhetorically before continuing. "It can be seen in various ways: a cubicle factory ruled by alpha males with loud voices. It's the last call for the Willy Lomans of the sports world, with years spent ironing worn shirts and driving countleskilometres behind them. It's a wake-up call for the MBA grads straight out of school who believe their education will give them an edge. No offence to you or Rusty, but it doesn't. Not here, at least. Your education may open doors and build credibility, but will it lead to real change? Probably not."

"Has it always been like this?" Kristina asked.

"Like what specifically? Limiting? Thankless? Stressful? Heart attack-inducing? Yes. All the above, and so much more. There's definitely a yearning for change, and that's where the sales pit becomes a double-edged sword," Dan replied, leaning forward with a glint in his eye.

"More like a snake pit," Kristina added.

"Well, if we use the fairy tale description of a snake pit being a place of horror, torture and death, then yes."

Kristina giggled.

Dan continued. "On one hand, it's a place of camaraderie and teamwork. On the other hand, it's a space that can suppress individuality and breed complacency. Those who dare to push back or propose radical ideas often find themselves at odds with the very system that claims to encourage collaboration."

Kristina reflected on her ideas, the ones she had been hesitant to share for fear of rocking the boat or facing scrutiny.

"So, what do we do?" she asked quietly. "How do we break free from this stifling environment?"

Dan smiled. "It starts with small acts of bravery, Krissy. It's about seizing opportunities to voice new ideas, however unconventional they may seem. We need to create a ripple effect, encouraging others to let down their guards, challenge the status quo, and breathe life back into the sales pit. I think it's within our power to shift this narrative if we approach it collectively rather than as isolated individuals."

"So, are you saying we try to cultivate a culture where taking a chance is okay?" Kristina asked, her curiosity piqued.

"Yes," Dan affirmed, leaning forward with conviction. "Jimmy was arguably the first domino to fall in the entire organization. Hopefully, not the last."

"Tell me about it," Kristina started. "It's an opportunity to reclaim the very essence of why we're here— to innovate, to inspire, and to make an impact that goes beyond the metrics on any spreadsheet." At that moment, Kristina felt hope ignite within her. Both she and Dan knew it wouldn't be easy, and there would be obstacles along the way, but perhaps they could rediscover the possibilities waiting to be unleashed.

"I want you to break through this glass ceiling; there should eventually be a woman leading this department, someone with a different perspective. You have that in you. Moreso than anyone else in the department."

"Even Shane?" Kristina asked, half serious.

Dan looked unamused but noticed a fire burning in her eyes. "Krissy, you're not just good—you're great at what you do. I don't even need to say this, but being a woman in a male-dominated office is tough, and you handle it well. You're ambitious, smart, funny, and you hold your own with everyone, even Shane."

"Thanks, Dan. No doubt, being a woman presents challenges. It's not just the guys in the sales pit; being taken seriously by prospects and clients can be tough, too. People see me and think, 'Who's this hot chick trying to sell me sports? Get me a cocktail, baby.' Don't get me wrong, I can handle that bullshit, and it doesn't phase me. It's just sad and unfortunate that this is the world we live in, where women and sports are an oxymoron," she said calmly.

"But those challenges encourage me to be better than anyone else at what we do. I like it here. I'm not looking elsewhere, so no need to worry. I want more responsibility, and I want to be a catalyst for change."

Dan continued. "I would fully support that. I strive to give everyone a real shot at success. You know, projects that go beyond our daily scope face intense scrutiny and rarely come to fruition. Remember

Rusty's project during the strike when he evaluated suite programs from every professional sport?

When he presented his findings to the suite and marketing departments, he was told he had made the old VP of Marketing sour."

"Sour?" she asked.

"He was scolded and basically told not to tell them how to do their fucking jobs."

"I think we all learned a lot from his findings, but it's obviously unfortunate that his out-of-the-box thinking was not welcomed because it made the marketing department, you know, the department that was supposed to be creative, look like they didn't know what they were doing."

Dan exhaled, shaking his head. "It's been the same problem for years. The marketing department prioritizes short-term ticket sales, and our sales team is often left to pick up the pieces when season ticket holders feel undervalued. There's no continuity, no unified strategy. It's a game of quick fixes."

Kristina folded her arms, nodding. "Right, and meanwhile, we're expected to justify the price of full-season memberships when people can just pick and choose their games at a discount. It's frustrating. Everyone passes the buck and the bucket of responsibility."

Dan leaned back, rubbing his temples. "Exactly. And every time someone suggests a change, it gets buried in a never-ending cycle of meetings, emails, and half-hearted 'we'll consider it' responses. That's why Rusty's project during the strike was dead before it even had a chance. The suite and marketing departments didn't want to acknowledge that someone in sales—someone outside of their little bubble—might actually have a better idea than them. Which he did."

Kristina sighed. "Rusty's bachelor party suite idea was brilliant. I mean, a fully branded partnership with a hardware store. Decking out a suite with toolboxes, bar stools, and power tools? A man cave on steroids? That thing would've sold out every game. But nope—too innovative, I guess."

Dan smirked. "God forbid we actually try something that makes sense."

Kristina chuckled, shaking her head. "It just proves that change around here is more about politics than actual results. And I get it—some people are just comfortable. But comfort breeds complacency, and complacency kills growth. You know...I guess that's why I want more responsibility, Dan. Like I said, I don't want to just sell tickets; I want to be part of the change."

Dan studied her for a moment. "Then let's work on that. I'll make sure you get positioned with management to take on bigger projects beyond your account manager role. But you have to be ready for resistance."

"I can handle resistance. I just want the chance."

"Good. Because this department needs someone like you to shake things up."

"You ever regret getting into this business, Dan?" Dan let out a dry laugh before downing the remainder of his now cold coffee. "All the fucking time." She raised an eyebrow, prompting him to continue.

"Look, professional sports seem glamorous from the outside, but it's exhausting. Late nights, endless stress, pressure from ownership and constant pressures from family and friends looking for freebies. I mean, hell, if I had taken a different path, I'd probably have less stress, be home more, maybe still be married. Some days, I wonder if I'd just be happier doing something else."

Kristina held his gaze. "Then why stay?"

Dan sighed, running a hand through his hair. "Because despite all the bullshit, I love this game. And I love this sales team. I care about the people here—at least, the ones who give a damn. But if you ask me whether professional sports is a career that ages well? I'd have to say no. Most of the guys in the sales pit would never admit it, but deep down, they all know it too."

Kristina nodded, absorbing his words. She had only been in the industry for a few years, but she had already felt the weight of it—the highs, the lows, the grind that never stopped. She knew Dan was right.

Dan continued, "You'd think a mid-sized market like ours would be hungry for change, but instead, it's just a revolving door of outdated ideas. People here protect their jobs by resisting innovation. And when that mentality runs the show, nothing ever evolves.

"It's called cesspool syndrome, Dan," Kristina explained. "Organizations that fail to renew themselves ultimately fail because all the shit floats to the top. That's not how it should be."

"Agreed. But it's not just this organization, though. It's every organization resistant to change. In successful organizations, the cream rises to the top, oooh yeah," Dan said, channelling his best Macho Man Randy Savage voice. "Not this organization. Not yet."

Kristina shook her head. "Oh, I know. I realized that in my first month here. Half the programs we run are completely backward. Why is marketing responsible for casual fan ticket sales, while sales handles season ticket holders? It makes zero sense. We should be one department. Instead, marketing floods the market with game-day deals, free hats, stuffed animals—whatever gimmick they can think of—just to move a few hundred extra seats because that's all they know. All they feel comfortable doing."

Dan leaned forward, nodding. "And then season ticket holders see that and wonder why the hell they're paying full price. We've spent years convincing people that season tickets are an investment, but marketing undercuts us at every turn."

Kristina laughed bitterly. "Perfect example: my neighbour. I was talking to him about a flex pack, and guess what he did? He bought tickets to individual games instead—and marketing threw in two bonus games for free just for buying online! Why would anyone buy a five- or ten-game pack from the inside sales team when they can get a better deal as a casual fan?"

Dan groaned, rubbing his face. "This. This right here is the bane of my existence. And nobody in upper management wants to admit it's a problem. Or is capable of admitting that."

Kristina exhaled, shaking her head. "So... what do we do?"

"We keep pushing. We keep finding ways to work around the bullshit. And maybe, just maybe, we change the game."

Kristina nodded. "Okay. I'll start putting something together and touch base with Rusty about his research. If I can integrate some of his findings, maybe we can build something compelling enough to start a conversation."

Dan smiled. "That's the spirit. Just don't let it consume you. A good idea is only as valuable as those willing to listen to it. And around here..." He leaned back in his chair, exhaling. "Well, you already know how that goes. But for what it's worth, Krissy, if anyone can shake things up in this department, it's you."

"Alright. Challenge accepted."

Outside in the pit, Kristina passed Shane, who was mid-conversation with Jay, likely scheming another half-baked idea. She overheard just enough to know that whatever they were planning was bound to go sideways.

She shook her head, smiling as she sat down at her desk and opened a new document. She wasn't sure how far this proposal would go, or if it would go anywhere at all. But if Dan was willing to give her the platform to push for real change, she'd be damned if she didn't take the shot.

CHAPTER 7

"The Fucking New Guy (FNG)"

Shane power-walked back to the pod, careful not to draw too much attention from the rest of the pit. "Jimmy's canned," he announced softly but loud enough for Rusty and Jay to hear. Neither of them had heard the news yet. "I'm sure they're going to split up his book of clients... it's draft time! I call dibs!"

"What? Really? What's going on?" Rusty asked, his eyes narrowing. "I knew something was up. I just hope we actually get a say in who we take over this time. Remember when Frank got shafted with all of Jeff's old clients?"

"I highly doubt we'll get any input," Jay said flatly. "They're probably just going to do what they always do—arbitrarily reassign them."

"Ok, then I'm going to argue for a snake draft. Fantasy football style, baby!" Shane declared, doing a little celebratory shuffle in place.

"Yeah, good luck with that, too," Rusty said, unimpressed. "And they won't 'arbitrarily reassign them,' Jay." He shot Shane a knowing look. Everyone in the office knew that Shane managed to weasel his way into those account reassignment conversations with upper management.

He had a knack for showing up at the right place at the right time—like the time he had 'accidentally' walked into Dan's office with Egg McMuffins while Dan and Kent were discussing Jeff's accounts. Or the time he conveniently needed to grab signed items for a golf tournament while Kent and Wally, the executive vice president of sales, were deep in conversation about bonus structures. Just a few days earlier, he'd conveniently appeared with an Americano coffee for Dan while Dan and Lena were discussing Jimmy's fate.

Shane also had the inside track because he went out for lunch with Dan often enough to be privy to upcoming news. Like his conversations with Kristina, Dan trusted Shane and figured he'd hear everything soon anyway.

"Jimmy was dead weight," Rusty added. "If I had to hear him offer the moon to a client one more time just to close a sale, I was going to lose my shit. That's not good business and doesn't set the right example for anyone—rookie or vet."

"If I had a dollar for every time Jimmy cut my grass..." Jay muttered, rolling his eyes.

"He was a seasoned vet who cut everyone's grass," Shane said with a smirk. "It's what seasoned vets do."

"I remember my first real sale," Jay started, leaning back in his chair. "It was a walk-in to the front office. Carin? Liz? Whoever the receptionist was at the time called the sales line, and I was the only one logged in, so I picked up. Sold my first flex pack in the 200-level. Then, the next day, Jimmy pulls me aside and tells me he had spoken to that client at a game the week before, so the sale was his." Jay shook his head. "There was nothing logged in the CRM. I had to create the client's account and take down all their info. No way he had talked to the guy before. And if he did, he sure as hell didn't follow up."

"The cardinal rule of sales," Rusty started. "If it's not logged in the CRM, it never happened. So what ended up happening?"

"I argued my case, but Kent overruled Dan and said I had to split the commission with Jimmy," Jay said, still bitter. "The time wasted arguing with Jimmy over $117 before tax wasn't even worth it."

"I don't think Kent or Wally even talked to him about it," Shane said.

"When do you think they'll announce Jimmy's gone to the team?" Jay asked.

"Who knows? Why are we always the last to know these things?" Rusty grumbled. "Actually, I'll answer my own question—because they think we don't pay attention or know any better. Same thing happened with Eric and Jeff. One day, they were just gone, and we didn't get an all-team email until we started asking questions. They even spelled Jeff's name wrong. 'Jerf.'"

"Jerf?" Shane repeated, chuckling. "I like that."

"Why do we act like only sales, marketing, finance, legal, and ops are completely messed up around here? HR is ass-backwards, too."

"This place, man. Fuck my life," Jay muttered. "You can't make this shit up."

"I give them until noon," Shane predicted. "Everyone saw Lena walking Jimmy back to his desk. And his waft of cheap cologne and cigarettes was hard to miss, too."

"Noon today?" Jay asked. "I'll take the over."

"Double or nothing?" Shane asked excitedly, grabbing his crotch. Like so many others in the department, he was a compulsive gambler. Gambling was ingrained in every aspect of the culture as well.

"Absolutely not taking double or nothing," Jay shot back. "Way too many variables at play."

Kristina's phone rang as she walked past their cubicle pod after her one-on-one. Shane watched her as she strode away. Since it was game day, she wore her usual Tuesday power pantsuit with stiletto heels. With them on, she stood at least six inches taller than him. She was effortlessly coordinated in the team's colours, finishing the look with a short scarf around her neck.

"Son of a bitch," Shane muttered.

"You're lucky she didn't catch you eye-fucking the hell out of her, Shane," Dan said as he walked past the photocopier on his way back to his office. "You know she'd destroy you or at the very least, beat the shit out of you."

"Nobody beats Shane," Shane muttered, referring to himself in the third person.

Moments later, Kristina walked past Jimmy and Lena wrapping things up and entered Dan's office.

"Excuse me, Shane," Dan said, smirking. "I've got business to take care of." He winked before following Kristina.

"Wait, what?" Shane called out, suddenly panicked. "Pics or it didn't happen, Dan!"

Dan turned around just before shutting the door, shaking his head in mocking disappointment.

Inside Dan's office, Kristina passed Dan a contract. "This arrived during our one-on-one. I need you to approve it."

Dan skimmed the details as she continued, "I gave Hadley Scientific Corp. 10% off for buying four full-season golds for the rest of this year and automatically renewing for next season."

"Good job, Krissy. You're leading the monthly sales contest now, right?"

"Third month straight," she confirmed, grinning. "I'm sure that's grinding Shane's gears—losing to a girl."

"Nicely done," Dan said, signing the override form. "Just keep up the great work and momentum. This team needs all the help we can get right now."

Meanwhile, over at Capshaw Chemical, an environmentally insensitive paint manufacturer and distributor, Max Walker leaned back in his chair at his cubicle. It was his first job out of college, and it showed—khakis, an Old Navy polo, and a sparse desk with only his backpack and a Pop Vinyl figurine of Wolverine next to his desktop phone.

Max spent most of his day answering calls from concerned citizens complaining about Capshaw's less-than-stellar environmental record.

"Yes, miss, I absolutely agree that all mammals normally have eyelids," he said, rubbing his forehead. "Mmhmm. And how close is your home to the factory? Mmhmm. I see." He rolled his eyes, already exhausted. "Yes, of course, I've taken notes... Yes, I'll send them to my manager. Of course, your concerns are very important to me." He sighed. "Mmhmm. Yes, please call if someone doesn't arrive to remove the fish floating in the lake tomorrow. Mmhmm. Okay. Thank you for sharing your concerns. Mmhmm. Yes, thank you. Mmhmm. Okay. Bye."

He hung up the phone and let out another sigh. His head hurt from all the nonsense. Seconds later, Max stood up and glanced around. The old fluorescent lights buzzed overhead, casting a sterile, lifeless glow on the endless rows of drab grey cubicles. The air felt thick, almost suffocating. Or maybe that was just the weight of collective misery pressing down on him and everyone else.

Ever since the most recent 'accidental' chemical spill into the city's sewage system, morale had hit an all-time low. Max and his colleagues spent their days getting screamed at by the public, drowning in a never-ending loop of damage control. He wasn't sure who suffered more—the residents downstream or the employees trapped inside this godforsaken cubicle farm.

He flopped back into his chair and glanced at the clock. 3:45 p.m. Almost there.

Softly, he started singing his own twisted version of Skinnamarink.

"I hate my job in the morning, and in the afternoon, I hate my job in the evening, underneath the moon..."

Then, as if struck by divine clarity, he sat up straighter and declared, "I fucking hate my job all the fucking time." He glanced back at the clock. 3:45 still. Jesus, time was standing still. "I really hate my job all the fucking time," he repeated, only much louder this time. Heads turned. Eyebrows raised. A few smirks flickered across exhausted faces while others simply returned to their screens, resigned to their fate.

Max surprised even himself, and the realization hit him like a slap—Capshaw Chemical wasn't just a company. It was a graveyard for dreams. A place where ambition went to die, buried beneath spreadsheets and corporate memos. Why didn't anyone warn him about this?

Yet. He refused to let it consume him. He refused to be its next victim.

With a sudden spark of energy, he clicked furiously at his keyboard, the thought bubble in his mind expanding with each keystroke. A few minutes later, he hit print.

Standing up again, he quickly walked past the kitchen and towards the photocopier. He passed one colleague being berated by a customer over the phone while another banged her head against her desk in frustration. It was just another Tuesday in the trenches. Good times.

Max grabbed the warm, freshly printed page and, without hesitation, marched straight to his manager's office, closing the door behind him.

Moments later, he emerged, walking backwards as he finished his conversation. "Thank you for the opportunity," he said, calm but firm. "I appreciate your support... and thanks for the reference." For the first time in a long time, he felt alive. He had just made arguably the biggest decision of his young professional life.

Thirty minutes later, Max sat in the passenger seat of his sister Sarah's car, heading home.

"I had the best day at work," he announced, grinning.

"Oh yeah?" Sarah glanced at him. "What happened?"

"You could say I turned over a new leaf."

"Uh-huh," she smirked. "Is this 'new leaf' still employed?"

Max leaned back dramatically. "I like to think of this leaf as floating on the winds of opportunity."

"No more saving the world from toxic sludge?" Chad, Sarah's brooding, unnecessarily macho boyfriend, chimed in from the backseat. Chad leaned back against the worn upholstery of the car, his muscular arms crossed and an eyebrow arched above his sunglasses like The Rock. He had the kind of swagger from a lifetime of being left to his own devices. A cocky smirk played on his lips as he looked at Sarah's unimpressed gaze through the rearview mirror. "What did I say? Sar-bear?"

"There was no saving that company," Max shot back. "I worked for toxic sludge, Chad. I had to save myself from becoming toxic sludge."

Chad whistled. "Well, well. How are you going to celebrate?"

"I dunno," Max said casually. "Maybe I'll put my feet up and watch the game tonight. You guys in?"

"Fuck the team," Chad scoffed. "Bunch of sack-less, no-heart losers going nowhere fast."

Max gasped in mock horror. "Wow. Doesn't your dad work for the team?"

Sarah rolled her eyes. "Oh, don't mind him. Chad's just bitter because his dad got let go from the sales department today. No more free tickets for Chadwick."

"I'll sell you my tickets cheap," Chad muttered softly.

Max smirked. "I did just quit my job. Not exactly swimming in disposable income right now, pal."

Chad leaned forward. "Listen, man, I can't go for obvious reasons," he whispered. "But I promised your sister I'd take her. So... El Cheapo, pay for parking, and the tickets are yours. Deal?"

Max nodded, flashing a half-smile. Chad reached into his leather satchel and pulled out an envelope with two tickets inside.

Ten minutes later, Max and Sarah arrived at their mom's house, where they both lived. Their twin teenage sisters were home, mindlessly scrolling on their phones at the kitchen table.

"Max?" their mother called from the living room. "You're home early. Is Sarah with you?"

"Yep," Max replied, popping his head into the room. "Took a long, hard look in the mirror and made a change—for the better."

"That's nice, dear," she said absently. "Garbage day tomorrow. Don't forget to take it out before you leave for work."

Max blinked. His mother had entirely missed the life-changing decision he had just made.

"Mom," he said, walking over and kissing her forehead. "I'm a man now. The man of the house. And that, my dear mother, is enough responsibility for me to handle at the moment."

"Uh-huh." She barely looked up.

"Sarah and I got tickets to the game tonight. So, we've gotta go get ready, byeeeeeee!" He sprinted up the stairs before she could respond.

He poked his head into Sarah's room. "You better not take long to get ready! We need a parking spot near the exit, and I want to catch warmups. We've got lower bowl tickets! Might as well take full advantage of them, right?"

"Patience, little man. I'll meet you in the car—give me five minutes!" Sarah called, applying a fresh layer of makeup.

Max rolled his eyes. "What for?"

"Gotta look my best."

"'Look your best'?" Max snorted. "Look your best?"

Sarah shot him a deadly glare, and he knew that look all too well.

"No, no, no! I meant because—you already look your best!" he stammered, dodging a hairbrush that flew past his head.

"Fine. I'll meet you in the car!!" Max yelped, retreating.

Now sitting in the driver's seat of the beat-up Honda Civic he shared with his sister, Max drummed his fingers on the wheel. The cassette player reminded him of childhood fishing trips with their dad, the best of the Bee Gees filling the silence.

As Sarah finally closed the front door, Max muttered, "You know, Sarah, Chad is a total tool. He thinks way too highly of himself and doesn't appreciate you. You deserve better."

Out loud, he said, "Took you long enough."

Sarah shot him a smirk. "Oh, I'm sorry. Normally, I just stand behind the front door, waiting for someone to ring the bell so I can swing it open and yell, 'Surprise!'"

Max rolled his eyes. "Uh…"

"Relax, chief. We'll get there when we get there." Sarah glanced at him. "Oh my God. We're wearing the same outfit. This is so embarrassing."

"We're going to a hockey game with thousands of people all wearing the exact same thing," Max deadpanned.

"Yeah, but… not with those cutesy wittle Girl Guide gloves, Max."

Max looked down at his thin mittens—clearly made for children. "Yeah, maybe."

Traffic was unusually light, thanks to the team's recent losing streak. When they arrived, Max parked as close to the exit as possible—this was his tried-and-true strategy to get home faster.

Inside the arena, their lower bowl seats weren't bad, though the angle of the glass partially obstructed their view.

"I'll give Chad one thing," Max admitted. "He did have a good ticket hookup."

Sarah smirked. "Had. His dad got canned today, remember? No more job, no more tickets."

Max grinned and started taking his shot. "So... what good is he to you, anyway?"

Sarah narrowed her eyes.

"Kidding! Not kidding?" Max backpedalled. "Maybe."

"Maybe what, Max?"

"Yes," he mumbled as Sarah narrowed her eyes yet again.

The game was a snooze fest. Max, one of the team's biggest fans, sat slumped in disappointment as they fell behind by three goals.

Max sighed. The concession popcorn was unnecessarily too salty. "I'm getting a Sprite," he muttered.

"You want anything? Popcorn? Hot Dog? New boyfriend?"

"Nope," Sarah said, texting Chad a thank-you with an 'xo' at the end.

Max lunged up the stairs two at a time, making his way toward a narrow concourse with long tines, which created chaos and congestion. He noticed a simple black table draped with a team-branded tablecloth as he waited in line. Drawn to it, he noticed team pocket schedules, arena maps, and glossy printed sheets detailing ticket package options scattered across the table.

He scanned the materials before glancing at the young inside sales representative standing behind the table, completely engrossed in his phone. He and Max were likely the same age.

"Hey, mind if I grab one of these?" Max asked, pointing to a ticket package form.

The rep barely looked up. "Yeah, go for it. Take all of them if you want."

Most inside sales reps played a crucial role in generating revenue and building relationships with fans and corporate clients. Their job was to sell ticket packages—mini plans, flex packages, suites, group tickets, and corporate partnerships—while learning the nuances of the sales process in a fast-paced, high-pressure environment.

Dan had always expected his inside sales team to analyze casual ticket sales data and develop targeted pitches to convert single-game buyers into package holders. If a fan purchased multiple box office tickets, they could often apply the cost toward a flex package, unlocking season ticket holder perks like discounts at the team store and priority access to exclusive events.

This was how most Fucking New Guys—or FNGs—started their careers in the pit. It was a grind that toughened them up fast. Salty, Shane, and Rusty had each played a key role in mentoring new hires, showing them how to navigate the high-pressure, cutthroat world of ticket sales. Reps were held to the usual strict performance metrics—call volume, follow-ups, conversion rates, and revenue targets. Those who excelled could move into account management, outside sales, or even leadership roles.

After flipping through the sales sheet for a moment, Max spoke up.

"So, how long have you worked here?"

The sales rep finally looked away from his phone. "This is my second season. Well... I guess, technically, we're still in year two."

"Rough one, huh?" Max said.

"Way worse than last year."

"Well, I mean... one bad year after eight straight playoff seasons? Still not a terrible run, right?

Besides, this season isn't over. We could go on a run!"

"I guess," the rep muttered, already on his phone.

About twenty feet away, Dan was crossing the concourse, carrying a gift bag for the young son of one of the team's season ticket holders. He had been on his way to the guest services office when he noticed Max striking up the conversation.

Intrigued, Dan stopped and observed for a few moments.

"Hi, I'm Dan, the team's Sales Manager," he said, extending his arm to shake Max's hand.

Max extended his hand. "Max. Nice to meet you."

Dan shook it firmly. "You're outgoing. Knowledgeable, too."

"I could talk about this team all day and night, sir. Ask me anything."

Dan chuckled. "I believe you. I like your energy," he said. "What do you do?"

Max hesitated for only a second before smirking. "Currently? I'm a free agent."

Dan raised an eyebrow. He had heard plenty of potential hires fumble through answers, but anyone who spoke in sports metaphors caught his attention.

"A free agent, huh?" Dan nodded. "Any interest in discussing some opportunities here?"

Max's eyes widened. "Here?" he asked, now almost stumbling over his words. "Like... now?"

Dan grinned. "Easy, Max. Let's set something up this week." He motioned toward the table. "I run the department—season ticket sales, group sales, corporate partnerships... and the team Mike over here is on," he said, subtly acknowledging the still-disinterested sales rep, who now tried to appear engaged.

"My team's about twenty-five strong," Dan continued. "We're looking to fill a few vacancies—mostly on the account management and retention side."

Max nodded, eager but shocked by the sudden turn of events.

Dan's account managers maintained, grew, and renewed the team's season ticket base. They upsold existing clients on group nights, suite shares, additional tickets, and premium experiences throughout the year. During renewals, their job was to retain customers for the following season, often by upgrading their seats or increasing their package size—from Flex 20 to Flex 30, from half-season to full-season.

These upgrades didn't just drive revenue; they deepened the fan's connection to the team, making renewals easier in the long run.

Each retention rep managed between 450 and 700 accounts with an average book value of around $2,500,000. Their books often representing multiple seats per client. Their job was to build strong relationships with season ticket holders through at least four meaningful touchpoints each year— phone calls, in-game seat visits, lunch or dinner meetings, in-office consultations, or hosting clients in a suite.

The busiest season for retention representatives was the renewal period, which generally ran from mid-February to the end of March. This was a critical time, and Dan's representatives were expected to establish live contact with every client, providing reminders about the renewal package that would soon arrive in the mail. The renewal package typically included an invoice and a specially produced marketing brochure highlighting the numerous benefits of maintaining a season ticket. Additionally, it featured various incentives for clients who renewed by a specified date, encouraging prompt action.

Max's mind swirled as he struggled to contain his excitement about this serendipitous encounter. He wondered if one of the vacancies Dan mentioned was to fill Chad's dad's position. Part of him wanted to showcase his connections and knowledge but decided against it in case there was animosity surrounding the dismissal.

"Look, Max, the period's about to start. I need to run and drop this off to a client, but here's my card; when you get back to your seat, send me a text so we can set something up."

"Thanks, Dan, I'll do that!" Max said, trying to keep his cool despite his face feeling flushed.

Dan stopped in his tracks and turned back towards Max. "Actually, if you are free tomorrow afternoon, why don't you come by around 3 p.m. It's a dreaded back-to-back, mid-week match-up against a Californian team. If you're available, I'll reply to your text with directions. You can experience life in the sales pit, and we can discuss things while watching the game from our suite."

Max couldn't believe the opportunity that had just presented itself, but he briefly paused to compose himself, quietly cleared his throat and said, "Thank you, Dan! You can expect a text in a few minutes, and I'll see you tomorrow." The two shook hands, and Dan turned around to continue his mission. Max stood in the middle of the concourse as the crowd rushed back to their seats before the third-period puck drop.

He took it all in and looked at the concessions, team shop, and inside sales table, which started it all. He basked at how life had a way of happening when he wasn't expecting. Just as he had faced moments of disappointment and closed his own employment door earlier in the day, he had learned in high school and college that setbacks often paved the way for new opportunities.

Max felt high. His body buzzed with adrenaline flowing through his veins as he looked down at Dan's business card with the team logo to the left of his name and credentials. Somewhere in the distance, the arena horn blew, and the third period began. He couldn't wait to tell his sister the news. He quickly power-walked back to the tunnel at the top of his section and could see Sarah in their seats watching the action but was stopped by an usher who asked him to wait until a stoppage in plan. His news had to wait. For now.

Moments later, Max hustled his way down twenty-something steps and flopped back down next to Sarah. His face was flush. He wore a smile from ear to ear.

"You finished your drink already?" Sarah asked as Max returned to his seat empty-handed.

"Oh, dang!" Max exclaimed.

"Are you ok?"

"Yeah, yeah, yeah...I didn't get a drink, but I got something better. I got the Sales Manager's business card."

"You did?" Sarah asked in disbelief.

"Yes! We even had a quick chat about working here. He wants me to text him my number."

Sarah looked into Max's eyes and placed her hands on his shoulders. "Please tell me you didn't talk to him like a little boy telling Santa what he wants for Christmas," Sarah joked but didn't allow her brother to respond. "Woah, wouldn't it be strange if you got a job the same day Chad's dad lost his? Chad would be so angry, especially since his tickets got you into the game in the first place!"

"Well, I guess if you put it that way..." Max said, glancing at the business card again. 'Ah, screw it, and screw Chad and his unemployed dad,' he thought as he began sending Dan the text.

For the first time in a long time, Max was excited. The game in front of him was suddenly the second most exciting thing happening that night.

CHAPTER 8

"The Consultant"

The next morning, Dan reluctantly sat in on another marketing-led season ticket holder renewal newsletter meeting. He had asked Kristina and Rusty to join him—partly for support, partly because he didn't want to be stuck alone in a room with three marketing team members. Dan knew Kent would contribute little, but he was still surprised to see him waiting in the room before the meeting started. The only certainty in meetings like this was that another unproductive meeting would be necessary.

The discussion embodied a clash of perspectives—where ambition and strategy collided with the realities of day-to-day execution. Roger Wallstein, the Club President and CEO, presided over the meeting. Sitting at the head of the table, he exuded a mix of a beginner's enthusiasm and the seasoned wisdom that came with tenure. His presence commanded respect, but even he could sense the simmering tension from both sides of the table.

Dan glanced at Kent—the embodiment of everything irritating him lately. Kent wore a slight frown. His fingers steepled thoughtfully as he reviewed the presentation slides filled with metrics Dan found irrelevant. *So that's why you're here, Kent,* Dan thought, *full of piss and vinegar.* He had little interest in what the marketing team was about to unveil, knowing it would likely be another hastily put-together campaign requiring additional resources without a clear execution plan.

Roger had witnessed the ongoing battle between 'good' and 'evil' countless times. However, the debate over who belonged to which side was always open to interpretation, depending on who you asked at that moment.

Kristina and Rusty shared Dan's frustrations—the marketing team consistently missed the mark, failing to provide the quality support that would actually translate into signed season ticket contracts. Conversely, the marketing team saw themselves as advocates for customer relations and community development. They often accused sales of not properly utilizing the resources they provided.

Mark Anderson, the team's Senior VP of Marketing, began his presentation, outlining an elaborate strategy to boost brand awareness and engagement.

"This has nothing to do with supporting the renewal campaign," Dan muttered to Kristina and Rusty.

As Mark continued, arguing the importance of long-term brand loyalty and presenting impressive metrics—social media engagement, website traffic—Dan shifted in his seat, his frustration already bubbling.

"These are highly relevant prospects," Kent noted confidently.

Dan nearly rolled his eyes. *Does he even know what social media is?* He shifted again, struggling to keep his irritation in check.

"Metrics don't close deals. They don't put food on the table," Rusty whispered to Dan and Kristina as Mark and his team rattled off case studies, industry trends, and past campaign results in a presentation that felt passionate yet entirely disconnected from the sales pit.

When it was finally his turn to speak, Dan seized the moment.

"We need immediate actions that push deals across the finish line—new sales and renewals alike," he said firmly. "Do you think our prospects care about our click-through rates?" His voice rose slightly. "They care about solutions to their problems—about how our product on the ice serves as an escape from the daily rigours of life. Your metrics, while important, don't close deals or put food on the table." He glanced at Rusty, who nodded in agreement. "Right now, we're not on the same page."

Kristina and Rusty murmured their agreement. Even Roger seemed to acknowledge the disconnect.

Kent, predictably, remained silent while the marketing team looked stunned.

Mark leaned forward. "How do you expect to build relationships with these fans without brand awareness, Dan? We need to position ourselves as industry leaders—not just someone who swoops in when they're ready to buy."

Rusty scoffed. "Is this our inaugural season?"

That got Kent's attention.

"No, it's not," Rusty continued. "It's our twenty-fifth season, including an incredible run eight out of the past ten years, Mark. The city—no, the region—knows exactly who we are. The league knows who we are."

The friction in the room thickened. Dan raised his hands slightly, making a subtle gesture for calm.

"Let's take a step back," he said evenly. "Rusty, I don't think anyone here disagrees with you. We all know how successful this team has been," he said, his gaze moving around the room. "It's clear we need to align our objectives more effectively."

Dan turned to Rusty. "I appreciate your passion and insights, so I asked you to sit in on this meeting. But we need your insights to guide our strategy, not just to vent frustrations. Trust me, I'm just as irritated as you are, but there's a bridge to build here."

With that, the tension in the room slowly shifted. The discussion, once combative, turned more collaborative as both sides began to realize that their perspectives—though seemingly at odds— were interconnected.

By the end of the hour-and-a-half meeting, the sales team begrudgingly learned the final direction of the upcoming fan newsletter. Despite years of pleading, the marketing team still hesitated to promote season ticket sales, focusing instead on casual ticket buyers and upcoming promotions.

Dan, as always, pushed for more season ticket holder content. According to marketing's precious metrics, over 60% of the newsletter's readers were already season ticket holders. To Dan, this was a perfect opportunity to engage the team's most loyal fans—generate referral opportunities, distribute customer service surveys, and reinforce the value of their memberships.

To Dan's relief, this newsletter edition focused primarily on the renewal campaign, set to officially launch early the following week. In response to the team's poor record—or perhaps as a reward for loyal ticket holders—the team had decided to freeze season ticket prices for the next season. This meant current season ticket holders would not face the 6% price increase that had frustrated them last year.

With renewal season now just days away, Dan committed his sales team to directly contacting all 5,600 season ticket holders before the campaign ended.

Touchpoints—unsolicited interactions between the organization and the client—were essential to bridging communication gaps. They allowed fans to ask questions, voice concerns, and—most importantly—reinforced that the team valued their investment, input, and loyalty.

After the meeting, Dan, Kristina, and Rusty walked back toward the pit. Dan whistled and gestured for his team to gather around.

"The renewal campaign starts next week. It's going to take a full-team effort—renewal calls, face-to-face meetings, and everything in between to retain as much of our season ticket holder base as possible."

He paused, looked toward the ceiling, clasping his hands together.

"Please, eight-pound, eleven-ounce baby Jesus... we don't ask for much, but if you could grace this team with a few wins between now and the end of the month, that would be swell. We've blessed this fanbase with years of outstanding regular-season success yet questionable playoff performances. And while you're at it, an improbable run to make the playoffs this year would be splendid." He made the sign of the cross. "Yours truly, these mutts."

A few chuckles broke out as most of the sales team followed suit, making the sign of the cross. Everyone knew that a winning team significantly improved their chances of meeting sales targets.

"Also, ownership wants as much money in by the start of April," Dan continued, his tone turning serious. "So, we're setting April 2 as the deadline for season ticket holders to renew if they want to be eligible for prizes and bonus tickets."

"Whoa—bonus tickets?" Shane asked, eyebrows raised.

"Prizes?" Jay echoed, leaning in.

"I know, right?" Dan smirked. "We have six additional games this season to use as renewal incentives, and the schedule over the next three weeks gives you guys plenty of chances to get face-to-face with clients. We're not expecting high demand for the California teams—including tonight's game—so if you need an excuse to meet with your clients, make some calls and then come see me for tickets to leave at will call. This is a perfect opportunity to invite half-season and flex holders to games that aren't in their package."

"What about full-season ticket holders?" someone asked from the back.

"Invite them out. Encourage them to use the extra tickets to reward staff, consortium members, or neighbours. Hell, tell them to delight whoever they want. Also, I suggest using these tickets for seat upgrades—upper 300s down to lower 300s, lower 300s to the 200s, and so on. Just use them to get face-to-face with your clients. That's all I care about."

"Okay, but aside from bonus tickets," Jay started, "you mentioned something about prizes?"

"That's right," Dan nodded. "Thanks, Jay. We're rolling out a contest for..." He hesitated, struggling to remember the details. "Help me out here," he said, turning to Kristina and Rusty.

"There are over 500 prizes," Kristina jumped in. "Big-screen TVs, round-trip train tickets, a chartered road trip with the team, signed jerseys, and a bunch of other experiences. It applies to all renewed or new season ticket holders."

The team exchanged skeptical glances. The prizes were appealing on paper, but the real concern was whether the April 2 deadline was too soon to make a significant impact.

After dismissing the team, Dan returned to his desk, closed the door, and sat alone in the dark.

"This is a complete waste of time," he muttered, staring at the schedule he could barely make out. "Fifteen wins in the next twenty-two games just to have a shot at the playoffs? Not a fucking chance. Overpaid, underperforming idiots—all of you. The rookie sneezes, and it costs us five grand. It's infuriating. Just do your fucking job."

With a defeated sigh, he flicked the lights back on and reached for his phone. He dialled Wally's extension, hoping he had taken stock of the frustrations expressed in the meeting. If anyone could lobby ownership for better support, it was Wally.

"DC, what's up?" Wally answered. "Everything sorted out now?"

"Wally, do you genuinely think we have a shot at making the playoffs?" Dan asked.

"Listen," Wally exhaled. "Whether we have a shot or not, our job is to show ownership, and we're doing everything possible to extract every last dollar from this market."

"What's with the April 2 deadline?" Dan pressed. "We've never faced a renewal period this tight— even in Cup-contending seasons. The market's desperate for a winner; we're clearly not one. You really think offering tickets to games people already have, or bonus tickets to a California road trip no one cares about, will motivate anyone?"

"You're asking what the real incentive is without playoff access, huh?" Wally asked, his tone unreadable. "A chance to win a flatscreen TV? Everyone already has one!"

"Knowing this team, it's probably a damn old monitor scavenged from the concourse," Dan snapped. "This isn't selling off wooden seats from an Original Six barn—we need to give people real reasons to renew."

"We need renewals—plain and simple," Wally shot back. "Even if we miss the playoffs, those deposits are critical for keeping this team afloat in the offseason. You remember what happened the last time we missed the playoffs for three straight years? We were hanging by a thread. Nearly missed payroll that summer."

Dan exhaled sharply. He hated how right Wally was.

"We've been lucky with good seasons lately, but we can't let it get to that point again," Wally continued. "Sure, 25% of the league is thriving. But for those of us outside that bubble? It's dire. Compared to other sports, we're fifth—maybe sixth—in popularity. You know why baseball and basketball players make four- or five times what hockey players do? TV broadcasting rights. Merchandise. It all adds up. Our league? It's weak. Running on chemo and radiation. If the Canadian dollar drops any further, we're all in trouble."

Dan sat back, absorbing the weight of Wally's words.

"Salaries have been a mess for years," he admitted. "But to say the future looks bleak..."

"I wouldn't say it if I didn't feel something was about to give," Wally cut in. "If we don't get better revenue-sharing fast, we're not just talking about struggling teams—we're talking about losing teams. Ours included."

Dan swallowed hard. This wasn't the conversation he'd expected to have. "What do we do?"

"We must be relentless," Wally insisted. "We need every sales rep talking like we're in the playoff hunt—like it's a given. We must sell belief, even if deep down we know it's bullshit. Ownership won't accept excuses for missing revenue targets."

Dan scoffed. "Respectfully, Wally, I can't remember the last time we actually hit our targets before the fiscal year ended."

"I get it," Wally said firmly. "But you know what needs to be done. Get your team out there— meet clients, build relationships. And if they can't handle that? Maybe we do need to shake things up beyond just Jimmy Bennett."

Dan hesitated. "Speaking of upcoming changes... what do we know?"

Wally sighed. "I'll be blunt. Ownership hired a consultant. New VP of something. He starts next week. Cutthroat. No loyalty except to the owner. He's here to clean house. No one is safe—not you, not me, not Kent."

Dan's stomach turned. "Jesus Christ."

"Just do your job, DC," Wally said. "Keep your top guys out of meetings that might trigger them. I don't fault Rusty for speaking up, but he's got cache with you and me. He won't with the new consultant."

Still holding the headset, Dan stared blankly at a team poster. A losing season. A looming lockout. A market that doesn't care. And now a consultant here to burn it all down.

"This won't end well," he muttered. "We need everyone's help—and fast."

CHAPTER 9

"The Pokémon Master of Disguise"

After wrapping up his call with Wally, Dan was furious. He was certain Kent had known about the new consultant for over a week and had deliberately kept him in the dark. Dan needed answers but wasn't about to give Kent the chance to dodge the conversation.

Kent's knack for escaping uncomfortable discussions—bathroom breaks, urgent tasks, mysterious meetings—was well documented. He always had an excuse. If he caught wind of Dan's inquiry, he'd disappear faster than usual. So, instead of calling, Dan decided to corner him in his office. He stepped inside with a smirk. "Kent? Didn't expect to find you here, buried in your work."

Kent glanced up, startled but recovering quickly. "Just about to head out," he said, gesturing toward the clock above his whiteboard.

"It's 1:30 in the afternoon," Dan shot back, raising an eyebrow.

"Noted," Kent replied. "But maybe you can help me with something."

Dan folded his arms. "What's that, Kent?"

"What do you get a 13-year-old for his birthday?" Kent asked flatly.

Dan blinked. "Seriously? I'm your birthday consultant now?" He scoffed. "Our whole world is about to crash and burn, and you're worried about a 13-year-old's birthday present?"

"My nephew," Kent clarified with a shrug. "I'm at a loss."

"Well, I'm at a loss too, Kent," Dan snapped. "I just got off the phone with Wally and need some clarity on a few things."

Kent waved a hand dismissively. "We'll find time to discuss."

"No, we will find time now," Dan pushed back. "There's a tsunami heading our way, and I am beyond disappointed that you didn't think to tell me about this consultant. You run this department, Kent, but I'm holding the sales team together. You could've looped me in at any time."

Kent's phone buzzed on his desk. "Hold that thought," he said, raising a finger. He skimmed the text before setting his phone down, his attention shifting to Dan.

"What's a Pokémon?" he asked, completely serious.

Dan's eye twitched. "Jesus, Kent...,"

"Seriously."

"I'm sure your nephew will like Mimikyu. It's a small Pokémon that is considered the master of disguise," Dan growled.

Kent looked up from his seated position completely missing Dan's sharp reference. Their eyes caught each other, and there was a quiet pause. "Noted. Thanks for the suggestion." Defeated, Dan rubbed the back of his neck. "Or make it easy. Just get him a jersey."

"Jersey it is!" Kent chirped, already moving for the door.

Dan's patience snapped. "Where the hell are you going?" he called after him. "I need answers, Kent!"

"Then walk with me," Kent said over his shoulder. "I've got places to be."

Dan exhaled sharply, then picked up his pace. "Kent! Kent! Slow down, for God's sake!"

"What's the rush?" Kent asked casually. "Look, I get that things aren't ideal. But if we go on a run, we can put ourselves back in the playoff conversation."

Dan shook his head. "That's not the point, Kent! What do you know about this consultant the owner hired? Wally made it very clear that this guy doesn't care about us or anyone in this office."

Kent shrugged. "Now that you mention it, I think Wally said something. Didn't think much of it."

Dan clenched his jaw. "You didn't think this was important? This affects our entire sales team. That's twenty-plus families potentially impacted, Kent. And Wally insinuated you've known for over a week." Kent finally stopped walking. His expression remained unreadable, but he let out a small sigh.

Dan seized the moment. "You know, I talked to Kristina yesterday," he said, his voice quieter but still firm. "It got me thinking about where I am and where I'm going here. Moments like this—when I'm left completely in the dark? That doesn't just affect me; it affects everyone counting on us for 'leadership.'" He made air quotes, sarcasm dripping as he pointed behind him towards the sales pit. "You're never the most transparent guy, but keeping this from me? That's a betrayal."

Kent exhaled through his nose and placed his hands on Dan's shoulders. "Listen," he said. "You make the rest of us look good. You're the sharpest, most visionary guy in this office. But vision alone? Not enough. Sometimes you have to act instead of analyzing. I knew you'd handle it. And really, that's all anyone can do."

Dan searched Kent's face for sincerity.

Kent smirked. "I've been around long enough to see a lot of shakeups. Trust me, the people who need to be taken care of will be taken care of. Some things might change, but most will stay the same."

Then, as if the conversation had never happened, he clapped Dan on the arm. "Now, if you'll excuse me, I have a jersey to buy."

Dan watched Kent stroll past Jimmy's empty desk and toward the stairwell. His blood boiled.

Dan ran to catch the door before it closed completely. He stood at the bottom of the stairs and directed his frustration upwards. "It doesn't have to be this way, Kent," Dan called after him. "You think I can just handle it? Maybe if I had resources, or time, or—hell—even basic information from you, I wouldn't have to struggle to hold your department together."

Kent paused at the door. He looked back, his face unreadable. "Keep your chin up, son. Everything will be fine. Trust me."

Then, he quickly turned away, gripping the stairwell railing. "Oh, and Dan?"

Dan didn't respond.

"Keep your chin up," Kent repeated, "but also keep your head down and push through whatever it takes to get us past this next hurdle. It doesn't matter if we make the playoffs. You're pivotal to this organization. I'll make sure everyone knows that."

And with that, he disappeared up the stairs.

Dan stood there, fists clenched. "So, what is it, Kent? Keep my chin up or keep my head down?" he muttered. "Thanks for absolutely nothing."

Seething, he turned sharply on his heel and strode toward Frank's desk.

"Hey, Frank. Got a minute?"

Frank leaned back, grinning. "Always for you, my man Dan. What's up?"

Dan exhaled sharply through his nose.

"I've had a few meetings today, and as you know, the renewal campaign will be its usual abomination. Ticket sales for this extended homestand are an abomination. Something needs to give beyond bonus tickets. Have you seen next Tuesday's numbers?" Dan asked as Frank turned to the ticketing system and entered next Tuesday's date.

"An abomination?" Frank asked, looking up at his boss. Frank squinted at his screen, then zoomed in on an entire upper section. "Well, they're nowhere near where they need to be," he muttered. His eyes widened. "Oh, that's not good. Total abomination."

"Yeah, that's another section I noticed, too," Dan said, pointing to a different area with fewer than thirty tickets sold. "What are your thoughts on getting some out-of-market restaurants on board for team-sponsored bus trips? Cheeks in seats."

Frank exhaled loudly. "Oh, Jesus, Dan, we tried those before. For next week?" Frank laughed loudly. "We got some of the pubs to chip in for beer and wings, threw in a ticket for $50, and we covered the bus, but it was a total flop after three months," he explained. "We can't go back to that poisoned well, especially for next week's games. It'll never work. Sorry, dude."

"How many of those bang buses did we try?" Dan asked.

"Oh, just one," Frank admitted.

"Isn't that a small sample size to call it a total flop?"

Frank gave Dan a deadpan look. "When you sell three tickets for a bus that holds fifty-two, yeah, I'd say that's a total flop of majestic proportions." He gestured dramatically, miming an explosion with his hands as if a bomb were falling onto his desk, scattering papers everywhere.

Dan ignored the theatrics. "Up until recently, our brand had never been stronger. Our community programs and commitment to charity were all driving factors with local businesses. What the hell gives?"

Frank sighed as he scooped up the papers. Back at his desk, he searched for a spreadsheet. "Okay, here. If you must know, we had twelve confirmed sales at the start of that experiment. But after the first losing streak, nine either didn't show up at the pickup location or just came for the $50 beer and wings." He frowned.

"Well, that doesn't make sense." Dan folded his arms. "Can we do it differently this time around? Is there anything we can do to ramp up interest in other communities? Maybe send a healthy scratch to meet the group after the game? Throw in some swag? Desperate times call for desperate measures, Frank."

Frank shook his head. "Not with less than a week's execution time." Frank grimaced, then let out a long, rumbling fart.

Dan recoiled with a gasp.

"We reek of desperation," Frank said with a smirk. "That also will reek of desperation."

"And old rotisserie chicken, oddly enough," Dan grumbled.

"Took the wife to Swiss Chalet this past weekend," Frank said, tilting his head in thought. "Not sure how that's still in there, but I'm impressed you know your fecal matter so well."

"It's your brand," Brad giggled as he turned his chair around. "Your digestive tract is something else, man."

Dan smirked dryly. "Well, when your ex-wife, her family, all her friends, and some of your own friends think you're a piece of shit, you kinda get to know what you're talking about."

Frank's smirk faded into something more thoughtful. "You and I both know you're not a piece of shit, Dan." He hesitated for a beat before adding, "Besides, it's not your fault your ex plays for the other team now."

Brad's eyes widened as Frank turned back to his screen, entering more data. Before he could process anything, his screen flickered, then went blue. Moments later, the computer shut down completely.

Frank stared blankly at it. "Well. That's also not good."

Dan snorted. "Quite possibly an omen of things to come."

Frank leaned back in his chair. "I hate going to those IT guys. I really dislike techies. Almost as much as I dislike going to those out-of-market bars and trying to put programs together with less than a week's notice." He shook his head. "Besides, isn't that Rusty's gig now? Doesn't he have anything to say about a restaurant program?"

Dan frowned. "Frank, the restaurant program is your program. You have all the connections. You're supposed to know what to do in this situation."

Frank turned in his chair, clearly puzzled. "My program?"

Dan just stared at him, unblinking.

Frank sighed. "Alright, alright. I'll make a few calls, but my gut reaction?" He started to question before squeezing out a quiet fart. "That's how my gut reacts. Interest will be low—again."

Dan nodded. "Don't waste too much time on this. You've got pre-renewal calls to make, so you can give away more free tickets." He shot Frank a look. "You need to get in touch with every single one of your clients this year. And for fuck's sake, Frank—please make sure you tag them properly this time."

With that, Dan left the pod, walked toward the main reception area, and went to the bathroom.

Dan shoved the bathroom door open, muttering under his breath about Kent's evasiveness and the absurdity of asking about Pokémon when there were far more pressing matters to address. In fact, mentioning Pokémon felt like a complete insult. He moved quickly to the nearest urinal, desperate and eager to take a moment to gather himself.

After relieving himself, Dan splashed cold water on his face. That's when the room began to tilt. The walls seemed to close in, his perception turned cloudy, and a strange warmth radiated from the core of his body, quickly spreading outward. A sudden wave of detachment took over. He felt weightless like he was floating—looking down at himself from above.

As a fluorescent light flickered overhead, its harsh buzzing hum sliced through the silence. The disorienting glare pulled him back down, grounding him in the present—but barely.

Dan's hands trembled slightly at first as he gripped the edges of the sink. He stared into the mirror and barely recognized himself. The man staring back at him was haunted—hollow-eyed and pale, a stranger cloaked in exhaustion. The deep shadows under his eyes were a testament to months of intermittent sleep—going to bed too late, waking up too early. His body on constant high alert. Alert status red. His mind never fully at rest.

'Ground yourself, Dan,' he pleaded to himself. "One thing you can smell. Taste. See. Feel. Hear," he said aloud.

He tried to follow the steps he'd learned in therapy—court-mandated but helpful nonetheless. Smell? That was easy. The scent of a urinal puck. No longer blue. It appeared faded and could not mask the strong smell of urine. What about taste? Nothing but dryness and regret. The thought of tasting something mixed with the stench of stale urinal made him feel even sicker to his stomach. He stumbled out of the bathroom, away from the suffocating stall-lined walls, and into the hallway where at least the space felt less claustrophobic.

His legs now felt weak. He forced himself forward. Carefully moving toward the leather couch just outside the doors connecting the hallway to the reception area.

The distant ringing of phones from the sales pit droned in the background. The cold tile beneath his feet gave him something to focus on. "Anchor yourself, Dan. Come on," he desperately pleaded.

Now seated, Dan fixated on the wall of crooked pictures of the team's championship run hanging on the wall. Had it always been like that? Oddly tilted? Or was Dan the pinball machine whose cabinet was pushed and nudged just a little too much and about to tile? Why had no one fixed it? His thoughts drifted, but then he caught himself—this was another distraction.

He forced his attention back to touch. The leather beneath his fingertips felt cool to the touch. The seams pressing into his palm. "Just focus on the texture," he reminded his hands. "Focus on the texture," he willed. At least he could feel his racing heart as it thudded beneath his Adam's apple, pounding against the walls of his throat. "Ugh"

His body felt heavy and his first attempts to move his extremities proved futile. However, he kept pushing, and his right hand slowly and instinctively found his pocket. A familiar plastic pillbox felt like salvation. He fumbled it out, nearly dropping it. What a waste that would be. Still gripping the small bottle between his trembling fingers, he concentrated on keeping it tight between his fingers.

He could see the little blue lorazepam shining bright like a diamond through the transparent orange bottle. He carefully popped open the lid as his hands continued to shake, now more than before. Tipping two tiny, 2mg rapid-release pills into his palm, he delicately handled them like they were shards of broken glass.

"Just a little to take the edge off," he whispered, pleaded and prayed.

He placed both pills under his tongue. Closed his mouth. Waited.

A single bead of sweat rolled down his spine and divided his ass cheeks like a kicker splitting the uprights. A cloudy yellow aura grew behind his eyes. The aura tightened.

Would the lorazepam work this time? Was this a panic attack? Dan squeezed his eyes shut. The office noise faded into a low, indistinct hum. Slowly, his breathing steadied. The world, once tilted and suffocating, began to level out. The crooked picture on the wall remained crooked.

As the pill dissolved, his pulse slowed, and his fingers finally stopped trembling. He had dodged another bullet. For now.

Moments later, Dan attempted to stand up slowly. Still unsteady, he grasped the couch's armrests for support as he lifted himself up. He shuffled back to the bathroom and turned on the faucet again. He splashed another handful of cold water on his face. As the water dripped from his chin, he stared into the mirror. He could barely recognize his reflection.

'Keep your chin up but your head down.' What the hell did that even mean? Kent's words echoed, looping endlessly in his mind. Dan ran a hand through his hair, took a deep breath, adjusted his tie, and squared his shoulders. He needed to push through. He willed himself to push through as he always did.

As he stepped out of the hallway and into the reception area, his gaze landed on a man waiting near the entrance. Something about him set Dan on edge immediately.

The man was in his mid-forties, of average build, with balding salt-and-pepper hair recently cut short. He wore thick Tom Ford eyeglasses, a tailored Paul Smith blazer and a crisp dress shirt without a tie. It screamed corporate professional, but it was not flashy. Yet, there was something eerily familiar about him that Dan couldn't quite place.

"Oh, good afternoon," the man said, his voice smooth, friendly—but measured.

Dan, still shaken, nodded slightly. "Afternoon. How are you?"

The man's smile was faint. "You work here, don't you?"

Dan cautiously paused. Something about the question also felt off. "I do. What about you? Are you a fan?"

The man's smile widened slightly. "I guess you could say that. I'm in town for business—I thought I'd check out the arena, see what it's all about. If I end up moving here, I'd consider season tickets."

Still wary, Dan studied the man for another moment before slipping into his professional persona. "Season tickets, huh? Great choice. What are you looking for? Premium seats? Maybe something closer to the glass?"

The man chuckled. "I'm not getting ahead of myself yet. I'm still exploring my options." His eyes followed the wall behind the receptionist as he pointed out a few team photos from years past. "I've been watching this team for a while—seen some great seasons... and some not-so-great ones."

Dan reached for a business card in his pocket. "Well, I'm Dan, the Manager of Sales. If you're serious about season tickets, I can have one of my reps meet with you."

The man took the card, glancing at it briefly. His smile lingered a second too long.

"Dan... good to meet you. I'm Michael."

Dan narrowed his eyes.

Michael. Something was unnerving about the way he said Dan's name. There was also something unnerving about how he said his name. "Nice to meet you too...Michael." Michael slipped the card into his breast pocket. "Looks like you've got quite the operation here. I've already spoken to a few people. Your receptionist over there is a stunner," he added with a wink as Kelly frowned.

Dan's stomach twisted.

Michael didn't give him time to respond.

"Let me ask you something, Dan," Michael continued, his tone shifting slightly. "What's the vibe like here? Among the staff, I mean. Everyone's upbeat, right? Motivated?"

Dan stiffened.

'That's a... weird question,' he thought. The subtle emphasis on 'vibe' really irked Dan.

Michael's smile didn't waver.

"I mean," he added casually, "A team's success starts from the inside, doesn't it? How's this year been on the front office?"

Dan forced his expression to stay neutral, but his instincts were screaming that something was off.

No fan asks about morale.

Michael checked his watch. "Well, Dan, I'll let you get back to it. I've got a bit more exploring to do before I head out."

Dan watched Michael leave, his gut twisting with unease. Something wasn't right.

As Michael walked up the stairs, he passed Rusty. They exchanged friendly glances. Rusty arrived at the reception at just the right moment, coffee in hand and an amused grin tugging at his lips. "What's up, Dan? You look like you've seen a ghost. You good?"

Dan motioned for Rusty to follow him back toward his office. "Close enough," he muttered.

Rusty fell into step beside him, his curiosity piqued. "Alright, spill it. Who was that guy?"

Dan glanced over his shoulder as if expecting Michael to re-materialize out of thin air. "I have no idea,

Rusty," he admitted. "He said his name was Michael. Claimed he's in town for business, considering season tickets. But Rusty..." Dan trailed off, his mind still trying to untangle the unease gnawing at him.

"But?" Rusty prompted, taking a slow sip of his coffee.

Dan exhaled sharply. "But he didn't seem... genuine. He wasn't asking about seats or packages but about us. The staff. Morale. The vibe of the front office." His voice dropped slightly. "Who the fuck asks that?"

Rusty let out a low whistle. "Maybe he's just one of those arrogant rich dudes who loves asking questions he doesn't care about. You know, the 'I'm smarter than you' type."

Dan frowned. "Maybe," he conceded, his tone far from convinced. "But he really didn't act like a typical prospect, you know? He was too...calculated or...methodical."

Rusty raised an eyebrow, leaning against the doorframe of Dan's office. "Okay, yeah, I'll admit, that's a little weird. Maybe he's scouting for something?"

Dan ran a hand down his face. "Scouting for what, though? He's either the strangest fan I've ever met or... I don't know. And we've got some real crazies. But this feels like something else."

Rusty's casual grin faded slightly as Dan continued. "Wally mentioned the owner hired a consultant. You think that's him?"

Rusty hesitated. "A what?"

"A consultant." Dan's words tasted wrong even as he said them. "Wally said the guy was cutthroat. No loyalty. Sent here to clean house. If that's true, wouldn't he want to keep a low profile? Why pretend to be a fan?"

Rusty's concern deepened. "A consultant pretending to be a season ticket prospect?" He shook his head. "That's a bit dramatic."

Dan leaned forward, elbows on his desk. "Is it, though?" He locked eyes with Rusty. "Think about it. If you were hired to evaluate a department...or an entire front office—figure out where the weaknesses were—what better way than blending in and gathering intel before anyone knows who you are?"

Rusty didn't answer right away. He swirled the last bit of coffee in his cup, staring down at it as if it held some deeper truth. Finally, he looked up. "Okay. If that's the case, what's your move?"

Dan hesitated. "I don't know yet."

Rusty set his empty coffee cup on Dan's desk with a deliberate tap. "Well, if he's some undercover consultant, that's your chance to impress the hell out of him." He smirked. "I'm sure you did just that."

Dan huffed out a dry laugh. "Yeah. Right."

Rusty clapped a hand on Dan's shoulder. "I wouldn't lose sleep over it."

Dan leaned back in his chair, exhaling slowly as the lorazepam fully took effect. "You're probably right," he murmured, though his mind refused to settle.

Rusty shrugged. "Trust your gut, bud. But until we know for sure, maybe keep it on the down-low. The last thing we need is Shane going full conspiracy theorist about some corporate mole infiltrating the office."

Dan snorted. "Fair point." As something about the man still lingered in his mind—like an itch he couldn't scratch. A whisper of unease he couldn't quite shake. Perhaps a snake in the woodpile.

CHAPTER 10

"It's Okay Not To Be Okay"

While Dan's out-of-body, mind-warping moment unfolded, Max was in his Civic, navigating a nerve-wracking drive to his first professional sports interview. The weather—a miserable mix of light snow and freezing rain—meant crawling traffic and no time for the mental prep he preferred. He knew he didn't need to prepare, but his last interview for an entry-level customer service job had gone well precisely because he wasn't stressed and prepared. He'd arrived with twenty minutes to spare to collect his thoughts and calm his racing heart. Now? Not a chance.

As the car in front of him slowed, Max slammed his palm against the steering wheel. "Leave the house earlier, check the weather before bed. Jesus, Max. You're better than this." He exhaled sharply and tried to quell his growing frustration, but the usual highway bottleneck near the arena made that impossible. This traffic wasn't new, and he knew he'd left too much to chance.

The local sports radio station hummed in the background. "It's a slippery one out there. Higher than normal volume on the highway. Give yourself extra time to get where you need to be."

"Shut up!" Max snapped, jabbing at the dial and changing the station.

Back at the arena, Kevin—a former sales team colleague and mentor turned elusive entrepreneur— called Rusty about what he claimed was an "important business opportunity."

"Hey Rusty, it's Kevin! How the hell are you, man? Is now a good time to chat?"

Rusty leaned back in his chair, grinning. "For you, Kev? Always. Everything okay? You in jail?" he teased.

Kevin chuckled. "Nah, no jail this time. But yeah, man, sure as shit, everything's great—just really great, thanks." He paused. "Hey, I know this is short notice, but I thought you might be interested in this new business I got involved with last month. We're doing an event Friday night, and we've got a really great guest speaker coming to talk about leadership, technology and goal setting. Right up your alley."

Rusty furrowed his brow. "Leadership and goal setting, eh? What's this 'business' all about, anyway? Wait, did you also say technology?"

Kevin hesitated for half a second too long. "Well, it's...so hard to explain, man. I mean, it's tech, communication, leadership, and owning your own life. I think you, of all people, would really enjoy what Bob is going to talk about."

Rusty smirked, sensing the sales pitch coming. "Uh-huh. And why me, exactly?"

Kevin's voice took on a practiced sincerity. "Well, I respect your opinion, and I think you respect mine, right? You said it yourself—I've always been a mentor to you. Did I ever lead you astray?"

Rusty laughed. "In the office, no. Never. Outside of the office? Maybe a different story."

Kevin laughed harder. "Fine— out of the office shenanigans, not included. Let me ask that again. Have I ever led you astray in business?"

Rusty paused. "Come on, man. I just established that," he said. "Alright, let me run it by the ol' ball and chain and give you a shout shortly, okay?"

Kevin's enthusiasm shot through the receiver. "Great, Rusty, really, really great! Hey, how's Amy, anyway?"

Rusty grinned. "Amazing, man. We're expecting our second this August."

A beat of silence. "No shit! That's great, man. Congrats! I'm thrilled for you, bud! Look, let's catch up more soon. Hoping it works out, eh? I'll send you the directions now so you can plan."

They hung up, and Rusty turned toward Shane's desk, where Shane was deeply engrossed in a Skype call.

"Oh yeah, I love the eggshell white; that's totally going to match the cream leather couches you ordered." Shane nodded approvingly at his screen. "When do those arrive again?"

A warm voice replied, slightly distorted. "They're coming in April, Shane."

"Oh, hang on, Janice, Rusty's here. Say hi to Janice, Rusty."

Rusty glanced at the screen and smiled. "Hi, Mrs. Sanders, how are you?"

"Oh, very well, Rusty, thank you. How's that beautiful wife of yours?"

Rusty beamed. "Oh, you know... she's glowing these days. Just a bit more 'cooking' time. Baby number two is due in August."

"Oh, how lovely!" Janice said. "All the best to you and yours! Look, Shane, I'll let you go.

We can talk later," she abruptly hung up before Shane could respond.

"Love and kisses to you, too," Shane said softly.

Confused, Rusty tilted his head. "Love and kisses? Janice? You call your mom Janice?"

Shane shrugged. "Yeah, obvi. We have a very professional relationship. Why?"

Rusty raised an eyebrow. "Uh... well, respectfully, isn't it kind of weird to call your mom by her first name?"

"No," Shane shot back quickly and firmly.

"It doesn't feel like you are both pretending?" Rusty asked cautiously.

Shane forced a chuckle. "Pretending? No one is pretending." Shane's expression stiffened. "She calls me by my first name, doesn't she? She called you by your first name, didn't she? What's your point, Richard?" Shane blinked rapidly.

Rusty hesitated. "My point is... she's not my mom."

Shane's jaw clenched. "Well, she hasn't really been mine either. Not in the way you're thinking. That's just business as usual. That's just...how we are. It works."

Rusty studied him. "Does it, though?"

Shane shifted uncomfortably. "Did you have a point to this interrogation, officer?" Shane's gaze dropped to his screen, now dark from inactivity. He didn't like the reflection staring back at him.

Nobody had ever challenged him like this.

Rusty sighed. "Look, it just seems... distant, you know? Like you're talking to a colleague rather than your own mother."

Shane's voice hardened. "Like I said. It's business as usual, man. Being emotionless and distant is easier. It avoids...unnecessary complications."

"Complications? Like feelings? Like history? You don't think that affects you? You don't think that has affected you your entire life?"

"Fuck you. You're not my shrink, Rusty. You didn't grow up in my house. You wouldn't understand."

"No, I'm not your shrink, Shane. But I've been where you are.

Shane looked up, surprised.

Rusty exhaled. "I bet when you were growing up, your mom was always charming to everyone else— strangers, colleagues, neighbours. But behind closed doors?" Rusty shook his head. "Nah, it was different, right? Nothing was ever good enough. Any mistakes you made were a catastrophe. You should have known better."

Shane's brow furrowed. "That sounds... familiar." He nodded.

Rusty nodded back. "Yeah. Narcissists can light up a room with their charisma, but at home, it is always about control. You are either an extension of them or a complete disappointment. No in-between. You are left asking yourself why I am not worthy of love or attention, and it fucking sucks, man. You and your mom... you're two people who can't connect. You avoid real emotions. I did that, too, for years."

Shane swallowed hard, feeling a strange mix of validation and unease. "So... how'd you deal with it?"

Rusty offered a small, knowing smile. "It took me a long time to figure out that their version of me wasn't real. I suddenly realized I had the power to break the cycle. I couldn't live with the façade. Are you sure your façade is serving you?"

Shane sat still. His shoulders slumped, and he tried hard to hold back tears. Shane clenched his jaw, another flicker of vulnerability breaking through the bulletproof vest he thought he tightly wore. Holding back tears, Shane tried to convince himself and Rusty that it was nothing new. "It's not a façade. It's just our way."

A shadow crossed Shane's features as he considered the unspoken truth behind Rusty's words. "Maybe," he admitted quietly, a tear dripping down his right cheek. Blinking rapidly, he tried to reset and regain his composure but struggled to do so. "I just don't know how to change it."

Rusty leaned forward, his voice steady. "It starts with recognizing it, man. You don't have to accept a relationship that leaves you feeling empty."

Shane clenched his fists in his jacket pockets, feeling isolated in the empty office. Thankfully, Jay wasn't in the pod; it was just him and Rusty. He lowered his head, a familiar dread pooling in his chest. Shane let out a long breath and a fake laugh, his internal struggle evident. He felt like something inside him had broken. His mind quickly raced back to a recessed moment in his brain from his childhood when he was disciplined because, according to his mother, he 'should have known better.' It wasn't his fault; he was nine and accidentally got on the wrong bus to go home from school. The more Shane paused, the more his mind raced, and suddenly, memories he had buried deep began clawing their way to the surface.

<< Flashback <<

He was nine. Or was it twelve? He wasn't sure. It didn't matter because the feeling was the same.

Rusty stayed quiet. He knew Shane wasn't with him anymore—he was trapped in his past.

And for the first time in years, Shane let it in.

He saw his younger self glancing out the window of his elementary school's office. He saw children joyfully playing on the swings and jungle gym—their parents watching over them. Those happy kids were not the same as the ones who had laughed and teased him for taking the wrong route. Even at his young age, he observed how the parents supported their little ones, always ready to catch them if they fell.

His mother had come to pick him up from the school office. "Oh, my goodness, I am so sorry for all of this," she said to the secretary with a warm, practiced laugh. "I don't know where his head was today! He's usually so responsible. Thank you so much for keeping an eye on him—I swear, I'd lose my own head if it weren't attached!"

It was a different story moments later. Her face was fuming with frustration and anger as they now briskly walked out of the school. "How could you be so careless? You should have known better than to get on a strange bus." The words cut deeper than any physical blow he had received from his father. This was her routine —profound disappointment and frustration rather than empathy towards her young child. As he cautiously shuffled toward the car, he tried to explain, but like most other words he used, it just wasn't good enough.

"I-I was just trying to get home, mummy, I-I" younger Shane said. But her mind was already racing ahead, planning her next reprimand, her next chance to reinforce consequences and how he could never live up to her expectations.

"Stop being a baby about this," she scolded, tone ice-cold. "How old are you? I'm not your 'mummy, grow up,'" she said mockingly. "You're lucky I didn't just leave you there and let you find your own way home. You need to pay attention and take responsibility for your actions."

How old was he? Shane struggled with the memory. But if he was in elementary school, so he was likely nine. A deep-rooted feeling of inadequacy welled up inside him; it was clear now that nothing he did would ever be good enough. For close to fifteen years, now maybe more, Shane had buried that memory deep down years ago, but now, as an adult, it came back harder than ever.

>> *Flash Forward* >>

Rusty tried to bring Shane back. He softened his tone. "Sorry." He briefly paused to think how he could rephrase his last point. "Okay, look. I just want you to see—breaking down walls makes us vulnerable."

It's okay to be vulnerable. It's okay to not be okay.

Shane swallowed hard. He blinked rapidly as tears pricked his eyes. The floodgates opened. "But it's all I know," he said finally, sounding both defeated and resigned.

Rusty's voice softened. "That doesn't mean it's right." He held Shane's gaze. "There's more to family than formality. You deserve that."

Shane's throat tightened. "Did I deserve it back then?" he whispered, the weight of unanswered questions pressing against his ribs.

Rusty grabbed Shane's shoulders, using them as leverage to roll his chair closer. "You deserve better. Don't let Janice's way define all your other relationships."

Shane hesitated. A flicker of hope fought against a lifetime of conditioning. "I guess I never thought of it that way."

Rusty offered a small smile. "Then maybe it's time to start."

They sat silently for a moment before Rusty gave Shane's shoulder a reassuring squeeze. "It's okay, Shane. None of this was your fault. None of this is fair."

As Rusty let go, Shane's grip tightened, his head briefly pressing against Rusty's shoulder before exhaling deeply. When he pulled away, his gaze fixated on a small, wet stain on Rusty's jacket.

Rusty followed his stare, then let out a dramatic groan. "Jesus Christ, Shane, that's disgusting." He grinned. "Keep it together, man."

With pent-up emotions finally released, Shane sighed—a strange mix of satisfaction and exhaustion—before chuckling. "Go fuck yourself, Rusty."

Rusty smirked. "And he's back." He clapped Shane on the back. "Better than ever."

Shane wiped his sleeve against the damp spot on Rusty's jacket. "I've always been better than you, Rusty." His voice was lighter now, steadier. "So, why did you even come over here, anyway?"

Rusty blinked, momentarily thrown. The rawness of the moment had fogged his own memory. "Uh, oh yeah—Kevin called." He sat back in his chair. "Something about an event on Friday. Leadership, technology, communications—some business-y bullshit."

Shane snorted. "Yeah. Total pyramid scheme."

Rusty raised an eyebrow. "A pyramid scheme?"

Shane nodded, deadpan. "Yeah, I humoured him and told him I'd go. Also suggested he invite you." He winked.

Rusty sat up. "Wait. You know it's a pyramid scheme. You know it'll be a complete waste of time. And you told him to invite me?"

Shane's eyes widened innocently. "Is that not what I said, Rusty?" He blinked rapidly. "Besides, he said it's a killer networking opportunity. Lots of prospects. Lots of young, impressionable babies looking to meet studs like us." He paused. "Actually, I take that back. Studs like me." He threw his fists in the air. "Besides, isn't leadership and technology and communication and whatever other bullshit he said kind of your thing?"

Rusty rolled his eyes. "No, not really."

"Oops. I told Kevin it was." Shane smirked. "Who cares what the event is about? I say we go, eat some free food, drink some free booze, and grab some business cards. Worst case? We hate it. Sneak out the back once the presentation starts. Simple. I do this all the time. Keep track of your mileage and expense that shit."

Rusty sighed, already regretting what he was about to say. "Alright, fine. I guess there's nothing better to do on one of the only nights off this week than waste time at a pyramid scheme meeting."

Shane beamed. "What time are you picking me up?"

Rusty threw up his hands. "I don't even know if I'm going yet!"

Shane smirked. "You remember our road trip conversation?"

"Vegas and Oakland. You and Jay trying to drag me into that disaster."

"Ohhh, right. That road trip." He grinned. "What about it?"

"Amy shut it down. Hard no. But I should check in with her before committing to this, too."

"Dude. This one is actually a work thing. Tell her you just have to go."

"You mean exactly like I was supposed to tell her about Vegas?"

"Exactly."

Rusty shook his head. "You're impossible."

Shane pressed. "What time are you picking me up?"

"You live on the other side of town."

"Wow. I didn't realize our friendship was based on geography."

"You absolutely would NOT drive across town for me."

"I totally would."

Rusty snorted. "Bullshit. You've used that same excuse to bail on poker night. And when I left my wallet at your place last year. Should I continue?"

Shane folded his arms. "Fine. I don't need a ride."

Rusty sighed, defeated. "I'll pick you up at seven."

CHAPTER 11

"Sell Yourself, Kid"

Dan re-entered the same bathroom where he'd had his out-of-body experience earlier. He took a glance around, let out a long breath, and... farted.

A few moments later, he realized he wasn't alone. A voice from the corner urinal spoke. "Hey."

Dan stiffened. "Hi." He winced. There was an awkward pause. "Shhh... That didn't happen." He pressed a finger to his lips.

The man zipped up and walked past him. "What didn't happen?"

Dan nodded. "Exactly."

Moments later, the two men were reunited in the main office lobby. Max made up time by taking an alternate exit and calmed his racing mind in the parking lot before heading inside to freshen up in the bathroom before his meeting with Dan. The weight of this opportunity wasn't lost on him— interviewing for a job with his favourite team. Max sat up in the leather chair as Dan walked into the reception area. He was ready to pounce up to his feet. If he were a dog, his tail would have been wagging wildly.

Unfortunately, the weight of this opportunity was lost on Dan. It had already been a hell of a day, and his brain felt like it had been through a blender. He still didn't immediately recognize Max. Dan stood by Kelly, the receptionist, skimming a message on his phone. "Running behind, are we? No surprise there."

Max misunderstood and thought Dan had started talking to him. He sprung up, and in one lunge, was in Dan's face. Dan blinked, trying to process why this stranger was so comfortable and...energetic. "Uh... okay?"

Max stepped back and cocked his head. There was a long pause. Then Dan finally placed him.

"Right. Max! Didn't recognize you without your jersey. Weren't you wearing a hat under a toque?"

"And gloves...I may have also been wearing gloves," Max mumbled. "And by may, I mean yes."

"Right...I didn't think those came in adult sizes," Dan chuckled. "Give me a few minutes, okay? Can Kelly get you a coffee?"

"Thanks, but no thanks. I'll never sleep tonight. Not just because I'm excited about this opportunity, but because—" Max stammered.

It grew more difficult as Max made eye contact again with Kelly, the receptionist, who raised her right arm to wave and smile politely. It was the same kind of wave Wendy Peffercorn gave Michael 'Squints' Palledorous in the coming-of-age classic The Sandlot—a scene that had been burnt into Max's brain ever since he found the movie on Netflix and watched it twice in the past week.

<< Flashback <<

Squints had a crush on Wendy Peffercorn, the eighteen-year-old lifeguard at the local pool. With her red bathing suit, blonde hair, and glamorous white sunglasses, Wendy was the childhood crush of every boy born between 1975 and 1983, including Dan and Rusty, when the film was released in 1993. In the memorable scene now playing in Max's head, Squints intentionally jumps off the diving board and pretends to drown. This action prompts Wendy to jump in and rescue him from the bottom of the pool. The drama unfolds as she pulls him from the water and performs CPR on the pool deck. After three or four mouth-to-mouth breaths, Squints' eyes suddenly open, and he grins. He boldly kisses Wendy, causing gasps around the pool and Wendy to recoil. "You little pervert!" she exclaims before dragging Squints out, a grin on his face from ear to ear.

In 1993, that moment played for laughs—a cheeky, mischievous act of childhood bravado. But times had changed, and watching it now, Max couldn't help but see it differently.

>> Flash Forward >>

Back to reality. Max cleared his throat and returned to his conversation with Dan. "Uh...because caffeine hits me...really hard," he finished, his eyes locked with Kelly's for possibly too long, feeling flustered and drawn to her.

"I have a delayed ejaculation—oh God—a delayed reaction to caffeine," Max blurted out, completely embarrassed, his face turning red as he closed his eyes and quickly looked away.

"Right." Dan nodded slowly. "Okay, no coffee. Bottled water instead? Actually, you look like you could use some, so hold that thought. I'll be right back."

"Yes, bottled water is fine. Tap water is fine too, whatever you h—" Max started again, only to stop mid-sentence as he noticed Kelly biting her upper lip.

"Hey, relax," Kelly said as Dan walked back toward the pit. "Stay cool, dude. Dan's awesome. You've got this," she said with a wink.

Max took a seat again, noticeably flustered. "Breathe, Max," he whispered. He started focusing on his breathing. He tried to use the time to refresh his memory on the team personnel he hoped to work with. Thankfully, he had bookmarked an online media guide on the team's site and scrolled through it intently.

He looked up from his phone and saw Kelly loudly chewing gum, still smiling at him while the reception phone rang three times. She didn't pick up. He smiled back, then noticed all the framed photos on the wall behind her were slightly tilted. The urge to fix them itched at him.

"You all set, Max?" Dan asked as he returned with a bottle of water.

"Yep, sure am," Max said, springing to his feet. In fact, he sprung to his feet so quickly that he fumbled his phone, barely catching it before it hit the floor.

"Great. Hope you don't mind. I invited a few from my team to sit in on the meeting. This is Kristina and Shane."

Max stood, eyes widening slightly. "If this isn't intimidating enough, then how the hell are you going to cut it in the professional sports world?" Kristina teased, smiling as she reached out to shake his hand.

"Yeah, this is the big leagues, kid. Welcome to the bullpen," Shane added, pointing toward the hallway where the interns and inside sales team worked. He extended his hand to shake Max's now sweaty palm. "And over there? Well, that's the sales pit. That's where you'll be if you can land a job!"

The four entered the boardroom. Shane and Kristina took seats at the table. Dan settled into a chair in the corner behind Kristina, arms crossed. Max remained standing by the boardroom doors. "Well, have a seat," Shane motioned for Max to sit down.

"You prepared, rookie?" Kristina called out before whispering, "Remember your training, young Padawan."

Max nearly lost his composure. While he tried not to objectify Kristina, he couldn't believe that a gorgeous, confident woman working in professional sports was sitting directly across from him, speaking Star Wars to him nonetheless—was this real life?

"I'm not going to lie; I'm pretty excited," Max said, reaching for his water—only to knock it over.

Water cascaded across the table.

"Quite possibly an omen of things to come," Dan muttered from the back.

"Uh…" Max stumbled, face flushing.

"Relax, let's start this one over, okay? We didn't just see that," Dan said, winking.

"Nope, didn't see or hear anything, right Dan?" Max said, grinning sheepishly.

"Didn't hear anything?" Dan asked.

"Exactly," Max replied, squinting slightly, nodding like a detective in a crime drama.

"Alright, sell yourself, kid," Shane said, leaning forward, his expression sharpening with curiosity. "You like role-playing, don't you?"

"Like Dungeons and Dragons?" Max asked.

"That's not what I had in mind," Shane scoffed with a sheepish smile as Kristina kicked his foot from underneath the table.

"Sure, let's do this," Max said enthusiastically. "Are you a fan or a business owner?"

"I'm a contractor. Actually, I run a daycare," Kristina interjected, crossing her arms.

Max nodded. "Got it. So, what's your plan for the tickets?"

Shane sighed. "Honestly? I don't think we need them. My wife's pushing for it, though," he said, acknowledging Kristina as his office wife. "She thinks it could help with business." He nodded in her direction. But I read on Twitter that nobody really wants tickets. So...there's that."

Max raised an eyebrow. "Well, how many games have you been to?"

"This year?" Kristina asked.

"Yes."

"Two," Shane admitted.

"How many clients do you have?"

"Several."

"I'd recommend starting with a Flex 20 package. It's a great way to see how the whole experience could benefit your business. You said you run a daycare, right? Let's break it down."

"Sure," Kristina nodded.

Max pulled out a flex package form he had grabbed from the sales table the previous night. He turned it upside down towards Kristina and Shane and explained how a Flex package worked.

"Okay, so the Flex 20 gives you twenty ticket vouchers to use however you'd like. You can distribute them across different games—four for gold-level, ten for silver-level, and six for bronze-level games," Max explained confidently.

Shane leaned in, intrigued. "I'd like to hear more. Please...go on."

"I think you'd want to keep the four gold tickets for you and your spouse..." he said, acknowledging

Kristina. "Those are usually premium games."

"Excuse me?" Kristina interrupted, raising an eyebrow. "Are you totally assuming he has a spouse?"

"You're right. I'm sorry. That was a gross assumption. Let's pivot." Unfazed, Max recalibrated smoothly. "Keep those four gold tickets for your best clients or a night out with three of your friends. Gold games are in high demand. Even if it's a tough matchup, those games can be really special," Max explained. "Then, split the six bronze tickets into two sets of three. Invite two loyal families from your daycare as a thank-you for their support. Share a game night with them; it builds relationships."

"And the ten silver tickets?" Kristina asked, intrigued.

"You can reserve those for future use. I don't think you need to pick them all at the same time." Max shot a look over at Dan, the fly on the wall. Dan did not acknowledge.

"I looked at the schedule," Shane interrupted. "I have no interest in attending any of those games or watching those teams." He aggressively pointed at the majority of the schedule. "I want to exchange those ten for gold tickets."

Max paused, glancing at Dan again, who observed the conversation with his usual unreadable expression. Dan responded with a small shrug. "Don't ask me, I don't work here."

"Uh, don't feel pressured to decide right away," Max continued. "Even if you don't want to go to those games, use them for business development purposes—invite prospects or clients in small groups of two...or two games of four or five even."

"Parents don't have time for hockey games," Kristina countered.

"That's fair, but what about grandparents?" Max suggested. "Other caregivers who step in when parents need a date night or have a work commitment? I'm sure a grandfather would love to experience a game with his grandson."

Shane frowned, rubbing his chin. "That all sounds appealing, but...money's tight right now."

Max respectfully waved a hand. "No worries! I've got a payment plan ready for you— monthly or quarterly— whichever works best. There's a financing fee, but since these tickets are for your business, they can be written off as a promotional expense. You enjoy those tax returns, don't you, Shane?"

Shane's eyes lit up. "If there's anything I love more than sports, it's getting money back on my taxes. Woo-hoo!"

"See? It's a win-win," Max said, extending his fist for a bump. Shane left him hanging.

"Alright, Mr. One-Sided Partnership." Dan choked on the gulp of water he was drinking. He chuckled, glancing at Shane. "I think he gets everything you two are throwing at him."

"But I haven't even talked about half-season packages or access to exclusive season-holder events."

"Impressive," Shane admitted, his interest piqued. "How do you convert casual buyers into season ticket holders?"

Max laughed lightly. "I noticed you bought twelve tickets at gate price this season. Did you know we offer flexible packages with discounts up to 40% off gate prices, plus playoff access and even a free autographed jersey?"

"We're out of the budget for jerseys, right?" Shane asked, glancing at Dan. "Asking for a...uh...client."

"Yeah, negative. No room for that," Dan confirmed.

Kristina shook her head. "Still not convinced. What if someone like me, who used to have season tickets, wanted to come back?"

"Hmmm," Max paused, then smirked. "Ring, ring, ring," he said, motioning for Kristina to pick up the phone.

"Hello?"

"Hello, is this Kristina?"

"Y'ello. You'll have to speak up; I'm wearing a towel," she quipped.

"Nice Simpsons reference, Krissy," Shane whispered.

Hiding his grin, Max pushed forward. "I'm calling you today because, well, it's quite obvious—I want to win you back. I know you didn't renew your previous season ticket package for some very important reasons, but I'd be happy to discuss your past experience and explain how things have improved since then."

"I've told you assholes a thousand times—I am NOT renewing those season tickets! You guys fucked something up every single year!" Kristina shot back, crossing her arms.

"Mmhmm, I can appreciate your previous experience wasn't the greatest, and as someone who's just starting with the team, I need to understand those reasons—even if you have to tell me one more time." Max's voice softened, but he kept his composure. "I promise, I'm here for you..."

Then, turning to Dan, he explained, "I would just ask them to vent, listen to them, and try to solve objections as they arise. It's what I did in my previous role, but honestly, talking about hockey tickets is a hell of a lot sexier than talking about environmental policies and floating fish."

Dan interrupted, "The message to communicate is that, as an organization, we are committed to ensuring that each season ticket holder has an enjoyable experience at the games and gets the most value possible. We're willing to do what it takes to atone for past mistakes and win them back," he said, looking at the rest of the panel for concluding thoughts or questions.

"Who do you know in this town? Any connections?" Shane asked.

"Never mind that," Dan interjected. He reached for his phone and dialled a number. "I'm putting a real prospect on speaker. Sell them." He slid his phone across the table. "Careful, you're on speakerphone."

A moment later, Rusty's warm voice answered, "Hello? Who's this?"

"Hello, it's Max. What would you say if your name was drawn for a discounted season ticket pass— AND one of those games is at glass level?" Max asked smoothly.

"I might be pretty excited about that. Did I win tickets?"

"You won the opportunity to buy tickets...at a discount, of course," Max continued, grinning as he picked up steam. "And I'll throw in a bronze-level game for you and a guest—on the glass."

"Okay, okay, we get it. You're good at this," Dan said, cutting the call short before the prospect could say another word.

"Well researched," Shane noted, his expression suddenly suspicious. "Who tipped you off?"

"Nobody tipped me off. This team is all I know—it's all I've ever wanted to know. I've paid out of pocket for eight games this season, plus I was given tickets for last night. Over the past three or four years, I've probably been to another thirty games, back when the team was making the playoffs every year."

"Why didn't you have a season ticket package, Max?" Kristina asked, tilting her head slightly.

"I didn't really think about it, and nobody ever called me to discuss my options, despite using the same email and phone number for all my ticket orders. I guess the opportunity was there to convert me from a casual buyer to a season ticket holder, but nobody ever reached out."

"Interesting," Dan said, clasping his hands together and glancing at Shane. "Very interesting indeed. Isn't the casual buyer program one of yours, Shane?"

"Maybe." Shane shifted uncomfortably in his seat.

"Regardless, I think we've seen and heard enough, Max. Thank you for your input." Dan leaned back slightly. "Shane, Kristina, and I will debrief this interview. In the meantime, you can sit in the lobby while we discuss whether you get upper-level tickets for you and a friend or whether you get to sit with us in the Owner's suite for the full experience tonight. Sound good?"

Max's jaw dropped. "Oh, wow. Absolutely. Thank you, Dan. Thank you, Kristina. Thank you, Shane."

Dan stood up and extended his hand. Max shook it firmly, his grip a little too eager.

"Can I...can I just sit here for a minute?" Max asked, his voice almost euphoric.

"Sure, kid. Take your time. Krissy, walk him back to the lobby when he's ready."

"Sure thing, boss."

Dan and Shane left the room, heading toward Dan's office.

"He's a bit of a lamb, eh?" Shane asked. "Aren't you worried he's too much of a fanboy?"

Dan shrugged. "No, not really. I think his passion and knowledge are infectious. We could use that kind of energy in the pit. Plus, I'd rather a lamb straight up than a lamb dressed in a wolf suit."

"So, same question posed differently—you don't think he'll be eaten alive?"

"What are our other options?" Dan asked, nodding toward the interns and inside sales reps down the hall. "Shane, we need fresh talent; he knows what he's talking about. It took you two years to figure out what a flex package was, and even now, I'm still not sure you fully understand how they work."

"I know how club seats work, though," Shane grinned, subtly honking his crotch.

Dan exhaled sharply. "I think I'm going to take a chance on this one. He's got the raw tools—reminds me a little of you when you first started... aside from the flex packs. We can teach him. You, Rusty, Krissy...you can train him, mould him into a superstar.

"And if not?" Shane asked.

"If not, then we cut him loose after the renewal campaign. Worst case, he walks away with a lifetime of memories from his cup of coffee in professional sports."

A few minutes later, Dan walked over to Rusty's desk. "Hey, thanks for playing along, man," Dan said before updating him about Max and laying out a plan. Begrudgingly, Rusty rose from his chair and headed toward the reception area, where Kelly and Max were making small talk.

"Hi, Max?" Rusty's familiar voice called softly. Max turned to face him.

"Yes, this is me. Err... that is me. I mean, yes, I'm Max," he stumbled, extending his hand.

"Hey, I'm Rusty." Rusty shook Max's hand before sighing. "Unfortunately, Dan had to run home to deal with a family emergency. But before he left, he asked me to come find you and thank you for your interest in the role you discussed with Kristina, Shane, and Dan."

Max's body stiffened, and the hairs on his neck stood on end. A sinking feeling crept into his chest.

"Dan's going to go in another direction," Rusty continued, his tone measured. "And given Dan's circumstances, he just wanted me to let you know sooner rather than later. You know, not to keep you waiting."

A wave of self-doubt crashed through Max like a tidal wave. 'Of course, this was too good to be true!' he thought. 'Why are you such a fucking fanboy?!'

"Oh..." Max said softly, his voice barely above a whisper. "I'm sorry to hear about Dan's emergency. I hope everything is okay. I appreciate you letting me know in person."

Rusty glanced down, faking a sombre nod. "Dan said he'd really like to keep in touch whenever the time is right."

"Of course, Rusty. I'd like that. You know, if it's ever the right time for me to come on board in some capacity. I probably came across as a fanboy—I'm sorry."

Kelly and Rusty exchanged a glance.

"Well," Rusty paused, dragging out the silence. "I guess...it's a good thing I'm just messing with you because we'd like to invite you to stay for tonight's game as our guest in the Owner's suite."

Max blinked. "Excuse me?"

Rusty grinned. "If all goes according to plan, come into the office tomorrow and shadow Shane and me for the day."

Max's breath caught in his throat. He looked between Rusty and Kelly, whose eyes were wide with excitement.

"Besides, I'm curious to hear your review of your experience tonight. Whatever plans you have for tonight and tomorrow, change them. We need you sharp."

Max leaped into the air, throwing his fists up before clapping his hands together in pure joy like he had just won 'a new car!' on the Price is Right. Kelly reached over for a high-five. Their hands clenched.

"I guess that's a yes?" Rusty chuckled. It was like he was Howie Mandel and had just told someone they had the golden ticket and were going to Hollywood on America's Got Talent. "Kel, what do you think?"

"Oh yeah!" Kelly cheered, smacking Max's hand.

Max nodded furiously. "Yes, I can make tonight work. I can make tomorrow work. All day tomorrow... and the game tonight. Yes! Yes! Yes!"

"Great," Rusty said. He checked his watch. "Hey, it's 4:45; we normally move our cars over to the staff lot across the street now. Come with me. I'll grab you a parking pass."

"This is crazy, Rusty," Max said.

Rusty clapped him on the shoulder. "Welcome to the sales pit, Max."

CHAPTER 12

"A Simple Twist of Fate"

Max got into his car and followed Rusty to the staff parking lot across the street. They walked back to the building, down the stairs, and sat at Rusty's desk.

"Sales is a numbers game, Max," Rusty began. "Management evaluates us on what we pitch, who we close, and how much business we have in our pipeline. You'll quickly figure out what works best for you. Everyone develops their own style. Did you learn anything like this in school?"

"I never took sales in school or anything like that," Max admitted. "But I know there's cold calling, networking, door-to-door sales, contests or giveaways, and taking data from those contests for prospecting. Uh... casual buyers, former customers, lapsed customers," he finished, his voice tinged with excitement.

"Ok, so you know more than most FNGs."

"What's an F-N-G?" Max asked.

"You're the Fuckin New Guy," he said with a wink. "But your knowledge will help. And those last three? Those are your low-hanging fruit. They may have been season ticket holders before or purchased tickets here and there. They already know the product. They've been here before, so they know what to expect. Calling them and asking about their experience would be a great way to start the conversation. Just because they walked away once doesn't mean they won't come back. Life circumstances change." Rusty gestured to Frank, who returned from the mailroom with a stack of return-to-sender envelopes.

"How do we keep fucking up replacement tickets?" Frank groaned, throwing his arms up.

"Exhibit One," Rusty nodded. "We screw things up a lot. But people will give you a whole slew of reasons why they didn't come back, and I'd say seven out of ten times, it's money or life circumstances. They lost their job, they had a baby, they bought a house, they moved across town, or they died. The other three times? We probably messed up. Lost replacement tickets, perceived discounts not applied to their account, or worse, applied to the wrong damn account."

"How about we promised them this but gave them that?" Frank muttered, slamming the stack of envelopes onto the round table in the middle of the pod.

Rusty nodded. "And then there's the 'team performance' excuse. Some will claim they're unhappy with the team's direction. Given our success in previous seasons, those complaints are rare—relatively speaking. Everyone's a fan in one way or another."

"Right," Max nodded. "I think I just need to give them a chance to speak—to really hear them out. People just want to be heard. At my old job, whenever someone complained, I learned that the key was to not focus on what they didn't like but to remind them what they loved."

"Exactly. Ask about their family. How much their kids love the experience. Get them talking about the memories." Rusty smiled. "Tell them about a time you went to a game with your dad."

Max hesitated. "My dad died when I was eight."

Rusty's face fell. "Oh, Jesus. I'm sorry, Max. That was insensitive of me."

Max shook his head. "It's okay, man. You didn't know." He exhaled softly. "A drunk driver killed him. It was late afternoon, and he was coming to pick up my older sister, Sarah, from an intramural volleyball tournament. My twin sisters were three at the time."

"Holy shit, Max," Rusty said, his voice barely above a whisper. "I didn't mean to—"

Max gave a small, sad smile. "I do remember one time with him, though. It was actually the year he died. I think I was seven." He paused in thought. "He'd won these terrible seats in the upper 300s— Family Zone. So, we got to the arena, and I was decked out in my jersey, hat, and toque. Sarah had probably painted my face too. When we reached the main gate, this older gentleman stopped us and asked to see our tickets."

Max paused, thinking fondly of that memory.

"I'll never forget this," Max continued, his voice warming at the memory. "The guy said, 'How would you like to sit in my seats tonight?' Then he looked at me and asked, 'Have you ever sat at the glass?'"

"Amazing," Rusty said with a smile.

"My dad and I agreed, and as we walked to our section, I remember feeling completely overwhelmed. I was seven, so everything seemed huge, but I took it all in. As we walked down the big steps, my dad saw his boss sitting in the 18th or 19th row, and for once, he looked like the king of the castle."

Rusty grinned. "That's a hell of a moment."

"That's not it, though," Max chuckled, eyes glistening. "Our seats were right next to the visiting team's bench. It was Dad, me, a glass partition, and their backup goalie.

"Warmups began, and both teams took the ice. Some players fired pucks at the net. Others stretched right in front of me. I never realized just how tall hockey players were until then."

"This is why we do what we do, Max," Rusty said, shaking his head. "That memory from fourteen years ago is still vivid for you. That's what we're trying to create for every fan."

"What I remember most..." Max paused, his voice thick with emotion. "One of the players pointed at me and flipped a puck over the glass. My dad caught it and gave it to me. I still have that puck on my bookshelf in a plastic holder."

Rusty exhaled sharply. "Jesus."

"The player was from the area. He scored his first professional goal that night. We won 3-1, but he was named the third star. As you know, opposing players normally don't come out for the three stars, but he did that night. As he skated off the ice, he reached over and handed me an autographed stick before disappearing into the tunnel. That stick is still in my room."

Max chuckled. It was bittersweet. "Dad and I talked about that moment the entire way home. We were giddy, still in disbelief over the twist of fate that put us in those seats. And then, a few months later... he was gone. Killed in a different twist of fate by a drunk driver."

Rusty sat back, stunned. "Jesus Christ, Max."

Max's voice hardened. "The driver survived. That piece of shit was three times the legal limit. His lawyer argued he was a low risk to reoffend and got him counselling. He pleaded guilty to impaired driving causing death. They gave him ten years."

Rusty's fists clenched. "I remember reading about that. Devastating. The justice system failed you."

Max nodded grimly. "He had multiple driving violations. Two years before the crash, he was arrested for public intoxication."

"He's out now, isn't he?"

"Yeah. He served four years. Now he's the same age dad was when he died.

Now he works at a fucking bakery.

Dad always told Sarah and me that there's good in everything. That there's good in everyone. And I know that's true for most people. But to this day, I can't find the good in that piece of shit."

Rusty nodded solemnly. "You're justified in feeling that. Your whole family is."

Max exhaled. "It's why I don't drink. Kind of a tribute to dad."

Rusty smiled, his voice quiet. "That's painfully beautiful, Max."

Max's eyes flickered with sadness. "Sarah still blames herself. None of it would have happened if she hadn't had that volleyball game. She's carried that guilt her whole life."

Rusty let out a slow breath. "We all have a story, don't we?"

Max nodded. "Yeah. Speaking of stories... let's change the subject. What's the story with your name?"

Rusty paused before answering. "Well... my real name is Richard, but my last name is Geare."

Max squinted. "Sounds the same but spelled differently?"

"Yeah, exactly. And I hate dealing with the constant, 'Hey, do you know your name is the same as that Hollywood actor? Do you know the Dalai Lama? What was it like working with Julia Roberts?'" Rusty sighed dramatically. "But anyway, it's getting closer to game time. We should probably start heading up to grab a bite to eat."

"Speaking of which..." Frank suddenly appeared in the pod, looking expectant. "You owe me dinner. Let's go!" He pointed to the ceiling before realizing his mistake and redirecting his hand down the hall.

Rusty sighed. "Frank, this is Max. Max, this is Frank Washburn."

Max extended his hand. "Nice to meet you, Frank."

Frank grabbed Max's hand in an iron grip and yanked him closer. "You are Maximus Decimus Meridius," he declared theatrically. "Commander of the Armies of the North, General of the Felix Legions, and loyal servant to the true emperor, Marcus Aurelius. Father to a murdered son, husband to a murdered wife. And you will have your vengeance, in this life or the next."

Frank pulled Max even closer—uncomfortably close—until the tip of their noses touched.

Rusty, suppressing a laugh, finally interjected. "Hey, Gladiator, how exactly do I owe you dinner?" He reached in between them to pry Max free. "I bought last time. And the time before that, too!"

Frank released Max and shrugged. "Fair. Then I owe you dinner! Let's go!" His enthusiasm was even greater this time as he pointed toward the back stairs.

Rusty narrowed his eyes. "Why the sudden rush?"

Frank exhaled dramatically. "Well, for one, I'm starving, and I could eat the ass of a horse right now."

Max's eyes widened slightly. "...Okay."

Frank ignored him and continued. "Two, I need to get out of this basement—stat! Christ, we see the sun once in the morning when we arrive, and if we're lucky, we catch it again when we leave. But on game days? It's like being in a fucking casino—I have no idea if it's sunny, raining, snowing, or if the world is ending in giant flames. And C..." Frank paused dramatically before pointing at Rusty. "... Let's just get out of here. Bring the kid with you."

Max scoffed. "Frank, I'm not a kid. I'm twenty-two years old."

Frank smirked. "I know you are, kid. That was the point. You're still just a wee tadpole."

Max hesitated. "...K."

Frank's face twisted in sudden fury. "Excuse me?"

"Whoa! That changed quickly!"

Rusty stifled a laugh. "Yeah, you just broke one of Frank's cardinal rules."

"What cardinal rule?"

Rusty smirked. "Never respond with a 'K' or a thumbs-up. Especially on BBM or Messenger."

Frank shook his head in disgust. "Absolutely unforgivable."

Max raised his hands in surrender. "Duly noted."

Frank exhaled, seeming to let it go. "Alright then. Now let's go before I actually have to eat a horse's ass."

CHAPTER 13

"Tales of 'Rink Reuben,' Chili Con Carne-ton Heston, and Meatball Mike"

Back in real time, Shane was getting hungry. "Alright, who's catering this meeting anyway?" Shane asked, leaning closer to his camera. "Has anyone tried Skip the Dishes or Uber Eats yet?"

"Frank, we're all looking at you," Steve, a former inside sales representative, added. "Wait... why are you a potato?"

"I don't know what I did," Frank admitted.

The gallery view of familiar faces erupted in laughter.

"Okay, leave it alone before we lose you for good!" Jay pleaded. "We're all dying to know if you prepared anything for this special occasion."

"Number one, what am I, your personal chef?" Frank shot back. "No one's catering this, Shane. Number two, Jay, last time I checked, we were in the middle of a goddamn pandemic. And C, we haven't had gatherings in person like this since the Toronto Raptors started their title defence! Grab a bag of chips like a normal person, Jay."

"Hold on," Salty cut in, smirking. "Frank, didn't you tell me you made your legendary chili last week?" He scrolled through his phone and then held it up to the camera. "Yeah, here it is—you sent us all photos in the group chat. Said something about it needing to 'stew for days' to reach full flavour?"

Frank straightened up. "That's one of my cardinal rules: you gotta let things stew. The longer you stew, the more flavourful your brew. Rinse those beans in your sink because if you don't, you'll have farts and shits that'll really stink. Now that's a true story, folks. Wash the starch off the beans, and you're good to go."

Shane groaned. "Here we go. You had to mention food, Salty. Now he's gonna start dispatching unsolicited advice."

"Why are you being a dick, Shane?" Frank asserted. "Actually, I've answered that already."

Shane rolled his eyes. "What does this have to do with m—"

Frank cut him off, raising a hand. "Dut-dut-dut-dut, young grasshopper."

Salty exhaled and rolled his eyes. "Okay, Frank, we get it. Now, please, remind us all of your culinary masterpieces before you go full philosopher on us."

Frank grinned. "Well, since you asked..." He took a deep breath. "I remember some of the culinary masterpieces from back in the day..."

Frank, Rusty, and Max made their way up to the concourse in search of dinner. It was 5:20, and the arena hadn't yet opened to the public. This was an advantage—they avoided the lively, chaotic atmosphere of eager fans flocking to their favourite stadium concession stands. However, many of the vendors weren't fully set up yet.

Dinner choices among the sales team varied, but even a FNG like Max could tell that the longer someone had been with the organization, the more discerning their palate became.

The unpaid interns and inside sales reps often stuck to the classic hot dog and pop combo—the most affordable option at the arena. Frank liked to call this group "The Cold Cut Club" because, while technically "hotdogs," those stadium wieners were barely warm. And the term "fountain" was accurate for describing the pop—because more often than not, the machines were low or out of syrup altogether, leaving nothing but carbonated water with a vague aftertaste of what once was Coke.

But to Frank, a hotdog and pop combo was pedestrian at best. Tonight, Frank was on a mission.

Despite being much older and larger than most of his colleagues, he moved with the determination of a maid of honour leading her bride and bridesmaids through a bachelorette pub crawl. Nothing was going to stop him from reaching his destination.

As they turned the corner, Max caught the tantalizing aroma of smoked meat and pulled pork sandwiches wafting from a stand nearby. The price? Sixteen bucks a sandwich.

Max swallowed. "...That smells unreal."

Rusty nodded. "Yeah. But wait till you see where he's taking us."

Frank, still laser-focused, didn't even break stride.

This was no ordinary food hunt. This was a pilgrimage.

No surprise, Frank was adventurous, and he always looked forward to ordering from the secret menu he believed was personally concocted by the man he fondly referred to as 'Rink Reuben.' It should be noted that Rink Reuben was not to be confused with American record producer and Def Jam Recordings co-founder Rick Rubin. While Rick Rubin produced Run-D.M.C. and the Beastie Boys, Rink Reuben produced Frank's favourite sandwich from the secret menu, the 'Half' 'n' Half.'

Today, Frank ordered the 'Half 'n' Half'—a decadent mix of half-smoked meat and half-pulled pork piled high on sourdough bread. The sandwich came with a generous handful of kettle chips and two crisp, sour pickle spears, all pressed together in a chaotic medley of flavour.

Although they didn't do it for everyone, Frank always requested two pickle spears. This was largely because, when his first request was denied, he had demanded to see Reuben's pickle policy.

"Which I'm sure clearly states only one pickle spear per person," Frank had argued.

This strategy wasn't born out of sheer stubbornness—it was actually a sales tactic Frank had picked up from one of Kent's sales trainer friends. That trainer had once been denied a free piece of pie at a restaurant, so he confidently requested to see their written policy stating that dessert was not included. Long before Google Reviews, perhaps afraid of him causing a scene—and with no such policy to show—the manager had caved and given him a slice of lemon meringue pie on the house.

Max couldn't deny how amazing Frank's sandwich smelled, but the thought of mixing smoked meat and saucy pulled pork made him slightly queasy. He and Rusty stuck with a safer choice: a classic Montreal smoked meat sandwich stacked high between two slices of rye bread with a healthy smear of mustard. It was served with a single pickle spear.

Frank took his first triumphant bite, unleashing a symphony of sound: the satisfying crunch of the chips, the squish of the saucy pulled pork, and the rhythmic chewing that followed. "You both are a bunch of amateurs. You should have asked to see his pickle policy!"

Leaning back in his seat, a satisfied grin spread across his face.

"Reuben's done it again." Frank sighed in pure bliss, nodding approvingly. "You guys have to try this." He offered up his sandwich, holding it out for Max and Rusty as they looked on in mild horror.

Unbeknownst to them, Rink Reuben was not the actual name of the delicatessen samurai behind the counter. His real name was Jim.

But that never bothered Frank—nor did it seem to bother Jim.

Frank often quipped, "A name is merely a formality. But a good nickname? That's a badge of honour."

And this honour was extended far and wide to a cast of culinary characters and establishments inside and outside the arena.

Rather than remember people's real names, Frank used a system of mnemonic devices, associating them with a related food item that whet his appetite.

In this particular case, 'Rink Reuben' was Frank's go-to sandwich haven inside the rink.

Max, still wrapping his head around it all, chuckled. "You seem... really attached to your food choices, Frank."

Frank nodded. "Absolutely! You have no idea. I've got a system."

He gestured dramatically, leaning in as if unveiling a grand secret.

"I call it... my culinary nickname catalogue," he whispered, eyes wide with excitement.

Max raised an eyebrow. "Go on..."

"It's how I remember all these incredible places!"

"Alright, give me two examples."

"First off, we've got Chili Con Carne-ton Heston—my go-to Mexican food truck. It's holy ground for tacos."

Rusty snorted. "Of course it is. Birria Tacos, right?"

"The finest birria tacos, with the finest consommé on the side."

"Oh yeah, the consommé!"

Frank continued, undeterred. "I can only go there when my wife is at yoga. But when I do, I order with authority—like Charlton Heston in The Ten Commandments."

Suddenly, Frank threw his hands into the air, mimicking Moses parting the Red Sea.

"BEHOLD HIS MIGHTY HANDS!" he bellowed. "I COMMAND YOU... BRING FORTH THE HEAT!"

Max and Rusty burst into laughter while Frank, completely unfazed, took another triumphant bite of his Half 'n' Half.

"I don't understand The Ten Commandments reference," Rusty said, shrugging as if he'd just been asked a question in a foreign language.

Max raised an eyebrow so high it nearly jumped off his forehead. "Actually, Rusty, that's a high-risk, low-reward question."

Now finishing the last bite of his sandwich, Frank wiped the sauce from his mouth and the meat sweats from his cheeks. He leaned forward slowly, deliberately—like he was about to share yet another grand secret.

"If you must know—"

"Oh, no, never mind, I remember now. Disregard! Abort!" Rusty interrupted flatly, now remembering why.

Undeterred, Frank lowered his voice, his expression dead serious.

"That Mexican feast is so good that when I'm finished, I drive back home, walk straight into the bathroom, part my ass cheeks like they're the Red Sea... and I pray for divine intervention."

"Oh, God!" Max gasped, choking on his final bite and recoiling.

Rusty buried his face in his hands. "Frank, for the love of all things holy, why?"

"Alright, alright," Frank chuckled, holding up his hands. "Here's a few tamer examples..."

He cleared his throat, adopting a more professional tone— if that was possible for Frank. "There's Meatball Mike's, right off Saint Michael Street—best spaghetti and meatballs in town."

Max nodded, relieved. "That makes a lot more sense."

Rusty smirked. "Oh, Frank, tell Max about your annual football watch party."

Frank perked up instantly, his eyes gleaming.

"Sunday Sub Day," he declared dramatically, "just wouldn't be complete without my mega power creation."

"Get ready for this." Rusty grinned, patting Max on the shoulder.

Frank's eyes sparkled with excitement as he painted the scene like an artist unveiling his masterpiece.

"Picture this! Layers of thick-cut smoked ham and grilled steak piled high and seasoned with the kick of 'Slap Ya Mama' seasoning. Then, I add applewood-smoked bacon, chipotle mayo, fresh lettuce, juicy tomatoes—all smothered in melted sharp cheddar cheese."

Rusty squealed with delight. "Go on, Frank, faster! I'm almost there."

Frank held up a dramatic finger. "And it's all cradled in my freshly baked, homemade Hulk hoagie bun, ready to deliver an elbow drop to your taste buds."

Max shook his head, laughing. "Tell him what it's called, Frank!" Rusty urged.

Frank sat up proudly. Very seriously. "The Macho Ham Randy Sandwich!"

Max nearly fell off his chair.

Rusty, still grinning, looked at Frank in amused disbelief. "You know, I once asked you—how is it that the guy who can effortlessly recite obscure movie lines and niche pop culture references struggles to remember the names of actual people?"

Still chuckling, Max shook his head. "So, do you expense these meals or what?"

Rusty and Frank turned in unison, staring.

"Or what?" they asked together.

Unfortunately, team employees didn't enjoy any discounts on concession food, nor could they expense meals unless they were with a client. Even the occasional $10 concession voucher barely covered a hot dog and pop.

Further adding to their frustration was that the team didn't even oversee the arena's concession stands or parking lots—both were outsourced to major vendors with contracts with most professional sports teams.

As a result, fans and employees alike found themselves trapped in an overpriced web of expensive, underwhelming food options and lacklustre perks.

After dinner, Rusty took Max on a tour. As they took a lap around both concourses, Rusty highlighted several notable areas, including the best bathrooms in the venue and the only bathroom that offers hot water. He also pointed out the location of the guest services desk and the upper-level inside sales table.

During their walk, they encountered a few of Rusty's clients. Rusty seamlessly included Max in these conversations, which primarily revolved around the team's recent road trip, during which they managed to win a game—just barely. They also discussed the upcoming season ticket renewal campaign. Max valued this experience, appreciating the opportunity to witness first-hand interactions between a season ticket holder and an account manager. It didn't take long for Max to notice something distinctive about Rusty's sales style.

"You talk to each of your clients like they're your friends," Max observed.

Rusty nodded, unfazed. "That's how I build strong relationships. It's intentional."

"I can see that." Max glanced at Rusty, intrigued. "But doesn't that blur the line between professional and personal?"

Rusty shrugged. "Maybe in some industries. But in this one? Friendliness makes things a lot easier."

He gestured toward one of his clients, still waving as they walked away.

"It's a hell of a lot harder to say, 'I'm not renewing my season tickets' to your buddy than it is to some random account manager you've only spoken to once a year at renewal time."

Max nodded.

It made sense. Relationships were everything. And in the world of ticket sales? Sometimes, being a "friend" was the biggest competitive advantage.

Max noticed that Rusty carried a tiny notebook and pen, carefully making notes after every interaction. Everything from what they spoke about, client concerns, games to trade, or special requests was meticulously recorded.

If Rusty had time, he would return to his desk during an intermission to log the touchpoint into the CRM. Otherwise, he'd input everything after the game, ensuring no detail slipped through the cracks. Afterward, Rusty led Max to the gallery level—an area of the arena Max had never explored before.

Perched high above the ice, the gallery level offered a panoramic view of the entire rink. This vantage point was essential for the general manager and coaching staff, allowing them to evaluate player performances in real time.

Beyond team strategy, the gallery level was a hub for media professionals. The press box, located above centre ice, served as the nerve centre for sports journalism. Reporters and broadcasters delivered play-by-play commentary from this perch, sending real-time updates to television and radio audiences.

The gallery level also featured over 20 private suites available for rental, each accommodating up to twelve guests. These suites provided a premium experience for corporate clients and high-profile fans, offering a private restroom, comfortable seating, and a cozy couch.

The highlight of the gallery level was undoubtedly the exclusive Alumni Suite, a distinguished space dedicated to honouring franchise legends and serving as a shrine to the team's storied past. Boasting optimal sightlines and plush couches, the suite also featured large flatscreen TVs mounted on the walls, creating an inviting atmosphere for fans and former players alike. As ambassadors for the team, these alumni often attended games here, thus elevating the experience for select clients who had the unique opportunity to mingle with hockey royalty.

Despite its allure, Rusty acknowledged that the Alumni Suite was underutilized compared to the bustling 200-level and club-level suites. "The real reason?" he smirked as they stepped into the elevator. "The wait for this damn thing is agonizing."

Back on the 200-level concourse, Rusty and Max passed Jay and Salty, each engaging in conversations with their clients.

"So, this is what you guys do every home game?" Max asked, keeping pace with Rusty's power walking. His voice carried a hint of awe.

Rusty chuckled, a playful glint in his eye.

"I'll use this term very loosely, but one of the 'perks' of working here is access to the games. All account managers are encouraged to be here every night to interact with clients and fans."

He dodged a group of opposing team fans.

"Not those fans."

Max laughed.

Rusty continued, navigating through the crowd effortlessly.

"Some guys leave after the first period; others stay till the end. Personally? I stick around as long as I can. The real work happens in these interactions."

Max took in the energy of the arena. Tonight's atmosphere felt different—subdued.

"Weird vibe tonight."

Rusty nodded knowingly.

"Second game of a back-to-back. Fans are exhausted We are exhausted, too."

They veered off the concourse and entered a 200-level hosting suite. Inside, Kristina and Shane chatted with clients over a beer while Frank was elbow-deep in a plate of chicken fingers, blissfully unaware that plum sauce was now decorating his tie.

Rusty excused himself, disappearing into the crowd.

Max, momentarily alone, watched as Rusty navigated the seats immediately in front of the suite like a pro.

Spotting an older gentleman seated alone, Rusty approached. The two talked for twelve minutes, their exchange punctuated by nods and laughter.

By the next TV timeout, Rusty had returned to his seat.

Max leaned in. "Client?"

Rusty grinned. "Longtime season ticket holder. Comes solo every game. His dad played for the original team in the 1920's."

In the same row but on the other side of the suite seating, Dan glanced around the arena, shaking his head. He waited until the clients Shane entertained left the suite before addressing the team.

"Can we take a moment to mourn the upper bowl?" he said, facing the group. The attendance was dismal—just over 11,000 fans. "We all collectively failed this one, folks. I'd bet actual gate numbers are closer to 9,850, but they'll probably announce 12,000. That is a generous estimate at best."

Rusty leaned toward Max. "You were here last night, right? They announced 14,443, and some fans laughed—me included."

Dan, still frustrated, as the group shifted uncomfortably. "It's embarrassingly quiet in here. They might as well stop announcing attendance altogether."

"We clearly need to do better at filling this place up. Now, if you're telling me you've exhausted every avenue, I want you to be damn sure you've done that. Don't—" He took a deep breath. "Don't grin-fuck me."

The suite fell silent. Frank lowered his head. Shane and Kristina exchanged knowing glances.

Max, mid-bite into his egg roll, froze. He leaned toward Shane. "I'm... not familiar with the term grin-fuck."

Shane looked a bit sheepish. "Uh... well... grin-fucking is when someone pretends to agree or act on something when they really aren't going to."

He paused. "Wait. That's a bad definition. Hey, Frank—what does 'grin-fucking' mean again?"

Frank, barely looking up from his phone, responded in a mock British accent. "Don't be a grin-fucker,

Max. According to Urban Dictionary..." He cleared his throat dramatically. "It's when someone smiles and shakes your hand, assuring you they've heard and will act upon your recommendations or concerns, when in truth, they've already ignored and dismissed you."

Frank waved his hand dismissively as if shooing away Shane and Max altogether.

"Ah, good day, sir! You are dismissed!"

Rusty chimed in, grinning.

"For example…"

He adopted a high-pitched customer service voice.

"You get a stack of tickets thrown on your desk and say—'Thanks, Dan! I know this homestand has some exciting opponents, and I'll reach out to all my group leaders and get rid of these—I mean, give them away!'"

Shane smirked. "Plot twist: He doesn't reach out to his group leaders. And all hell breaks loose when only 11,000—sorry, 9,800—fans show up on a Thursday night."

Rusty sighed, shifting his focus back to the ice.

"I cannot believe we're still in this game. We've taken six more penalties and been outplayed all night."

Shane deadpanned:

"The referees need to get off their knees because they are blowing the game."

"We are terrrrrrrrrrrrrrrrrible," Frank added.

Moments later, Dan walked over to Rusty and Max. "So? Thoughts on your first suite experience?"

"This is so legit, Dan," Max said, his excitement evident. "Thanks for the invite. These guys are showing me a great time… and they told me all about what grin-fucking is."

Dan chuckled. "Yeah, don't be a grin-fucker, Max." His tone turned more serious. "Listen, I know you're here tonight, and hopefully, we haven't scared you off. You'll be back in tomorrow, but I also wanted to see if you're available tomorrow night. There's a sports dinner—Wally's being recognized as an outstanding community leader or some shit like that—and we've just had a cancellation from one of his guests. So, if you're up for it, would you like to attend the dinner with me, Salty, and a few players?"

Max's eyes widened. "Holy shit! Yes, Dan. I will absolutely make that work."

"Great. Suit up again tomorrow, and you can ride with me," Dan said. "If I were you, I'd take the bus to the office tomorrow because there's no way you'll be legally allowed to drive home after tomorrow." Max felt a lump form in his throat.

Dan's offhand remark seemed harmless on the surface, perhaps even a joke. But it cut deeper than Dan could ever know.

Max's chest tightened. His mind raced back to that night— the night that shattered his family.

He had spent his entire life avoiding alcohol because of that night. It wasn't a preference; it was a necessity, a promise to himself.

And now? Here he was, stepping into a world riddled with the very vices he had worked so hard to avoid.

The carefree banter of his peers, the casual drinking culture of the pit, the jokes about intoxication— they all felt like sharp, unwelcome reminders of what had been stolen from him.

Dan had no idea. And now was certainly not the time to bring it up.

Max forced a tight smile. "Thanks for the ride, Dan." Inside, he felt a mix of anger and disappointment.

He wanted to shout, to explain how deeply that remark resonated with him.

But instead, he clenched his fists and kept his mouth shut.

Moments later, Shane scooped a takeout container of stale nachos and wandered over to Max, Rusty, and Dan.

"Suite tickets to the game and an invite to the sports dinner tomorrow? Wow, look at this guy—Mr.

Big Shot." He nudged Max playfully. "You don't think you're showing him all the shine up front? Doesn't he need to earn his way?"

"As if you've ever earned your way, Shane," Rusty quipped.

Just then, the opposing team scored two quick goals on an extended 5-on-3 power play, 14 seconds apart.

The game was officially out of reach.

The mass exodus began.

Fans poured toward the exits with seven minutes still left on the clock.

"Beat the traffic!" Shane yelled into the crowd before clapping. "Beat the traffic!" Clap, clap, clap, clap, clap.

Then, grinning mischievously, he turned to Max. "Well, it's about time I hit the old dusty trail. Rest up and prepare yourself, kid. Hope you like it weird— because it's going to get weird tomorrow."

He then stuffed a handful of popcorn in his mouth, shoved three egg rolls into his coat pocket, and bolted out of the suite, take out container of nachos in hand.

As the final seconds ticked away, the arena emptied, leaving just Rusty, Dan, and Max in the suite.

Dan turned to Max, his tone direct but encouraging.

"Alright, Max. We'll treat this like an internship, and the first few weeks will feel like training camp." He leaned in slightly.

"We expect you to dive deep into our organization's rules, regulations, and—most importantly—our sales strategies."

Max nodded, listening intently. "You'll attend meetings, read manuals, and shadow not just Shane but also Rusty, Frank, Kristina, and a few others. Each of them has a unique approach to sales, and it's important for you to learn from all of them."

He sipped his drink.

"This will start as an unpaid internship, but you'll earn commission and performance bonuses. Our internships typically last four months. Consider this a trial run—now until the end of the season, and then some."

Dan's eyes locked onto Max's.

"If this isn't clicking for you—or for us—we'll have to part ways. Sound fair?"

Max nodded again, this time more confidently. "I just ask that you see past my lack of sales experience. I'm eager to take on tasks that will help me grow into a seasoned account manager."

Rusty leaned in, his expression serious.

"You'll need to learn quickly, Max. This job isn't just about the high-fives and celebrations. There's a lot of freedom here, but with that comes responsibility—and the possibility to stumble."

He paused.

"It's not always puppy dogs and ice cream."

Rusty's voice softened slightly. "You're stepping into the world of professional sports. Trust me, you'll feel the envy from a lot of people. But we've all been told the same thing— a long line of people want what you're about to have."

Max swallowed hard.

"Getting to the sweet spots means experiencing the bitter ones first."

Dan nodded. "Shane's right—you're getting a taste of the good stuff now, but it won't last."

Max raised an eyebrow. "In what way?"

Rusty leaned back. "You'll start to see things differently. Beyond just wins and losses."

He gestured toward the arena.

"You'll notice the empty seats. The signs that need renewing. The bathrooms without hot water. You'll see the grind behind the scenes. Selling tickets is cutthroat—and you might get your grass cut."

Max tilted his head. "Grass cut?"

Rusty smirked. "Just wait."

Dan clapped Max on the back. "You'll learn a lot about yourself really quick, Max."

Then, standing up, he stretched. "Anyway, gents—duty calls. I need to get home."

He pointed at Max. "Thanks for your flexibility tomorrow. Hope you like it weird."

Rusty packed up the last few slices of pizza for the drive home.

Max, meanwhile, stared out into the emptying arena.

He watched as the cleaning crew moved down the aisles, large clear plastic bags in hand.

Pop bottles, beer cans, and plastic cups were shovelled in for recycling.

Others followed with mops and brooms.

And for the first time, Max realized—

This was just the beginning.

CHAPTER 14

"Coffee is for Closers"

The next morning, Max woke up too excited to sleep past 6 a.m. —even after getting home close to midnight. After a hot shower and a hearty breakfast of three scrambled eggs with feta cheese and four slices of turkey bacon—cooked, as always, by his mother—he and Sarah left the house by 7:15 a.m.

As a result, he was the first person to arrive at the office.

But when he found the doors still locked, he quickly scurried back into the warmth of the car.

Sarah side-eyed him, adjusting the rearview mirror. "How are you feeling, Max? You good?"

She then leaned over and casually messed with his hair.

Max immediately at her hands. "Will you quit it!?"

Sarah rolled her eyes. "Well, if I don't help you out, who's going to look after you?"

"Fine but be quick. Please be quick."

Sarah fluffed a final strand and sat back, satisfied. "Well, at least there's not much traffic this early in the morning."

"Yeah, noted," Max muttered, glancing at his watch.

"I know this is just kind of a trial run…"

Max cut her off. "Training camp."

"Excuse me?"

"If I'm going to work for a professional sports team, I have to use sports clichés."

Sarah snorted. "You're such a loser."

Max smirked.

Sarah rolled her eyes again, this time adding dramatic air quotes. "Fine. Training camp."

Then, her voice softened. "But as I was saying… I know this is just kind of your training camp, but for what it's worth? I think you're gonna make the team. And go on to be a Hall of Famer, Max." She smiled, nudging him gently. "I'm proud of you. You took a huge risk quitting your job. You showed you weren't afraid to follow your heart, and I truly believe this is your chance to show everyone who you really are."

Max swallowed hard. Her words meant more than he could say.

"Aww, thanks. I appreciate that beyond words." His voice wavered slightly, but his smile was genuine.

Sarah held up a finger. "Now—don't fuck this up, okay?"

Max laughed. "Ha! Deal."

He reached over, pulling her in for a quick hug.

Sarah glanced toward the parking lot. "Look, someone's coming, so you should probably stop crying and follow them in."

Max went in for another quick hug. "Love ya, sis."

"Love you too, Max. Just remember…never compromise who you are. Alright?" She grinned. "Now, get out. I gotta get to work."

Shane had also arrived early, casually strolling past Max and Sarah in the car on his way to the entrance. Max hurriedly stumbled out. "Hey, Shane! Wait up—I got here super early, too."

Shane barely turned before pausing mid-step.

His head cocked as he watched Sarah slowly drive away. Then, his entire demeanour changed.

"Woah, woah, woah—who may I ask was that?"

Max groaned. "Forget about her, Shane. She's out of your league."

Shane gasped, clutching his chest as if personally wounded. "I'm offended! You don't even know me."

"Sorry. That's my sister. I'm just... super protective of her."

Shane narrowed his eyes. "That's your sister?"

He pointed dramatically toward the Honda Civic disappearing down the road. "You and her came out of the same vagina?"

Max stared at him, eyes wide. "What the fuck? Eww! What?! You're right—I don't know you!"

Shane shrugged, sipping his coffee. "I had to ask."

Max shook his head, still recovering.

"Actually... there were complications, and I was a C-section baby, so... I guess there's that?"

Shane winced. "Dude. I wasn't even going to ask that." He pointed his coffee cup at Max, eyes serious.

"But since you've overshared—please never do that again." Max chuckled despite himself.

"So... is she married?" Shane pressed, wiggling his eyebrows.

Max's smile disappeared instantly. "No."

Shane grinned. "I must know everything about her. She isn't a lesbian, is she? Not that's stopped me before! If you know what I mean. Actually, no, don't tell me. It'll be fun to try. Actually, no, it's ok if she's bi. I need to know there's a chance."

Max groaned. "For starters, I have no idea what you just said. Secondly, No! You will get nothing other than the fact that she has a boyfriend."

Shane perked up. "Who's the guy?"

"You may know him...Chad Bennett. Jimmy Bennett's son..."

Shane froze.

"That smoke show?" His voice dropped to a whisper. "She's dating... Chad fucking Bennett?"

Max narrowed his eyes. "Hey, hey, hey—that smoke show has a name."

"And her name is?"

Without thinking, Max quickly replied. "Sarah."

Shane smirked, satisfied. "Well, that's one more piece of information I didn't have. So— thank you for that, Max." Then, he winked.

Max rolled his eyes. "Another piece of information?" He crossed his arms. "She's learning Spanish." Shane raised an eyebrow. "And how exactly is that relevant?" Max grinned. "At least that's something you can't make weird."

Shane immediately perked up.

"Ah, Español. The language of love." He took a dramatic breath. "Sólo el pensamiento de ser con usted por la mañana me ayudó a conseguir mediante hoy."

Max stared. "Uh... what?"

Shane sighed dreamily, placing a hand over his heart. "Just the thought of being with you tomorrow is enough to get me through today."

Then, he closed his eyes, dramatically blowing a kiss to the heavens. "Sarah...with an H," he whispered softly.

Max rubbed his temples. "We just met."

Shane grinned. "Love is a journey, Maximus."

Max exhaled sharply. "Do you seriously know Spanish?"

"Not at all. That's all I know."

The two then walked silently into the office as Shane punched in the door code.

They passed the empty reception area and headed toward the kitchen, where they found Bryan brewing a fresh pot of coffee.

Bryan—an early bird by nature—lived a three-minute drive from the office and often arrived before most of his colleagues had their first sip of caffeine at home.

He greeted Max warmly, pouring him a steaming mug.

"Oh, thanks, Bryan, but I don't drink coffee," Max said, raising his hands. "I have a delayed reaction to caffeine."

Shane nearly choked on his Americano.

"Hey! You didn't say you have delayed ejaculation! Well done, squirt."

He gave Max a playful slap on the ass. "It's okay, we play sports!"

Max flinched, eyes darting around the kitchen.

"Dan told you?" he asked.

Shane winked.

Max sighed.

"Yes, obvi. It's okay—I've never had that problem, so I cannot possibly empathize with you," Shane said, smirking. Then, his tone shifted to mock seriousness. "But hey, come on, Max. You're better than that. You need to start drinking coffee because it's going to be a late night."

Before Max could protest, Shane grabbed Bryan's cup and thrust it toward him.

"Remember—coffee is for closers."

Max's eyes lit up instantly. "Glengarry Glen Ross!" he exclaimed, grinning.

"ABC!" Max and Shane shouted in excited unison.

Max pointed dramatically at Shane. "'A'—always. 'B'—be. 'C'—closing. Always. Be. Closing."

Shane hopped onto a chair in the kitchen, arms outstretched as he pressed his palms against the ceiling tiles.

"A-I-D-A!" he bellowed. "Attention! Interest! Decision! Action!"

Bryan shook his head, amused.

A brief silence followed.

Then, Shane sighed dramatically, stepping down from the chair. "Oh man, Glengarry is a great fucking movie." He pointed at Max. "But never repeat any of that in its entirety in my presence ever again."

He then ripped four sugar packets open and dumped them into his coffee, adding three creamers, and another shot of vanilla Coffee Mate.

Max chuckled. "Fine. We'll agree that it's a great fucking movie, and David Mamet is one hell of a playwright."

Shane turned abruptly, eyeing the vending machine. He inserted his change, punched in his code, and watched in pure horror as the Mars bar got stuck halfway down.

"Oh, you've got to be fucking kidding me."

He smacked the glass, then tried shaking the machine.

Nothing.

"I swear to God," Bryan muttered, watching from the counter, "one day, I'm just gonna say 'fuck this' and go back to my family's farm."

Shane snorted. "Bullshit. You wouldn't last a week without WiFi, Bry!"

Bryan shrugged, unfazed. "Oh yeah? I'll grow potatoes. Or weed. Yeah, nothing but weed for acres. You'll all be begging me for marijuana in five years. Just watch!"

Shane quipped. "We'll have dispensaries on every street corner in five years, Bryan. You'll drive down any street past a Tim Hortons, weed store, then a Starbucks, a convenience store, another weed store, and finally...a sex shop." He gave the vending machine a final, well-placed hip check as the Mars bar finally tumbled free.

He grabbed it triumphantly before turning back to Bryan with a smirk and a, "Wooooooooo!"

"Uh-huh. Sure, Shane." Bryan held up his hands.

With the coffee situation still not properly handled, Bryan offered to show Max around the 'bowels of the stadium.'

Max happily obliged; however, he did not take a sip.

They visited storage rooms, dressing rooms, and the loading dock area, where Bryan introduced Max to the security office, which was staffed 24/7. Max got his temporary staff pass, which allowed him to move freely throughout the arena and stairwells.

Next, they walked into the lower bowl, where Bryan pointed out the seating assigned to his season ticket holders.

This was an extension of what Rusty had shown Max the night before, but Bryan, ever the professional, went through the price levels and sightlines all over again.

They sat nine rows up, watching the operations team patch some rough spots on the ice, likely damaged during the previous night's game.

Bryan leaned back in his chair. "Later, we'll come back and watch the team practice." Max perked up.

He had never seen a professional team practice from this close. The idea thrilled him.

As they walked back to Bryan's desk, a familiar voice stopped them. "I heard you've earned a spot at the sports dinner tonight... is this true?" Max turned to see Salty standing there, arms crossed.

"Yes, sir!" Max replied.

Bryan chuckled. "Max, this is Sal, but we call him Salty. Salty, this is Max."

Salty rolled his eyes. "We met last night, Bryan." Bryan shrugged. "You and I were in the same suite...with Max." Crickets.

Salty quickly focused back on Max. "Look, kid, word of advice—the dinner is one thing. But the afterparty?" He leaned in. "That's a whole different experience."

Max raised an eyebrow. "How does one prepare for something like the afterparty?"

Bryan and Salty exchanged knowing looks.

Then, in perfect unison, they said:

"You don't."

Max laughed nervously. "Should I be concerned?"

Salty clapped a hand on his shoulder.

"Probably."

CHAPTER 15

"The Caffeine Spiral, aka The Jitters and the Shitters"

After their tour, Bryan and Max stopped in the kitchen, where they found Shane pouring himself another coffee. He quickly filled Bryan's travel mug and topped up Max's mug. He had only taken a few gulps in front of Shane and Bryan an hour earlier, but it felt like he was already on his second cup of the morning. Something about this coffee was... off.

Shane pointed to an empty seat in the inside sales hallway. "Sit here, Max."

Max lowered himself into the chair, eyes locking onto the cold cup of coffee in front of him. He hated the way he felt. What Max should have admitted was that coffee was a wild card. He never knew how it was going to affect him. But now? Chocolate rain was inevitable.

He sighed, disappointed in himself. He had been warned that he'd have to do things he didn't want to do in this job—but he hadn't expected it to start this early.

'It's just coffee.'

Then why did it feel like a betrayal? Everyone else seemed fine after caffeine. They functioned like pros. Why couldn't he?

The jitters weren't just physical. They started in his limbs—twitchy fingers tapping the desk, a bouncing knee that shook the floor. Then, they moved inward.

Like wildfire, his thoughts ignited. 'What if I missed an email from Shane?' 'What if things get weird tonight, like Salty warned?' 'How does Frank know so much random pop culture trivia?' 'What if I make an ass of myself at the dinner?' 'In front of Dan? Or worse... Wally?'

He shook his head hard. The more he focused on the sensations—the rapid heartbeat, the faint dampness in his palms, the tightness in his chest—the worse it got. He clenched his fists, gripping the desk, knuckles turning white.

"This is fine. Totally fine. I'm fine," he quietly said to himself.

He wasn't fine. His breathing turned shallow. Every inhale felt insufficient. Every exhale left him light-headed. His gaze darted to the coffee mug as if it were the enemy. How could something so small trigger this tidal wave of chaos? 'I didn't have more than four or five gulps!' 'Maybe it was the lack of sleep?'

It didn't matter. None of these racing thoughts matter. His therapist's voice echoed in his head.

"Breathe, Max. Four seconds in. Hold for four. Four seconds out. No... two seconds in, four seconds out?" He spoke to himself just a little louder and more impatient.

At least he tried. But regardless of the amount of caffeine, it had rewired his nervous system, nonetheless.

Fuck.

He needed to flush this poison out. He hurried to the kitchen, desperate for anything to reclaim control. The water cooler was out of order.

He flung open the fridge. Inside? Three bottles of red Gatorade. A glass container with someone's leftover salmon. A tub of margarine.

"What the hell kind of fridge is this?!" he said aloud, looking at the three bottles of red Gatorade again.

"Ah, fuck it."

He grabbed all three Gatorades and chugged the first bottle in short order on his way back to his desk. Did they belong to someone? Not his problem.

He scribbled a note in his notebook: 'Replace three red Gatorades.'

Then he sat back down, trying to sit upright—but instead found himself leaning against the wall.

Unlike the sales pit reserved for the top sales staff, as he was told the day before, the hallway was for inside sales reps—the rookies, the ones still "learning the ropes" in training camp."

Max appreciated the calm and quiet of the hallway when he and Shane arrived early in the morning. Unfortunately for Max, that tranquillity was about to change. Two of the loudest and most obnoxious inside sales reps, Steve and Scott, strolled into the reception area, parading down the hall like rampaging elephants.

Max had met them briefly the day before, but that wouldn't help him in this situation.

Scott and Steve lived together with two other colleagues—Ryan from group sales and Brittany, Ryan's girlfriend who worked in the catering department. Scott and Steve sat back-to-back in a tiny pod, already mid-conversation.

Scott leaned back in his chair, crunching on a Fun Dip stick. "Hey, do you ever feel like you're stuck in this weird place," he mused, "where, like, work takes up so much of your time that even your free time feels like work?"

Steve nodded immediately. "I know! Like, here we are, working on a Friday, and on Monday, we'll come back feeling like we didn't do any of the shit we needed to do over the weekend."

"Yeah... and we're just going to keep falling further and further behind." Scott rubbed Fun Dip powder on his gums like a deranged addict. Now noticing Max for the first time, Scott suddenly popped his head over his cubicle wall, looking straight at Max. "Hey, Max! I heard you're going to the sports dinner tonight."

His grin was pure chaos. "That's pretty fucking epic, eh?"

Max groaned.

It was only 9:03 a.m. And he already felt like he was hanging on by a thread. He needed to rally.

Tonight was important. But how?

Scott wasn't done. "Hey, what do you think they'll serve tonight?" He leaned in, eyes sparkling with curiosity. "I heard it's always some fancy fucking meal!"

Max blinked. His brain struggled to function.

Was this guy serious?

He stared at Scott, half-dazed. "I... don't know, man."

"Yeah... it's probably going to be steak or some bougie shit, eh?" Scott said, lifting an imaginary teacup to his lips with a raised pinky finger.

Steve laughed, already scrolling on his phone.

Max sighed. It was going to be a long fucking day.

"Was there a specific food from your childhood that you absolutely loved, but after eating it as an adult, you got absolutely obliterated, puked it all up, and have never touched it since?" Steve asked openly.

"Chicken pot pie. Fuck, I can't go near that flaky crust and creamy chicken shit inside anymore," Scott replied. "The thought of it totally makes me want to yack!"

"Ugh...." Max groaned a second time before reaching for the garbage can. He wasn't quick enough and vomited red Gatorade and coffee all over the side of the bin and onto the carpet.

"Woah, dude!" Steve exclaimed before laughing and snapping a photo of Max face-down in the garbage bin as Rusty walked by.

"Hey," Rusty said delicately, placing a hand on Max's shoulder. "I've seen good friends struggle with the pressures of this job, but not this quick. Jesus, you okay, Max?"

"I'll be okay," Max answered, wiping up the mess with every Kleenex from the box on his desk. "Bad reaction to coffee. Must. Rally. Now," he added in a hopeful yet clearly defeated tone.

"Hey, Rusty?" Steve asked. "Have you heard the rumours that they're going to announce a new concert today at ten?"

"That's the word around here, yeah. Terrible timing, per usual, but we don't control any of that."

"Why is it terrible timing?" Max asked, starting to rally now that the coffee had evacuated his body.

"It'll sewer this renewal campaign because clients will want us to get tickets for them before the public, and we can't. They'll want to leverage their renewal to get tickets, which we won't do, and since they don't know the rules, even if we could, they'll ask if we'll sell them more tickets than their account entitles them to—which we won't."

Moments later, everyone's phones and computers dinged as they received the same email from Kent. There was no actual message aside from Kent's email signature. Instead, it was all laid out in a lengthy email subject line.

Re: "Yeam, mandatory sales meeting on the sales floor, 9:15."

"What does that mean?" Max asked Steve.

"He means there's a mandatory sales meeting on the sales floor." He looked at his phone. "Now, in eight minutes," Steve replied confidently. "'Yeam' is a typo for 'team.'"

The small sales floor quickly filled with twenty or so colleagues standing next to each other as Kent and Dan positioned themselves in front of the photocopier to address the group.

"I guess I'll start off with the worst-kept secret in the office," Kent began. "On Wednesday, we let Jimmy Bennett go. After twenty-plus years, it was time to mutually part ways. Yesterday, Dan brought in someone who feels he's ready to fill Jimmy's shoes. He thinks he's ready to make a difference. Dan? Do you want to introduce him?"

Dan wasn't prepared for the introduction, and the impromptu meeting surprised him. Which was odd because nothing seemed to surprise Dan in those days. He was also confused as to why Kent had framed Max's arrival as filling Jimmy's shoes. Nevertheless, he pointed Max out and announced: "Max is passionate and without the emotional baggage some of you mutts seem to have," he added with a laugh. "I've asked Max to come in for two weeks as a trial—to help make some calls and take some of the load off of you, especially with some of Jimmy's clients. As Kent said, we're down a man in the sales pit, and hopefully, Max can get a full experience of what it's like working for a professional sports team. Be kind to him. Help when you can. But he's not necessarily here to fill Jimmy's shoes."

Dan paused, taking stock of the room. "Like I said, it's a two-week training camp to start, and he's coming in at an opportune time because we've got a long homestand ahead of us. You know how those stretches go—lots of long hours, lots of terrible food choices over the next two weeks, and maybe some hazing for this pledge."

"I'll go first!" Shane called out, quickly standing up and holding a paddle with 'FOR SPANKING' hastily scribbled on the front in red spray paint.

"You weren't actually supposed to bring that to the office," Dan laughed. "Anyway, Max'll be starting like most of you mutts did—in the hallway. He'll learn as much as possible and be involved in as much as possible. For the most part, Rusty, Bryan, Kristina and Shane will be showing him the ropes, and I expect you all to give him a warm welcome," Dan said, pointing again to Max. "Everyone, this is Max. Max, this is your new family. Anything else you want to add, Kent?"

Kent was frantically typing an email. "Okay, guys, let's be clear on one thing here," he said, launching into a completely different speech. "We want to give you all the tools you need to be successful. We've invested in you—bought you the best sales lists in town, given you a number of prospecting event opportunities—and where are we?

"We all have a job to do, but I understand that some people in this room are uneasy. I know what happened yesterday—I mean Wednesday—with Jimmy caught a few of you by surprise. I don't want you to feel like you're working in fear of losing your job. But professional sports is cutthroat. I get it."

"Uh, Kent?" Dan tried to interrupt.

"One minute, Dan." Kent dismissively held up a full hand. "Look, the management team isn't in the business of giving ultimatums or threatening you to do your jobs," he said, scanning the room.

Some of the sales reps nodded slightly, seemingly relieved, while others—like Salty and Rusty— exchanged unimpressed glances and shook their heads with arms fully crossed. Their body language could have told Kent all he needed to know. But Kent didn't notice and continued to drone on.

Now, Max looked even more confused, trying to read Dan's expression, but Dan simply blinked quickly and gave a subtle shake of his head, almost to say, 'Well, I tried.'

Kent finished his monologue by circling back to how he started. "We are, however, in a business where we need to drive revenue, and for us to be successful, we must hit that target. That target influences who we sign in the offseason, our capital expenditures on the stadium, and the programs we put together.

"So... if you're not prepared to stand at the bottom of this enormous fucking mountain with your backpack on, ready to start climbing, then it's time you looked elsewhere. Let's be clear—I'm only asking you to look at yourself in the mirror and ask yourself if this is really for you. If you're prepared to give it your all—come to work, be productive, be hungry, and be aggressive for your next deal—then we're on the same page.

"And just to be clear, after you've looked at yourself in the mirror once, look again and ask yourself if you've truly been giving it your all. If I asked myself that same question right now, I'd give myself a D. Is that good? No way. Can I improve? Absolutely."

"Will you?" Salty muttered under his breath. "Absolutely not."

"So, in conclusion," Kent continued, ignoring the comment, "if you're struggling to find your place in this organization, then come see me or Dan. No sense in mixing business and pleasure. I know I'm always more receptive to honest conversations, and I'd respect you for coming in, shaking my hand, and saying this isn't for you."

Pausing, Kent took an extra long gulp of coffee, inevitably keeping everyone hypervigilant and on their toes. "I don't need to say this, but I will anyway," he started. "We've got a whole line of people dying to get into this business, so just be honest with yourself and with me, and I'll do what I can to help you along."

"Is he seriously telling everyone to quit if they don't like the situation?" Max quietly asked Frank.

"There's really no way of knowing, Max. In true Kent fashion, yes. He's doing his usual semi-quarterly 'shit or get off the pot' address."

"Semi-quarterly? That doesn't make any sense, Frank," Max said, raising an eyebrow.

"Nothing makes sense here," Frank muttered, walking backwards and disappearing to the other side of the room.

Seconds later, as Kent was still talking, everyone's phones dinged simultaneously. An internal email had just arrived, announcing the worst-kept upcoming concert secret.

"There it is. Fuck my life," Rusty whispered to Salty reading the press release on his Blackberry. "This concert is going to cripple us, and tickets go on sale during renewals?"

"Are you fucking kidding me? Just cancel Christmas," Salty mumbled, shaking his head.

As Steve had alluded to fifteen minutes earlier, inappropriately timed concert announcements were nothing new. Rusty knew all too well that every time they faced an uphill battle—season kick-off, renewals, playoffs, etc.— some poorly timed concert announcement would come along and derail their efforts nine times out of ten.

After what was supposed to be Max's introduction—but had instead been hijacked by Kent's 'we're not going to fire anyone, but if we don't hit our targets, somebody's going to get fired' speech, along with the concert announcement— Shane walked back to his desk to grab something, addressing Rusty and Jay as he passed.

"Well, if you'll excuse me, I must shit. I need to babysit Max this afternoon, and then you and I have that thing tonight, Rusty. The last thing I want to do is leave him alone in this pod with you two while I take a dump, or worse, must shit somewhere in the wild...or in public."

When it came to using the bathroom at work, everyone had their preferences. Many used the washroom outside the main reception area, as it was close and the only one in the basement with hot water. Others, mostly Shane, went out of their way to use a different facility in the arena. Since it was the morning after a game, the cleaning staff would have thoroughly disinfected overnight, making this the safest time to avoid getting herpes from a toilet seat—or so Shane believed.

The private club washroom was arguably the closest and least used, but for Shane, it wasn't good enough. He often ate there while hosting clients and prospects, and 'don't shit where you eat' was one of his own cardinal rules. Instead, Shane took the elevator upstairs to the gallery level and used the press box shitter.

"Players make fifty, I make a dime. That's why I shit on company time," Shane mumbled to himself as he walked into the elevator.

Reaching into his pocket, he pulled out his old MP3 player and scrolled through his special 'shitting' playlist. His go-to track? 'The Lonely Shepherd' by Zamfir. The instrumental classic helped him relax and get into the 'Kill Bill' mood. Given his poor diet, mostly of coffee, Egg McMuffins, and arena food, he needed all the help he could get to get past his regular, irregular bowel obstructions. When the playlist failed, he had a case of enemas at home, and four emergency bottles were in his bottom desk drawer next to the Imodium, Pepto-Bismol tablets, and Rolaids.

Meanwhile, over in Frank and Salty's cubicle, Frank was losing his own shit over the concert announcement.

"You can't make this shit up!" Frank exclaimed.

"Can't make what up, Frank?" Salty asked, barely glancing over.

"This email I just got from the owner of McKenzie Hardware. His kid heard the leaked news and is demanding I find him twelve front-row seats for the boyband concert. Twelve! Can you believe that?"

"The show hasn't even been officially announced yet, and he's already demanding twelve front-row seats?" Salty asked incredulously. "He knows you can't do that, right?"

"Don't be ridiculous," Frank said, slipping into his best Balki Bartokomous impression from Perfect Strangers. "His thirteen-year-old daughter doesn't care! She's on the up and up with that band and knows everything before everyone else. So, how would I do that?"

"You can't," Salty replied flatly.

Frank slowly stood up. He was determined to lift the weight of the impossible tethered to him. So he walked over to the other cubicle pod to speak with Rusty. But Rusty was on the phone, so he quickly pivoted to Jay.

"Jay, I need your help," he said, tapping Jay on the shoulder. Jay was also in mid-conversation with a client. "Please hold, just one sec," he said into the phone before covering the mouthpiece. "What is it, Frank?" he asked, clearly annoyed. "I'm on the phone!"

"You're the program guy. How would I get twelve front-row tickets to the concert they're announcing tomorrow?"

"You can't, Frank!"

"I don't understand."

Jay sighed, adjusting the microphone on his headset and covering it even more despite putting the call on hold. "Because the concert promoters keep all the best seats for themselves. You've got fan clubs, radio stations, contests, charity allocations, the band's family and friends, and then there's the stage layout—they always keep the best seats until they release them closer to the show, sometimes even on the day of the show. That's what Springsteen does!"

Rusty, not finished with his call, swung his chair around. "You know all of this! This has been the way it is for each of your twenty-plus years," he whisper-yelled. "Now get back to work, Frank! Or, at the very least, let Jay!"

About an hour later, at 11:03 a.m. Kent sent another all-staff email. The email subject line now advised of another emergency meeting at 11 a.m. "Well, we're already three minutes late," Dan told Kristina as they walked to the board room.

"Sounds about right," Kristina acknowledged.

Frank, Salty, Kristina, Rusty, Bryan, Max, and Jay were already seated around the boardroom table, waiting for Kent.

"Ladies and gentlemen, in advance of tomorrow's concert announcement, it must be stated that under no circumstances are you to communicate seating locations or guarantee access to anyone. Are we clear?" Kent demanded as he entered the room.

"Jesus, Kent, what's the rush? You couldn't have waited two more minutes for the already late meeting to start so everyone else could get here?" Dan muttered. It was loud enough for Kent to hear.

Kent ignored him and continued. "The promoters are holding their cards very close to their chest on this one and are being extremely selective with the details they've given us. This show is going to be worse than Madonna and the Rolling Stones...combined."

"What does that mean, Kent?" Frank asked.

"It means we're in the dark," Kent replied flatly. "I wouldn't expect too much. Apparently, this is the hottest tour in the world right now, the highest-grossing. Has anyone even heard of this group?" The room stayed silent.

"We can't even guarantee club seat holders their usual seats for this one. That's going to be a problem during renewals. Val, can you elaborate?"

Valerie from the box office, who had successfully navigated the Madonna, Rolling Stones, and Pearl Jam fiascos, stepped in. "A lot of you have already come to me asking for holds and early access. We just can't do it," she explained. "Kent and I felt the need to clarify that this will be a clusterfuck of epic proportions. Given the official announcement is tomorrow, details are still subject to change. But we've asked Melanie from EQqo Entertainment to also give you what she knows."

Melanie stood and addressed the group. "Thanks, Val. Tomorrow's concert announcement will be nothing short of the biggest concert this city has ever seen. These guys won International Group of the Year on Making the Band, and they've sold out stadiums and arenas everywhere—Europe, Asia, South America, Australia. When they hit North America this summer, they'll be bigger than The Beatles in the '60s. We're the first stop on their North American tour, so this is a concert nobody over here has likely ever seen before!"

"Sounds about right," Salty mumbled to Rusty, who simply nodded.

Having finished his business in the washroom, Shane weaselled his way into the back of the boardroom, listening intently to the details Melanie was presenting. Moments later, he casually raised his hand to make it seem like he had been there the whole time.

"When you say 'played,'" Shane started, "you really mean—and I mean this very, very loosely— 'performed' or 'danced,' right? Do these guys even play instruments, or do they just parade around and lip-sync their way into the hearts and minds of teenagers and their overworked, underpaid, and overwhelmed parents who would rather drink battery acid?"

"Well, uh... no," Melanie admitted. "They're mostly a pop act, no instruments. I mean, they have a backup band, but you know what I mean. We've heard great reviews about their production value."

"And these guys are talented how?" Shane pressed. "Can they even speak English?"

"Well, they won the—"

"Yeah, yeah, we know. They won some popularity contest, mostly thanks to social media and a large Korean population. I mean, their name is ma#tag—Smashtag—for Christ's sake!"

"ma#tag's '#OutOfControl' tour is currently the highest-grossing tour in the last calendar year," Melanie explained. "Their concert movie was incredibly popular when it was released at Christmas, and it continues to top the box office. We'll be holding back the first five rows on the floor, plus the first ten rows on each side of your club seat sections for promotions, fan clubs, contests—you know, the usual." She made eye contact with Rusty, who nodded at Frank. "Additionally, we'll be holding back the first four rows of your 200 and 300 levels as well. Any questions?"

"What about our club seat holders, Mel? What do we tell them? What do we say when they ask why the best twenty-nine rows aren't available?" Dan asked.

"They'll be given seats as close to their original location as possible, in the quantity of their account," Melanie continued. "So, four full-season seats equal four concert tickets. Two half-season seats, two tickets, and so on." Sally exchanged a knowing glance with Frank. "We'll do our best to keep club seat holders in their general area, but some may be seated behind the stage or on the side. We cannot guarantee exact locations, as Kent said earlier."

"This is like when the league held back seats for the All-Star Game," Valerie added. "We managed that event well enough but obviously had fewer restrictions. And every possible seat in the house."

"And if I need, say... twelve seats in the front row, how do I go about that?" Frank asked.

"You can't," Melanie said bluntly.

After the meeting, Frank slumped at his desk, practically in tears, while Salty chatted with Brad nearby.

"No, no, no, no!" Frank panicked, scrolling through another email.

"What now, Frank?" Brad asked, looking over Salty's shoulder.

"Another email. Same client. The thirteen-year-old is restless and needs an answer. NOW. She wants to know what progress has been made for her bat mitzvah party."

"Christ, Frank, tickets don't go on sale for a few weeks. We haven't even officially announced the concert yet. Tell your client to calm their tits!" Salty said dismissively.

"Do you have a thirteen-year-old?" Frank asked, dead serious.

Brad and Salty exchanged a look.

"No," Brad said flatly.

"You know neither of us do, Frank," Salty said with growing frustration.

"Then you don't know what I'm dealing with," Frank sighed, rubbing his temples. "Also, and I mean this sincerely, Salty...." Frank paused. "Telling a pre-pubescent girl to 'calm her tits' is like telling a fish to 'take a deep breath' or a snowman to 'cool it'.

Salty raised both eyebrows, struggling to understand Frank's point. "Didn't you explain to your client that you have zero—and I mean zero—access to tickets?" Salty asked.

"Kinda," Frank admitted.

"It's a simple yes or no answer, Frank," Salty said, folding his arms.

"I told him I'm working on it—which I am," Frank insisted, pointing back and forth between them. "The rest is just details."

"There's really nothing to work on, and there aren't any other details, Frank. You heard Kent, Melanie, and Valerie yourself. If you can get him tickets—and that's a big if—he won't be anywhere near the first five rows. We just talked about this not even twenty minutes ago!"

CHAPTER 16

"Brown Balls"

A few hours after his first trip to the washroom, Shane realized the issue wasn't his lunch—it was the unholy amount of expired cream he had dumped into his coffee. Seated at his desk, he felt something brewing in his gut, a pressure mounting with each passing second.

Then, suddenly—

A loud, thunderous fart ripped through the office.

"Oh my God," Shane groaned, face flushing crimson. "This is it. I'm going to die in this office and from my own stink."

"What the hell, Shane?!" Jay shouted, recoiling in horror. "How is that smell even possible?"

"It must be something I ate," Shane winced, clutching his stomach. "I'm pretty sure something died inside me... I definitely need help."

"Okay, just breathe," Rusty chimed in, feigning a calm, meditative state. "In through your nose... hold it... now exhale. Just push the pain away... but maybe aim in Jay's direction."

Shane shot Rusty a look, equal parts mortified and amused. "I think I need to... take care of business again," he admitted, standing up and taking a deep, shaky breath. "If I'm not back in forty-five minutes, send a search party."

"Forty-five minutes?!" Jay's face twisted in disbelief. "Is it really going to take that long?"

Shane chuckled weakly. "Well, if I'm lucky, I'll be back in ten. But you know, sometimes these things just can't be rushed. Even when you think you're finished...you're not. It's...it's like a canal locks. You close the gates around the boat, the water fills up, the boat floats in, then you wipe, then the canal gates open to allow the boat to pass."

Neither Jay nor Rusty knew what to say and remained speechless as Shane made a hasty retreat, leaving his colleagues to ponder the terrifying battle unfolding between the human body and lactose intolerance.

In this emergency, Shane did his best to waddle towards the bathroom outside reception. There was no time to risk waiting for the elevator. But the second he pushed the bathroom door open, he stopped dead.

Two of the three stalls were occupied.

"Oh, Jesus Christ," he muttered, stomach twisting violently. Turning sharply on his heel, he had no choice and beelined toward the elevator.

"Gotta relax, gotta relax," he whispered, reaching into his pocket and fumbling with his MP3 player again. Rather than the usual calming melody of Zamfir's pan flute, he accidentally hit play on Out of Control—the chart-topping hit from ma#tag.

Visibly sweating, he practiced the breathing technique Rusty had just taught him. He felt like an expert. "In through your nose... hold it... out through your mouth," he murmured, exhaling with force. "Why is this elevator taking so long? C'mon, c'mon!"

Finally, the doors slid open—

And Melanie from EQqo Entertainment stepped out.

The two exchanged smiles. They'd met plenty of times before, and she clearly hadn't forgotten his earlier rant in the boardroom.

"Oooh, is that a boyband in your pocket?" Melanie teased, raising an eyebrow.

Shane, momentarily distracted by one of his many weaknesses—rocker chicks in jean jackets—felt his stomach lurch.

"Where'd you get that jean jacket?" he blurted out, unable to stop himself.

"What's wrong with my jean jacket?" Melanie questioned insecurely.

"What's right with your jean jacket? I mean, who wears jean jackets these days anyway? What are you, from the '80s?" he smirked painfully.

"Are you Levi Strauss?" she laughed. Then her expression shifted. "Wait... why are you sweating?"

Shane wiped his forehead. "We really need to stop meeting like this," he joked.

Just then, the chorus of Out of Control blared from his pocket.

Melanie grinned as she mockingly sang along, barely in English, "Girl, things are gonna get out of control..."

"Terrrrrrrrrrible song," Shane replied, trying to ignore the pathetic fallacy of the situation.

Melanie bit her lip. "So terrible."

She looked him up and down, eyes flickering between his drenched shirt and the undeniable swamp-ass situation happening in his pants.

"Why do you have that song playing in your pocket, Shane?" she asked, crossing her arms. "Are you a closet ma#tag fanboy?"

"That song is playing at just the right time and place," he said smugly.

Melanie smirked. "Girl, things are gonna get out of control..." she sang softly.

Shane leaned against the elevator wall. "Just wait till you see what's really playing in my pants."

Melanie's eyes twinkled.

"What if I can't wait?" she murmured.

"Ugh..." Shane exhaled.

And with that, she grabbed him by the jacket and pulled him into the elevator before the doors slid shut.

Five minutes later, the stench of Shane's fart still lingered as Max walked over to the pod Shane shared with Rusty and Jay.

"Shane might be a while," Rusty said as he tagged a pre-renewal call in Salesforce.

"Yeah, he hasn't returned from the upper levels yet," Jay added. "We'll send him over to the bullpen when he gets back, Max."

Max returned to the bullpen, settling back into his seat near Scott and Steve, who were deep in very loud conversation.

"Man, I was playing poker online last night and made sick money. Dude, I was on such a roll!" Scott exclaimed.

"Online poker is for babies. I went to the casino last weekend, put down three hundo, came away with six hundo playing roulette," Steve bragged.

"You still play the outside?" Scott asked.

"Yeah, man, it's the only way to play."

"You do realize that requires, like, zero skill? It's either red or black," Scott scoffed.

"What happens when it lands on green?" Max whispered. "And why do you need to yell? You're sitting right next to each other!"

"Man, if I could go to the casino every day, I would. If I could make more money there than in commissions... I'd fucking retire! See ya!" Scott declared.

"See ya!" Steve echoed before the two shared an explosive fist bump.

Dan walked by moments later, stopping next to their desks. "Scott, you got your sales numbers in?"

"Not yet, but I'm feeling hot—like I just hit my third blackjack in a row. That's when you double down."

"Dude, that's literally when you walk away," Dan said, shaking his head bitterly.

Steve waved him off. "You don't walk away when you're up. You chase the heater. Keep going, Scotty!"

Max mumbled, "That's also how you lose your house."

Scott turned to his deskmate. "You 100% don't know what you're doing."

Steve just grinned. "Bet on red, baby."

"You literally just said you play the outside, Steve. Is it red? Is it black? Which is it?" Max asked, unable to hold back.

"You may have been up this time, but didn't we lose big last time we went?" Scott added, concern creeping into his voice.

Steve exhaled, rubbing his face. "Listen, it wasn't my fault. I was up. Way up. I was going to leave."

"Steve..." Scott started.

"But then I lost one roll. And then another. And then... well. You know how it goes."

Dan sighed. "Goddamn it, man."

Steve leaned back, shaking his head. "I should've walked away." He chuckled bitterly. "Yeah, yeah. Lesson learned, I s'pose."

About thirty-five minutes after leaving for the washroom, Shane finally returned to the pit—still visibly uncomfortable.

Max tried to stop him as Shane passed his pod. "Are you okay? Where are you going? Why are you sweating so much?" he asked. "You've sweat through your shirt—and you know you have swamp ass, right?"

"So, I've been told," Shane muttered before reaching his desk, throwing his MP3 player back in the drawer.

"Jesus... I've got fucking brown balls," Shane groaned, which immediately caught the attention of his pod mates.

"What the fuck are brown balls, Shane?" Jay asked as Max walked into the pod. "And seriously, why are you sweating so much?"

"You've heard of blue balls, right?" Shane asked.

Jay and Max looked confused, but Rusty nodded knowingly, frowning.

"For our uninitiated friends," Shane started, looking at Jay and Max, "blue balls are what happens when your love life takes a detour at the almost exit without actually getting off the highway! Thankfully, that hasn't happened to me since grade school, but basically, it's like your body threw a pants-off, dance-off party... but nobody hits the music to start the dance, ya know what I'm saying? Now you're just stuck, awkwardly waiting, and at the same time, you start experiencing severe swelling of the scrotum. You lose all sense of time and place and can't concentrate on anything else."

Shane pulled out his phone and showed the group an old black-and-white photo of an Indian man sitting on his own enormous testicles.

"That's inappropriate, Shane," Rusty said, pushing the phone away. "Also, you've got blue balls confused with elephantitus of the nads," he said, quickly Googling it. "Actually, it's called elephantiasis—e-l-e-p-h-a-n-t-i-a-s-i-s," he said. "Scrotal elephantiasis is a rare condition that causes severe swelling of the scrotum. It's a type of lymphedema, which is a condition where lymphatic vessels are obstructed, causing fluid buildup."

"Thank you, Dr. Google," Shane said dismissively, rapidly blinking as sweat dripped into his eye. "It's apparently a serious problem, but again, I wouldn't know anything about it," he added, grimacing in pain. "That poor bastard's balls are full. He's just a squirrel saving up all his nuts because you know...he can't...he doesn't know whether he is uh...."

Jay quietly raised his hand, waiting his turn. "Because he doesn't know if he is going.... or cumming" Shane finally said in between winces.

"No! Shane. Stop. Right. Now." Rusty angrily pleaded. "This is over the top."

"I prefer to use the phrase 'out of control.'" Shane corrected before noticing Jay's hand, still extended patiently. "Yes, in the back," Shane said, pointing at Jay three feet away. "What is it?"

"Asking for a friend... and more for clarification," Jay began. "You haven't had blue balls since grade school? That's my first question. Follow-up question: can you finish explaining what brown balls are?"

"Why?" Max asked, knowing instantly this was another high-risk, low-reward question.

"You know when you need to shit or fart," Shane said, shifting uncomfortably. "But you can't because you're with someone else who wouldn't appreciate you shitting or farting in that moment... notably a woman. Or a dude, I guess," Shane said, casting a shy look at Jay.

"And this causes blue balls?" Jay asked, completely oblivious to Shane's comment.

"No, Jason! Let me finish," Shane snapped.

"Yes, please," Rusty cut in before Shane glared at him. "Like I said, that's enough."

"Maybe you haven't said I love you yet, so it's all sunshine and fucking rainbows up to this point."

"Oh, so that's what the first three months of any relationship is called?" Steve asked, walking into the pod.

"What?" Max asked, startled.

"Well, if you must know, I've got more bluish-grey balls right now. Or maybe ugly brown balls. Or...chocolate mocha balls."

"Chocolate...mocha? Oh, come on, Shane!" Rusty was about to lose his own shit on Shane.

"Oh Jesus, I can feel it deep, deep in my plums," Shane groaned, gingerly sitting down—only to immediately stand back up, shifting his weight from foot to foot.

"So... you haven't shit, then?" Max asked.

"No," Shane breathed heavily. "I literally ran into Melanie—if you know what I'm saying. And let's just say...things got out of control."

"Ah. So that's why you prefer the phrase 'out of control.' Rusty giggled. "I'll allow that."

Just then, Frank walked down the hallway, returning from reception with an Amazon package.

"How'd the shit go?" he asked. "Ya drop the kids off at the pool?"

"It didn't happen! Not yet, at least!" Shane replied. "Massive, elephantiasis brownish-mocha balls, now. Frank. I may die."

"You didn't shit?! Where the fuck were you all that time?"

Shane hesitated, now unable to speak. Sweat dripping out of every pore.

Rusty smirked.

"Things got out of control," he said.

CHAPTER 17

"And Boom Goes the Dynamite"

As the day wound down, Kristina returned to the office after several pre-renewal meetings at the technology park a few kilometres away. She had coordinated three separate meetings to prepare for upcoming deals. Like so many of her colleagues, she had a lot of work to do as she tried to get ahead of the looming challenges in the weeks and months ahead.

About an hour later, Frank burst out of his cubicle and rushed into Dan's office. He was carrying a notepad, donning a green plastic visor—popularized by Asian tourists in Las Vegas—and, for some inexplicable reason, had an unlit cigarette dangling from his mouth. Even more perplexing, given that Frank neither smoked nor gambled, two more of his cardinal rules: 'Never smoke'm even if you've got'm' and, 'If you are going to give away your money, give it to Christ.'

When Frank crashed in, Dan was sitting at his desk with Kent, discussing their expectations for the sports dinner.

"Hey, Dan! Got a sec?" Frank asked. "I ran some numbers and made some calls." He was clearly out of breath.

"As in, pre-renewal calls?" Kent asked, leaning forward.

"No," Frank replied sternly.

"And?" Dan replied, also leaning forward, knowing full well it wasn't about pre-renewal calls. "How's it looking?"

"Like my first wife on the eve of my second marriage," Frank said, a hint of humility in his tone.

"Ah, yes. I remember that train wreck—should I be concerned?" Kent queried.

"Probably," Frank admitted.

"So, what are the pubs saying?" Dan pressed further.

"They're on board... 'ish'."

"What does 'ish' mean?" Kent raised an eyebrow.

"Well, we need to consider some advertising and marketing support during the broadcasts, now and for the rest of the season. It would really help if we had a few prizes to raffle off—maybe some signed jerseys."

"Hmmm, we've already depleted our stash of signed jerseys for this season, and there's no time for broadcast or marketing support given their other pressures. How about a hat and a polo shirt?" Kent suggested.

Frank paused for a moment. "They'll do fifty bucks for a ticket, a pint of beer, and a pound of wings."

"Fifty bucks for a pint of beer, a pound of wings, and a seat?! We could probably swing that," Dan said confidently.

"I've actually tackled a pound of beer before," Frank laughed, shaking his head.

"One of the next three games during this homestand starts next Tuesday," Kent noted. "That's an ideal opponent but not enough time to promote and execute."

"Arizona, Los Angeles, or Tampa?" Frank clarified.

"Exactly. I'll never understand how those markets can support a franchise while we struggle so much," Kent shrugged. "But I think Tampa is the only one we can expect some sales."

"Here's the thing: if we use those two bronze games and one silver game for the tickets, accounting for bus costs, we'd need to sell... sixty tickets to break even," Frank calculated.

"Well, alright! That doesn't sound too bad, does it?" Kent asked, smiling at Dan and Frank.

"Buses hold fifty-two," Dan stated matter-of-factly.

"Jesus..." Kent muttered, his optimism dwindling.

After Frank left, Dan moved over to Bryan's desk and settled next to Max, who was observing Bryan at work.

"How are you holding up, kid? Ready to get wild?" Dan asked.

"I think so?" Max replied. "But I've been warned about the afterparty by just about everyone. And now you're also saying it's going to get wild? Honestly? I have no idea what to expect," he admitted, looking bewildered.

"It's probably best you don't," Bryan said softly.

Later, Rusty drummed his fingers impatiently on the steering wheel of his SUV. It was 7:04 PM, and Shane was surprisingly late. As annoyance bubbled inside him, Rusty glanced at the modern condo where Shane lived. Just then, the back door swung open, startling Rusty.

"What the hell is this? A car seat?" Shane exclaimed incredulously. "Since when have you had a kid? Isn't Amy pregnant?"

"Shane, we talked about this like, yesterday! We also have Emma, our daughter; she's four! And I am not a taxi! Why did you go for the back door?" Rusty asked.

"I always go for the back door, obvi!" Shane replied.

Shane clambered over the car seat, dramatically scattering Emma's toys and other clutter around the back. But just as he was about to regain his balance, his hand landed on a particularly soft, well-loved stuffed bunny. He forgot what he was doing for a moment, absentmindedly squeezing its worn ears between his fingers, lost in the comforting nostalgia of childhood toys—until Rusty's impatient huff snapped him back to reality.

"You know, you can always sit shotgun," Rusty suggested.

"Not a chance! You think I want to be seen in this mom-mobile? Of all the vehicles you could have brought, why this one?" Shane retorted.

"Dude, you asked me for a ride. Do you want a ride or not?" Rusty snapped. "Besides, what's wrong with my SUV?"

"It's a Honda!"

"It's actually a fuel-efficient Nissan, you donkey!" Rusty kept his gaze on Shane. "Well? Do. You. Want. A. Ride. Or. Not?"

"Yes, please! Tally-ho, driver!" Shane said, pointing vaguely in the direction of the street.

Around the same time, Dan and Max settled into their seats at the Sports Dinner. In addition to recognizing local community champions, the event also raised funds for the local children's hospital and other groups for at-risk youth.

The tastefully arranged table was adorned with centrepieces designed by children from the hospital, a postcard explaining the supported charities, and the evening's meal printed on linen paper.

Off to the side, Kent engaged in animated conversation with several guests while Wally nervously mingled among the crowd of local sports and business dignitaries. Three seats at their table remained conspicuously empty.

Max glanced at Dan, a smirk playing on his lips. "Kent and Wally sure know a lot of people."

Dan chuckled. "They have to. Almost everyone at this event has hooked up with someone else in the business."

"So, who are we missing?"

"Salty's off schmoozing somewhere," Dan said, motioning to the seat to his right. "We're still waiting on the players."

"Dinner's about to be served. Shouldn't they be here?"

"Considering they were supposed to be here an hour ago, I'd call it a ten percent chance they actually show up," Dan predicted with a dry laugh.

Just then, Kent returned, pocketing his phone.

"The overpaid divas are no-shows. Looks like it's just the six of us tonight," he declared, a hint of irritation in his tone. "Losers."

"What happened this time? Aren't they required to be here?" Dan inquired.

"Coach is bringing them all on a Zen retreat to change their mindset or some shit like that." Kent scoffed. "Considering how they're playing this season, it's probably best they stay away."

"Well, I hope you brought your appetite, Max," Dan said as the catering staff began serving the first course: a vibrant antipasto dish featuring olives, assorted deli meats, cheeses, and an elegantly wrapped cucumber-julienne salad.

One of the servers leaned closer. "Is this person here, sir?" he asked, his eyes drifting toward one of the empty seats.

Dan waved his hand at Salty's seat with a hint of eagerness. "Uh, yes, thank you. He's just at the bar ... and the other two spots as well," he said, acknowledging the seats reserved for the players.

The server placed additional plates of antipasto on the table, and Dan observed with satisfaction as the plates piled up.

"And boom goes the dynamite!" he grinned, grabbing two fluffy dinner rolls from the basket. He tore them apart, tossed the utensils from the empty seats onto their respective places, and poured the remnants of the olive oil onto their plates.

"There's plenty more where that came from."

"Take notes, kid. Dan's a genius," Kent said, his mouth half-full, clearly enjoying his appetizer.

Amidst a mouthful, Dan gestured towards the wine bottle at the centre of the table. "Max, do you mind?"

Max eagerly passed him the bottle, and Dan poured a few splashes into the two empty glasses before finishing the remaining wine.

"Garçon, une autre bouteille de vin, s'il vous plaît," Dan requested, his accent faltering but earnest nonetheless.

With the start of his meal finally laid out before him, Dan relaxed and savoured the moment.

"So, how did your day go? Did you learn a lot?" Dan asked, stuffing his mouth with a mini sandwich of French bread and thinly sliced meat.

"The calls I sat in on were interesting—lots of similar conversations. The team needs to improve. My clients aren't fans... they're not keen on tickets..." Max trailed off, lost in thought, hypervigilant for the moment things would inevitably get weird.

"And what do you think of the mutts? Your first impressions?" Kent prodded.

"Well, they're... unique," Max replied cautiously. "I'm still getting the hang of things, but I can see that everyone brings something different to the table. Bryan, Rusty, and Shane are showing me how to navigate the hurdles. I look forward to shadowing Kristina and Frank next week."

"Yeah, those guys are great teachers. Kristina especially. Don't be shy to ask questions," Dan added, winking encouragingly.

"Why aren't they here?" Max asked, glancing around.

"First off, it's vital for everyone to share these experiences. Besides, those guys attend enough events—if you ask Shane, he'll say he's at a hundred each year. Trust me, he could use a night off."

Meanwhile, the twenty-five-minute drive across town now complete, Rusty's SUV pulled up outside a rundown strip mall in the city's east end, illuminated only by a lone light from a second-floor office. Rusty exited the SUV and walked to the other side to find Shane still inside, jiggling the door handle with mounting frustration.

"Fuck off, Rusty! Come on! This is embarrassing!" Shane's voice was muffled, clearly annoyed, still trying to engage the door handle.

Rusty paused to tie his shoe and checked his phone for the address. With a sigh, he swung the door open. "Childproof doors? Are you kidding me?"

"I offered you shotgun! You turned it down because you didn't want to be seen in this thing. Now you need some tough love," Rusty gestured emphatically at the SUV. "You act like a man-child, so... childproof doors it is."

Shane stumbled out of the back, gasping loudly.

"What the hell? Where are we?"

"If only I had a shotgun! I'd feel a lot safer," Rusty quipped, trying to lighten the mood.

"Jesus, there's a homeless shelter across the street! Don't look them in the eyes!" Shane urged, his voice rising with urgency.

"Where did you come from, Shane? They're real people!" Rusty countered, exasperated. "And look, one of them is coming over to say hello!" He pointed at a homeless man on the corner, panhandling.

"Let's get the hell out of here," Shane declared. "This is exactly why I didn't drive!"

Throughout dinner, Dan engaged in a subtle yet intricate dance of manipulation, orchestrating the food on his plate with practiced finesse. Each bite was an opportunity to engage in playful experimentation as he expertly rearranged the colourful dinner of perfectly cooked prime rib, garlic-herb potatoes, heirloom carrots, and peppercorn gravy, creating visually appealing compositions that piqued the curiosity of those seated around him.

As they savoured the flavours, the servers moved gracefully, offering tantalizing additional courses— for Dan, Max, Kent, Wally, and Salty, plus two additional servings for the players to be named later.

Max took mental notes as Dan's slightly slurred interaction with the servers was surprisingly effortless. He seamlessly directed their attention, ensuring wine glasses remained full and plates replenished as often as possible.

The atmosphere buzzed with a lively hum, punctuated by laughter and the clinking of cutlery against fine China plates.

Dan's manipulation took on a strategic flair as the final course approached, balancing indulgence with the anticipation of dessert. His suggestions to the servers brimmed with enthusiasm, ensuring every guest was engaged and each dish celebrated in excessive quantities.

A few moments later, Rusty and Shane navigated using the pulsing techno music emanating from a narrow staircase as their guide. Shane stopped short at the top, staring wide-eyed at the scene before them.

"Oh my God. The bears are who we thought they were. Let's just go, man. Cut our losses. Tell Kevin we got lost... or that I had diarrhea."

"I'm surprisingly okay with that decision," Rusty conceded, turning to head back.

But before they could escape, Kevin appeared, bounding up the stairs with an enthusiastic bounce, holding a paper Staples bag filled with sheets of paper.

"Hey, guys! You came! So great to see you! Come on in!" Kevin exclaimed, beckoning them eagerly.

"Uh, I'd love to," Shane began, "but something I ate at lunch isn't sitting well with me. Rusty, you go on in without me. I'm going to find a bathroom to destroy. And boom goes the dynamite. Gimme your keys."

"Actually, Shane, the diarrhea meds you took at the pharmacy will kick in any minute now," Rusty bluffed smoothly. "But I forgot my phone in the SUV, so... I'm going to go get it. I'll meet you inside."

"Oh, you won't need your phone in there, Rusty! Shane, there's a bathroom for you to use, too! No worries!" Kevin insisted, ushering them into a room buzzing with attendees in their 20s. It was an overwhelming sausage party. There were no beautiful babies in sight, aside from three women who Shane would have ranked as 2s or very generous 3s. The walls were adorned with motivational posters, and an overly chipper PowerPoint presentation displayed serene scenes of oceans, sunsets, and mountains, interspersed with phrases like leadership, excellence, and teamwork.

"Oh no," Shane gasped. "What the hell is this, Kevin?"

"Hey, wanna see my new business cards? Just be careful! They're hot off the presses 'cause I just printed them on photo paper until the official ones come in," Kevin said, bubbling with pride.

"No, Kevin! I don't want to see your business cards. What is THIS?" Rusty waved his arms dramatically, overwhelmed at the unfolding scene.

"I told you, Rusty!" Kevin said, with a dreamy, smooth vibe.

"Are you high, Kevin?" Rusty asked.

"Nah, man, just super chill with my new direction in life. We have a speaker tonight! It's going to be great! He's not actually here in person, but you know... he's talking to us from San Diego using his technology!" Kevin replied, his excitement infectious. Or intoxicated.

"This better not be a timeshare presentation," Shane warned, glancing nervously at Rusty.

"What's a timeshare?" Kevin asked.

"Is this a pyramid scheme?" Shane pressed, skepticism no longer dripping from his voice but flooding the space.

"Well, Shane, I'm glad you asked! We're an accelerated wealth company specializing in emerging technologies and the Internet of Things to grow our business and the business of others," Kevin beamed, reading proudly from his prepared card.

"Totally a pyramid scheme," Rusty groaned, glaring at Shane.

"No, man, we don't believe in pyramids! It's all about opportunities—great opportunities! I don't want to work for someone else forever; I want to be my own boss, and this, man... this is a fantastic opportunity to do just that."

"You should have known better," Shane pointed accusingly at Rusty.

"Me? You encouraged this!" Rusty shot back. "He wouldn't even have invited me if you hadn't told him to! I will never forget this."

Kevin guided Shane and Rusty past a group of late-twenties dudes wearing cheap suits, texting on their phones.

"Here, you can sit here," Kevin said, pointing to the second row in front of the projector.

"Wait! Let's grab a—oh fuck my life," Shane groaned.

"What? What now?" Rusty asked.

"Where the hell are the free refreshments?!"

Meanwhile, it was a much different scene at the sports dinner across town. After dessert, Max stood by the bar, sipping a Sprite, waiting to get Dan a drink before the awards ceremony began. Grabbing a complimentary cocktail, he turned to walk back when he found himself in the orbit of a group of giggling, thirty-something women who had clearly had too much to drink.

"Ooooooh, well, hello, handsome! Whatcha got there?" one of them purred.

"Oh, this?" Max held up his glass. "It's a Sprite."

As soon as the words left his mouth, he regretted them.

"Here, maybe it could use some sugar," another woman teased, reaching into her purse and dropping a pinch of a mysterious powder into her drink, her friend's drink, and—before Max could react—his.

A ripple of unease washed over him as his drink fizzed. His mind flashed back to earlier in the day, to Salty's ominous words: 'Whatever happens tonight, happens.'

Off to the side, Dan quickly finished his newest drink and watched Max interact with the woman, grinning to himself as he pulled out his phone and texted Shane.

As the presentation dragged on, Shane's phone buzzed. He glanced down to see a text from Dan: 'Tell me it's NOT a pyramid scheme!'

It was quickly followed by an onslaught of laughing and poop emojis.

Shane held up his phone, showing Rusty with disbelief and amusement. "Don't tell him the 'emerging technology' is video phones! Please don't tell him!"

"I don't want to hear the end of this, either." Rusty moaned, shaking his head. "We ride and die together on this."

"Apparently, these clowns haven't heard of Skype or FaceTime," Shane muttered.

"Not to mention Facebook Messenger, Zoom, Google Meet, WhatsApp... what a joke! I can't believe I traded future considerations with Amy for this... for fucking video phones," Rusty lamented.

"None of this would have happened if we went to Oakland!"

"That has nothing to do with this," Rusty said, pointing carefully around the room. "And that was supposed to be next weekend!"

"I haven't been fucked like this since high school," Shane admitted, shaking his head. "We're never getting this time back. Ever."

"Hey, at least it's not a timeshare presentation," Rusty mocked.

Shane remained irate. "Hi-tech Mormons selling to family and friends, and you get a cut of every one of their monthly bills? Are you kidding me? It breaks my cardinal rule: don't sell to family or friends!"

"I'm not forking over $500 to kick off my own video phone company," Rusty insisted, his face etched with incredulity. "I can't believe Kevin roped us into this. I can't believe you roped me into this, you jackass! He led us astray!"

Just then, Kevin bounded over, beaming with enthusiasm. "What did you think, guys? Wasn't it just amazing?"

"Oh, yeah, great! Just... great," Rusty forced a smile, trying not to roll his eyes.

"So great, Kevin. Thanks for thinking of us," Shane added, his voice dripping with sarcasm.

"This is going to be huge, guys! Rusty, you're going to love it!"

"Going to love what?" Rusty retorted, suspicion creeping into his voice. "Why me and not Shane?"

Twelve seconds later, both Shane and Rusty received a text from Dan:

'Drop whatever you're doing. Just get over here now! SHIT'S GOING DOWN!!!'

Twelve seconds after that, another message followed:

'Rookie's landing us some trophy bass; shit's going crazy! I have wet panties! We need to tear this motherfucker down! Get over here as fast as you can!!!'

"Wooooooo! I'll drive!" Shane shouted, leaping onto the rickety banister and sliding down at high speed—only to crash into the door with a thud that echoed down the narrow hallway.

Max stood awkwardly with the two women, who giggled coyly at him.

"He looks a bit nervous, doesn't he, Cindy?" one teased.

"I think he's kinda cute, Jill," the other replied, eyeing Max up and down.

"You're not a cop, are you?" Max asked.

"This is a party, baby! Just relax and enjoy," Jill purred, leaning in to grope and kiss Cindy passionately.

Max's eyes nearly popped out of his skull. "Are you hookers? Lesbians? 'Because I'm all for women's rights and the LGBTQ+ community!" he blurted, throwing his arms up.

Before he could process what was happening, something across the room caught his eye—Salty, sprinting toward him, appearing out of nowhere like a shirtless mirage.

"Whatever happens tonight, happens. Just saying," Salty declared before striding toward the bar, chest bare, confidence unchecked. Salty didn't seem like the tattoo type, but there it was, a giant family tree tattooed across his entire back. It was strikingly beautiful. Max hoped and prayed that Salty's unexpected tattoo would be the weirdest thing he saw that night. It wasn't.

Jill smirked, nudging Cindy. "I'm sure your friend over there can show you a thing or two."

Max followed her gaze toward Dan, who was watching the chaos unfold with pure delight. He stood tall, his right foot planted firmly on the chair. Knee bent, with his right elbow resting lazily atop it. His posture was casual yet commanding, like a captain surveying his crew or a strategist weighing his next move. His gaze was steady, watching intently, exuding quiet confidence with just a hint of amusement.

Jill pointed at Dan and beckoned him over. Taking the hint, Dan mimed his way across the room, pulling himself closer with an invisible rope.

"Well, well, well. Hello again, ladies," Dan announced, his voice dripping with machismo. "Is this kid bothering you?"

"Actually, no, we—I mean, they were—" Max stammered.

"Well, then, he must be trying to take advantage of you!" Dan accused, pointing at Max before randomly tossing three ice cubes into the crowd. "Max, you magnificent slut! You're outnumbered."

"He couldn't take advantage of us if he tried," Cindy pouted.

"Allow me," Dan said, moving closer and closer to the group.

"He's nervous! Poor fella," Jill giggled, playfully ruffling Max's hair.

A few minutes later, Shane hastily parked Rusty's SUV across three spaces in the hotel parking lot, leaving the engine running as he jumped out and sprinted towards the venue.

"Oh, don't worry about me, Shane. I've got this!" Rusty called out , left to fend for himself and properly park the car. "Just make sure you tip your valet!"

As Shane burst through the banquet hall doors, his eyes darted around. It didn't take long to spot Dan, Cindy, Jill, and Max. Salty was there, too, sitting alone at an empty table, watching the mayhem unfold like an amused spectator. He was eating a Kit Kat. Max caught sight of Shane and waved him over.

The dinner had rapidly devolved into a hedonistic fantasy—older couples grinding together, half-clothed people dipping various body parts into the chocolate fountain, and Dan enthusiastically giving Jill a lap dance.

"Female empowerment, I say! This is why the vote counts!" Dan bellowed. "I would've voted for Crooked Hillary in 2016! Harris in 2020! Michelle Obama in 2024! WOOOOO!"

After properly parking the SUV, Rusty calmly walked up the stairs and into the hallway, pausing at the banquet hall entrance in stunned disbelief.

"Did we leave a bad place and somehow end up somewhere worse?" he muttered, shaking his head.

His eyes roamed the scene, quickly finding Shane—who had already discarded his pants and was pounding drinks at the open bar. To the left, Kent and Wally were tearing around in nothing but their underwear and business socks. Rusty squinted, recognizing George, a former colleague fired for paying off a suites department employee for leads. Inexplicably dressed in a long trench coat, George swayed to no particular music as he devoured an oversized bag of Skittles. Under any other circumstances, it would've been a hilariously odd sight, but here? At this sports dinner? He blended right in.

Rusty sighed and turned back towards Shane, just in time to see him down his fourth shot in a row to the cheers of the crowd.

"WOOOOOOOO! I'M THE KING OF THE WORLD!" Shane howled.

"WOOOOOOOO!" the crowd echoed back.

"BRING ON THE GINCIDENTS!" he bellowed.

"Gincidents! Gincidents!" the crowd chanted.

"The monkeys have escaped their enclosures and taken over the zoo," Rusty muttered as he grabbed a beer from the open bar and reluctantly joined his coworkers.

Dan was now giving Cindy a lap dance while Jill wildly licked Max's face. Max, wide-eyed and giggling uncontrollably, looked both amused and terrified.

"Your skin is so soft! What's your skincare regimen?" Jill asked, licking him again.

"Noxzema girls get noticed. Am I right, Max?" Dan yelled over the noise.

"I just wash my face!" Max sputtered between giggles.

"Oooh, I love facials!" Jill purred. "Will you give me one, Max?"

"No, me, me, me!" Cindy slurred.

"SKEET, SKEET, SKEET, SKEET!" Dan yelled out. "How about you both at the same time?"

"WOOOOOOO!" Shane cheered from across the room.

"WOOOOOOO!" Dan responded as if he and Shane were exchanging moose mating calls in the wild.

"Your tongue... it's like my cat's," Max observed, laughing again hysterically as whatever the ladies had dropped in his Sprite started to take effect. Then Jill suddenly pulled back, playfully clawing at his clothes.

"Oh my God, your shoulder feels ah-mazing!"

"Oh my God, you smell like a rainbow!" Max declared.

"SKEET, SKEET, SKEET, SKEET!" Dan repeated.

Still in his boxers, Shane dashed up behind Jill and started kissing her face. Realizing he was essentially trapped beneath her, Max looked up uneasily. Jill still had her weight on him, pinning him in place. And now, Shane—reeking of cheap cologne and alcohol—was far too close for comfort.

The rainbow sweetness had turned sour.

"Whatever happens tonight, happens, right?" Salty quipped, not even looking up from the last stick of his Kit Kat bar.

Just then, Kent darted past the group and delivered a stinging slap to Rusty's ass.

"SHAG TAG! YOU'RE IN!" he cackled, sprinting away—only to be immediately smacked on the ass by Dan.

"You're it, Rusty! Better go got'om!" Max called out.

"Right... go get'em, Rusty; rookie's landing some trophy bass!" Rusty grumbled. "Shit's going down, they said. This is totally normal," he added, carefully setting his drink down before chasing after Kent.

"This is totally awesome!" Max shouted, ducking as a shoe flew by and a bra landed squarely on his face. He ripped it away and swung it round in the air. "And spectacular!"

"Totally legit, bro!" Shane replied, now playfully shoving Jill into Cindy and Max.

The three collapsed onto a couch in a tangled heap, Cindy and Jill's lips quickly finding each other. It was like something straight out of a raunchy adult film—or one of those steamy scenes from the 1998 movie Wild Things starring Neve Campbell, Denise Richards, and Matt Dillon. Just Google it.

Max's pupils dilated to the size of old silver dollars. He stood frozen, his brain desperately trying to process the insanity unfolding around him.

"I hope you like it weird," Shane and Salty declared in unison.

CHAPTER 18

"About Last Night"

The next morning, Max groaned as sunlight streamed through the slats of poorly adjusted blinds, landing squarely on his face. He blinked against the brightness, groggy and disoriented. The leather couch beneath him creaked as he shifted, his suit rumpled and stained with what appeared to be chocolate and...was that glitter?

"Ugh," he groaned, sitting up slowly and clutching his pounding head. His tie hung loosely around his forehead, and one of his shoes was missing. His other sock, inexplicably, was on his hand like a puppet.

The air was thick with the stale scent of cheap beer, sweat, and something oddly fruity—Skittles? It was a pungent cocktail of regret or just another weekend for Shane and Jay. There was really no way of knowing. Blinking blearily at the unfamiliar room, Max struggled to reconcile his hazy memories with reality. He hoped they didn't overlap.

Empty pizza boxes littered the coffee table, along with a half-eaten McNugget box where six lonely survivors remained. A hot pink Victoria's Secret bra spun lazily on the ceiling fan above.

Max fully sat up with a groan, only to realize he was chewing something. He pulled a half-eaten slice of pizza out of his mouth and stared at it in horror.

"Oh God, I could have died," he whispered, dropping it onto the plate like it was radioactive.

Dan was sprawled out on the floor, face down and spooning a potted plant like it was his high school sweetheart. He wore a towel, haphazardly tied, as if mid-interpretive dance or striptease.

"Dan," Max croaked, nudging him gingerly with his sock-covered hand.

Dan groaned but clung to the plant. "Five more minutes, coach," he mumbled before rolling over and dumping dirt onto the carpet.

Rusty was slumped on the couch, hugging a throw pillow like a life preserver. His Blackberry silently buzzed. It was his seventh missed call. All from Amy.

Meanwhile, Salty, the picture of serenity, sat in a recliner flipping through a dog-eared issue of Popular Mechanics. "Morning, sunshine," Salty murmured. "Coffee's in the pot. Help yourself."

Max rubbed his temples, trying to summon any coherent memory from the night before. Flashes surfaced—Dan doing the Macarena on a table, someone yelling Gincidents! at the top of their lungs, and a conga line that ended when the chocolate fountain toppled over onto the dance floor. He vaguely recalled arguing with Jill about the definition of charisma while Cindy attempted to braid his short hair. Was this before or after the orgy?

His phone now buzzed in his pocket, startling him. He fished it out and saw Shane's name flashing on the screen.

"Shane? What the hell happened last night? And where are you?"

Shane's voice, hoarse but chipper, crackled through the speaker. "Bro! LEGENDARY night. You killed it at karaoke. The crowd went wild. Oh, and Cindy says hi."

In the background, Jill's voice rang out. "Hi, Mark!"

Max pulled the phone away, grimacing as his headache intensified from her now irritating voice.

Hanging up, he staggered into the kitchen, catching his reflection in the chrome toaster. His face was smeared with glitter and lipstick, and someone had expertly drawn cat whiskers on his cheeks.

He groaned. "Oh no. Who...? Jill? Cindy? Salty? Shane? Please tell me it wasn't Shane."

Behind him, Dan stretched and yawned, bits of dirt cascading off him like confetti. "You were majestic, man," he said, grinning. "Also, you look like shit." He turned towards Salty and raised a weak finger to point. "I blame you." He gagged slightly, then swallowed. "Ugh, I just threw up in my mouth!"

"Don't blame me," Salty said without looking up. "I'm not the one who sang Celine Dion like it was a fucking TED Talk."

Max groaned, leaning against the counter. "Whatever happens, happens, right?" he muttered in shame. "Never again."

From the living room, Dan snorted. "Never again until next time, you mean!"

Max froze, the faint taste of early this morning's pizza still haunting his mouth. He sighed deeply, rinsing his mouth under the kitchen tap.

"Yeah," he muttered under his breath. "Until next time."

Max spent most of the weekend buried under heavy blankets, trying to piece together the sports dinner. By Monday morning, the mere thought of facing his colleagues made him vomit. He vomited again at the smell of the breakfast his mother had prepared—or maybe it was the creeping realization that he still had no idea what actually happened Friday night.

His mom dropped him off at work since he still wasn't feeling well enough to drive. Her parting words—"You're too old for this nonsense."—echoed in his ears.

Equally echoing in his head? Scott and Steve's loud conversation from Friday morning.

Max realized they were right.

He'd come back to the office thinking, 'I didn't do any of the fucking things I needed to do this weekend.'

Yeah... and we're going to get further and further behind, he thought grimly.

Ironically enough, perhaps truer words had never been spoken. At least, spoken about Max's first 36 hours in professional sports.

He slumped into his chair, regret weighing heavy in his brain.

Out of nowhere, Shane appeared, perched on the edge of Max's desk like an overly enthusiastic golden retriever ready for a walk. He had a smoothie in one hand and an infuriatingly smug grin.

"Well, look who survived the sports dinner of doom," Shane announced cheerfully, loudly slurping his Booster Juice. "How are we feeling, big guy?"

Max groaned, pulling his chair closer to his desk to physically block out Shane's relentless enthusiasm. The smell of strawberries, bananas and spinach made him feel sick to his stomach. "Don't call me that. My mom had to drive me to work this morning because I still feel like death. And stop smiling. It's physically painful to look at you."

"Hey, I'm just basking in the afterglow of Friday's shenanigans," Shane said. "Which, by the way, you were the star of."

Max shot Shane a withering look. "I was? Wait. Please, for the love of God, don't remind me."

"Oh, I'm going to remind you," Shane said, leaning in like he was about to share the juiciest secret of all time. "Dude, you owned the karaoke stage. Celine Dion? I didn't know you had it in you."

Max's head hit his desk with a dull thud. "I didn't have it in me, Shane. That's the point. And now I'm pretty sure I'll never live it down."

"Are you kidding? Everyone loved it!" Shane exclaimed. "Even Cindy and Jill! They said you were adorable. Or did they say you were doable..." Shane shrugged.

Max's face went pale. "Oh no. Not Cindy and Jill. Please tell me they were the ones who drew on my face."

Shane's grin turned mischievous. "Jill did the whiskers. Cindy handled the glitter. Honestly, you looked majestic, like Mr. Mistoffelees. Like some kind of fabulous party bear."

Max sat up, glaring. "A bear? Mr. Mistoffelees is a cat. Are you even listening to yourself?"

"Welcome back, bro, relax," Shane said, patting Max's shoulder and gently pushing him back into his chair. "It wasn't even the weirdest thing that happened to you that night. Remember Dan and the potted plant?"

Max groaned again. "How could I forget? He was spooning it like it was his prom date when I woke up."

"You arm-wrestled him for it," Shane recalled.

"I did?"

Shane laughed. "You challenged him. Said you were fighting for the honour of... I don't know, some kind of pizza king or something?"

"And that explains why my arm still hurts. Great. What about the chocolate fountain? That wasn't me, was it?"

"Nah, that was all Salty," Shane said. "A lot of it was Salty, actually. What a fucking legend. He knocked it over while trying to climb on one of the tables with the same potted plant in hand. Honestly, we should've seen it coming. Classic, classic Salty."

"Unbelievable," Max muttered.

"Oh, and you should know," Shane added, lowering his voice like Frank sharing a secret, "George says you owe him for that pizza you 'earned.'"

Max buried his face in his hands. "I'm never going to hear the end of this, am I?"

"Probably not," Shane said brightly. "But hey, at least you didn't join Dan for his interpretive towel dance slash striptease."

Max looked up, horrified. "Towel dance? Striptease? Is that why he was wearing a towel Saturday morning?"

Shane nodded. "He said it was about freedom of expression. Honestly, it was pretty moving. You may or may not have passed out by then, though."

Max leaned back in his chair, staring at the ceiling. "I can't believe I woke up on Dan's couch with glitter on my face and the distinct smell of Skittles in my nostrils."

"And you wouldn't trade it for anything," Shane said, grinning. "Except maybe some more nostril candy."

Max paused, and then he felt like vomiting again.

Meanwhile, over in the pit, Salty and Frank were busy working on pre-renewal calls.

"How was Friday night?" Frank asked, eyes on his spreadsheet.

"Good food. The usual sports dinner. Disappointingly, it was rather tame this year," Salty replied.

"That is disappointing!" Frank said. "I think Phil is still missing in action from three years ago. But what can you do? How did the kid do?"

"He held his own just fine," Salty said with a small smile.

Moments later, Kristina walked down the hallway and stopped beside Max's desk. "I heard stories from the sports dinner, Max. Tell me they aren't true," she asked, legitimately concerned.

"We've just established that he had a great time, Krissy, and we'll just leave it at that," Shane reassured her before Kristina rolled her eyes and physically pushed him away from Max.

Once Shane was out of earshot, she turned back to Max. "How are you really doing?"

Less than a week in, Max was already seeing the not-so-glamorous side of professional sports that Dan and the others had warned him about.

He was also realizing what he wanted from this job—and what he didn't.

Just like Friday, Max loved how quiet the building was when he got in early in the morning, but that peace was completely shattered as soon as Scott, Steve, and a few others arrived. The volume was one thing, but their constant laughter, crude jokes, and casual profanity made it almost impossible to concentrate.

It wasn't his place to say anything. At least not yet. But he worried that when he started making regular calls to his own season ticket holders, they'd be able to hear Scott and Steve's bullshit in the background.

"Honestly?" Max said softly. "I wish I knew." He hesitated, then added, "Can we go somewhere quieter, please?"

Sensing his frustration, Max watched as Scott and Steve walked down the hallway like Stone Cold Steve Austin heading to the ring, ready to unleash a can of whoop ass. Just like the beginning of Stone Cold's theme music, Max heard glass breaking as they entered the hallway. Kristina nodded. They left the hallway and slipped into the empty arena, finding a quiet, unlocked suite.

For the first time since that damn cup of coffee on Friday morning—Max felt relief.

Max sat back in the plush suite chair, exhaling a long breath. For the first time in days, the hum of his nerves began to settle.

Kristina, perched on the edge of her seat, gave him a knowing look. "Alright, Max. Let it out. What's on your mind?"

He hesitated, staring out at the empty ice rink. "I don't know... I guess I'm just already overwhelmed.

It hasn't even been a week, and I feel like I'm already messing this up."

Kristina tilted her head, her tone calm but direct. "What makes you think that?"

Max sighed, rubbing his temples. "A lot of things. For starters, Scott and Steve—I mean, they're nice enough, but the way they talk? It's like they don't care who hears them. The jokes, the swearing...Scott is always clearing his throat. I can't imagine a season ticket holder being okay with that if they overheard. And if I ever get to that point—making calls, talking to people—I don't know how I'd handle it. What if it reflects badly on the team? Or worse, on me?"

Kristina nodded slowly and methodically. "That's a valid concern. Have you talked to them about it?"

"No," Max said quickly, shaking his head. "It's not my place. I'm just the intern. Plus, I feel like if I said anything, they'd just laugh it off or think I have something stuck up my ass. And maybe I do, but I don't think I'm wrong."

"You're not wrong," Kristina said firmly. "But you're also right that it's tricky. It's not easy being the new guy, especially in an environment like this. The culture can be…" She paused. "This culture is a lot. But it's okay to feel the way you do. I think we all do and have at various points in our time here. I don't want to take anything away from what you're saying because I am validating that we have all experienced this—and it sucks."

Max let her words sink in before continuing. "I agree, the culture is a lot, but it's not just that. Friday night at the dinner… I didn't want to drink. I just wanted to experience something new, take it all in, you know? But everyone acted like I had to. Coffee on Friday—I hate coffee. Then alcohol and drugs later—I don't even know if I did any. I didn't have a chance to think, let alone say anything, because I just wanted to fit in, show that I'm a team player, prove I can handle the role and all its glory. I didn't want to say no because I thought it'd make me look weird. Or weak." He ran a hand through his hair. "I hate feeling like I'm not in control of my own choices. And I hate that I'm so worried about screwing this up that I'm doing things I don't even want to do."

Kristina leaned back, crossing her arms. "Max, let me ask you something. Why do you think you're here?"

He blinked at her, confused. "Because I want to work in sports?"

"Sure," she said with a small smile. "But why do you think Dan invited you—without you even applying or asking for this opportunity outright?"

Max hesitated. "I guess... because he saw something in me? Untapped potential. A passionate, outgoing, and honest twenty-two-year-old ready for my next challenge." He attempted to inject some confidence into his tone.

"Exactly," Kristina said. "You earned this. Not by being like Scott or Steve, pretending to like coffee, or going along with things that don't feel right to you. You got here by being yourself. And that's what's going to keep you here."

Max looked at her, unsure. "But what if being myself isn't enough?"

Kristina leaned forward, her voice steady. "Then it's not the right place for you. But trust me—most of the time, being yourself is enough. Focus on what you can control. You can't change how Scott and Steve talk, but you can control how you react. You can't make everyone stop drinking at events, but you can choose not to, and if anyone gives you a hard time, you can stand your ground. It might initially feel uncomfortable, but the more you stick to your values, the more people will respect you." Max frowned. "What if they don't?"

Kristina shrugged. "Some might not. But those people don't matter. The ones who do—the ones who recognize your integrity, your passion, and your team spirit—are the ones worth impressing."

Max leaned back, mulling over her words. "I guess I've been so focused on not messing up the past few days that...

you're right. I let all that affect me. Thanks, Kristina... for helping me remember why I'm here in the first place."

Kristina smiled. "It's easy to lose sight of that in this environment. You were also thrown to the wolves very, very quickly. You were here as a casual fan on Wednesday, and by Thursday, you were interviewing for your opportunity to experience the trials and tribulations of professional sports. I know you want to do everything all at once, but it's not sustainable.

"I was invited to the sports dinner but politely declined because I was picking up my new puppy from the breeders— and, quite frankly, because of all the reasons I mentioned before. I just needed some 'me' time. And it's okay to do that. It's not a weakness. Try to remember that and give yourself some grace. What you experienced last week? Not a typical week."

Max nodded slowly, the tension in his chest easing slightly. "Thanks again, Kristina. I needed that."

"Anytime, Max. Here's one last thing about this job—it's a grind. Like you've seen, it's long hours, constant demands, and not a lot of the right kind of glamour. If you don't stay true to yourself, it'll chew you up and spit you out. But if you find ways to navigate, you'll find your way," she said, standing up and gesturing toward the suite door. "Now, let's get back to it. And remember—you don't need to drink coffee to fit in. Red Gatorades exist too, you know."

Max chuckled. "Noted."

CHAPTER 19

"Fans First"

Feeling more like himself by the middle of the afternoon, Max sat quietly, shadowing Dan and Rusty in a meeting that felt different from the start. The team's owner had flown in over the weekend to introduce Garry Breckenridge, the new Vice President of Sales and Service. He would also be attending the game the following evening.

Garry Breckenridge, a serial business executive, had built a storied career across two major industries: pharmaceuticals and professional sports. His résumé read like a masterclass in business operations and change management. Garry Breckenridge wasn't just experienced—he was transformative. In short, he required no introduction.

In moments, Garry Breckenridge would sit at the head of the boardroom table, having just been introduced to the management team as the one granted oversight over the business side of the organization with carte blanche to implement changes. That word—changes—hovered like a storm cloud over the room. What sort of changes were coming? Dan had spoken to a few of his counterparts in other organizations to calm his racing thoughts. He spoke to colleagues from other sports teams, including two that worked at organizations Garry had been, and one former season ticket holder who worked with Garry about a decade earlier. Dan's goal was to learn more about this new executive. No doubt, everyone he spoke with respected Breckenridge's accomplishments. What made Dan's thoughts race even more however was when two advised him to watch his back.

Then, the two men entered the room. The hairs on Dan's neck stood up. He could now place the mid-forties man with the tailored blazer, crisp dress shirt, and thinning salt-and-pepper hair he serendipitously met minutes after his panic attack the previous week.

Officially known as Garry Breckenridge, unofficially known as 'Michael.' He and Garry locked eyes. Garry offered a soft nod of the head, which Dan sent right back. Breckenridge exuded the same confident swagger as before, but only now, with the full context of his role known, did Dan try not to feel sick.

Their first encounter had begun with a lie.

He was advised to watch his back by multiple people. Now, Dan wasn't sure who or what he could trust, or what would happen next. Dan found himself staring intently at Garry as the Owner spoke. Dan couldn't look away or shake the sense that this meeting wasn't just about strategy.

The uneasiness wasn't lost on Max or Rusty either, though Max found the atmosphere anything but inviting. Breckenridge stood at the head of the table, flanked by the owner and a mix of sales and marketing representatives, as well as key department heads: Kent, Wally, Valerie from the box office, Meghan, the marketing coordinator, and Jeff Price, the team's financial controller.

"Good afternoon, everyone," Breckenridge began, his voice smooth yet commanding. "First, thank you for the introduction and the warm welcome. I'm excited to start because I see tremendous potential in this organization."

He scanned the room, his gaze sharp enough to cut glass.

"I've heard there are a lot of hardworking people here, and I look forward to meeting each of you," he said as he caught and held eyes with Dan. "The team's performance on the ice hasn't been what we'd like, but with the right tools in place, we can accelerate improvement—not just for the team, but for the fan experience."

Max leaned toward Dan and Rusty, whispering, "What does he mean by 'the right tools?'"

Dan shook his head. "We'll find out soon enough," he replied grimly.

As Breckenridge's introduction concluded, the owner chimed in. "You know, I'm a fan first and an owner second. All I care about is that our fans leave entertained. That's why I asked our marketing department, 'What more can we do for them?'"

He gestured to Meghan, who advanced a slide on the presentation.

"We're proud to introduce the Fans First campaign," Meghan began. She clicked to the next slide, unveiling bold graphics featuring supporter sections, group memberships, chants, and drums.

To Dan and Rusty, it reeked of a marketing department desperate to curry favour with the new VP, mimicking the strategies Breckenridge had used in the past. But it also reeked of something else: a lack of understanding because Garry had very little experience with professional hockey.

Breckenridge had spent much of his career in big cities, working with teams that drew from broad, diverse populations willing to embrace new traditions. But this was a different world—smaller, more conservative, and fiercely proud of its hockey roots. A program designed using flashy gimmicks and groupthink might not resonate with a hockey fanbase that valued authenticity, grit, and tradition over showmanship.

Rusty leaned back in his chair, stifling a sigh as Meghan continued her pitch. The slides were slick, the graphics vibrant, but the substance. It felt forced—like trying to jam a square peg into a round hole.

"We'll be introducing value-priced tickets for children, with 10,000 available across the final ten home games," Meghan explained. "Community groups, sports teams, and schools can purchase these tickets for $20, which includes a drink and a hot dog. Accompanying adult tickets will be priced at $30."

Dan raised a hand. "What's the plan to make sure this actually works? Are we targeting the right demographics? And what about our season ticket holders?"

"The rest of the Fans First incentives will be announced later," Meghan replied curtly.

Dan and Rusty's frustrations simmered beneath their stoic surface. Breckenridge's ideas might have looked good on paper, but they didn't reflect the realities of hockey culture—or the challenges of their market. Dan knew what the fans wanted because he'd spent years listening to them. Rusty fielded their complaints about cold concessions, narrow concourses, and parking lot gridlock. They both knew the fan frustration with rising ticket prices and lacklustre on-ice performance.

And yet, here they were, being sold on drums and supporter sections.

For all of Breckenridge's credentials, it was clear he didn't yet grasp what made hockey fans in this market tick.

Dan glanced at Max, who was quietly scribbling notes beside him. Max leaned over and whispered, "Do you think this will work?"

Dan gave a slight shake of his head. "It might look good in a PowerPoint, but whether the fans buy in? That's a whole other story."

"It's a great way to fill empty seats while giving back to the community," the owner added. "And we'll also be opening the stadium for free game-day practices on our last five Saturday home dates."

Max noticed Dan's jaw tighten.

The conversation shifted, but old grievances and new tensions remained, particularly around one of Dan and Rusty's recurring points of contention: whether to send out a physical newsletter to season ticket holders and fans alike. Marketing pushed for it, citing its use as a vehicle to distribute discount cards for fan shops and restaurants. Dan countered, arguing that past newsletters had caused more confusion than they were worth and questioned why casual newsletter subscribers would get the same discount cards as season ticket holders.

"By the time those cards get to our season ticket holders, the season's 75% over," Dan pointed out. "Shouldn't these have gone out before Christmas to encourage holiday spending?"

Kent surprised everyone by siding with Dan. "Look, I just don't want the newsletter coming out of our sales budget. We could distribute the discount cards at games instead, creating even more touchpoints for account managers."

Meghan pressed her lips together in a thin line. "The cards need to be activated in advance, and we'd have to ensure your reps know what they're doing."

Rusty snorted softly. "Oh, like the last time the newsletter advertised—" He cut himself off, shaking his head.

Max leaned toward Dan and whispered, "What's her problem?"

"Where do I even start?" Dan muttered.

Meghan advanced the presentation with a pointed look at Dan and Rusty. "Now, onto the playoff ticket templates," she announced, unveiling a vibrant design featuring the team's colours and logo.

Max thought they looked sharp, but Dan leaned toward him. "Looks nice, but printing 213,000 tickets for a playoff run we're not making? Wasteful. And marketing's excuse that they'll use the leftovers for flex tickets next year? Classic spin."

Toward the end of the meeting, Rusty brought up fan complaints about concessions. "If we're serious about putting Fans First, let's start with the ones we already have," he argued. "Cold food, long lines, and overpriced concessions are recurring themes in our feedback. Imagine taking your kid to their first game and getting a pizza with raw dough or a pink, frozen burger."

"Why are you even telling us this?" Meghan snapped.

"Because these are the issues our season ticket holders tell us about—every day," Dan said, coming to Rusty's aid.

"We're so focused on adding gimmicks that we neglect the basics."

Breckenridge finally spoke. "What else are you hearing, Dan?"

Dan exhaled sharply. "No hot water in bathrooms. No vegetarian options. Parking lots are a mess. The concourse is too narrow. People can't get out of the lots after games without sitting in traffic for an hour. Should I go on?"

Breckenridge leaned back in his chair, nodding slowly, though his expression gave nothing away. "Noted," he said.

Max studied Dan and Rusty. For the first time, he fully understood what Rusty meant about emotional strength. Both he and Dan were driving the struggle bus, and it showed. It wasn't surprising either.

The work-life balance as an account manager in professional sports was a precarious juggling act at best. Unfortunately, for many families, the scale almost always tipped toward work. In just a few days, Max had quickly learned how all-consuming—and random—the job could be.

Salty once broke it down in a way that was impossible to ignore: the average game day started at 9:00 a.m. and didn't wrap up until 10:30 p.m. or later, adding an extra five and a half hours to the typical eight-hour workday. With forty-one home games a season, that totalled an additional 205 hours—or the equivalent of over 25 full workdays. And those numbers didn't even account for the extras: season ticket holder events, corporate dinners, community appearances, or family skates. Adding those events would bring that total to almost thirty full workdays.

"No wonder so many of these guys are divorced," Salty had quipped, half-joking but with an undeniable edge of truth. The relentless hours made it hard to leave the stress at the office and even harder to nurture relationships outside of it. Burnout wasn't just a risk—it was a reality for many. Four sales reps had taken time off for mental health reasons, Max learned, struggling with issues ranging from anxiety to full-blown PTSD triggered by the high-pressure demands of the job.

The stakes were high, and the margin for error felt non-existent. For Max, watching the tension play out in real-time among his coworkers, it became clear how easy it was for work to creep into every corner of life—until there was nothing left to call your own.

CHAPTER 20

"A Charlie Hustle-Like Attitude"

The following Tuesday, Kristina was well ahead of everyone else. She had the chance to dive deep into a new project—leading the charge on an upcoming charity ball hockey tournament. The event aimed to raise funds for the team's foundation, which had already distributed over $650,000 to local programs this season. With teams of top clients and community members already signed up, she coordinated with the fan and community development department to bring it all together.

While Kristina orchestrated the broader tournament, Rusty had been tasked with assembling the sales team's entry. His plan was simple: pull together a team that wouldn't completely embarrass themselves. But, in true pit fashion, even a charity game was proving harder than expected.

"Alright, boys," Rusty announced, leaning against the partition of the sales pod next to Frank and Salty's desk. "Salty's out, so we're down a player for the ball hockey tournament. We need to find someone to fill his spot."

"Poor Salty," Frank said, shaking his head. "I remember my first and second vasectomy. Word of advice—never, ever go to Mexico for surgery. I don't care how minor they say it is."

Shane's head slowly popped up from behind the cubicle wall like a whack-a-mole.

"Kristina's athletic," Jay offered, unaware of Shane's sudden appearance. "Didn't she play softball?"

Rusty shook his head. "No dice. She had a soccer scholarship, but she's organizing the tournament. Apparently, that's a conflict of interest."

A soft "Wooooo" floated over from Shane's desk. The sound was strange enough to make the group pause—but not strange enough to derail them.

"Brad, you in?" Frank asked.

"Can't. Sorry. I'm behind on my calls. What about Kyle? Didn't he play junior hockey?" Brad replied.

"Yeah, Kyle!" Frank said with sudden enthusiasm.

Rusty sighed. "Kyle hasn't worked here for three months, Frank."

"Really? You don't say."

Another, slightly louder and longer "Wooooo" came from Shane's cubicle. The group exchanged glances.

"We can't let Shane play on the team," Frank whispered.

Rusty nodded. "Agreed. But we may have exhausted every other option..."

"You remember the last time we let him play, right?" Jay whispered back.

Rusty smirked. "Yeah—beer duty, Shane. Twelve players, seven random cans of beer, one bottle of Smirnoff Ice, a can of kombucha, all in a plastic grocery bag. No ice. No cooler. No class."

"Actually," Frank quipped, "Shane put the ass in class."

"Maybe he's learned?" Brad offered cautiously.

Rusty frowned. "Doubt it."

From his desk, Shane stood and made a grand show of walking to the printer. "What's up, boys?" he asked with a smirk.

"You hear anything we just said?" Jay asked.

"Can't hear you over me closing deals, boys. Hot sales. Ring the bell. Closed! Won! Wooooo!" Shane hollered, thrusting his hips like Jim Carrey in Ace Ventura: Pet Detective.

Rusty groaned. "Shane, tone it down, will you? This place sometimes resembles a professional organization!"

"Wooooo!" Shane replied even louder before mimicking air push-ups. "Whatcha planning?" he asked, snatching the registration form from Rusty's hand. "Wow! A ball hockey tournament?"

"We were actually about to ask the new kid to fill Salty's spot," Jay muttered.

"You're that desperate, huh?" Shane said, stopping mid-push-up. "Tell you what, I'll clear my schedule. You need me. I'm ready. Always in game shape."

"We're really not that desperate," Rusty said flatly.

"What if someone gets hurt?" Jay offered.

"Exactly!" Shane said. "Hold onto your tits, boys. I've been preparing for this."

Before anyone could respond, their phones all dinged.

"What the hell is this?" Brad asked, opening the email.

Rusty clicked the attachment on his desktop. A video popped up. It was Shane—shirtless, doing push-ups in his condo's underground garage while the Rocky theme blared.

"Oh, hello there, gentlemen," Shane said to the camera, wiping sweat from his brow. "I'd like to formally announce my candidacy for the...." There was a long pause. "Uh, I'm announcing my candidacy for the charity ball hockey team," Shane said enthusiastically, filling in the blank before the video continued. "...team. Allow me to demonstrate why I am the only choice."

The video transitioned into a montage: Shane playing tackle football against small children, lifting weights, karate-chopping planks of balsa wood, and inexplicably cooking eggs in slow motion. The scenes faded into each other with surprising professionalism, Eye of the Tiger playing dramatically.

"Meet my good friend, Pete Rose," Shane said as a clip of the disgraced baseball legend appeared, wearing a white Cincinnati Reds hat.

"Hi, I'm Pete Rose," the video began. "And I support Shawn Sanderson's application to join your team. Shawn, hustle hard and don't let these guys down. I'm counting on you, big guy," Pete Rose said, pointing at the camera.

Rusty paused the video, staring at the screen. "What the actual fuck, Shane? How did you get Pete Rose?"

"What? I called in a favour," Shane said, unpausing the video. "Shhh.... keep watching."

The video resumed with a clip of hockey legend Doug Gilmour.

"Hi, Shane, I remember the last time we played on the same team. Way to keep your stick on the ice!" Doug Gilmour read from cue cards off-screen.

"You don't know how to skate!" Frank accused.

"Do I really need to skate for this ball hockey tournament, Franklin?" Shane dismissed as he blinked rapidly. Suddenly, Shane reappeared on the monitor before a lacklustre green screen, riding a surfboard in a way reminiscent of The Fonz jumping the shark. Like Arthur Fonzarelli, Shane wore a leather jacket and surfed over a shark, giving an exaggerated thumbs-up.

"Eh? Eh?" Shane nudged Rusty.

Shane thought his retro coolness was avant-garde, but in reality, the reference was completely lost on him—he had never even seen an episode of Happy Days and had no idea that scene had been done almost fifty years prior.

The video took a bizarre turn into an unnecessarily long, dramatic montage of animals fighting, culminating in a black-and-white clip of bears playing hockey on ice skates. The camera zoomed in tight on Shane's face, capturing a twinkle of determination in his eyes.

Jay mouthed the words Why? at Rusty, Brad, Salty, and Frank, who all shrugged.

Finally, bold words materialized on the screen.

"I bring... beverages," a deep voice announced.

"I bring... a Charlie Hustle-like hustle with the relentless spirit and attitude of Charlie Hustle," the narrator continued as black-and-white highlight reels of Pete Rose played, including his infamous headfirst slide into Ray Fosse at home plate during the 12th inning of the 1970 All-Star Game. The play won the game for the National League, but Fosse suffered a fractured and separated shoulder, an injury that went undiagnosed until the following year.

With a confident flair, the camera zoomed in on Shane's sunglasses one final time as he lowered them, delivering his Pete Rose-inspired punchline with an infectious grin:

"Most importantly, I bring... an obligation to do everything I can to win the game within the rules."

As the words GUARANTEED WINS flashed triumphantly on the screen, Shane blew an air horn for seventeen agonizing seconds while large-font words like beautiful babies, dill pickle sunflower seeds, tapes, lotions, bandages, ice packs zoomed in alongside a stock photo montage of an oversized trophy. The finale featured a fully clothed Shane superimposed standing next to three girls in bikinis, giving a thumbs-up as images of sports supplies flooded the screen, all while a Canadian flag flapped dramatically in the background.

The group sat in stunned silence.

Finally, Brad clapped. "I mean... it's the worst thing I've ever seen. But also... amazing."

"How?" Rusty asked, turning to Shane. "How did you even put this together?"

"Resourcefulness," Shane said, grinning as he leaned against the pod barrier nonchalantly. "A true mentalist never discloses how he made the effect."

"Yeah, but you can't even run an invoice or use the photocopier," Salty added. "What the hell?"

Shane winked. "Guess you'll just have to draft me and find out."

As the afternoon dragged on, Shane remained glued to his desk, still clinging to the dream of playing in the charity ball hockey tournament. His monitor displayed a YouTube video of ball hockey highlights, and he mimicked the drills with small, awkward movements in his chair.

Then it happened.

A loud, wet fart ripped through the air just as Shane sneezed.

Rusty froze mid-typing and turned to look at him, his face a mixture of horror and amusement. "You know, Shane," he began, deadpan, "if you sneeze and fart at the same time, it takes a screenshot of your soul."

"Oh my God," Shane replied, wide-eyed.

Rusty leaned back, his eye twitching slightly. "Did you know that if you spend just ten minutes a day pooping at work, by the end of the year, you'll have been paid a full forty hours... just for pooping?"

Shane stared at him. "Oh my God."

Rusty burst out laughing just as his phone began to ring.

"You should probably answer that," Shane said, trying to stifle his own laughter as he struggled to stand.

"I can't!" Rusty wheezed, unable to stop laughing.

"Oh my God," Shane said again, his voice tinged with alarm. "I think I just shit myself. Did I just shit myself?"

Rusty doubled over, his face red with laughter. "I'm not looking, man! You're on your own."

"These are new pants!" Shane exclaimed, patting himself down. "I may have shit myself! I promised Mess I wouldn't do this!" he added, wiping away a tear the same way Wayne Gretzky had at his press conference when he was traded from the Edmonton Oilers to the Los Angeles Kings.

"Stop! You're killing me," Rusty managed between gasps, tears streaming down his face as well.

Overhearing the commotion from her nearby desk, Kristina walked into their pod, arms crossed. "What is wrong with you two? What did I miss?"

Now panicking about the smell wafting through the cubicle, Shane opened a drawer and grabbed the nearest bottle of cologne. He sprayed it liberally—twice in the air and once directly onto himself.

"Mind your business, Krissy," Shane said, coughing as he waved the cologne cloud away. "Nothing to see, but if you must know, Rusty may have just shit himself."

"Judas!" Rusty yelled.

Kristina wrinkled her nose. "Nothing to see, huh? But a whole lot to smell. You two are disgusting. It smells like sample day at The Bay, but with... a hint of mustiness."

"It's CK One," Shane announced proudly, holding up the bottle.

Kristina tilted her head. "I had a bottle of that... like 15 years ago."

"Why would you have cologne, Krissy? Something you want to share with the class?" Shane teased.

"CK One is unisex, moron. For guys and girls," Rusty chimed in.

"Oh, so that's why I always get hit on."

"By dudes," Rusty added, smirking.

Kristina rolled her eyes and changed the subject. "Anyway, any word on whether you're playing in the tournament, Shane?"

Shane's enthusiasm visibly deflated.

"He might've gone a little too far in his campaigning," Rusty mentioned with a smirk. "Nobody's mentioned it this afternoon, so... probably not happening."

Kristina raised an eyebrow. "Campaigning? Do I even want to know?"

"Absolutely not," Rusty answered before Shane could speak.

"Fair enough," Kristina replied. "But since you're not doing anything productive—per usual—I could use some help with the tournament planning. You owe me big time, though."

Shane straightened up, his grin returning. "Why yes, Krissy, I'd be honoured to assist however I can. Anything for you."

"She's not going to sleep with you, Shane," Rusty chirped without missing a beat.

"As if!" Kristina added, shaking her head.

"This isn't a quid pro quo, guys. I'm doing this out of the kindness of my heart," Shane said, flashing Kristina a toothy smile.

Kristina smirked. "He's right. I'm not going to sleep with you, Shane."

"Well, now I'm defensive and offended," Shane said. "Don't back me into a corner, Krissy. Don't make me—"

"Shane!" Kristina interrupted. "I've heard stories. Even if 10% of them are true, you'd sleep with any female who has two feet and a heartbeat."

Rusty jumped in, grinning. "And don't forget the dudes who hit on him, too!"

Shane shrugged dramatically as he flipped the pages of his journal. "What can I say? I'm an equal opportunity charmer. But let's not forget the intern with the peg leg. That was special."

Kristina groaned. "Oh my God. Should I come back later?"

"No, no, no! Stay!" Rusty said quickly, laughing. "He's just messing with you."

Kristina shook her head. "I don't even know how we got here."

"You came...,"

"That's it!" Kristina threw her hands up. "Rusty, make your calls. Shane, if you're serious about helping, slot the teams into divisions. Four teams per division—make it fair."

"Piece of cake," Shane said confidently.

As Kristina left, Max appeared with Shane's shoe in hand. "Is this yours? Is this even real leather?" he asked, dropping it near Shane's foot.

"Busy, Max," Shane said dismissively. "Trying to get laid."

"What?"

"You wouldn't understand, kid. Too young. I'll tell ya when you're older," he said, winking.

Max rolled his eyes and turned to Rusty. "What's wrong with him?"

"Nothing new. Same question we've all been asking for as long as I've been here," Rusty replied, grabbing his headset. He then turned back to Max, who was still standing there. "Oh! Did either Frank or Jay ask if you were free for the corporate ball hockey tournament?"

"What tournament is that?" Max asked.

"It's a charity ball hockey tournament Kristina is organizing. We've entered a team. We're going to be called the Sales Mutts. Frank was going to invite you to join today."

"Ooh! Is the spot still open?" Max asked excitedly.

"No! You can't play in that tournament. You're, uh... not free! Yeah, I set you up with a prospect meeting right before the first game. So, yeah, that was before we even, uh, knew about the tournament, and it's an easy sale for you. It was the only time they could meet. So, I figured I owed you one."

"For what, Shane?" Rusty asked.

"Mind your business, Rusty!" Shane said dismissively. "Look, Max, I'll send you the details momentarily, okay? Now get going!"

As Max returned to his desk, Shane picked up his phone and dialled quickly. "Hey, Jack. Need a favour. I need you to buy a ticket package from one of my guys, okay? Don't worry about it. I'll pay for it. Don't ask questions."

Rusty groaned. "Really, Shane? This is your strategy?"

"Closed-won, baby!" Shane yelled, throwing his arms in the air.

Rusty shook his head as he turned back to his computer. "We're doomed."

The following day, Jay, Salty, Rusty, and Frank were huddled together, discussing strategy for the upcoming ball hockey tournament as highlights played of the team surrendering a three-goal lead late in the third period in Long Island.

"It's probably safe to say the only thing choking worse than the team last night would be a couple of wannabe amateur porn stars," Salty said, dropping an unexpected zinger that sent the entire pod into shock.

"So, uh, wow," Rusty said, wiping a tear from his eye.

Moments later, the highlights on the television ended, and they returned to building their roster.

"Okay, we know I'm playing goal," Rusty began, tapping his pen on the desk. "It's three-on-three plus a goaltender, so Jay, you'll play wing or centre. Scott and Steve are on the second line. Frank, you're our stay-at-home defenceman."

"No problem," Frank said, inspecting his sizable frame. "I hardly move anyway. But we should have a spare D."

As if on cue, Shane walked into the sales pit.

"I don't understand how he does it," Frank said, wide-eyed. "It's like he knows!"

"Don't let him find out we need him," Jay whispered. "We'll never hear the end of it."

"You know," Shane announced, desperate for attention, "the referees needed to get off their knees because they blew the game last night!"

Rusty groaned. "You say that every game, Shane. Once, well done. Eighteen times? Come on, you're better than that."

"Alright, alright," Shane said quickly, raising his eyebrows. "How about this: The ref must be pregnant because he's missed the last two periods. Eh? Eh?"

"No," Rusty replied flatly.

"Hey, Shane..." Rusty rolled his eyes. "Speaking of babies, there's something we need—uh, would— like to ask you."

Shane blinked rapidly. "Yes, Richard? What is it?"

Rusty hesitated, but Frank jumped in. "Have you seen Max? We want to see if he'd play on the ball hockey team."

"Oh, Max?" Shane asked, a smirk creeping across his face. "I'm sure he would. Great guy. But, uh, pretty sure he's busy that day."

"How's the new kid busy when all of us aren't?" Frank added.

"I dunno, you tell me." Shane sprawled on his desk awkwardly, arms behind his head, grinning smugly.

"You're so embarrassing," Salty said, glaring. "Get up."

Shane shrugged. "Meh, I heard he's got a hot prospect meeting that day. Only time they could meet. Good for him, bad for you guys."

"Do we know anyone else?" Jay asked, exasperated.

Rusty sighed. "Shane? We've exhausted all our options. I can't believe we're doing this. Frank, do we have to?"

"It's okay, Rusty," Frank said solemnly. "We promised ourselves, but as I told my first wife the night I met my current wife, sometimes we have to break a promise... or it's a simple process of elimination—I honestly have no idea."

"Ugh, Jay, can you please finish?" Rusty pleaded.

"Begrudgingly, and only due to alleged scheduling conflicts—Shane..."

"Yes, Jason?" Shane said innocently, sitting up.

Frank hesitated, hand on his chest. "Why is this causing me heartburn?"

"It's okay, Frank... Jay. Take your time," Shane said.

"I can't... Rusty, please advise," Jay exhaled.

Rusty composed himself. "Shane, are you able to play for us?"

Shane sat up straighter, face serious. "Well, as I said, I'll need to make some calls and rearrange my schedule. But I'll get back to you."

Frank groaned. "Do it fast. This offer turns into a pumpkin in four minutes."

"Okay, okay," Shane said, pulling out his phone. He opened his calendar, where the ball hockey tournament was already scheduled. "Well, you know, I'll just... move a few... you know, a few things around." He gestured theatrically, swiping at his screen. "Switch this here... cancel that. Copy, paste... Done. I'm in, boys!"

"Alright, fine," Rusty said, exhaling sharply. "But you can't take this so seriously, okay? Like Krissy said yesterday, it's a fun charity ball hockey tournament. We don't need another incident."

Shane waved him off. "Relax. That guy deserved what he got at that softball tournament. I know my role: seventh man, fourth liner. I get it. I won't let you down, Dad."

Moments later, Kristina walked into the pod, holding the finalized tournament schedule.

"You guys know that the elite division refers to an exceptional and/or privileged group of athletes, right?" she asked, raising an eyebrow.

"What are you talking about, Krissy?" Frank replied. "We're none of those things. Combined."

"I thought you idiots would sign up for the corporate rec division," Kristina said, pointing to a list that included IT professionals, property managers, and American Sign Language interpreters.

Rusty frowned. "We didn't?"

"Then why did you sign up for the elite division?" she asked.

Rusty stared at Shane, "Shane?"

Shane ignored him.

"Shane!" Rusty repeated, this time with much more aggression.

"Oh, hello, I didn't see you there, Rusty. How are you doing?"

"So let me get this straight—you signed us up for the elite division? On purpose?"

"Of course," Shane said proudly. "Go big or go home, boys. This is our shot at greatness."

Kristina scratched her head. "You're playing against former junior players, ex-college athletes, and guys who actually train for these things."

"Good," Shane said. "That means they'll underestimate us. Classic underdog story. Have you never seen Mighty Ducks?"

Frank threw up his hands. "Oh, for the love of—Shane, we are not the Mighty Ducks!" He paused.

"Actually, we're more like the team they were because they couldn't afford good equipment!"

Jay shook his head. "So what happens when we get annihilated?"

Shane grinned. "Then we lose with dignity. And maybe break some of their bones in the process. But mostly dignity."

Rusty exhaled sharply. "We can't change this?"

Kristina sighed. "No. Schedule was finalized earlier today. You don't have a shot in the elite division."

"No, we certainly do not," Frank said. "She's right, boys. Playing in the elite division breaks one of my cardinal rules."

"What cardinal rule is that?" Rusty asked.

"Never play above your level," Frank explained. "One, we're not physical specimens, especially Rusty and me."

"I agr—" Rusty began.

"Rusty, let me finish. Two, how did this happen? Are we stupid?"

"Never mind, you just answered your own question," Kristina said dryly before sighing again. "Games start that Saturday morning. You're in the elite division, whether we like it or not."

Shane stood up in the middle of the discussion. "First of all, you already begged me to play, so there's no going back," he tried to affirm. "Second, adversity builds character, lads. And you're welcome."

"You can't build character if you're already a character," Frank muttered, shaking his head. "I hate you, Shane."

"No, you don't," Shane said smugly. "And if, no—when— we win, I expect a statue in my honour. Or at least free drinks for a month. But trust me. We've got this. And just to be clear, we're playing for keeps. I expect blocked shots, elbows in the corners, and bodies on the line. This is our shot at glory!"

"It's a fun charity tournament!" Rusty shot back.

"I am, and I can't stress this enough, Rusty, disappointed in you. Truly," Shane said, shaking his head.

Rusty muttered under his breath as Kristina handed them the schedule. "God help us."

"Boys," Shane said, clapping his hands. "It's time to get serious. We need training. Strategy. War paint. Frank, you still have that military-style playbook from your old flag football league?"

Frank stared at him. "It was a beer league, Shane. The strategy was 'don't throw up on the field.' That remains another one of my cardinal rules to this day." Rusty groaned and looked at Jay. "This is a disaster, isn't it?"

"Oh, absolutely. It's an abomination." Jay said.

"But at least it'll be fun." Shane threw an arm around Rusty's shoulders. "That's my spirit! Now, first order of business—matching headbands. I was thinking camo. Or maybe neon pink. Thoughts?"

Rusty shoved Shane's arm off him and walked away. "I'm going home."

"The game isn't even over," Shane called after him. "But think about it! Also, who's bringing beer for the bench?"

Kristina crossed her arms. "This is a family-friendly event!"

Shane quickly blinked. "Define 'family-friendly.'"

Kristina rolled her eyes. "Try not to embarrass yourselves too much. You Sales Mutts represent every one of us in the sales pit."

As she left, Shane grinned at the rest of them. "Boys, this is going to be legendary."

Jay shook his head. "More like a complete shitshow."

CHAPTER 21

"Crying in the Office Again"

With only a week left until the charity ball hockey tournament, the sales team was feeling the pressure—not just to field a decent team but to survive the chaos brewing in their personal and professional lives.

Frank, Rusty, and Shane were sweating in the team's workout room. One of the few perks

Dan had fought tooth and nail for was gym access when the team was on the road. Unfortunately, Dan's request was met with a resounding no. But that morning was made possible because Shane had sweet-talked the team's video coach into sharing the passcode so they could represent the team with the utmost pride. By 5:30 a.m., he was already texting, calling, and borderline harassing the team to drag themselves to the stadium for a "mandatory" workout.

By 7:15 a.m., Rusty and Frank begrudgingly arrived, blurry-eyed and grumbling. On the other hand, Shane was practically vibrating with energy, bouncing between machines like a drill sergeant with a whistle in hand.

At 7:20 a.m., Max entered the room wearing Lululemon yoga pants, a fitted shirt, and a yoga mat tucked under his arm.

"Who invited you? You're not on the team," Shane barked mid-squat.

"Kristina invited me. She thought your email was a mistake but said we should come anyway," Max replied, setting up his mat.

Perplexed, Shane quickly scrolled to his sent emails folder and after noticing he had made the mistake, decided to accept Max instead of admitting he fucked up. "Fine, it's good team building...and, uh...puck bunny building," Shane said, nodding to Max. "But did you have to wear those pants?"

"I'm no sexual deviant, but I wouldn't walk around like that," Frank muttered, inspecting Max's outfit.

Moments later, Kristina burst in, clad in neon green Lululemon yoga pants and a pink tank top. She looked like an ad for athletic wear, full of energy as she unrolled her mat next to Max.

"Morning, boys! Nice to see you up and at 'em!" she chirped before sliding into a perfect downward dog.

Rusty looked up, whispering to himself, "I'm a married man. I'm a married man..."

"That is one majestic ass," Shane muttered.

Frank inhaled deeply, "I am absolutely a sexual deviant."

Later that morning, Max sat at his desk, rehearsing a sales pitch. He was still finding his footing and felt the growing weight of expectations.

"You close that one or what?" Shane asked, walking past Max's desk with a banana in hand.

"You just heard me practicing. Still nothing," Max replied, deflated.

"If you ever need help, just swing by my desk," Shane said. "Just kidding. Absolutely not."

Rusty and Frank watched the exchange from their desks.

"Should we feel bad for the kid?" Rusty asked.

"I don't know. He gives me that funny feeling in my tummy," Frank replied. "Wait, is he crying in the office again?"

"Like, you want to tell him, 'It's going to be okay,' but also, 'Welcome to hell. This is your life now,'" Rusty said, shaking his head.

Kristina walked by, also noticing Shane and Max's conversation. "What's up with Max?"

"Just a sad little guy," Frank quipped.

Kristina smirked. "Maybe I'll cheer him up."

Frank muttered softly, "You can cheer me up anytime, Krissy."

"Frank!" Rusty whispered, having heard Frank's suggestive comment. Frank thought he had spoken inside his head.

Kristina stopped by Max's desk as he packed up later on. "Still nothing?" she asked. "Not yet. I thought being here would be high-paced and exciting, but it just sucks being at the bottom," Max admitted.

"You're still in the high-paced environment. It just takes time to find your groove, dude," she said.

"Trust me, those easy wins—what we call 'bluebird sales'—are rare. You've got to grind."

Max nodded. "What's a bluebird sale?"

"An inbound call where someone basically throws money at you," she explained. "But most of the time, those are ticket brokers. You should talk to Jay about it—he knows everything there is to know about brokers. I'm not 100% sure where we are now, but last time I checked, there were, like, 130 (give or take) confirmed ticket brokers representing approximately

1,700 full-season equivalents. Take him out for lunch, and he'll spill the tea."

Max did a quick calculation on his notepad. "That's, like, almost 10% of the building!"

"Actually, it's a little less than that, but yeah, when you talk about the sheer number of seats. But we only have around 6,000 season-seat equivalents, so 1,700 is closer to 30%."

"30%?" Max questioned. "Why do we sell to brokers?"

"Because we need the money...and we like transferring risk," Kristina explained. "Actually, hold that thought. Let's get Jay on the horn." Kristina picked up Max's desktop phone and called Jay, putting him on speaker.

"Yeah?" Jay answered.

"Hello to you too, Jay," Kristina replied.

"Krissy! Didn't know it was you. How's it going?"

"You had your chance, and you blew it, Jay," Kristina said dryly.

"I feel shame."

"Anyway, I'm with the FNG, and we're talking ticket brokers. I also suggested he take you out for lunch so you could tell him all about the program—without me," Kristina said, smirking. "But I didn't want to give you any weird ideas that he was actually trying to take you out for lunch."

Jay raised an eyebrow. "I don't really know what that means, Krissy."

"No, Jay, you wouldn't."

"Okay..."

"Anyway," she continued, "how many 'professionals' do you think we're dealing with? Twenty?"

Jay shook his head. "No. At the end of last season, I'd say we were closer to thirty 'professionals.' I mean, there are a few bigger networks, so... yeah, maybe twenty individuals who are professional scalpers. These are the big-ticket brokers from all over North America. A lot of them have multiple accounts to take advantage of old policies—playoff ticket access, ticket maximums, that sort of thing."

"Ah yes, good to see the old policies still applicable to ticket brokers. Weren't some of those the old legacy accounts we should have gotten rid of?" Kristina said with a sigh before adding, "How's that cleanup project going for you?"

"This year, I've determined we need to consolidate accounts whenever possible. It'll make management so much easier," Jay said. "I'd also argue we need to identify professional brokers who actually add value and find ways to work with them even more. Then we can clean out the clutter of non-professional resellers."

"Ticket sales across the secondary market are down everywhere in North America," Kristina noted. "This season's been brutal. The market's flooded with events. Think back to past seasons—like when the NBA strike limited the number of events for sale. Or the NHL lockout, when there was no hockey from September to December. When those seasons resumed, demand for tickets exploded. But now? It's completely oversaturated."

Kristina rolled her eyes. "This year's schedule hasn't helped either. Hardly any weekend evening games. And don't get me started on the matinee games. Those are a hard sell unless you're marketing to daycare groups."

"Hey, but Fans First, right?" Jay added sarcastically.

Kristina groaned. "Don't even start."

Jay leaned back in his chair. "Some of my brokers are saying consumers have a very specific price in mind for tickets. If they find what they're looking for, great—they'll buy online or at the box office. But if they don't? They'll just stay home and watch the game on TV. And with 4K TVs and cheaper entertainment options, staying home is becoming more and more appealing."

"That sounds a lot like what I read in The Elusive Fan," Max chimed in.

Jay perked up. "The Elusive Fan by Rein, Kotler, and Shields? That book is the bible of professional sports sales. Everyone should read it. At least twice. It's from 2001, but I keep a copy in my desk. Anyway, where were we? You know what, screw it—I'm coming over."

"No, we'd prefer not to see your ugly face," Kristina joked.

"Wow. Okay then," Jay said in a soft tone that Kristina mistook for sadness.

"I'm just kidding, Jay. Sorry. Get over here when you have a chance... please."

Jay hung up and, moments later, strolled into the hallway, dropping into a chair and kicking his feet up on the desk.

"What are your brokers saying, Jay?" Kristina asked.

Jay sighed. "Brokers are used to getting shafted. Almost every team has policies that, let's face it, discriminate against them. Whether limiting the number of seats per account, requiring them to pay in full instead of using a payment plan, restricting season ticket holder benefits, or cutting out ticket exchange privileges—for brokers, it's a constant struggle."

Kristina turned to Max. "The truth is, Max, teams and brokers have a love-hate relationship. Teams rely on brokers to move inventory, but brokers can also undermine box office sales if the secondary market gets too hot."

Jay nodded. "Exactly. The bad brokers will panic and unload tickets at $5 or $10, but that's not just their fault—it's what the market dictates. The good brokers? They'll see underpriced inventory, scoop it up, and resell it at their usual prices. I have a few brokers who refuse to sell off their inventory, even at the last minute for pennies on the dollar, so they don't give other brokers an advantage."

Max leaned forward. "So, you're saying there's no way to create a price floor on StubHub?"

"Exactly," Jay said. "That's why the relationship between brokers and the team must stay. We can't just cut them out when so much of our full-season equivalent numbers depend on them. Can you imagine if we had less than 5,000? Yikes!"

Kristina added, "This season, we made a conscious effort not to offer comp tickets, so a lot of seats went dark. It's tough because an empty arena is a bad look, but the brokers are the ones willing to fill those gaps."

Max nodded. "Dan and Rusty heard the same thing during their focus groups. People hate seeing the empty seats, but they're also part of the problem. They gave up their season tickets."

Jay sat up. "Look, there are brokers who want to do more with us. I've spoken to five who could each move between $125,000 and $500,000 in tickets annually. That's a mix of season seats and group tickets. Other teams work with brokers to unload tough inventory. Why can't we?"

"What's your plan?" Kristina asked.

Jay leaned forward. "We identify the pros—guys who never miss payments, don't resell tickets multiple times, and don't flood the market with trades. Then, we give them priority access to unsold inventory. We set a minimum price to cover our costs, tack on a 15% margin, and let them sell for whatever they want."

Kristina raised an eyebrow. "Not bad. We're in a good spot if we control the messaging, build trust, and remove unprofessional sellers."

Max chimed in, "What if we gave brokers the option to receive all their tickets electronically? The current system is a nightmare—logging in, initiating transfers, accepting links—it's clunky. We'd save on printing and shipping costs, too, right?"

Jay grinned. "Fucking right! We should make hard tickets an option but charge for the privilege. Most brokers prefer electronic delivery anyway. Far less hassle and fewer opportunities for them to fuck it up with bad PDFs."

"Why would they even want hard tickets?" Max asked.

Jay shrugged. "Some clients still like having a physical ticket for trust or as a keepsake. But that's not our problem. Anyway, this has been fun, but I've got a Hot-N-Ready waiting for me."

CHAPTER 22

"Coming Out of your Comfort Zone"

After Jay left to pick up his pizza, Kristina grabbed her coat from her desk and walked back to Max's. "Sorry," she said. "I didn't mean to hijack your end of the day with that ticket scalper talk. I actually had a reason for coming over. What do you do for fun, Max?"

"Me? Uh, well... you know, mostly just stay in my room, crying into my pillow with my cats."

Kristina smirked. "No, seriously. Maybe you need a fun night out."

"I have plenty of fun... again, mostly crying at home over my lack of social life. Pretty entertaining, I'd say. Princess Penelope is good company."

"Stop! I mean it," Kristina said. "Come out tonight. Say, nine? That gives you enough time to put on all your makeup but not enough time to overthink it. I'm heading to a karaoke bar with some friends. I'll pick you up. Also, wear something tight." She smiled and walked down the hallway.

Later that evening, Kristina pulled into Max's driveway in a sporty Volkswagen Jetta with a spoiler on the back. Max was already waiting by the front door.

"You know," Max said as he got in, "this is exactly the kind of car I pictured you driving. Fast, sporty, sophisticated. Plus, I think Cher's an incredible artist and humanitarian," he said, turning up the volume to "Strong Enough" and singing along.

'Strong enough
And I quit crying
Long enough
Now I'm strong enough
To know
You gotta go
There's no more to say
So save your breath and
Walk away'

Kristina grinned. "The fact that you know who Cher is gets you ten points, dude. The fact that you know the lyrics gets you ninety more!"

They drove downtown, listening to pop music and talking shop.

"So," Kristina said, glancing over. "Have you figured out what you've gotten yourself into?"

"I've learned the sports industry isn't just for 'fans' of sports." Max made air quotes around "fans."

"Be prepared to be overworked and underpaid," Kristina warned. "Be prepared to have your grass cut. Be prepared to start hating the team. If you're not ready to outwork everyone else in the sales pit, you might as well leave now."

Max nodded. "Watching guys like Shane and Rusty, you can see that practice makes a difference."

"Exactly. Just like the players on the ice, you've got to dedicate yourself to breaking into this world. Knowing a lot about the team helps, but don't get so deep that you can't see anything else."

After about twenty minutes, they pulled into an outdoor parking lot outside a flashy club.

"This it?" Max asked.

"Yes, sir."

They parked and walked to the entrance. Max stepped up to the bouncer and gestured to the line.

"Hey, man, how much is cover tonight?" Max asked.

"Guys are free tonight," the bouncer said, winking at Kristina and giving her a high-five. "Your hot friend might have to pay, though. Or not—she's good. Enjoy!"

Max blinked. "Okay, Kristina, when did we travel to an alternate dimension?"

"I know, right? Nice to have a night out. Come on. I know the bartender."

They stepped into the club and walked down a short corridor. A vibrant energy filled the air, but most attendees were men. Max froze mid-step.

"This is your idea of a fun night out?" He gestured toward the groups of men dancing together.

Kristina rolled her eyes. "So, you're another homophobe, huh? Perfect."

"What are you talking about?" Max protested, glancing nervously at two men making out on the dance floor. "Uh, okay, now I get why I've never heard of this place. Is this even a karaoke bar?"

Kristina smirked. "Listen, sometimes, if what you're doing isn't working, you've got to change things up. Am I right?"

"I appreciate that, but I'm not switching sides, Kristina."

She rolled her eyes. "That's not what I'm suggesting, dummy. Nobody's taking you by the hand here—well, maybe that guy... or that guy... or apparently, this guy already has!" She gestured at Max, who quickly pulled his hand back from another man's grasp.

"Seriously, man? I'm clearly here with her!" Max said, motioning to Kristina.

"Yep, he's with me," Kristina said without missing a beat, pointing toward a tall, stunning woman in a red sparkly dress. "But I think he's leaving with her. Now grab us some drinks and pass me that songbook, rookie!"

'I've got to break free
I want to break free, yeah
I want, I want, I want
I want to break free'

Max belted out the final lines of Queen's I Want to Break Free as the crowd danced and cheered. He grinned as he made his way back to the table, where Kristina and a male friend were sitting.

"Was that so hard?" Kristina asked.

In response, Max downed his virgin Long Island Iced Tea in one large gulp.

"Oooh! We're up next! Eeeek!" she squealed, sliding out of the booth with her male friend and heading for the stage. Max slid into her spot.

Moments later, a man in glasses slipped into the booth beside him.

"You were really good," the man said.

"Thanks! I feel kind of overwhelmed right now." Max wiped the sweat from his forehead with his cocktail napkin.

"Need another drink or anything?" the man asked.

"Oh! No, no, I'm good, but thank you." Max paused, suddenly remembering where he was. "Sorry, man. I appreciate it, but I'm not... you know... gay."

"Neither am I. I just came here to read your fortune."

Max blinked. "Really? Is this, like, a thing here? Or did someone send you?"

The man pointed to Kristina, who was mid-performance onstage. "She did. Now give me your hand."

Max hesitated, then extended his hand. "Krissy...." he mumbled. "Okay..."

The man studied his palm. "Hmmm... interesting."

"Right. Wait, what? What do you see? Is it a fire? Tell me it's not a natural disaster!"

"It's nothing like that. I see... the colour red in your future," the fortune-teller said with a cryptic smile.

Max blinked, unsure how to react. Was this supposed to be encouraging? Vague prophecies weren't exactly his thing, but for some reason, the words sparked a small, unfamiliar surge of confidence deep within him. He turned back to Kristina, who was already watching him with a knowing smirk.

"Did you see that, Max?" she asked, leaning closer.

"See what?" Max frowned, genuinely confused, a wave of panic rising inside.

"Woah," Kristina said, her voice low and exaggerated for dramatic effect. "She just fucked the shit out of you with her eyes, Max. Did you see that?"

She gestured towards the same woman in the sparkly red dress across the room—'Tall Red,' as Kristina would later dub her.

Max glanced over, and his stomach did a somersault when he saw the auburn-haired beauty looking in his direction, one eyebrow raised like she was daring him to make a move.

"What would I possibly say to her?" he whispered, already second-guessing himself.

Kristina clapped him on the shoulder. "I dunno, ask her to sing a duet with you. Don't Go Breaking My Heart, maybe? Or how about I've Got You Babe? Nobody hates on Sonny and Cher, am I right? Plus, you love Cher!"

Max's cheeks turned another shade of crimson. "I can't ask her to sing a duet with me! Wait—are we sure she doesn't have an Adam's apple?"

Kristina scoffed. "Trust me, she's real and spectacular," she said, playfully licking her lips and giving Tall Red another appraising glance.

Max looked down at the drink in his hands, searching for the courage he couldn't find.

"I'd love to take you up on your suggestion, but I can't. You saw how I get when I'm excited—I'd make a complete ass of myself." He sighed. "Seriously, Kristina, tonight's been fun as it is. Thanks for bringing me here. Totally out of the blue, and I loved that."

Kristina rolled her eyes and reached for his glass, downing the rest of his new virgin Long Island Iced Tea in one go.

"Oh my God, that was delicious," she said, smacking her lips. "What are these called again? I want four more. You need to order four more—and make sure to get one for her, too."

Max's eyes widened. "You want me to order four more? You realize there isn't any alcohol in them, right?"

"Okay, then order a ninety-two Octane for me, an... unleaded for you, and whatever Tall Red wants."

"Are you sure?" Max asked.

"Yes, yes," she said with an impatient wave. "I've only had three, and I'm surprisingly a girl with a shit-ton of alcohol tolerance. Things you learn in professional sports, am I right? But fine, you're right, I'm driving, so maybe don't order four. But go up to gay Jeff Bezos over there and order one for you and one for her! Do it, or you're walking home."

Max groaned but slid out of the booth. "Fine," he muttered, heading to the bartender—a Jeff Bezos lookalike in a mesh shirt who nodded as Max approached.

Max returned with two tall glasses of Long Island Iced Tea a few minutes later.

Kristina wasn't impressed. "Jesus Christ, Max. You're such a wimp!" she yelled, shoving him playfully. "What? I didn't do anything!" Max protested.

"Exactly! You didn't do anything! You didn't say anything, either! Where's your head at, man? Nobody's going to hand you anything—not here, not in the pit. So you got a job that dozens of kids competed for. You think you've made it? Think you've earned something? No, you haven't closed shit! Stop sitting on your ass and feeling sorry for your cheek meat. You haven't made it. You never make it in this business. You just have to keep hustling!"

Max sighed, her words hitting harder than he wanted to admit. "You're right," he said quietly.

"Right?!"

"I've been sitting on my ass," Max admitted. "That guy tried to read my fortune... said something about destiny. He told me he saw the colour red in my future. Whatever that's supposed to mean."

Kristina froze for a moment, then leaned back with an exasperated laugh. "There's no such thing as destiny, Max. You're in control. You can do anyone or anything," she said, motioning towards the drink she'd made him carry. "Wait—he said he saw the colour red in your future?"

"Yeah. Why? I don't get the reference."

Kristina grabbed Max by the cheeks, turning his head forcefully towards Tall Red. "You don't need another sign from the cosmos that this is supposed to happen. Look at her."

Max's pupils dilated. "Jesus Christ!" he whispered, his voice barely audible.

"Snap out of it, man!" Kristina barked, slapping him lightly across the face.

Max blinked rapidly, shaking himself. "You're right," he said, standing up abruptly. "I'm the man. I'm in fucking control. I can do anything—or anyone. And it starts with that lady in red!"

Kristina slid out of the booth, laughing as Max strode confidently onto the dance floor. Lady Gaga's Born this Way began playing over the speakers as Max approached Tall Red. Up close, she was even more stunning—auburn hair cascading over her shoulders, sparkling red dress clinging perfectly to her figure, no visible panty lines, and a confident air that screamed untouchable.

"Hey," he said, his voice cracking just slightly. He cleared his throat and extended the glass of Long Island Iced Tea. "Thought you might like this."

She glanced at the drink, then at Max, a curious smile playing on her lips. "That's bold," she said, her voice smooth and amused as she accepted the glass.

"Well, uh, I figured bold was the move here," Max replied, forcing himself to keep eye contact even though his palms were sweating. "And given what you are wearing, you seemed like someone who appreciates boldness."

She raised an eyebrow, taking a sip. "You're not wrong. I'm Michelle," she said, extending a perfectly manicured hand.

"Max," he replied, shaking it—perhaps a little too enthusiastically. "So, uh, do you come here often?" Michelle's laugh was melodic but laced with irony. "You're really going with that one? At a gay bar?"

Max froze, his face heating up. "I—I mean, no! I didn't mean—" He floundered for a second before she cut him off with a chuckle.

"Relax, Max. I'm just fucking with you," Michelle said, her smile widening. "But no, I don't. My friends dragged me here tonight," she said, rolling her eyes. "Something about me needing to blow off steam."

"Same," Max blurted, then immediately winced. "Not the 'dragged' part—I mean, my friend Kristina thought I needed to loosen up. Not that I'm stiff! I mean—we work together, and I've been working hard without much luck."

Michelle took another sip of her drink, clearly entertained. "Relax," she said again, holding up a hand. "So, Max, what's your deal? You don't seem like you're a karaoke guy, but holy shit, you absolutely crushed Tom Jones!"

"Am I a karaoke guy?" Max repeated. "Not really," he admitted. "Let's say that I just want to break free, though."

She tilted her head with intrigue. "Oh yeah? How's that working out for you?"

Max hesitated. "Not great, honestly. But hey, there's always tomorrow."

Michelle laughed again, and for a moment, Max felt like he was in the clear. His attempt at boldness and innuendos hadn't fallen flat, and Michelle was still talking to him. Then the music shifted to a sultry Latin beat, and Michelle's eyes lit up.

"Well, you made it this far, right?" she said before adding, "Do you dance?"

Without waiting for an answer, Michelle grabbed his hand and pulled him towards the centre of the dance floor.

Max's mind raced as they moved into the crowd. The floor was packed, the music loud, and every instinct told him he was out of his league and should cut his losses and retreat. But Michelle was already leading him into a rhythm, her movements fluid and natural.

"Just follow my lead," she said, her tone light but commanding.

Max tried to mimic her steps, but his awkwardness became glaringly apparent when he nearly stepped on her foot.

"Sorry! I'm more of a freestyle guy," he joked, though it came out weak.

Michelle smirked. "Freestyle, huh? Let's see it."

Max's brain short-circuited. His version of "freestyle" was mostly a combination of awkward shuffling and the occasional head bob. But he was pot-committed now. With a deep breath, he launched into a series of moves that could only be described as a hybrid of The Robot and a failed attempt at salsa.

To his surprise, Michelle laughed—not a mocking laugh, but one of genuine delight.

"Oh, you're something else, Max," she said, shaking her head as she kept moving closer to him.

Somehow, the tension broke. Max stopped overthinking and just let himself go; mirroring Michelle's movements as best as he could. It wasn't graceful, but it wasn't terrible either. It was good enough to turn the evening up a notch.

By the end of the song, he was out of breath but grinning.

"Not bad for a first-timer," Michelle said, her tone teasing but warm.

"Thanks. You're, uh, a good teacher," Max replied.

Before he could say anything else, Michelle's phone buzzed. She glanced at it and sighed. "I've gotta go. Work calls."

"Oh, okay," Max said, trying to hide his disappointment. "What do you do?"

"I'm an exotic dancer."

Max blinked, his brain short-circuiting again. His face turned beet red, and he instinctively stepped back, bumping into a table.

"Oh. Wow. That's, uh... fucking cool!"

Michelle laughed. "Relax, Max. It's just a job. And hey, it pays the bills."

"Yeah, of course. That's—yeah," Max said, nodding furiously before he said something he'd regret.

Michelle leaned in and kissed him on the cheek. "You're adorable. What are you doing for lunch tomorrow?"

"Normally, I just pack my Ninja Turtles lunchbox," he said jokingly.

"That's hot. Okay, text me tomorrow, and I'll give you my address," she said, slipping a napkin with her number into his hand.

"Wait, what? Really?" Max was dumbfounded.

"Yes, really! I don't work 'til late and make a mean lunch!" she said before disappearing into the crowd.

Max stood frozen for a moment, staring at the napkin. Everything was legible, and this was legit! Then he turned and walked back to the booth, where Kristina and Gay Bruce Willis cheered him on.

Kristina raised an eyebrow as Max slid into the seat, still dazed.

"Well?" she asked.

Max held up the napkin like a trophy. "My first 'professional' close," he said, grinning. "And it happened at a fucking gay bar."

CHAPTER 23

"Condo Rules"

Thursday morning arrived, and the charity ball hockey tournament was now less than thirty-six hours away. Full of energy, Shane strolled past Frank's desk, waving a stack of papers like an old circus promoter.

"Gather 'round, everyone," Shane called as he reached his pod. "Hot off the presses, I present to you all—the ground rules for Saturday night."

"Ground rules?" Rusty asked, looking up from his screen. "What's happening Saturday night?"

"Our championship celebration," Shane said, as though it were the most obvious thing in the world.

"Obvi."

"That's assuming a lot," Frank remarked, leaning back in his chair.

"You know what happens when you assume, right, Frank?" Shane shot back with an eager smile.

"No, Shane, please enlighten me," Frank said, throwing his hands in the air.

"You make an ass out of you... and you," Shane quipped, pointing dramatically at Frank and Rusty.

Frank sighed. "You're the ass, Shane. But seriously, I don't know what's more improbable—the Mutts winning the tournament or surviving it. We're not exactly spring chickens."

"Doesn't matter. I called my shot like Messier in '94. Guaranteed a win," Shane said confidently. "I've drafted these in anticipation of our inevitable victory." He held up the sheets and passed them out to those within arm's reach. "Read, review, sign here, here, there, and initial there and there." He thrust the remaining sheets into Frank's hands. "Please take one and pass them along."

Frank adjusted his glasses. "Rule one: Bring a winning attitude," he read aloud. "Shane, you know a winning attitude isn't going to save this team's lost season, right?"

"We're not talking about this shitty team. We're talking about our championship ball hockey team,"

Shane corrected, unfazed. "Significant difference!"

Rusty snorted. "Rule two: No work or office talk of any kind allowed. What if we wanted to plan a championship parade inside the office on Monday, Shane?"

"Rusty, it's not just about winning the championship. It's about celebrating the championship as defending champions!"

"But we'd be talking about a championship parade... in the office... while at work," Rusty explained.

Shane remained unfazed.

Jay chimed in. "Rule three: Arrive with an empty stomach. Multiple rounds of food will be served. And—wait— 'do the right wing'? What does that mean?"

"That's a typo. That's supposed to say, 'do the right thing,' and it means don't show up full like last time, Jay," Shane replied, narrowing his eyes.

"Rule four: Jersey wearing is required and will be strongly enforced," Max read. "And by jerseys, I mean hockey jerseys. No CFL or NBA jerseys. You are all better than that," he continued.

"He's right, you know. We are better than this," Frank argued.

Kristina smirked. "Rule five: Bathroom use is available for standing up only. Obvious exceptions apply if you're a girl."

Rusty scoffed. "Says the guy who took a walnut-crunch-donut-sized shit at my place last time."

"Rule six: No complaining about rules, space, seating, or temperature of the condo."

Jay chuckled. "Rule seven: Props, bets, and parlays are encouraged. Oh, and apparently, Shane reserves the right to 'woo' without warning?"

Kristina folded her sheet. "Is this even worth it? Am I going to be the only girl there?"

"Sarah will be there," Shane offered.

"Who's Sarah?"

"Max's sister. She's coming with Jimmy's son, Chad."

Max blinked in confusion. "Why are you inviting my sister? She doesn't even know you."

"She doesn't yet, but she will. It's manifest destiny, Chief. Besides, you're inviting her," Shane replied, grinning.

Max sighed. "I'm out."

"Nope!" Shane cut in sharply. "If you don't show, you better take a long, hard look in the mirror and ask yourself why. There's a lineup of people waiting to get in!" He pointed dramatically down the hall for effect. "That goes for all of you jackasses!"

Kristina raised a hand. "Does your condo have a party room we could use instead?"

"No," Shane replied flatly.

"I thought you were about to add a screening room the last time we were there?" Rusty asked.

"I never said that!" Shane objected, now more visibly flustered than before.

"Turkish bath?" Frank asked.

"What? Stop!"

"Stop teasing, guys. His place is small. It's got a maximum capacity of—what—six?" Kristina teased. "I'm counting... six... seven... eight... I am counting ten," she said as she pointed to everyone in the vicinity.

"Don't start this with me, Krissy!" Shane warned, now clearly annoyed.

"Fine. I'm in," Max declared.

"But only if we win," Rusty added. "And Amy's driving me, so she'll be my DD."

"Are you mental? No! Why? Pregnant women are not invited! You have to work here to be invited! Also, and this is probably the most important question I have about this: doesn't she go to bed at ten? I repeat, are you mental?" Shane snapped. "I swear to Christ, Rusty. If you RSVP and then bail early because 'Amy's tired' or whatever, you'll be blacklisted from next year's championship repeat. Don't screw around. Do the right thing, Rusty!"

"Understood, Chief. But if Amy's not invited because 'you have to work here,' then why is Max's sister coming?" Rusty asked.

"See rule six, Rusty: no complaining about rules, space, seating, or the temperature of the condo."

"I thought rule six was you need to bring your own swimsuit," Jay quipped.

Now feeling more defeated than ever before, Shane pleaded, "A swimsuit? What are you guys talking about? Why are you doing this to me?"

"I thought you said yes to the Turkish bath," Frank added.

"Fuck off... fuck you, and you, and you, and you! This is a one-sided friendship." Now agitated, Shane snapped, "No complaining. No reserved seating. No complaining about the temperature. NO TURKISH BATH! Oh, and one more thing!" He handed Rusty another sheet, trying to shift the focus.

Rusty rolled his eyes. "Rule eight: stay until the end of our televised game versus Carolina. Rule nine: there's a five-minute grace period to leave after said game. Shane, do you even hear yourself?"

"Rules keep people in line," Shane said proudly, admiring the sheet of rules he had hastily typed up that morning.

"What rules keep you in line?" Jay asked with a smirk.

That same morning, Max opened his inbox to find an email from Dan. The subject line read: "You've Earned It, Kid." Attached was a spreadsheet containing three hundred client accounts of varying sizes, tenures, and locations.

Max stared at the list, his stomach flipping. These weren't just names but opportunities, obstacles, and his first real test. Most of the accounts were hand-me-downs from the team: Bryan, Shane, Rusty, Frank, Brad, Salty, Kristina, and others had each relinquished about twenty accounts. On top of that, Max inherited some of the remnants of Jimmy's old book—a graveyard of "hand grenades"—clients on the verge of cancellation or with long-neglected relationships.

Still, Max refused to feel daunted. Where others saw a hot mess or a dumpster fire, he saw potential... or, potentially, a hot mess dumpster fire. But his goal wasn't just to retain revenue; it was to win over these clients, one small victory at a time. The trust Dan and the team had placed in him was the fuel he needed to prove he belonged.

After skimming the spreadsheet, Max turned his attention to another challenge: the fallout from the focus groups Dan and Rusty had organized before his arrival. Reviewing the recordings and notes, Max felt the raw honesty of the attendees' feedback settle over him like a dark cloud.

"Honestly, I want to see the men of the NHL, not the kids of the junior leagues," one former season ticket holder had said, summarizing a common frustration with the team's highly publicized "youth movement."

Dan's attempts to sell the promise of a rebuild had been met with consistent pushback. The roster lacked the star power of years past, and the fans weren't buying into the "future potential" pitch.

"I'll go when it suits me," another participant admitted. "With the team losing and tickets easy to find, what's the point of locking myself into forty-one games? Or ten or twenty games, for that matter."

Complaints ranged from logistical—parking, concessions, and game-day entertainment—to philosophical: former season ticket holders felt overlooked and undervalued. The loudest frustration came from a younger attendee:

"You've made it so easy to buy tickets online that there's no scarcity. Why commit to a season when I can grab a seat anytime I want? And I don't need to scramble to find someone to go to a Buffalo game on a Tuesday in early December."

Max knew these insights would fuel Dan and Rusty's upcoming presentation to Garry and Kent, but it didn't make his job easier. He was now tasked with repairing relationships that had taken years to sour with passionate fans who he had no affiliation with. But Max had a secret weapon—his ability to create 'wow' moments.

Just then, Max's phone rang, and he recognized Lorraine's name on his screen. She was one of the accounts recently transitioned from Bryan. Max smiled as he answered.

"Lorraine! It's Max. How are you doing?"

"Oh, Max. I just wanted to thank you. Before the holidays, Bryan gave me two tickets for a game, and you helped put the package together. My husband and son had such a great time!"

"It was my pleasure," Max said warmly. "I loved chatting with Bob and Daniel during the intermission. They're great guys."

Lorraine chuckled. "Daniel couldn't stop talking about how you surprised them with drinks—and that pin you gave him? Wrapped in team paper? He was thrilled!"

"Honestly, I wish I'd known it was his birthday," Max said. "I'd have brought a cupcake or a card. But I'm glad they had a good time."

"They did. That was such a thoughtful touch, Max. It made everything special."

Max leaned into the moment. "Lorraine, I'm glad to hear that. I want to let you know that I've taken over your account from Bryan, and I'm here to make sure you always feel like a valued part of the team."

Lorraine paused, her tone softening. "You've got a knack for making things special, Max."

"Well, thank you. The only thing I ask in return is, please don't keep me a secret. Referrals are the best thank-you I could ask for."

Lorraine laughed. "I'll keep that in mind."

Max's personal touch extended beyond individual accounts. He was thinking big, looking for ways to address broader issues within the pit. While most of the team kept their heads down or were game planning for the upcoming ball hockey tournament, Max took Dan's advice to heart, doubling down on his calls and leaning into his creativity.

Still, distractions lingered. Steve and Scott's antics grated on him, their crude jokes and excessive swearing echoing through the pit. Max was still worried that their behaviour would spill over into client interactions, especially now that he was tasked with making even more outreach. To Max, Steve and Scott felt like a ticking time bomb he couldn't afford to let detonate.

Even so, Max stayed focused, drawing on the lessons he'd learned from the focus groups and, if necessary, making calls from Jimmy's old desk. Max heard firsthand how fans felt overlooked and undervalued. Now, with his own book, he aimed to change that, one client at a time.

As he looked up the next number to dial, Lorraine's words stuck with him: "You've got a knack for making things special." Max smiled again, leaning back in his chair. He was just getting started.

Around the same time, an elderly couple sat at a bistro table in the main reception area, quietly waiting. Kelly had phoned Salty, their account manager, who came to meet with them.

"Ian, Catherine, good to see you both. Thanks for your patience. I was on the phone with another client. Next time, how about we schedule a meeting?" Salty said, addressing the couple.

"Mr. Salvatore, we have a problem," Ian said as he slowly, pointing to the invoice he had brought.

"Okay, what seems to be the issue?"

"We're not happy with your giveaways," Catherine said from behind grey hair and large-rimmed glasses. "We never get picked to win anything and don't feel valued as season ticket holders. When we decided to purchase a package, we assumed there would be more perks than this."

"Are there specific perks or giveaways you're talking about? Or ones you assumed you'd receive? We have many contests and giveaways throughout the season."

"Well, yes," Catherine continued. "Throughout the game, your mascot shoots hot dogs, T-shirts, and other items from a cannon into the crowd. We never catch anything; nothing ever comes our way."

"I guess I just assumed items get shot your way," Salty replied.

"Oh no, never," she said, her voice trembling with age. "Just once, we want to have a chance to get something. It never happens where we sit. We have the net in our way."

"Well, Catherine, that netting is for your protection from flying objects like pucks," Salty interjected.

"A girl was killed in Columbus years ago, and that set forth massive changes league-wide. Unfortunately, there's nothing we can do about that. Unless we moved your seats?" Salty calmly explained.

"Pucks and prizes. It gets in the way," added Ian.

"It gets in the way," Catherine echoed, looking at her husband. "And no, we do not want to move. We have front-row seats in the 300 level. Nobody is in front of us."

"Except for the net, right?" Salty said with an unrequited chuckle.

"Can you talk to someone? Can you ask them to come to our section and give things away?" Ian asked. "There are a lot of people who would be absolutely thrilled to get something from the mascot."

"I'll see what I can do," Salty said with a polite smile.

After lunch, which consisted of sixty Wendy's Baconators and large fries, the sales team was summoned to the boardroom for yet another renewal update. When it started, twelve sales reps sat around the long table in a small room while ten guys stood, unable to find chairs. Like most impromptu meetings, there was an uneasy feeling in the room. Salty looked at his watch and noticed the 'emergency' meeting should have started five minutes ago. From outside the room, he could hear Kent's voice getting louder.

The doors opened, and Kent walked in, talking loudly on his cell phone while carrying an extra-large cup of coffee. Kent managed to sit at the head of the table, remove his jacket, all while still talking on his phone and holding his coffee.

"Look, Kyle is our stud left-winger. I don't care who Marty's dad is—he's not getting Kyle's spot. I'm heading into a meeting. I'll call you back," Kent said, hanging up his phone and throwing it on the table in disgust.

"Okay, guys, I'm not the kind of guy who likes to use corporate speak—you know, flowery language. Someone who uses great metaphors and imagery to get his point across. And I'm certainly not a guy who builds up a speech only to underwhelm you at the end. So, over to you, Dan."

"Uh, okay, guys, we'll make it quick this time," Dan started. "Given what's happened in the last week, we need to keep working on our touchpoints and building a sales pipeline. Regardless of the team record or the fact they're now thirteen points out of a playoff spot, starting today, we need another full-court press to get face-to-face with as many renewals as possible."

"Okay, guys, let's be clear on one other thing," Kent piped up. "We've got a mountain to climb, and if you're not prepared to stand at the bottom with your pack on your shoulders ready to go, then it's time you looked yourself in the mirror and gave yourself a performance rating. If I were to do it right now, I'd give myself an F+. With the team away on an extended road trip, you should be able to make the calls you need to make. You are supposed to have live contact with everyone by the end of next week. Right now, I think only Kristina is on pace to get through her list. That's unacceptable."

Dan turned on a PowerPoint presentation and showed the sales team the sales dashboard that Kent and Wally had asked him to prepare. Everyone looked at the screen to find their name and percentages.

"63.6%, 21.5%, 66.3%, 82.4%...," Kent explained. "These numbers are not good enough. Not good enough at all."

"These are your overall numbers that combine retention and new sales for the rest of this season," Dan said. "We need you to bundle this season with next season. We need you to ask your customers when they renew if they'd like to purchase extra tickets for games in March and April. The suite department will follow up with all former suite rental clients and communicate existing offers to your book of accounts. You had the chance to contact your leads, and most of you haven't, so they're gone. We're going to put a few of you on group night planning, and we'll aggressively push community groups to agree to certain games."

"We have a lot of tickets and suites to sell to push towards budget achievement. Balance your focus on renewals and work on new sales, suite nights, and extra tickets for the rest of the season. If all of this reeks of desperation, well, that's because we're pretty fucking desperate."

A quiet fell around the overcrowded boardroom. Everyone was dejected and defeated. Everyone stood at the base of a very large mountain, as Kent had put it, and some didn't even have parkas on, let alone a full pack of supplies.

CHAPTER 24

"Snowed In"

Frustrated with the mountain metaphors, Rusty and Frank grabbed their coats and went out the back exit, heading up the stairs to the parking lot. The door wouldn't budge—it was blocked with snow, unknowingly piled up by the snow removal company, which exchanged its services for four full-season club seats.

"What the fuck?" Rusty said. "That's our fire exit!" He panicked as he and Frank pushed as hard as they could.

"We're stuck here. Oh my God. This is my worst nightmare—being trapped in the stadium with you mutts," Frank cried again.

Moments later, Kent and Wally poked their heads out of Wally's office.

"How are the calls coming along, boys?" Wally asked.

"We need to be aggressive. Now's the opportunity to get people when we know where they'll be—at home," Kent proclaimed. "Make the calls, you!"

"No sense in waiting till next week. Get on the phones, be aggressive—we'll get these guys on board," Wally said.

Now, much later that day, the weather had not slowed, and Shane could read the room. He typed out a desperate email to Wally, Kent, and Dan to help motivate the sales team. It didn't help that the team was snowed in at the office, stuck making calls, or that the only leftovers from lunch were six-hour-old Baconators with wrappers turned translucent from grease. The sales team required motivation because the renewal board had not been updated in a while, and nobody had rung the sales bell in hours.

"Gentlemen, as we all saw earlier today, the team is dejected and upset with our progress. We know this must improve, but we are also losing steam. It's been a long season, and morale has never been lower at any other point this year. I feel a sales contest is in order. Any rep who sells $5,000 or higher before end-of-day Friday gets their choice of the following: any jersey they want, a $100 gas/gift card to a restaurant of their choice, 100-level seats and Captain's Club dinner for the WAGS (wives, girlfriends, significant others), or two train passes for anywhere Via Rail goes. This will work—trust me on this one. You just need to agree on the right variables, which will help turn things around! We could also break out a secondary contest: if the team sells $50K tomorrow, they'll get a free night in a hotel. Let's make it competitive but attainable... for everyone. If you hit your number by end-of-day tomorrow, you get to choose your prize. Roll this out via email tomorrow morning at 8 a.m., bring in funeral sandwiches for lunch, and boom goes the dynamite."

About an hour later, Kent replied to Shane's email, surprisingly in agreement.

'I like it. Thanks for your efforts and thoughts. Given the prize values and our budget (or lack thereof), I would prefer a higher amount. Train passes would be regular class (approximate value of $150), jerseys... fine ($150). We have a pile of $100 gas cards from an earlier giveaway, so we could use those (ideally, as we have already made the investment). The team element is fine, too—there will be some who lead the way while others don't. Most importantly, we need to ensure this is tracked DILIGENTLY to ensure execution. PLUS, this is not a prize for $5,000 in sales. Nor does one get a choice for every $10,000. It's one prize per rep that sells $15,000 in new or renewal sales by end-of-day tomorrow. Things like the jerseys and hotels should be expensed by rep. Maybe no expensing—we will need to investigate the contra-deals we have to use. No hard dollars can go out.'

Surprisingly, Kent and Wally were right. Making pre-renewal calls to clients at home proved to be more successful later in the day. Rusty felt he got points from his clients because they felt sorry for him having to work during the storm of the century. Shane was also finding success with his calls and had sold some extras for an upcoming game.

When Rusty got up to go to the bathroom, he noticed Shane stapling an envelope shut with two staples.

"What are you doing, Shane?" he asked.

"Sold some extras. A thousand dollars' worth... ring the bell."

"Yeah, but why are you stapling an envelope shut? You know there's glue on the back."

"There are only two things I like licking, Rusty—ice cream, and I'll let you figure out the other," Shane said, winking.

"A man's taint?" Rusty shot back.

"Wait, what? No!"

"Anyway... why did a six-year-old handwrite the address? You realize there's a window on the envelope where you can put the ticket with the address on it, right?! When you print out the tickets, there's another ticket printed with the client's address for that exact purpose."

"It's fine. I've been doing it like that for four years. I tagged it in the CRM as a wow moment. The client is going to get it, and he's going to be so happy."

"Have some pride in your work, Shane," Rusty chirped.

"Look, I just sell."

"Can you fucking believe this?" Jay asked.

"Jesus, Jay, what happened to you?" Rusty asked, throwing the envelope back on Shane's desk to be redone.

Jay continued, "Since we can't go home, I was out removing nameplates from seats that belonged to a client of mine who relocated... two seasons ago."

"You? Why were you removing nameplates off seats? That's an operations job."

"You'd think it would be, right? But no. I, the sales mutt— no, sales donkey—had to do this. When my new clients asked when they would get their nameplates on those same seats, I told them I had asked OPS to remove and replace them months ago. Well, fast forward... what, 14 months later?

And the client brought it up again during my renewal call. I mean, the season's almost over, right? Fuck my life. Those brass nameplates are sharp, and since our fucking department doesn't have any tools, I had to improvise."

"I think I know where this is going, unfortunately," Shane said, throwing the same envelope back in the outgoing mail pile, having not altered it at all.

"Only after cutting my hand—A SECOND TIME—did I realize I had left a trail of blood all over the 200 level, and I needed to get myself to the bathroom to wash and disinfect the cut... You with me so far?"

"We're with you. Please continue," Rusty said.

"So, I make my way back to the office, and yes, I'm still bleeding at this point. I go to the first aid kit, you know, for first aid—and maybe a Band-Aid—only to find that our first aid kit is empty except for a few wet naps and a pair of gloves, which appeared to have already been used. Obviously rattled and still bleeding, I make my way to my desk, feeling a little light-headed, you know, from the blood and shit, and I type out an email to Mike in Ops to see if we can get more Band-Aids."

"Yep, I definitely know where this is going," Rusty said.

"His reply, and I quote: 'Sorry, Jay, we won't be purchasing any additional supplies or Band-Aids for the first kids due to budget cuts.'"

"Did he mean to say 'kids'? Or 'kits'?" Shane asked jokingly. "Who are the second kids?"

"Honestly? I have no idea anymore."

This was not the first time budget cuts had come up in conversation. There was a time last summer when the external cleaning staff didn't empty the trash or clean the office for two months due to "budget cuts," and the sales team was left to take their own garbage to the disposal. That, too, had not been regularly serviced due to budget cuts, so some, like Jay, took their office garbage back to their apartment.

"This does not surprise me in the least, boys. It's sad, and it's funny, but not in the 'ha-ha' funny," Frank chirped.

Hearing the commotion, Wally popped his head out of his office. "What's going on out there?"

"Nothing to see, Wally. Jay just nearly sliced his hand off trying to remove nameplates off of seats," Frank spoke loudly, his voice echoing down the hallway.

"Oh, you'll live. You're just sensitive," Wally said dismissively.

"Sensitive?! Look at this!" Jay unwrapped the paper towel to reveal a gash, still oozing blood, while walking closer to Wally. "Is this sensitive, Wally?"

"Oof," Wally winced. "Yeah, you might want to tape that up, bud."

"Thanks, Doctor," Jay snapped, reapplying the paper towel and holding pressure on the wound.

"Ok, let's not get at each other. Just focus on making your calls and getting the hell out of here whenever the roads clear."

Frank checked his phone. "That won't be happening anytime soon. My wife just texted— the city's completely shut down. Plows aren't even keeping up."

"Guess we're here for the long haul," Jay groaned.

Shane grinned, rubbing his hands together. "Alright, then. Who's up for some shenanigans?"

Jay sighed. "I hate this place."

CHAPTER 25

"Shattered Dreams, Broken Promises"

Jay and the others were finally rescued around 11 p.m. the night before when the snowplows arrived to clear the parking lots again. Neither Wally, Kent, nor Dan had called for help. Everyone thought the other had made the call, yet nobody did. The snowplows came at their usual 10 p.m. schedule for non-game nights, only to find a haunting scene of stranded vehicles. They contacted the operations department for assistance, but when nobody answered, they reached out to the lone security guard stationed at the loading dock 24 hours a day, who then came over to investigate.

With the state of emergency now lifted throughout most of the region, Friday morning came as slow as Thursday night had ended. The sales pit quietly buzzed with the faint, artificial hum of fluorescent lights as the team dragged themselves to their desks for another day of grinding renewals. Thankfully, the snowstorm had mostly passed, but the oppressive weight of unmet quotas, dejected morale, and leftover Baconators from the day before made the air feel just as heavy as the weather outside.

For most of the team, Friday represented one last chance to scrape together numbers that might justify clocking out early to prepare for Saturday's charity ball hockey tournament. For others, it was just another day of biting through frustration, punctuated by the occasional ding of the sales bell that always seemed to come from someone else.

Jay and Max arrived at the office around the same time and found Dan asleep on the couch. Jay dropped into his chair and rubbed his head with a coffee in hand and his hair still a mess from a restless night. Across the sales pit, Shane was already pacing, sipping a protein shake that looked and sounded like it had been blended with rock salt.

"You ready for the big day tomorrow?" Max asked, barely lifting his head.

"Not even close," Shane replied. "My legs are toast from stair sprints last night. Had to prep for the tournament. Cardio is king, baby."

"Cardio won't help when you get a ball whipped at your face," Max explained.

Before Shane could respond, Rusty stomped into the pit, holding a thick manila folder. "Can you fucking believe this?" he fumed, slamming the folder onto his desk.

"What now?" Jay asked, taking a slow sip of his coffee.

"Wally forwarded me another relocation request. I swear to God, these nameplates are going to be the death of us. I'm sure you are still not over yesterday's bloodbath."

"You know," Shane grinned. "You should totally disinfect your hockey gloves tonight, Jay. That's an open wound on your hand. Nobody wants to see your hand oozing pus and infected with gangrene next week."

"Noted. I'll be sure to Lysol tonight and again tomorrow."

Shane grinned wider. "Also, you're not going to let a little 'budget cut trauma' take you down, are you? You're a warrior, Jay. So much better than that!"

Jay shot him a look. "If being a warrior means stabbing myself in the hand for the hundredth time, then sure. At least I brought some tools from home this time." He lifted two rusty screwdrivers and a bent pair of needle-nose pliers.

"Can I use those?" Rusty asked, reaching out to grab the tools.

At 9:00 a.m. sharp, Kent had scheduled an all-staff email to be sent out, officially announcing the sales contest Shane had pitched the previous day.

Subject: Let's Finish Strong!

Team,

Starting today, every rep who sells $15,000 in renewals or new packages by end-of-day will win a choice of the following: any jersey they want, a $100 gas/gift card to a restaurant of their choice, 100-level seats and Captain's Club dinner for the WAGS (wives, girlfriends, significant others), or two train passes for anywhere Via Rail goes (upgradeable to business class should you wish to do so on your own dime).

We're going to put you in teams of four, and for the team that sells $50,000 collectively, the entire group gets a free night in a hotel on the company dime.

Let's make it happen!

Best, Kent

The pit erupted into groans.

"Fifteen thousand?!" Rusty exclaimed. "Are they insane? That's like pulling a rabbit out of a hat— but the hat is Jari Kurri's old JOFA hockey helmet without a visor!"

Frank, who had been silently chewing on a granola bar, added, "And $50K as a team? Half this crew hasn't even cracked $2,000 all week."

"You're thinking small, guys," Shane interrupted, spinning his chair around dramatically. "This is our chance to rise up. Heroes are made in the fire."

"No," Frank shot back. "Heroes are made with budgets that include basic office supplies. What's the prize for whoever finds the last Band-Aid in the sales pit?"

Rusty laughed, but Jay's tension didn't lift.

By noon, as expected, the sales numbers were grim. The bell had rung only three times, and surprisingly, none were for Shane, Jay, Rusty, or Frank. The team gathered in the break room, picking over a sad tray of funeral sandwiches Kent had ordered to "boost morale."

"Best part of this contest?" Jay said through a mouthful of turkey and cheese. "Realizing I'd need to sell $15K just to afford a dentist's bill for when I grind my teeth down to nothing."

Rusty shook his head, eating an egg salad sandwich. "I made $2,300 worth of calls this morning, and all I got was one guy telling me he'd think about it."

"I got hung up on three times," Frank added, sipping a cup of lukewarm coffee. "One guy told me he thought our team folded two years ago. I didn't have the heart to correct him."

"You guys are focusing on the negatives," Shane chimed in. "Where's the hustle? Where's the grit? I am seriously worried about tomorrow with your negative Nancy attitudes."

"The grit?" Rusty said. "The grit went out the window when Wally's stupid snow removal trade deal buried us alive yesterday."

"That deal is almost as bad as this asinine sales contest is going to look when nobody wins shit," Jay muttered. "Who came up with this bullshit prizing anyway?"

"Eh, eh, eh, you got to experience the bitter to appreciate the sweet, Jason," Shane said, trying to remain positive.

As the day dragged on, the pit descended into even more chaos. Steve and Scott were arguing loudly over who had more Twitter followers, Salty was frantically typing an email to appease Catherine and Ian about non-existent mascot giveaways, and Kristina sat at her desk with her head in her hands, muttering something about "another goddamn group night."

Rusty, meanwhile, was on a call with a potential renewal client who was clearly stringing him along. "Well, Mr. MacPherson," Rusty said with forced cheer, "I understand you want to wait and see how the rest of the season plays out, but wouldn't it be great to lock in your seats now? That way, you're guaranteed—"

Click.

The dial tone buzzed in Rusty's ear. He hung up and slammed his phone down harder than necessary.

"That's it. I'm done. I'm out."

"Relax," Shane said, leaning back in his chair. "We've still got time."

"Time for what? To hit $15K in the next three hours? You're dreaming, Shane."

Shane didn't reply. He just adjusted his tie and turned back to his computer, determined to make the contest work.

Around the same time, Max went over to Kristina's desk and asked how she was doing with the flexible benefits program proposal. She had invested most of her time working on the ticket broker proposal, leaving little time for the other project that week.

"So, what exactly is the flexible benefits program?" Max asked.

Kristina sighed, pushing her chair back slightly. "It offers season-seat owners points based on account tenure and investment level. I think there should be bonuses for renewing early."

Max nodded. "When will I be able to make my selections?"

"If all goes well, this program would be in place for next season's renewals. I see there being an online portal—just like your ticket account—where you can access the program immediately after you renew or purchase your ticket package. So, if you renew on the first day, you can access the best variety of benefits. If you renew at the end of the summer, you'll get what's left. You'll also be able to log in at any time after your purchase, but I repeat—benefits are selected on a first-come, first-served basis."

Max considered this. "Do points expire? Can you carry them over to the next season?"

"No, the deadline for selections would have to be December 31. All points would expire as of January 1."

"Hmmm... do I have to select all of my benefits at the same time?"

Kristina smirked. "Good question, Max. No, I don't suppose you would have to. You could browse and not submit anything or submit one selection at a time over multiple visits. However, I would strongly suggest reviewing the choices in advance and selecting early to ensure you get the benefits that matter most to you. Plus, as long as you have enough points, you can select whatever you want—so long as there's still inventory."

"Last question for now—what if I'm, like, 50 points shy of the prize I want? Is there any way to top up the points? Like, buy the difference, kind of like Aeroplan points?"

Kristina shook her head. "No, I don't see how that would happen. You haven't been here long enough to know that our finance department is slow. I just don't see how we'd be able to assign a monetary value to points." She paused, then pulled up a document on her screen. "Here, this is a list of all the prizes I've come up with based on my own research and discussions with a few reps in Carolina." She opened a PDF file and moved her chair out of the way so Max could see the screen better.

"See, this is how I see the points allocated," she said, pointing to a chart. "Renewing early gets you a bonus of 500 points; if you buy a new package, you'll get a bonus of 150 points. If you've been with us for ten years or more, you get 500 points. Five to nine years gets you 250 points, etc. Then there are the investment bonuses, starting with packages worth $1,000 or less, all the way up to packages worth $20,000 or more. These points are just examples—we could choose to make them worth whatever."

"Very cool. Is that how Carolina does it?"

"Yep, pretty much."

"Let's see the list of prizes and benefits then!" Max said excitedly.

Kristina clicked on a Word document and presented the list of potential benefits for Max to see.

"Here's what I've come up with so far. The next step is determining what kind of budget we have to play with to allocate available inventory."

Max leaned in. "Some of those items are 'priceless,' and others would have a tangible cost. I guess depending on how many we'd order, we'd get better discounts. That might influence the number of available items, too, right?"

"Exactly." Kristina nodded.

By the end of the day, the renewal board remained largely unchanged. A few reps managed to scrape together a couple of small sales, but the big wins Kent and Wally had hoped for were nowhere to be found.

The pit was eerily quiet as the team packed up for the weekend, each person weighed down by their own private frustrations.

For Rusty, Frank, Shane, and Jay, the pressure of tomorrow's ball hockey tournament loomed even larger. They needed a win—not just on the court, but in the pit.

And yet, as they left the office, there was an unspoken feeling that something bigger was on the horizon. A storm no one could see coming.

CHAPTER 26

"The Limousine-Riding, Jet-Flying, Kiss-Stealing, Wheelin' and Dealin' Tournament'"

With the state of emergency lifted throughout the rest of the city, it was finally time for the charity ball hockey tournament. As expected, the inclement weather forced the games indoors, and three makeshift playing surfaces were created on the arena floor using wooden boards to cover the ice.

Predictably, it was a spectacle—starting with warmups.

Rusty had just finished gearing up, grumbling as he adjusted the bulky equipment. Warmups, for most goalies, were a crucial part of getting into the zone, tracking the ball, and preventing early-game injuries. For Rusty, it was an exercise in frustration. Nobody seemed to know how to properly warm up a goalie, especially in ball hockey. The lightweight ball moved unpredictably, and the mechanics were so different from ice hockey that he had to throw all his instincts out the window.

He had given the team one simple instruction: "Shoot gently so I can track the ball."

On the sidelines, Shane was wrestling with a small packet of gel, attempting to tear it open with his teeth.

"Dude, what the hell are you doing?" Jay asked, raising an eyebrow.

"It's testosterone gel," Shane replied matter-of-factly, smearing it liberally over his stomach. "Absorbs through the skin. Science, baby."

"Does this technically count as a performance-enhancing drug?" Frank asked dryly, watching Shane's antics.

"Watch this dangle, boyeeeeees!" Shane declared, suddenly springing into action.

"Oh no," muttered Frank.

Shane grabbed a ball and charged down the court on an uncontested breakaway, flipping the ball with a flashy move intended to dazzle. Instead, the ball whipped upward and smacked Rusty square in the mask.

"What the fuck, Shane?!" Rusty yelled, ripping his helmet off. "It's warmups, you plug!"

"Sorry, Rusty! Just trying to get used to the new twig. Not sure these specs are right, you know?" Shane replied, completely unfazed.

"You fucking Timbit!" Rusty bellowed.

Jay and Frank exchanged looks as they stood by the boards.

"Did he just rattle the goalie before the game even started?" Jay asked, incredulous.

"Unbelievable," Frank muttered.

The first game began uneventfully—aside from Shane, who promptly led both teams in penalty minutes. He was whistled for hooking a guy in the groin ("accidentally," Shane insisted) and twice for slashing opponents' shins, including one egregious slash during a breakaway. By halftime, the tournament coordinator had issued Shane a formal warning to "play with integrity."

Meanwhile, Jay and Steve quietly carried the Mutts to a 4–2 victory, each notching a goal and an assist. The highlight of the game came when Rusty made a highlight-reel stacked pad save in close and chirped the opposing forward: "Like my wife always says, 'not tonight!'"

By the second game, the Mutts had found their groove, jumping to a 4–1 lead. Inspired by Frank's rock-solid defence, Rusty nicknamed him "The Mountain" after Frank absorbed a shot with his shin and declared: "This is my house, and I did not invite you!"

But the championship game proved to be a nail-biter.

Both teams scored on their first shots, and while Rusty was beaten early, the ball ricocheted off the post. He shrugged it off and shouted: "Hey! The post has feelings too, boys! Take it easy!"

In the opposing team's zone, Shane missed a golden opportunity. Standing wide open at the side of the net, he whiffed a cross-crease pass and shot wide. Immediately, he pointed at the opposing goalie, yelling, "Did you move the net? You moved the net! He moved the net!"

The referee was unimpressed and issued Shane a warning for unsportsmanlike conduct.

"Maybe if you had the super whip instead of ultra whip flex, you'd actually score," the opposing goalie chirped, earning a warning of his own.

Undeterred, Shane redeemed himself in the second half, scooping up a loose ball and firing it past the opposing goalie to put the Mutts ahead 2–1. Moments later, he set up Jay for a snipe to make it 3–1.

"He's on fire!" Shane yelled, slapping hands with Jay.

"Razzle dazzle!" Jay gasped, out of breath.

"Boomshakalaka!" Frank screamed as the three players chest bumped.

"Next shift, I'm going to break that kid's ankles," Shane said confidently, pointing at Randy—the smallest player on the other team.

Randy, a former varsity hockey player, didn't flinch. On the next shift, he danced through Shane, Jay, and Frank before undressing Rusty with a top-shelf finish.

"Savage," one of Randy's teammates muttered.

Randy struck again minutes later, stealing the ball from Shane and unleashing a rocket into the top corner Rusty had no business attempting to save.

"Ohhhhh, somebody's heating up!" Randy taunted. "I'm gonna start trending on Twitter, baby!"

Shane, shaking his head, fired back. "I'm Shane Sanders, the stylin', profilin', limousine-riding, jet-flying, kiss-stealing, wheelin' and dealin' son of a gun! To be the man, you gotta beat the man.

Wooooooo!"

Frank rolled his eyes. "Why do you keep stealing lines from Ric Flair?"

"Who's Ric Flair?" Shane asked blankly.

"Classless. Sixteen-time world champion. That's who," Frank muttered.

Shane ignored him. "Rusty, we need you to step up. Three goals on five shots? Come on, man! Quit being a little bitch!"

Rusty groaned. "I'm doing my best, Shane. Maybe you could stop turning over the ball?"

With time winding down, Shane devised a plan: win the faceoff, dump the ball, and set up Frank for a slap shot from the point.

"Knuckle-puck time, baby!" Shane declared confidently.

"How do I even knuckle-puck a round ball?" Frank whispered to Jay.

"No clue. Just go with it," Jay whispered back.

The plan worked—almost. Frank's booming shot hit an opposing stick and deflected directly into Shane's upper thigh before grazing his crotch. Shane crumpled to the ground in agony while the deflected ball bounced to Jay, who buried it in the open net.

Jay and Frank celebrated with a dramatic hug and a few hearty butt slaps.

"It's okay. We play sports," Frank joked.

"Million-dollar move, two-dollar shot!" Jay quipped before noticing Shane writhing on the floor. "Are you crying, Shane?"

Shane gasped for air, clutching his groin. "You take the hit to make the play," he mumbled, hobbling to the bench. "It's not how hard you hit. It's how hard you can get hit and keep moving forward. That's how winning is done!"

Rusty sealed the victory with a miraculous glove save in the final seconds, collapsing to the ground as the buzzer sounded.

Watching from the sidelines, Kristina shouted, "You okay, Rusty?"

"Two minutes behind but three steps ahead, boys," Rusty panted, peeling off his mask as the Mutts celebrated their improbable championship win.

CHAPTER 27

"Celebrate We Will, For Life is Short But Sweet for Certain"

Having taken his role as "Commissioner of Fun" a bit too seriously, Shane spent the entire week preparing his condo for what he envisioned as "the greatest championship celebration the city had ever seen!" Unfortunately for Shane, the time from the end of the tournament to the party was spent icing his junk.

His fridge was packed with enough beer and coolers to hydrate a small army, and he had painstakingly arranged a "championship buffet" on his kitchen island and coffee table. There were nachos, sliders, wings, three kinds of dip (none of which really went with each other), and a mystery crockpot filled with something that Shane insisted was his "championship chili."

Shane greeted Frank at the door of his condo, wearing a velour tracksuit and a neck brace. Frank sighed, simply shaking his head at Shane's spectacle. "I don't even want to know, Shane," Frank said, walking towards the spread before stopping at the crockpot.

Stirring the mysterious contents of the crockpot with a wooden spoon, his face scrunched in concentration. "This isn't championship-worthy, Shane," he said, looking up with a hint of frustration.

"I thought you were better than this. How many times do I need to say it? You've got to let things stew! The longer it stews—"

"Yeah, yeah, Frank," Shane interjected, leaning back against the counter with a smirk. "The more flavourful your brew, magical and mystical as it may be. But I honestly think that's just your excuse for a science experiment gone wrong." He crossed his arms, puffing up as if declaring himself the culinary king.

"Did you at least rinse those beans in your sink? Because, as I often say, you're in for some serious gastrointestinal consequences if you didn't," Frank continued, feigning concern. "Farts and shits like they're nobody's business. Especially after all the protein shakes you drank before the tournament."

"But hey, thanks for this epic and delicious spread, Shane. It truly warms our hearts to see you work so hard just to impress us." Shane's eyes glinted with mischief as he trumpeted his own efforts to make today and tonight happen.

Frank's expression turned from frustration to disbelief. "You think this is a joke, Shane? There's a whole process to cooking. It's not about throwing things together and praying for a miracle!"

"Process? Come on," Shane scoffed, waving a dismissive hand. "All that simmering and stirring is for those who don't know how to truly elevate a meal. You see, I'm the culinary prodigy here, but don't worry—I'll let you take all the credit later."

"I'd rather have a flavourful dish than your 'culinary genius' any day of the week," Frank shot back, trying to keep his composure. "At least my food doesn't come with a side of obnoxiousness."

"Obnoxiousness? No, Frank, that's just called personality," Shane replied, his tone indulgent.

"No, Shane. Cheez Whiz has personality. You, sadly, do not."

"Hey, look, you don't like it, get out! I don't need your commentary, Frank."

"Woah, woah. Calm your tits, guys," Rusty got in between them. He had been knocking at the door but came in anyway. It was a good thing because now he was attempting to defuse the tension between Frank and Shane. "Can't we just appreciate what Shane's done here? Besides, next season, when you inevitably host your Sunday Sub Day, Frank, you can do things your own way, too, okay?"

"Sometimes, I think you just enjoy stirring the pot, Shane," Frank muttered, rolling his eyes.

"No matter how much flavour I add, Frank, it'll always taste bitter when you're around."

After losing interest in Shane and Frank's spat, Rusty investigated the spread himself. He also had his doubts about one of the dips as he lifted one of the lids, immediately recoiling. "Dude, what's in this?" Rusty asked. "Smells like feet."

Shane snatched the lid back. "You don't ask what's in the seven-layer dip either. You just eat it and appreciate the heart and soul I put into it."

Rusty raised an eyebrow. "By heart and soul, do you mean expired ground beef?"

Kristina, who had just arrived, looked at the spread and snorted.

"How is everyone inside the condo? Where is the doorman downstairs?!" Shane gasped.

"So let me get this straight... you have a chili crockpot on the coffee table but not a single coaster in sight?" Kristina jokingly asked.

"Coasters are a crutch," Shane replied. "You know what isn't a crutch? This fine Italian leather couch—imported from Florence. Pure elegance." Shane faked a sneeze, and a money clip with a thick stack of $20 bills fell out of his sleeve and onto the floor.

"Oops!" Shane smiled, bending over to pick the money clip back up.

"That was unnecessary, Shane," Kristina said, shaking her head in disgust.

"That was my Italian leather couch reminding me just how expensive it is."

"Yeah, we know all about this fucking couch, Shane," Kristina shot back.

"Florence, my ass," Frank chimed in, tossing his jacket onto the back of the couch as the condo was starting to feel much warmer than it had before everyone arrived. "That's a Wayfair special if I've ever seen one."

"Also, why don't you have anything on your bookshelf or art on the wall?" Kristina added.

Shane ignored both of their comments and turned his attention to the growing crowd filtering into his shoebox of a condo. Kristina hadn't been exaggerating—this place was small. Very small. The entire living room, kitchen, and dining area was basically just one large rectangle, and it was already at capacity before even half the expected guests arrived.

Nevertheless, Shane was too proud to admit he should have booked the party room on the penthouse floor.

Max looked around, surveying the situation. "So... where do we all sit?"

Shane beamed. "Anywhere you can find! Ideally, not on the couch."

Kristina raised an eyebrow. "Then why do you even have a couch?"

"For me to sit on," Shane said matter-of-factly. "And also, to have sex on. Obvi."

The first real incident of the night happened less than twenty minutes later.

"Jesus Christ!" Shane screamed, running down the short hall. "Alright, who clogged the toilet?!"

The party momentarily paused as all eyes darted around in search of a guilty expression.

"Not me," Jay said immediately.

"Not me," Rusty added. "Rule number four, or seven, or... you know what, I don't care."

Kristina took a long sip of her drink. "Didn't even use it. Actually, I will certainly wait."

Shane glared at Rusty. "I knew this would happen. I totally knew this would happen!" Shane said, collapsing to his knees. "This is why Rule Five exists! Stand-up peeing only!"

"Sorry, you're right, Rule Number Five! I was close," Rusty held up his hands. "Dude, I literally haven't gone yet either. Also, and I can't stress this enough, why isn't stand-up peeing only not rule number 1?"

"Well done, Rusty," Max cheered from across the room.

"Don't start with me, Rusty!"

"Look, I don't think it was any of us."

"Oh, really? Then who? Who didn't have the class to take a squeegee at their own place? Why did you have to foul my throne?"

A voice piped up from the kitchen. "Sorry, Shawn, it was me," Chad admitted sheepishly.

Max groaned. "Goddammit, Chad."

Shane threw his hands up in defeat. "Jesus Christ, Chad. You had one job and you blew it! You fucking blew it! Where's Max's sister?"

As the night progressed, the drinking games started. Beer pong, flip cup, and an impromptu hockey stick limbo contest had taken over what little space remained in the apartment.

Meanwhile, Shane was agitated as he kept a hawk-like watch over his possessions and precious, expensive Italian leather couch, which—so far—had remained untouched by food or drink.

Then it happened.

With a slurred celebratory "WOOOOO," Jay raised his drink for a toast and, in his enthusiasm, flung half his Long Island Iced Tea straight onto the pristine cushions.

The room collectively gasped.

Shane froze. His eye twitched.

Now realizing the full extent of his accidental crime, Jay attempted damage control. "Okay, okay, no need to panic—I got this!"

He lunged for the nearest roll of paper towels, knocking over a plate of orange Doritos in the process.

Kristina put a hand on Shane's shoulder. "Deep breaths, buddy."

"My... couch..." Shane whimpered. "My beautiful, expensive Italian leather couch!"

By the next morning, Shane awoke with a pounding headache and a large Long Island Iced Tea stain on his couch. Someone has also rewritten rule six to read: Rule 6: No Complaining About the Stain on Shane's Couch.

Shane groaned, removing the sleep from his eyes. "We're still doing the parade, though."

CHAPTER 28

"Rick Rolled"

Rusty sat at the kitchen table, sore and slightly hungover from the festivities of the ball hockey tournament championship win and the subsequent celebratory Shane-a-palooza immediately following. His four-year-old daughter, Emma, sat across from him, humming as she coloured furiously with a red crayon. The smell of bacon and pancakes filled the air as Amy, now six months pregnant, softly shuffled around the kitchen, her back turned to him.

Rusty had been home for less than six hours. The charity ball hockey tournament had drained him. His body still ached from the game, his head pounded from one too many post-tournament beers, and there was still something very off about Shane's mystery crockpot chili.

But right now, all he cared about was this moment. Being here. Sitting with Emma and watching her eyes and face full of wonder. She almost looked like Boo from Monsters, Inc., and her beautiful brown eyes could capture your soul just by catching you staring.

Emma's bright little voice cut through the silence, and no matter how hungover Rusty was, her tiny voice and the scratching of the red crayon were music to his tinnitus-ringing ears.

"Daddy, are you coming to my soccer game next Saturday?" she asked, tilting her head slightly up and to the side.

Rusty hesitated. He knew there was a home game next Saturday. He knew he wouldn't be there but couldn't bear to disappoint her.

"Of course, baby," he said, forcing a smile. "Daddy wouldn't miss it."

Across the room, Amy stiffened. She didn't turn around, and she didn't say anything, but Rusty could feel the weight of another one of his lies.

Emma didn't notice. She simply beamed and went back to happily colouring.

Rusty picked up his coffee, took a slow sip, and tried to savour this quiet morning. It was nice to be present in the moment—sitting at the table with Emma and Amy, sandwiched between the craziness of the previous week: the three-game homestand, the ball hockey tournament, and the pending renewal period of doom.

Then his phone buzzed.

Jay had sent a meme—some inside joke from work. And it buzzed again.

Salty had just sent a link, simply with the words: "Please advise."

Rusty tried desperately not to open the link but clicked anyway.

Salty had Rickrolled him.

Rickrolling was an internet bait-and-switch prank where someone tricked another into watching Rick Astley's Never Gonna Give You Up music video. Rusty sat there, slightly amused, watching the video in its entirety.

'Never gonna give you up
Never gonna let you down
Never gonna run around and desert you
Never gonna make you cry
Never gonna say goodbye
Never gonna tell a lie and hurt you'

As Rusty sat through the entire music video, the contrast between his life and the lyrics of Never Gonna Give You Up hit him hard.

"Never gonna give you up, never gonna let you down"—It was nearly impossible to break his commitment to his job, his clients, and his colleagues, but his commitment to his wife and daughter felt like a chain binding him to a promise he had made but didn't keep.

He wanted to be there for Amy and especially Emma, yet the grind of his career lured him away, intoxicating him with its sports entertainment allure. Rusty knew he was letting them down, betraying their trust—all for a fleeting taste of glory.

"Never gonna run around and desert you"—He noticed all the running around and desertion in his life and couldn't shake the shame when he recalled so many moments he had prioritized work commitments over family stability. He convinced himself it was for their future and had used Jay and Shane's excuse of "it's for work" far too many times. But watching his family suffer because of his choices cut deep—

even then, he couldn't fully grasp what it meant to be truly present, to stand by those he professed to love, because it was impossible to turn off from the job that consumed him almost 24/7.

The reality of "Never gonna make you cry" really stung. Rusty had caused pain, particularly to Amy. Her tears haunted him and were a constant reminder of the emotional wreckage from his pursuit of working in professional sports. He had thought his ambition would pave a path to happiness for them.

He had been lured in by the shine of working in professional sports, of being the envy of his friends— but it only became a source of heartbreak, a heavy weight in his chest.

And then there was "Never gonna say goodbye, never gonna tell a lie and hurt you."

Oof. It all hurt.

He struggled to confront the truth of betraying not just himself but Amy, and perhaps most painfully, Emma. Rusty's lies festered in his memory—a web spun from ambition that pulled him away from his values, leaving him hollow and hurtful for no reason at all.

Indeed, Rusty— and everyone in the sales pit— was caught in the contradiction, chasing a championship and their dreams while yearning for the connections they had lost.

Rick Astley echoed what he, Frank, Dan, Jay, Shane, Kristina, and others truly desired— a life filled with love and loyalty— but their chosen path had cost them dearly.

If only they could have a redo.

If only he could see now that lofty ambitions should never overshadow the commitment to those who truly cared about him.

But how could he reconcile these conflicting desires?

Was there a way to bridge the chasm between his dreams and his responsibilities?

Then, another buzz shook him from his period of enlightenment.

It was a text from Shane. "Come out tonight."

Five minutes later, moments after Amy placed a plate of pancakes and bacon in front of him, and just as he finished pouring maple syrup onto his pancakes—another buzz.

This time, from a client.

"The nameplate on my seat ripped a hole in my wife's jacket. What are you going to do about it?"

Rusty exhaled, setting his phone face-first, but he still felt the phantom buzzing.

"Thank you," Amy said as she sat across from him, close to Emma. "Thanks for putting that away, Richard." She acknowledged that, for once, he wasn't tethered to his BlackBerry.

Rusty forced a smile and reached for her hand. She was busy sipping her coffee, watching him.

"We should do a date night soon," he offered softly.

Amy's lips curved into a polite smile. She didn't believe him. They both knew it wouldn't happen.

Emma got up from her booster seat and ran over to her dad, holding a piece of paper in one hand and her red crayon in the other. She crawled into his lap and nuzzled into his armpit, maybe making up for lost time.

"Show Daddy what you drew, baby girl," he said, carefully taking her latest masterpiece from her tiny, clenched fingers—fingers that looked like little cheddar-smoked sausages.

Then he gasped.

It was a crayon picture of their family—Emma in the middle, Amy beside her, their house in the background.

But Daddy wasn't there.

Rusty stared at the drawing, something in his throat clenching.

For a moment, he thought about telling her. That he wanted to be there. That he hated missing her games. That he didn't know how to balance work and family.

But she was too young to understand—the same way Amy understood.

Instead, he forced another smile and told her she had done a great job.

Another lie.

Emma grinned and squealed as she slid down his leg and went back to colouring next to Amy, who just sipped her coffee.

CHAPTER 29

"Championship Parade"

When Monday morning rolled around, Shane's apartment was still in shambles. The stain had now set into his "very expensive Italian leather couch," which still smelled like regret and Frank's unrinsed bean farts. Yet, aside from the couch and Doritos dust now ingrained in Shane's carpet, most of the Mutts had survived the legendary, slightly disastrous, probably fire-code-violating championship party at Shane's condo.

But despite the hangovers, despite the poor decision-making that would occur the next night, and despite absolutely nobody else in the office giving a shit about their ball hockey tournament win, Shane had committed to the championship parade, and he was going to see that it happened.

Shane, of course, had gone all in. Not only had he brought in an actual championship trophy (that he had purchased from a thrift store the day he learned he had "made the team"), but he had also just printed out a "Championship Parade" banner on the office printer. Since the printer could only handle standard-sized paper, twelve separate sheets were taped together extremely unevenly—like something a group of second graders would bring to a pep rally. Or, more accurately, something his clients had come to expect when they received mail with their tickets enclosed.

Frank had somehow acquired a megaphone over the weekend. Rusty spent ten minutes in the old storage closet shredding old invoices from the finance department's recycling for "confetti." Jay, disappointed that the go-kart plan didn't pan out, had commandeered Jimmy's rolling office chair to serve as the "parade float." He sat proudly on it, wearing his ball hockey jersey, waving to imaginary fans like a discounted version of the Pope in his Popemobile.

At 10:05 a.m. sharp, Shane blew his Fox forty whistle, and the parade officially began.

"Alright, Mutts! We march!" Shane bellowed as he led the way while a portable Bluetooth speaker blasted:

'Ooh oh oh oh, ooh oh oh oh
So light 'em up, up, up, light 'em up, up, up
Light 'em up, up, up,
I'm on fire!'

Frank pushed Jay, who sat regally in the rolling chair float, waving dramatically. Frank engaged with the "crowd" using his megaphone, randomly shouting nonsense like, "HISTORY BEING MADE, PEOPLE!" Rusty followed, throwing shredded invoice "confetti," which fluttered uselessly to the ground in the saddest attempt at pageantry ever seen.

Kristina and Max carried Shane's makeshift Championship Banner, which immediately started falling apart because it was literally just printer paper held together by three pieces of Scotch tape and a few staples.

All the while, Shane led the charge, holding his fake thrift store trophy over his head like it was the

Stanley Cup. They stormed out of the sales pit, down the inside sales hallway, turned the corner— And immediately ran into Wally and Kent.

Kent, holding his ever-present XL coffee, did not look amused. Wally, on the other hand, looked genuinely confused.

"What... are we looking at?" Kent asked, rubbing his forehead with his free hand.

Shane stepped forward. "Kent. Wally. Welcome. You are witnessing history."

He gestured to the absolute shitshow behind him.

"This is the Mutts Championship Parade."

Wally blinked. "The what?"

"The Mutts Championship Parade, Wally. We won the ball hockey tournament on Saturday. Top division. This is a big deal. Like, a really big deal!"

Frank, still wielding the megaphone, chimed in.

"LADIES AND GENTLEMEN. THIS IS NOT JUST A CELEBRATION. THIS IS A CHAMPIONSHIP MOVEMENT!"

Kent snatched the megaphone from Frank's hands and immediately threw it into a nearby recycling bin.

Then he pointed at Shane. "You. My office. Now."

Shane opened his mouth to argue but thought better of it.

"Alright, Mutts, that's a wrap. Parade's over," Shane muttered, quickly handing the trophy to Jay before walking toward Kent's office.

Now holding the fake thrift store trophy, Jay stood awkwardly in the hallway as Rusty, Kristina, Frank, and Max returned to their desks. Jay looked at Max, now sitting quietly at his desk in the hall. "So... do we just... uh, do I just... go back to work now?"

Max sighed, looking down at the "trophy" Jay held. "Yeah. Probably."

And just like that, the 'Greatest Parade in Office History' ended in under four minutes.

After the parade disaster, Kent ripped into Shane for "a colossal waste of company resources" (even though zero company resources had been used outside of the printer and some old, shredded invoices).

Kristina and Max spent the next twenty minutes peeling tape off the walls from the now-destroyed Championship Banner while Rusty was politely asked to grab the vacuum from the storage closet to clean up all the shredded invoice "confetti"—which took way longer than expected.

Frank retrieved the megaphone and quietly returned to his pod.

And Shane? Shane walked out of Kent's office, straightened his tie, and walked right back to his desk like nothing had happened.

Jay looked up. "Well?"

Shane cracked open a Red Bull. "I've had worse."

Frank shook his head. "Was it worth it?"

Shane took a long sip and smirked. "Oh, absolutely. Despite the chaos, the yelling, the four-minute duration, and the absolutely minuscule level of company support, one thing was certain: Frankyboy... the Mutts are undefeated champions, and nobody can take that away from us."

He raised his can in a toast.

"We fly together! Quack, quack, quack, quack!"

CHAPTER 30

"Sexy Business Cards, Jell-o Shots and Dana the Intern"

Seconds later, Jay's cell phone rang. He looked at it quickly and, not recognizing the number, willed it to stop ringing. It kept ringing.

"Aren't you going to answer that?" Frank asked, peeking his head over the pod divider.

"I don't recognize the number. My cardinal rule is I don't answer a number I don't recognize. Can't deal with the hand grenade. Need time to prepare a response," Jay stated. "Have you ever been so unimpressed with a client that you searched for them on Facebook just to see how legit crazy they are in real life? That seems to be my entire book of clients. They all need psychologists."

"Speaking of psychologists, last week it took Jay an hour-and-a-half of motivational self-talk shit to make a call that ended in a 44-second voicemail," Rusty told Frank over the top of his pod divider.

"I think some of my clients just call me out of the blue so they can argue with someone," Jay said dejectedly.

"Is that why you always have, like, 18 voicemails a day?" Salty asked.

"I can't get sewered in real time; today especially, I am screening my calls."

"I was talking to a client and meant to say 'all good' and 'no worries,' but I accidentally said 'all worries,'" said Brad. "Coincidentally, that's the best description of most of us at any given moment working here," he continued.

Jay's phone dinged again, this time indicating he had a voicemail. Dialling in to check it, Jay listened and lowered his head shamefully.

"Oh my God," he muttered.

Replaying the voicemail, this time on speakerphone, Salty and Frank turned to listen.

"Heyyyyy Jayyyyyy, it's your favourite Jell-O shot girl, Dana! I just wanted to call and say it was great meeting you last night and that I'd love to take you up on your offer to work for you! Call me anytime, and we can work out the details."

"I may have hired an intern last night," Jay said apologetically.

"An intern?"

"Shane, Scott, and Steve went out to meet a bunch of sports business students with Dan and Krissy," Jay started. "Scott and I were late because there were pre-drink festivities at their place, so we just went to the bar with the intention of fake interviewing potential interns for next year."

"Please tell me a casting couch was not involved," Rusty pleaded.

"I hope not!" Jay said, scratching his head. "Shane was off his rocker per usual; we were passing out business cards left and right. So many business cards."

"Is Dana a student?" Frank asked.

"Hardly. She's the Jell-O shot girl. We must have bought a whole tray of them… or more! You know what? I'm just going to ignore Dana and never speak of this again."

"Out of sight, out of mind won't work here. She knows who you are, Jay. She works at your favourite bar," replied Salty. "She has your business card with your personal cell phone number!"

"I'm never going to drink again. There, I said it. I mean it this time."

Frank called Scott's extension and asked him to come over. Moments later, Scott appeared.

"So, how was last night, Scott?" asked Frank.

"Oh, you know, we did that thing with those people at that place."

"We may have hired an intern," Jay said.

"I don't remember that," Scott said, laughing. "I woke up on the bathroom floor at 3 a.m. with a wicked, wicked headache. No evidence of vomiting, though, so that's a bit of a win! But I was obviously sensing it was a real possibility. Took three Tylenol, and well, here I am!"

"I believe there were multiple vomit spells," Jay explained.

"No word of a lie, the eight vodka Red Bulls almost killed you and me. How our hearts didn't explode is a modern miracle!" Scott said, laughing.

"I also found a whole pizza in the front closet this morning," Jay added. "Don't even know where that came from!"

"Guys, I know we say this every week, but you really need to make some wholesale changes," pleaded Salty.

"I found some mangled cupcakes all over the house. Icing on the floor, all over the table. Sprinkles in my bed."

"Yeah, Courtney brought those over for the tailgate party," Jay said, rubbing his head.

"Who's Courtney?" asked Scott.

"The girl I'm seeing," Jay said proudly.

Everyone in the pod looked at Jay with astonishment and disbelief.

"Well, I invited her over last night. She came with Steve... and a few of her friends... and her boyfriend."

"Jesus," Scott said. "You know, I think we were probably drugged by that Jell-O shot girl, Rachel."

"The Jell-O shot girl is Dana."

"No, man, she said her name was Rachel," Scott said, rubbing his head.

Just then, Jay's phone rang again. It was the same number as before.

"Yep, you definitely sewered yourself," said Frank.

"I still don't understand how you felt the need to go back out the next night," Rusty said, throwing his question toward Jay, Steve, and Scott.

"You know what, Rusty? I'm starting to learn that I value sleep so much more than I did when I was younger," Frank acknowledged. "I couldn't have done what you idiots did. I wouldn't have done what you idiots did either."

"Yeah, Frank, it was pretty rough," Steve acknowledged. "What did you get up to anyway?"

"Sunday, I must have taken a late morning or early afternoon nap so good that when I woke up, I thought it was the morning and I'd missed the school bus. But it was obviously Sunday... and I'm 52."

"Yeah, you must have been asleep when I was knocking on your fucking front door!" Steve said, annoyed.

"What were you knocking on my door for?" Frank asked.

"You forgot your wallet at Shane's. I found it behind the couch. It must have fallen out when you threw your jacket over it."

"I did?" Frank said, confused as he patted his pants, looking for his wallet.

"Yeah, man. Here." Steve tossed Frank's wallet to him. "When I saw no other cars in the driveway, I didn't have high hopes. So, I stopped at the convenience store between your house and mine and proceeded to spend $40 on some prop bets."

"And? How did it go?" Frank asked.

"I woke up this morning with the same level of negativity and despair as before... and I owed you $40, so there's that," Steve said as he pulled two twenties out of his pocket and handed them to Frank, who quickly snatched them.

By this time, Jay's phone had rung for the fifth time, with yet another voicemail ready to be played. There was no time for callbacks, as he and Shane were in their pod, trying to access the online ticketing system. EQqo Entertainment, the promoter for the ma#tag! World Tour had just released tickets on the floor and other prime areas of the stadium due to a new stage setup. Collectively, Jay, Shane, and especially Frank had a list of forty clients who had all demanded tickets as a condition of their renewal.

"Why aren't you logging in?" a visibly rattled Jay said to his computer.

"What's wrong now?" Shane asked, unimpressed.

"It's asking me for my password to log into the ticketing portal. I haven't changed my password, and it's not accepting the one I'm typing!"

"Have you tried resetting it?" Shane asked.

"No need to reset the password. I know what it is!" Jay persisted.

"Let me try," Shane said, pushing Jay's chair out of the way with his foot. "What's your password?"

"I'm not telling you my password!"

"You're going to have to change it, anyway, aren't you?"

"Well, yes, but telling you my password will expose you to my brain's Pandora's box. Plus, I like my password, and I guarantee you it'll tell me I can't use one of the previous five."

"Okay, here's what you do," Shane said confidently. "Set the password to 'password123,' then switch it to 'password1234,' then 'password12345,' then '123password,' then '1234password,' and then you change it to the password you want. Boom goes the dynamite—five old passwords cleared, one ready to go."

"Amazing. Brilliant," Jay said as he pushed Shane's chair back to his desk.

"So, you got to the bar late last night and then left early?" Shane asked. "What gives? I thought you were better than that."

"Meh, I wasn't feeling it. After the 'Jell-O shot incidents,' I just went home, got really polluted high, and played video games until 5 a.m. this morning."

"You getting stoned? Shocking," Shane said, rolling his eyes. "Wait," he started, looking at his watch. "That was like less than five hours ago... are you still high right now?"

"No! God, no!" Jay said. "It was a bad trip, but not nearly as bad as the time Scott and I baked that weed cake. We ate the whole thing and felt nothing... so we hit the bong a fuck ton of times until we felt EVERYTHING. Turns out we totally fucked up the measurements and put enough weed oil in it for ten people. I was high for three days straight!"

"You know, if you are high for more than 24-hours straight it's permanent. Yes, I see no ill effects," Shane said comfortingly.

"Thank you. Anyway, it's fine because Sunday was almost a total write-off. After the championship party, I got home and slept well into the afternoon. By then, I missed all the early afternoon games and only had time to run to the corner store and buy a Pro-Line for our game and the rest of the schedule."

"And? How did you do?" Shane asked.

"I ripped the ticket up after the first period of our game. Devastated. Rattled. Just cancel Christmas."

"This is why I never bet on our games."

"What are your cardinal betting rules, anyway?" Jay asked.

"In reverse order," Shane began. "Cardinal Rule #5 – It's never your fault. No bad betting strategies. Rule #4 – Appreciate that there's a lot of luck and randomness in the outcomes of a game. Nothing you can do but get on your knees and pray."

"That's not the only thing you do on your knees, Shane," Rusty quipped from the other side of the pod.

"Grow up, Rusty!" Shane snapped, throwing a pen lid that easily missed Rusty. "Rule #3 – You can't live in the what-ifs. You play to win the game or don't play at all. No babies crying over the bets they never made, even if they would have won. Out of sight, out of mind."

"Interesting," Jay said, taking notes.

"Rule #2 – Garbage time in football will fuck you almost every time."

"Garbage time can lick my taint," Jay muttered.

"Rule #1 – I always look for value. Sometimes, Pro-Line is the better bet. Sometimes, sportsbooks are better. Sometimes, the

The Sales Pit | 343

Packers, for example, will be +8.5 on Pro-Line but only +6 on some sportsbooks. Always look for value."

"What else?"

"And finally, the golden rule—always bet with your head and not your heart. Remove yourself from the fanboy mentality and never bet on your own team, even if you think they're a lock."

"I know, I know. I give us way too much credit. Even as terrible as they are this season," Jay said, ashamed. "I think my only rule is to rotate my tickets. So, for example, if there are four games I want to bet on, instead of combining them all on a single ticket, I buy four smaller tickets and play all four possible three-game combinations. If I get three out of four picks right, I win one of my tickets!"

"Correct. But if you go four for four... come on, baby! See you later, alligator!" Shane said, honking his crotch as Rusty walked into the pod. "Hey, Rusty, are you ready for this? This is the most important thing you will hear all day—possibly all time."

"Ugh," Rusty groaned.

"You and Jay have just secured a coveted invitation to the final game of the season party I am throwing."

Rusty was unenthusiastic about the prospect of spending yet another Saturday night with Shane.

After all, the team's schedule saw them play at home on Saturdays about sixteen times. That was sixteen weekends that were totally shot for any kind of planning.

"Wooooooo," Rusty said softly and mockingly. "A glutton for punishment, eh, Shane? Has your condo association already recovered from our championship celebration?"

"I paid the fines!" Shane shot back. "No thanks to any of you cheap skates."

"As usual, I am disappointed in all of you," Rusty said as he sat down at his desk.

"Fuck off, Rusty. This is going to be epic!" Shane declared emphatically.

"We already established the ground rules for your use of the word 'epic,' Shane," Jay said, turning around to face the other two.

"Everyone knows that we have zero shot at making the playoffs, but we might as well embrace that and still get together to send this season off in style," Shane explained, still excited.

"Wait, we're not doing the get-together at your place again, are we?" Jay asked before adding, "Your place is so small."

"We already established that last week!" Rusty said. "Why don't we just do it somewhere else? Where we can have space to actually enjoy the tasty spread and the game without watching it on a 42' TV!"

"Nobody has stepped up to host the party yet, so by default, it falls back to the previous host."

"You just told us you were hosting this party!" Rusty argued, visibly confused.

"If it's back at your place, can we at least reserve seats?" Jay asked.

"Yeah, I am not sitting on anyone's lap again," Rusty muttered. "Not like last time!"

"No, boys, you aren't allowed to reserve spots. The same rules apply from before."

"Besides, the condo was very expensive. Premium hardwood, boys. Pree-me-um hardwood," Rusty said mockingly before grabbing his crotch and picking his nose.

"You're right, Rusty. Thank you for noticing; it is premium hardwood. Made in Italy or Bolivia—had it imported," Shane said smugly.

"That wasn't the point I was trying to make, Shane."

"Even still, you noticed, and I appreciate you noticing me, noticing you, noticing my hardwood floors underneath my expensive Italian leather couch in my very expensive condo." Shane faked another sneeze with a different crowd, and another money clip with a thick stack of $20 bills fell out of his sleeve and onto the floor.

"Oops!" Shane smiled, bending over to pick the money clip back up.

"Krissy told me about your money clip up your sleeve trick. I agreed with her then, and your shenanigans just reinforced how unnecessary that was, Shane."

Shane simply smugly shrugged.

"Have you not learned anything from the Mutt-a-palooza you threw last weekend?" Rusty asked.

"Actually, yes, thank you for allowing me to elaborate," Shane began. "I know you're probably asking yourself, 'How can you fit so many people in such a small space again?' 'How can anyone see the game?' 'Will there be a similar, or even better, spread?' 'Can I have the recipe for the layer dip you made?'"

"I wouldn't have asked any of those questions," Jay disclosed.

"If you recall, I have two TVs side by side for my annual Super Bowl party, with the potential for a third for the evening. That's a combined 82 inches of television, side by side, you know, for optimum viewing angles."

"Why don't we ever have a party at my place again?" Rusty asked. "Remember, I have a 100-inch screen with a much larger area and a much larger, more comfortable couch."

"Maybe if you planned an evening like that, we would," Shane interrupted.

"He did, remember?" added Jay.

"Right. The Doritos Incident, Part 1," Shane said, remembering that Part 2 had been on his turf.

"Speaking of Doritos, what'll be served at Fiesta di Shane?" Frank asked, poking his head above the half-wall. "No more of that mystery-meat chili, right? RIGHT?"

"I'm not going to get into the merits of my mystery-meat chili. But I will promise you that the end-of season party will offer nothing but the best and healthiest for you, Frank. Egg rolls, chicken strips, 'za, wings, plus various dips, sodas, cocktails, and, of course, Imodium on tap!" Shane announced.

"Your party better be worth the week-long bowel obstruction," Frank muttered, rubbing his stomach.

"I'm surprised and disappointed in you, Shane—you've refined your palate," Rusty chirped.

"Yeah, Shane. Do you remember your last failed attempt at a last-minute party and how it resulted in an aggressive order of 200 wings and eight greasy pizzas? After four hours, 170 wings and five pizzas were left," Jay reminded the group with a giggle.

"That 'mistake,' as you call it, handsomely fed me for the rest of the week."

"Wasn't the overdose of pizza and wings also the likely cause of Shane's bowel obstruction, which required an emergency enema at the hospital five days later?" Frank asked.

"I had to change, boys," Shane said earnestly. "I've humbly learned from my failed food ordering, and now I know that leftovers need to be refrigerated."

Jay let his phone ring to the end one last time before dialling in to check his voicemails. Unfortunately, there were three 'Jell-o Shot Internship' messages from Dana and two new messages from 'Rachel.'

CHAPTER 31

"Flexible Benefits"

Max's mind never stopped turning when it came to fan engagement. He wanted to take Kristina and Rusty's lead and reach the fans, connect with them, and make them feel valued—not just as customers but as a part of the team's identity.

Around 4 PM, Max made his way over to Rusty's desk, notebook in hand. Half-distracted by his screen, Rusty looked up as Max plopped down in Jay's chair across from him.

"Rusty, I've got a few ideas," Max began, his voice tinged with excitement. "They're still rough, but the goal is all about brand awareness, fan affinity, and season ticket holder recognition."

Rusty leaned back, arms crossed. "I assume you've already touched base with all your accounts?"

Max nodded eagerly. "Yeah. I've called everyone, met with as many as I could before the season ended. Now I'm just thinking about how we can build on that—over the summer, you know?"

Rusty studied him for a second before nodding. "All right. Whatcha got?"

Max flipped open his notebook. "First idea—Locker Room Cleanout. We randomly pick renewed season ticket holders and give them the chance to clean out their favourite player's locker."

Rusty raised an eyebrow. "You want fans to clean up after players?"

"No, no," Max waved his hand. "Not literally clean up after them. They'd get to go through the locker and keep whatever's inside."

Rusty leaned forward, intrigued. "Okay, that's interesting. But what if multiple people want the same player's locker?"

Max tapped his pen against the desk. "We could hold eighteen separate draws. That way, each winner gets a specific player's locker."

Rusty smirked. "So the fans don't get to choose—we assign them a locker?"

"Exactly," Max nodded. "When they show up, their player's locker could have, I don't know, a game-worn jersey..."

"Or practice jersey," Rusty added.

"Yeah, that too!"

"Not that too—one or the other," Rusty corrected.

"Right...okay, so maybe a signed stick, game-used gloves, socks, water bottle, a signed puck from the player—whatever's in there."

Rusty nodded, his mind turning. "Maybe a personalized thank-you photo?"

Max's face lit up. "That would really put this experience over the top!"

Rusty tapped the desk thoughtfully. "And it wouldn't cost much. Most of that stuff gets tossed or donated anyway. And for fans? It's huge. It's exclusive, personal, and unique. Nobody would be able to live that down!"

"That's exactly it," Max said. "Fans don't just want merch. They want experiences—something they can't buy in stores. Like this."

Rusty grinned. "Not bad, kid. Not bad at all. What else you got?"

Max flipped to another page. "Speaking of kid, didn't you and Amy have your ultrasound today?"

"That's right. It was supposed to happen last Thursday, but given the weather, they asked to reschedule for today. A little boy, Max. We're having a little boy!" Rusty said, holding back his emotion. "Million-dollar family!" Max acknowledged.

"Thank you! You're probably too young to know this reference, but as soon as I found out we were having a boy, I jumped up and down like I was on Jerry Springer," Rusty said with a laugh.

"Jerry Springer?" Max asked, confused.

"The show was known for its sensational and often controversial content. One recurring theme on the show involved paternity tests, where men would appear to find out whether they were the father of a baby. These episodes typically revolved around relationship turmoil, infidelity, and dramatic reveal scenarios."

"Ooh! Suspense and drama!" Max said excitedly.

"Those paternity test segments became a hallmark of the show," Rusty giggled. "Anyway, when the ultrasound revealed we were having a boy, I started crying and throwing fists in the air. It was amazing."

"I'm so happy for you, man! I didn't mean to go off on a tangent, but I wanted to know!"

"It's cool, Max. I appreciate you remembering. Anyway, what else ya got?"

Max flipped the page. "So, I've been thinking about season ticket holder recognition. I know people talk about hats, pins, lanyards, but that's all been done."

Rusty reached into his desk, pulling out a commemorative pin for the ten-year season ticket holder. He tossed it onto the table. "Yeah. Nobody cares about these."

"Exactly," Max nodded. "So, instead of a pin, what about a commemorative patch?"

Rusty looked up. "Like, iron-on or sew-on?"

"Yeah! Something fans can put on their jersey, hat, jacket—wherever."

Max flipped his notebook around, revealing a rough sketch of a round black patch with bold white lettering:

"Official Season Ticket Holder"

Rusty rubbed his chin. "Hmm. That's actually a pretty good idea."

"I've been watching our fans," Max continued. "You can tell who's a season ticket holder. They wear it with pride on their face. But a patch is a super-status symbol. It's something they can display proudly."

Rusty nodded. "Patches cost next to nothing when bought in bulk. I remember my Scouts days—we got patches made in China for less than a dollar. Who knows what they'd cost if we ordered a bunch from Alibaba."

"Exactly," Max agreed. "And we could sell extras. Most season ticket holders have more than one jersey or jacket, right? Surely, they'd buy more."

Rusty smirked. "That's smart. External revenue generation, and don't call me Shirley," a reference that flew over Max's head like an 'Airplane' in 1980.

Max flipped the page. "Okay, this one's called 'Cheeks in Seats.'"

Rusty laughed. "Cheeks in Seats?"

"Yep," Max grinned. "I got the idea in Chicago last summer. I was at the Taste of Chicago festival— thousands of people sitting on lawn chairs in Grant Park watching Stevie Wonder. And then I saw it— White Sox season ticket holder chairs."

Rusty's eyes narrowed. "Like...folding chairs?"

"Yeah, but branded. The team logo on the back, with the words 'Season Ticket Holder.'"

Rusty sat up. "You're telling me that camping chairs got you thinking about fan engagement?"

Max grinned. "You'd be surprised. It's genius. Think about it—our fans use chairs all the time. Camping, tailgating, kids' games, cottage weekends. It keeps our brand visible all offseason."

Rusty crossed his arms. "Okay, and what's the cost?"

"I checked. About $20 per chair."

Rusty whistled. "Not bad."

"I also didn't check that hard, so we could probably get them much cheaper. We could do different colours based on seating level," Max continued. "Gold for club seat holders, red for 100 and 200 level, blue for flex packs. Full and half-season holders get a chair for every seat they own. Flex plans get one."

Rusty nodded, impressed. "And if they want extras?"

Max smirked. "$30-$40 each. About 50% profit."

Rusty grinned. "You've thought this through."

Max leaned forward. "Rusty, this keeps us in our fans' minds. This is how you build fan engagement— year-round!"

Rusty shook his head. "Damn, kid. You and I think alike."

"Awesome. Thanks, Rusty."

"You're a pain in the ass, Max, but I like the way you think."

Max laughed, jumping up from his chair. "That's it for me right now. Congrats again! A boy...wow!"

Rusty watched Max skip back to his desk, shaking his head. The kid was onto something.

CHAPTER 32

"Conversations for Mutual Understanding"

It was Tuesday, and with the high of the Mutts' championship run and subsequent parade now in their rearview mirror, shit was about to get real.

Garry Breckenridge sat in his new office, its walls a shrine to his professional past. Framed photographs and awards hung in neat rows, each one showcasing a different chapter of his illustrious career. Here was Garry in his crisp blazer, shaking hands with a hockey legend after securing a record-breaking sponsorship deal. Next to it, a shot of him hoisting a minor league championship trophy, his face alight with triumph. A plaque commemorating his "Outstanding Leadership" at the NBA franchise hung prominently beside a group photo of him with a team of grinning executives.

The sheer number of accolades gave the room an almost museum-like quality—a testament to his ambition and drive. To an outsider and those in the industry, his résumé was nothing short of impressive.

He tapped his pen against his notepad, a shallow grin spreading across his face. The employees had been called in one by one for their individual "performance chats." Garry insisted they weren't reviews but "conversations for mutual understanding." Still, the air in the pit was tense, with whispers floating among the cubicles about what these meetings might mean.

-Shane's Meeting-

The first to enter was Shane, swaggering in as if he owned the place. His tie was askew, and his trademark smug grin was firmly in place.

Garry gestured to the chair across from him, his grin widening as Shane dropped into it with an exaggerated lean, crossing one ankle over his knee.

"Shane! Thanks for coming in. I've heard great things about your energy on the sales floor," Garry began.

Shane leaned back even further, the corners of his mouth twitching upwards. "Energy? Garry, I am the energy. The pit feeds off me. Without me, it's like a hockey team without a goalie—an empty net."

Garry chuckled weakly, jotting a quick note on his pad. "Interesting analogy. Tell me, Shane, what would you say is your biggest contribution to the team?"

Shane pretended to think for a moment, then shrugged with exaggerated nonchalance. "My sales, obviously. Renewed five accounts this morning alone. Plus, morale. You've seen me out there. I keep everyone laughing, keep things light. It's a gift, really."

"And how do you see yourself fitting into the organization's long-term vision?" Garry asked, pen poised.

"Long-term? Honestly, Garry, I'm aiming for bigger things. Maybe Director of Sales. Or VP. But hey, I'm open to negotiation," Shane said with a grin.

Garry's expression didn't falter, but his eyes sharpened as he jotted something down. "Ambition. I like that. Thanks, Shane. We'll be in touch. Can you send Rusty in?"

As Shane left, Garry scribbled something on his notepad, circling it twice before tapping his pen against his chin. He glanced briefly at a nearby frame featuring himself at a baseball stadium, mid-presentation, as a group of executives nodded along.

The grin in the photo mirrored the one he wore now.

-Rusty's Meeting

Rusty stepped into Garry's office with his usual air of defiance, his bold tie pattern practically screaming for attention. He was the kind of guy who wore his emotions on his sleeve—or, in Rusty's case, on his brightly coloured socks. He paused, glanced briefly at the wall of Garry's framed achievements, and then sank into the chair across the desk.

Garry greeted him with an effusive grin, one Rusty found unnerving. "Rusty! Thanks for coming in. I've been looking forward to our conversation. That is one hell of a shirt and tie combination!"

Rusty crossed his arms and leaned back. "Oh yeah?" Rusty said with a smile. The tension in his chest immediately released.

Garry chuckled as though they were old friends. "Is that amusing? I know fashion when I see it. I feel your confidence, Rusty, and I like it. I've heard you're a cornerstone of this team. Your numbers are impressive, but it's more than that. Your passion—it's what sets you apart."

Rusty raised an eyebrow, unconvinced. "Passion, huh? Never heard it called that before."

"Oh, absolutely," Garry said, leaning forward as if sharing a secret. "The way you put fans first, the way you fight for their interests—that's rare. I've been going through notes and reports, and it's clear you're having conversations that others just... aren't. I heard it straight from the horse's mouth at the Fans First meeting. You did not go unnoticed."

Rusty tilted his head, fixated on Garry's words. "Conversations about what?"

"Like the hard ones," Garry said smoothly. "The ones about how the organization might be failing its fans. Most of the people I've spoken with here don't seem to have the same level of interaction with our season ticket holders as you do, Rusty. I'd like to hear more about what you're seeing out there."

Rusty studied Garry, searching for a hint of sincerity in the polished veneer. "What I'm seeing? I'm seeing a lot of clients who feel like we're squeezing every last dollar out of them without giving much back—or at least giving them something exclusive. They're tired of broken promises and getting the runaround. Whether it's discounts to casual buyers or putting on events with players, only for the players to not show up, it's hard to feel momentum when expectations don't often meet reality." Garry nodded, his pen scribbling rapidly across his notepad. "Go on. Specifics are good."

"Take the new seat pricing tiers," Rusty said, leaning forward now. "We added all these extra fees, but what do fans get in return? Less access. Fewer perks. And don't get me started on the parking situation—it's a disaster. People are fed up."

Garry's grin tightened. "That's valuable insight, Rusty. And you've got to admit, it's not easy to hear. But that's why I need people like you. You're not afraid to call it like it is."

Rusty smirked. "Yeah, that's what gets me in trouble half the time."

"Not with me," Garry countered quickly. "I respect it. That passion, that drive—it's what this organization needs. Honestly, I wish more people here had the guts to say what's really going on. There's a difference between being a 'yes man' and being a 'company man.'"

Rusty's smirk faded, replaced by a flicker of surprise.

Garry leaned back in his chair, setting his pen down with a flourish. "Here's what I want, Rusty. Keep having those conversations with fans. Keep bringing me that feedback. If we're going to be the kind of organization that leads the league—not just on the ice but off it—it starts with knowing where we're falling short. And you're the guy who's in the trenches. You see it firsthand."

Rusty nodded slowly. "I'll keep doing what I do. But you're going to listen, right? I mean really listen? Nobody is making this shit up, Garry. Whatever you experienced elsewhere, I promise you that its nothing like this."

Garry placed a hand over his chest, his tone solemn. "Thank you, Rusty. I promise you; I'm listening. We all have a role to play in making this team the best it can be, and yours is vital. Don't ever doubt that."

The meeting ended with a handshake and a faintly genuine-seeming smile from Garry.

As Rusty walked out, he couldn't shake the feeling that he'd been both praised and played at the same time.

-Dan's Meeting-

With a look of confusion and concern, Dan entered Garry's office next, shutting the door carefully behind him. He gave Garry a curt nod before sitting down, his movements deliberate and composed.

"Dan, thanks for taking the time. How's everything going out there?" Garry asked, his voice as smooth as ever.

Dan leaned forward slightly, his expression flat. "Same as always, Michael," he said with a smirk. "I'm finding ways to support my team, making sure they're making calls, closing deals, keeping the ship afloat."

Garry leaned forward as well, mimicking a sense of camaraderie. "It's all right to feel duped, Dan. I know we started off on the wrong foot, but I hope you understand why I couldn't tip my hand then. I will say, however, that you handled yourself quite well. Let's put facades behind us and just cut to it, then. How do you feel about the team dynamic?"

Dan shrugged lightly. "It's fine. Could be better, but it's fine."

"Care to elaborate? I'm trying to understand the culture here," Garry pressed, his grin never wavering.

Dan hesitated, his gaze sharpening. "Honestly? The culture's been hit-or-miss this season. Normally, everyone is pretty jovial, but as the team goes, so does the culture. Not to mention, there's been a heavy feeling of distrust and anxiety presenting now more than ever—at least since you got here. Some folks feel like you're more focused on process than people."

The grin on Garry's face tightened. "Process is important, Dan. You know that. It ensures we're all rowing in the same direction. Don't you agree?"

Dan's lips twitched in what might have been a smirk. "Of course—if you know where the boat's going."

A flicker of irritation crossed Garry's features, but he nodded as though unfazed. "Noted. Thanks for your candour, Dan. That's exactly the kind of feedback I'm looking for." Dan nodded in return, his expression unreadable as he rose and left the room.

"Please send Frank in," Garry requested.

-Frank's Meeting-

Frank entered the office with the ease of a man who'd seen it all before. His salt-and-pepper hair gave him an elder statesman look. He wore a blazer that was just a touch too tight for the meeting, paired with a jovial smile that barely reached his eyes.

"Frank," Garry said warmly, rising from his chair to shake his hand. "Thanks for making the time. It's not every day I get to sit down with a true industry veteran."

Frank chuckled, sitting and leaning back as if the chair were his own. He quickly scanned the photos on Garry's wall. "Well, Garry, I don't know about 'veteran.' Seems like you've done more in this industry than me. But I have been around the block a few times."

"Yes, Frank. I have done more in the industry than you," Garry replied, his tone smooth, almost reverent. "But your experience... that's exactly why I've been looking forward to this conversation. Your experience is invaluable. You've seen this organization through ups and downs, highs and lows. There's a lot we can learn from someone like you."

Frank waved a hand dismissively, but his grin widened. "Ah, I just try to keep the wheels turning. Show up, do the job, and let the chips fall where they may."

"That's the kind of steady hand every team needs," Garry said, nodding as he jotted something down. Then he glanced up, his expression softening into something more inquisitive. "But, Frank, you know as well as I do—this industry is changing. Fast. Technology, fan engagement, the business side of things... it's all evolving. I've got to ask: how do you see yourself adapting to that?"

Frank gave a short laugh. "Adapting? Garry, when you've been in this game as long as you and I have, you don't adapt to the landscape—you shape it. Trends come and go, but relationships, trust—that's what matters in the long run."

Garry tilted his head, his grin tight. "Relationships and trust, sure. But I've heard... well, unconfirmed stories from before my time here. Things that might suggest, let's say, a more relaxed approach to professionalism. Particularly on work-related trips and activities."

Frank laughed heartily at that, his voice echoing off Garry's meticulously adorned walls. "Oh, those were the days! Back when things were a little more... let's call it flexible? But come on, Garry, that was ages ago. Different times, different rules."

Garry smiled, but his eyes remained sharp. "I get it. Times do change, and so do people. But I've got to be thorough, Frank. You understand. Are there any... details I should be aware of? Anything that might paint a clearer picture?"

Frank shook his head, still grinning. "Nothing you haven't already heard, I'm sure. And besides, it's all ancient history. These days, I'm about the work. Delivering results. That's what counts, right?"

"Absolutely," Garry agreed, his pen moving swiftly across the notepad. "Results are key. But culture, too. It's something I'm focused on—building a culture where accountability and trust are foundational."

"Accountability," Frank echoed, smirking. "Sure thing, Garry. If there's one thing you'll never have to worry about with me, it's me letting this team down. My track record speaks for itself."

"It does," Garry replied, leaning back and folding his hands together. "And it's impressive. Frank, I'll be honest—I appreciate everything you've brought to this team. Your history here is invaluable. But I also have to consider what comes next for this organization. You understand that, don't you?" Frank's smile didn't falter, but his eyes darkened just slightly. "Of course, Garry. Always looking ahead, right? Well, like I said, I'm here to do the work. Whatever that means for you and your plans."

"Good," Garry said, his grin widening again. "That's what I like to hear."

As Frank left the office, he cast one last glance at the wall of accolades behind Garry's desk, muttering something under his breath that might have been a chuckle.

Garry, meanwhile, sat in silence, his pen hovering over the page. Besides Frank's name, he scrawled and underlined:

Frank – Experienced, adaptable? Watch carefully.

-Salty's Meeting-

Salty eased into Garry Breckenridge's office, his well-worn polo shirt—with the team's logo from three redesigns ago—a subtle nod to his twenty-plus seasons with the team. He carried himself with humility and quiet pride, though his nerves betrayed him in the faint tap of his fingers against the chair as he sat down.

Garry greeted him with the usual wide grin, his pen poised over a blank notepad.

"Salvatore, or, I guess they call you Salty," Garry said, drawing out the nickname with exaggerated warmth. "A legend in this organization. Thanks for coming in."

"Happy to," Salty replied, shifting slightly. "Always glad to chat."

Garry nodded, setting the stage. "Twenty seasons is no small feat. You've seen the team through a lot—different managers, different eras, different... logos," Garry said, motioning to Salty's chest. "I bet you've got a unique perspective on some folks here. Mind if I pick your brain a bit?"

Salty smiled faintly, already sensing the direction this was going. "Sure. What do you need to know?"

"Let's start with Frank," Garry said, flipping through his notes. "Solid numbers. Strong reputation. But, as you might imagine, I've heard... stories. About the old days. You've known him a long time. What's your take?"

Salty's eyes flickered with hesitation. "Frank's... reliable. Always comes through when it counts. I respect him a lot. Knows the business inside and out."

"But?" Garry prompted, his grin sharpening.

Salty rubbed the back of his neck. "Well, he's... confident. Maybe too confident sometimes? Back in the day, that could get... complicated," he said softly before repeating, "Back in the day, that got complicated. But we've all grown up, right?"

Garry chuckled, jotting something down. "Right. Complicated how?"

Salty hesitated, then shook his head. "Nothing worth rehashing. Those were the days, as Frank would say."

Garry's grin widened. "I see. What about Rusty? He's... a character, isn't he? Outspoken."

Salty's demeanour shifted, his tone brightening. "Rusty's one of the best. Passionate, knowledgeable, and reliable.

Outspoken? He advocates for what's fair and doesn't say something unless it's well thought. He cares about the fans, the team, the work. You can't ask for more than that."

"And Dan?" Garry pressed.

"Same deal," Salty said firmly. "Dan's the glue that holds everything together. Smart, calm under pressure. Tremendous emotional intelligence. He knows how to get things done. If I'm brutally honest, he does more than his fair share."

Garry leaned back slightly, tapping his pen against the notepad. "Honesty is the only way to go, Salty. And what about Kent?"

Salty hesitated for a beat too long. "Kent... knows his priorities. He's here when he needs to be. He leaves work at the office. We could learn from Kent in that sense. That's gotta count for something, right?"

Garry tilted his head, clearly enjoying the visible effort it took for Salty to keep his tone even. "Anything else? What about Shane?"

"Well," Salty said, forcing a faint smile, "he's an acquired taste and the alpha male. He's... persistent, a little crazy. Likely undiagnosed ADHD, but it works for him because... you know he's not going to quit on something once he starts. He's a character but shows his character through his sales leadership. He's our top guy by leaps and bounds."

"Persistent," Garry repeated, his grin sharpening. "I'll make a note of that."

Salty shifted uncomfortably, eager to move on. "What else do you need?"

Garry leaned forward slightly, his tone softening. "Let's talk about you, Salty. Twenty seasons is a long time to stay in one place. What's next for you? Do you see yourself in Kent's role? Or Dan's? Or something else entirely?"

Salty's eyes narrowed slightly at the mention of Kent's position. "Kent's role? No. That's Dan's seat if he wants it. He's the only one who can handle it, and ... Dan's the only one who could make it better."

"And you?" Garry asked, his pen poised again.

Salty paused, gathering his thoughts. "I'd like to lead. But I don't think I'd bring much to the retention team—they're all great leaders already. Maybe if we were to create something new. A role in managing the inside sales team. That's where I could make a real difference. Mould those reps, help them grow, shape them into what the organization needs."

Garry perked up at that, leaning forward. "Interesting. Shaping the team in the organization's image. That's exactly what I'm looking to do—change the culture, align it with our vision. Tell me more about how you'd see that role working."

Salty relaxed slightly, sensing genuine interest. "It's about mentorship. Setting clear expectations ensures the younger reps have a roadmap to success and a path to grow their careers. Building a team that understands the organization's values and carries them forward. Yes, I get this is a sales department, but it can't be just about hitting numbers—it's about creating a culture of winners."

Garry nodded slowly, his grin returning in full force. "I like the sound of that, Salty. Very much. Let's keep this conversation going another time. I think there's real potential here."

As Salty left the office, he felt relief and cautious optimism. Behind him, Garry scribbled furiously in his notes, underlining Inside Sales Leadership and adding a star beside Salty's name.

-Jay's Meeting-

Jay stepped into Garry Breckenridge's office next, offering a cautious smile, his hands gripping the strap of his messenger bag. His suit jacket was slightly too large, and his tie hung just a little loose, giving him the look of someone still adjusting to the corporate world. He hesitated for a moment before sitting down, his eyes darting to the walls lined with Garry's framed photos and accolades.

"Jay! Come on in," Garry said, beaming as he gestured toward the chair opposite his desk. "Glad we could have this chat."

"Thank you, Garry. I appreciate it," Jay said, his voice earnest but tinged with a nervous edge. "It's nice to get some one-on-one time."

"Absolutely," Garry replied, leaning back and folding his hands. "I've been hearing great things about you. You've really hit the ground running since you joined. How are you feeling about things so far?"

Jay straightened up. "Uh... things are good, but... this is my sixth season with the team. I wouldn't say I've recently joined."

Garry froze for half a second, his grin faltering as he quickly glanced at the folder on his desk. "Ah," he said, recovering quickly. "My mistake. That question was meant for Max. I apologize. Let's start again."

Jay nodded, still slightly perplexed but willing to go along. "No problem."

"So, Jay," Garry continued, leaning forward slightly to re-establish his rhythm, "what's your take on the culture here? You've been with the team for six seasons, so I imagine you've got some valuable insight."

Jay paused, considering his words carefully. "I think the culture is… okay. It's shifted a bit over the years. People work hard, but there's a lot of pressure. Sometimes it feels like we're just running on a hamster wheel without a clear goal."

Garry jotted something in his notes, nodding. "Interesting. And what about the feedback you're hearing from the fans? Our season ticket holders, specifically. What are they saying?"

Jay relaxed slightly, encouraged by the change in topic. "Well, honestly? A lot of what I hear is frustration. They feel like the organization's priorities are shifting away from them. The pricing changes haven't gone over well, and some people feel like they're getting less for more money. Parking's a big one, too—there are constant complaints about that."

"Parking," Garry repeated, writing it down. "And the pricing changes?"

"Yeah," Jay said, leaning forward slightly. "It's not just the cost. It's that the perks aren't what they used to be. There's less access, fewer exclusive events. People used to feel part of something special, and now it's just… transactional. But so many of our fans are 'what have you done for me lately?' and the truth is, not much."

Garry tapped his pen against the desk, his grin returning in full force. "That's great feedback, Jay. Really valuable stuff. It lines up with some of the other conversations I've been having. Rusty mentioned similar concerns about fan engagement. Would you say you agree with his perspective?"

Jay nodded slowly. "Yeah, Rusty's got his finger on the pulse when it comes to our fans. He listens, he understands their frustrations, and honestly, he's not afraid to say what needs to be said. I think a lot of us feel the same way, but he's the one who actually speaks up about it."

Garry smiled, twirling his pen between his fingers. "That's what I keep hearing. And what about your own role, Jay? Where do you see yourself within this organization long-term?"

Jay hesitated for a moment, choosing his words carefully. "Honestly, I love working in sports. I love the energy, the fans, the way every day is different. But I also want to feel like I'm growing, like there's a clear path forward."

Garry leaned in slightly. "And do you feel like you have that path here?"

Jay exhaled, his fingers tightening around his bag strap. "I don't know. I've been here six seasons and had some great moments, but sometimes it feels like unless you're a top producer or in the right conversations, you're just... existing."

Garry's grin widened. "That's exactly why I wanted to meet with you. I want to change that, Jay. I want people like you—dedicated, passionate people—to feel like there's a future here. That this isn't just a stepping stone or a place to stagnate. If you could carve out your ideal role in this organization, what would that look like?"

Jay blinked, surprised by the question. "I mean... I love sales, but I also love the storytelling side of things. I'm always coming up with ideas for engagement and ways to connect with fans on a deeper level. Maybe something in branding, marketing, fan outreach? Something where I'm not just selling but helping build something."

Garry nodded thoughtfully, making a note. "That's good to know, Jay. I like the way you think. We'll have to talk more about this down the road."

Jay gave a cautious smile. "I'd like that."

"Great. That's all for now. Thanks for your honesty—I really appreciate it. Can you send Max in?"

Jay stood, adjusting his tie slightly. "Sure thing." He left the office, his mind racing.

As Jay left, Garry sat back in his chair, tapping his pen against his notes. Beside Jay's name, he wrote: Insightful, steady, aligned with Rusty. Keep engaged. His gaze flicked to a photo on the wall of him shaking hands with a league commissioner, a satisfied grin creeping back onto his face.

-Max's Meeting-

Max strode into Garry's office enthusiastically, clutching a notebook under his arm. He sat down, eyes bright with curiosity, looking around at the framed accolades as if he were taking notes on them, too.

Garry chuckled, leaning forward. "Max, you are an interesting guy."

Max grinned. "Thanks, I think?"

"You've got ideas. Big ones. I've heard from Rusty that you're already looking at ways to enhance the fan experience, build engagement, and create more brand affinity. That's exactly the kind of thinking I want in this organization."

Max straightened up, beaming. "I appreciate that, Garry. I just think that fans are the heartbeat of this whole thing. You make them feel special, and they'll stick with you through anything. But right now? I think we're making it harder for them to feel valued."

Garry nodded, his pen scratching against the notepad. "That's what I'm hearing. So tell me, what would you do to fix it?"

Max didn't hesitate. "I think we need to rethink our perks, our engagement strategies. We need to reward loyalty in ways that matter to fans, not just with another generic lanyard or lapel pin. We should give them experiences—things they can talk about, brag about, show off."

Garry smirked. "Like the locker room cleanout idea?"

Max's eyes lit up. "Exactly! Stuff like that. Things they can't get anywhere else. Make them feel part of something exclusive, not just another transaction."

Garry jotted down a few more notes. "And what about you, Max? Where do you see yourself long-term?"

Max hesitated briefly but then shrugged. "Honestly? I just want to be in a place where I can keep thinking creatively and making an impact. I love sales, but I also love strategy. If I could blend the two? That'd be the dream."

Garry's eyes gleamed. "Well, Max, I think you might just be in the right place at the right time."

Max tilted his head. "What do you mean?"

Garry set his pen down, his grin widening. "Let's just say I've got a few ideas too. Let's keep this conversation going. For now, though, great work. Keep those ideas flowing. We'll talk soon."

Max stood, shaking Garry's hand firmly. "Looking forward to it."

As Max left, Garry leaned back in his chair, staring at the list of names in front of him. He waited patiently for Kristina to walk in.

-Kristina's Meeting-

Garry's interviews—though they felt more like interrogations—continued with Kristina. Like others, Kristina took the opportunity to share her thoughts and helping Garry paint a clearer picture of processes, culture, expectations, and reality.

Kristina came in last, a folder of neatly organized notes tucked under her arm. She sat down without waiting for an invitation, her posture confident and professional.

"Kristina, I've been hearing great things about you," Garry began, flipping through a file in front of him. "Thank you, Garry. I've been working hard to keep things moving," Kristina replied with a polite smile.

Garry nodded as he scanned her numbers. "Impressive sales numbers this season. It's a nice mix of new and renewal. What's your secret?"

"Consistency," Kristina answered. "Staying ahead of renewals and focusing on relationships with clients. I try to meet with clients in their natural habitat. I find that shows them I want their business and that I won't wait for them to come to me."

"Relationships. That's key. And what about your colleagues? How would you describe your role within the team?" Garry asked, his pen hovering over the page.

"I try to lead by example. Help where I can, keep things professional," she replied steadily. "I've asked Dan for more responsibility, and I've sat in on several league-wide meetings lately to learn best practices that could potentially be implemented here."

Garry's grin widened again. "Drive and determination. I like that. Very professional. One last question—where do you see yourself in the next few years?"

Kristina didn't hesitate. "Growing within the organization. Moving into leadership roles where I can make a bigger impact."

"Interesting. Thanks, Kristina. Very insightful," Garry said, closing the file.

Kristina cautiously walked out of Garry's office. Now, Garry looked at the stack of notes he had taken with most of the sales pit. He had everything he needed from everyone in the sales pit. Everyone except for Kent.

-Kent's Meeting-

Garry picked up his phone and scanned a laminated sheet pinned to the back wall of his desk, listing extensions. He dialled Kent's number and asked him to come by.

As Kent entered Garry Breckenridge's office, he carried himself with a forced air of confidence—his robotic movements betraying the nervous energy he was trying to suppress. His tie was perfectly knotted, his suit freshly pressed, but the way he adjusted his cuffs and darted glances at Garry's wall of accolades gave him away.

"Kent," Garry greeted with his trademark grin, gesturing to the chair across from his desk. "Thanks for coming in. I've been looking forward to this conversation."

Kent nodded quickly and sank into the chair. "Of course, Garry. Me too."

"Good," Garry said, leaning forward slightly, his pen poised over his notepad. "You've been in your position for a while now, right? Overseeing the sales team?"

"Uh, yes," Kent replied. "It's been a great experience. Lots of moving parts, but I think we're doing well."

Garry tilted his head, his grin sharpening. "Doing well. Let's unpack that a bit. How would you define 'well' in terms of results? Will we hit the numbers we need to hit? And, more importantly, how are we keeping our season ticket holders engaged?"

Kent blinked, his mouth opening slightly before he spoke. "Well, uh, our renewal rates are... stable. Not perfect, of course, but we're holding steady. This year has been trying. And we'll have to see how things are going now that the renewal campaign is in full force. I'm hearing some early win renewals and escalation calls that will need to take place. And, uh, engagement—well, I think the team's doing a good job. They're reaching out regularly, keeping that line of communication open, ya know?"

Garry nodded slowly, his eyes never leaving Kent. "Stable. Not perfect. Hmm. Let me ask you this: what specific processes have you implemented to ensure our season ticket holders feel valued?"

Kent hesitated, fidgeting with the edge of his notebook. "Well, we've, uh, been focusing on... personalized touchpoints. You know, like in-seat visits, hosting, and... um, some targeted campaigns."

Garry raised an eyebrow. "In-seat visits," he repeated, his tone neutral, though a slight edge of skepticism crept in. "And these targeted campaigns—what kind of results are you seeing from those?"

Kent flipped hastily through his notebook, his movements a blur. "I don't have the exact numbers in front of me, but I think they've been... positive?"

Garry's grin remained, but his eyes hardened. "I see. Let's pivot to sales culture. It's something I'm focused on heavily. What do you think needs to change about our culture to drive better results?"

Kent sat back slightly, his brow furrowing. "Change the culture? Um... well, I think, uh, maybe more team-building activities could help? You know, get everyone more aligned and... and motivated. Not now, obviously, but yeah, the sales team could use a boost."

"How so? I've noticed a very cohesive group of sales professionals. The retention team is a tight-knit group, and everyone is a leader with drive, passion, and professionalism."

Garry's pen hovered over his notepad as he waited for Kent to continue before he deliberately echoed, "Team-building activities. Interesting." He slowly placed his pen down on top of the notepad. "Anything else?"

Kent shifted uncomfortably, his gaze dropping to the desk. "We could look at... streamlining some processes? Make things a bit more efficient?"

"Such as?" Garry pressed, his tone sharp enough to make Kent flinch.

"Well, uh..." Kent stammered, clearly grasping for an answer. "I'd have to... look into that more. Get feedback from the team. You know, figure out where the bottlenecks are."

Garry leaned back in his chair, studying Kent intently. "Kent, let me be honest with you. From where I'm sitting, it seems like there's a lot of room for improvement. And I have to wonder—how are you dividing your responsibilities with Dan? What's your role versus his?"

Kent swallowed hard, his throat bobbing. "Well, Dan's... great. He's very hands-on, so he handles a lot of the day-to-day stuff. I focus more on... the big picture. Strategy."

Garry's grin widened, though it was anything but warm. "The big picture. Strategy. Right. So, in your view, are we on track to achieve your big-picture goals?"

Kent hesitated again, his voice quieter now. "I think we could... be doing better. But with some adjustments, I'm confident we can get there."

Garry nodded, picking up his pen once more. "Adjustments. Noted. Anything else you'd like to add about your vision for the team or the organization?"

Kent shook his head quickly. "No, I think that covers it."

"All right," Garry said. "Thanks for your time, Kent. I'll see you at tomorrow's meeting."

Kent stood, smoothing his jacket as he left the office. His back was stiff, his movements even more robotic. Behind him, Garry scribbled furiously in his notes. Beside Kent's name, he wrote: Unprepared. Ineffective. Relies on Dan. Then he underlined it twice before tapping his pen thoughtfully against the desk again.

Garry stared at the pile of notes on his desk, his interviews now complete. He offered the pile a smile before turning his chair around to face the blank wall behind him. It was time to put things into motion.

And big changes were coming.

CHAPTER 33

"Rusty's Tipping Point"

That same day, Frank shuffled into Rusty, Shane, and Jay's pod and leaned against Rusty's desk, absently tossing a stress ball between his hands. His normally steady demeanour was frayed.

"Tell me I'm not the only one who felt like I was on trial in there," he muttered.

Rusty didn't look up from his monitor. "You're not the only one, Frank," he said, his voice clipped, the usual sarcasm absent. "It's like we were applying for our jobs."

"Jesus, Rusty, are you okay?" Frank asked. "You look like shit."

"Whatever, Frank. I'm just done with all of this."

"I've had more comfortable conversations with angry clients," Salty said as he clutched a stack of papers and mail. He stopped and turned around when he overheard Rusty's comment. "We're all done with this, Rusty. This isn't just about you, man. It's a long grind for all of us."

"Stay out of this, Sal," Rusty said dismissively.

"It's like he was digging for something," Frank said, quickly changing the subject, attempting to cut the tension. "You'd think twenty years with this team would count for something, but... I don't know, right, Salty?"

"Tell me about it," Salty said with an uneasy tone as he tossed a few pieces of mail onto Rusty's desk.

"He's a snake," Rusty started. "The kind who greets you with a smile but then stabs you in the back. Garry Breckenridge— he's the quintessential grin-fucker, amplified tenfold!" he proclaimed, gesturing dramatically as if pitching a movie to an eager audience.

Jay, seated at the next desk, chimed in hesitantly. "I don't know if he's that bad. I mean, he asked me a lot about the fans and culture. Felt like he wanted to understand, you know? Maybe he's just hard to read."

"Hard to read?" Rusty scoffed, finally turning away from his screen as he raised an envelope Shane had sent out last week. "This is hard to read... and embarrassing," he muttered, tossing the envelope onto Shane's chair with a snort. "Where the hell is Shane? We all need to yell at him!"

"He's too busy kissing Garry's ass," Frank chuckled darkly.

"That's probably the safest place for anyone to be right now," Jay added.

Beyond the pod, the air in the pit felt heavier than usual, weighed down by the lingering unease from Garry Breckenridge's one-on-one meetings. Conversations were quieter and more secretive. The usual constant banter had turned into sporadic, strained exchanges as the pressure of renewals took over. Everyone felt it—everyone felt off from the scrutiny, the tension, the looming sense of judgment.

The beer and wings bus trip Frank had been tasked with organizing couldn't be executed in time, nor was there much interest. The three home games against non-traditional hockey teams had netted the team three out of a possible six points— one win, one loss, and an overtime loss. Now, they were embarking on a five-game road trip with stops in New York, Long Island, New Jersey, Boston, and Carolina. Falling deeper in the standings and out of the playoff race altogether seemed like a legitimate possibility against a series of strong teams.

Yes, despite everything, the sales team tried to focus on their calls, emails, and pre-renewal follow-ups; they really had no choice in this thankless, what-have-you-done-for-me-lately sales environment. Yet their minds kept drifting back to their one-on-one meetings with Garry Breckenridge.

Rusty sat hunched at his desk, furiously typing away as he worked through his renewal calls. For Shane, the sound of Rusty's keyboard clicks was reminiscent of when he cut his toenails a few seasons ago. He remembered fondly how his overgrown big toe talon had hilariously shot into the air, over the fluorescent light dangling from the ceiling above the pod and onto Rusty's head. The thought amused Shane, and he started to laugh to himself. Beyond his quiet chuckles, a subdued silence filled the pit.

As Rusty finished one email, his focus was broken by a ping from his inbox. The sender was unfamiliar: Tammy.

"Dare I open this?" he muttered, squinting at the subject line.

With a resigned sigh, he clicked and opened the email.

Hello Richard,

My name is Tammy, and I just wanted to thank you for expressing interest in becoming a consultant for the great opportunity you attended a few weeks ago. Please find enclosed the start-up package, complete with a sign-up form and your invoice for $500...

Rusty's jaw tightened as his eyes scanned the email. "You fucking snake!" he hissed under his breath. "I knew you fucking sewered me, Shane!" His fists clenched as he imagined yanking Shane up by his collar and punching him in the face.

Before he could process his next move, another email came in, this one from Kent. Rusty rolled his eyes and clicked it open with little enthusiasm.

The subject line read: Donuts and Muffins...

Donuts and muffins are on the table in the sales pit.

There were another seventy-five renewals submitted yesterday—that's not nearly good enough, boys. We need three big days to get to our weekly goal, and you are all expected to do what you can to close business. Our deadline is in 10 days. Get at it!

P.S: An assortment of healthy wraps and sandwiches will be brought in every day this week for lunch so you can keep at it.

Salty, Rusty, Frank, Jay, and Kristina groaned audibly from all over the pit.

"Why don't you get on the phones and make some calls, Kent?" Rusty muttered to himself. "You think donuts, muffins, and sandwiches are going to make me work any fucking harder? Go fuck yourself."

"Fuck you, Wally," Frank muttered from the adjacent pod, not even looking up from his work.

Rusty returned to his renewal list, grinding his teeth as he tried to focus. Moments later, Max appeared at his desk, a powdered donut in hand.

"What's your favourite, Rusty?" Max asked, crumbs already dusting his shirt.

Rusty reached up, gently pushing Max's arm away from his face. His gaze was sharp, his patience thin.

"Any donut I can eat without hidden motives. They taste so much better."

Max, unfazed, pointed toward the table. "There's a whole box over there. All different kinds. If you hurry, the picking's still good. I can get you one if you want?"

"Yeah, I know. We all got Kent's email, Max," Rusty replied, his tone clipped. "No thanks."

"They're delicious," Max said, taking another bite.

"I bet they taste like broken promises and desperation," Rusty muttered, glaring at the glob of cream from Max's donut that had just dropped onto his desk.

"Sorry," Max said, sheepishly grabbing a napkin.

Rusty's expression softened slightly, though his tone remained firm. "It's not just the food, Max. Don't let these superficial gestures, like donuts and wraps, taint your judgment. They don't change the fact that the underlying reality remains thankless."

"What do you mean, Rusty?" Max asked, having now finished his donut.

"Come on, Max. They give us donuts and wraps today, tomorrow, and the rest of the week, but next week they'll tell us we didn't work hard enough, we didn't hit our goals, and we need to 'do better.'"

"You said taint," Shane said from across the room.

"Grow up, Shane," Rusty snapped, shaking his head.

Around the table of donuts, Salty and Kristina huddled, their conversation low but laced with tension.

"They can't keep doing this," Kristina said, her voice trembling slightly.

"They don't care," Salty replied, crossing his arms. "You think I will work weekends or past my bedtime for them? No chance. I've calculated it—we're working an extra 30 days a year for this so-called dream job." It was the same calculation he had shared with Max. Unfortunately, it didn't surprise Kristina or Frank nearly as much as it surprised Max.

Now hungry, Frank came by the table for a donut of his own. He shrugged, focusing more on the honey cruller in his hand. "It's brutal. But they don't care. We're expendable. Remember Ken's motivational speech? 'There's a whole lineup of eager beavers waiting, ready to take your job,'" Frank said in a voice that resembled Bullwinkle. "Fucking take it then!"

Jay also joined the group, visibly frustrated but now holding a donut of his own. "Do you not think it's kind of bullshit that it seems like they're waiting to see how renewals go before confirming our comp plan rates?"

"It's manipulation, plain and simple," Rusty said, popping up from behind the pod wall. The others nodded fiercely. "It's illegal, too."

"Retroactively denying bonuses? Changing targets after the fact? That's theft."

"Remember the sales contest last year?" Salty added.

Frank laughed bitterly. "Classic bait-and-switch. This place, man."

Now stuffing his third donut down his throat, Shane gave his thoughts. "Why hasn't anyone gotten used to this yet? You are all the moodiest whiners I've ever met. You kid needs to grow up!"

"What are you talking about?" Frank growled. "You're the least mature of any of us! Even me!"

"If you are expecting to be paid a bonus and it doesn't happen, even if you hit your target, wouldn't you be pissed off, Shane?" asked Rusty, still standing behind the pod wall.

"First of all, yes, I was pissed off because I hit my target, but I didn't sit around and whine about it. I took care of it."

"What do you mean, you took care of it?" Jay asked.

"Easy, I just started threatening to leave," Shane explained proudly.

"You threatened to quit?!" Rusty gasped.

"They can't afford to lose their top sales guy, can they? It was either me or not pay the bonus. They made the right call, Rusty."

"So wait, you blackmailed them to pay you your bonus?" Rusty asked, now getting in Shane's face.

"Paying me what we agreed to? Paying me what was in my comp plan? I don't call that blackmailing Rusty; more like collective bargaining."

Rusty's face hardened. "This is unbelievable, Shane! It's just another way to show us we're nothing but numbers to them. There is zero integrity and not even close to an even playing field either!"

"Speaking of integrity. Let's call a timeout here. We need to keep it down. I think now, more than ever, there are targets on our backs," Salty said, acknowledging Garry as he walked back into his office and shut the door.

The day dragged on, and the pit was still humming with keyboard clicks and hushed conversations. The fluorescent lights cast an unrelenting glow over the tired faces of the sales team, their expressions drawn and weary. Nobody wanted to be here this late, but nobody wanted to be the first to leave, either. The stress of the renewal campaign, the scrutiny of

Garry's leadership, and the creeping fear of job insecurity kept them tethered to their desks.

Rusty sat back down, rubbing his hands together, his breath shallow and uneven. He was still furious at Shane for admitting he had threatened to leave in order to be paid a bonus. It was such an ignorant thing to do.

Rusty's phone buzzed in his pocket. He didn't need to look to know it was Amy. He had ignored her last three calls, letting them go to voicemail. He knew what she'd likely say: 'Come home. Please', Why aren't you home yet?', 'Why aren't you talking to me?', 'We need to talk', 'Why aren't you home yet?'

But Rusty didn't want to talk. He didn't have the words, and he didn't have the strength. He swallowed hard and sent another call to voicemail. A second later, the notification popped up. 1 New Voicemail. 4 Total Messages. He stared at the screen, but his fingers wouldn't move to dial. Instead, he set the phone face-down on his desk and refocused on the renewal list in front of him.

Jay leaned back in his chair, cracking his knuckles as he glanced toward Rusty. "You look like you haven't slept in a week, man. Are you ok?"

Rusty forced a smirk, but it didn't reach his eyes. "I haven't. No. I am not."

Jay frowned. "Yeah, well... maybe you should."

Salty, who had been eavesdropping from his desk, glanced at Rusty. "You've been running yourself into the ground, dude. What's going on?"

Rusty shook his head and turned back to his screen. "Just trying to stay ahead of the numbers."

Salty wasn't buying it. "You're ahead of the numbers. You know that. This is something else. What's going on?"

Rusty exhaled sharply, his grip tightening on his pen. "Just drop it, Sal. Please," he begged.

Salty studied him, then sat back down as he shrugged. He should let a lot of things go and let it go with Rusty for now.

At the other end of the pit, Kristina closed out of her CRM dashboard and stretched. "Anyone else feel like this is the longest week of their life?"

Frank snorted, tossing a crumpled sticky note into the trash. "Longest? This place ages you in dog years, and I'm one of those old dogs whose back legs don't work, and now I need a dog wheelchair."

Shane sauntered over, finishing off the last bite of his fifth donut. "That explains why Rusty looks like he's pushing 60."

Rusty shot him a look but didn't bother responding. His eye began twitching.

Kristina rolled her eyes. "Shane, don't be a dick. Besides, dogs in wheelchairs get me every time." She held her heart.

"Relax," Shane said, holding up his hands. "I'm just saying. We're all stressed, but Rusty's got that thousand-yard stare going on. Like he's been through some real shit."

For a moment, nobody spoke. The silence was palpable.

Then, out of nowhere, Rusty laughed. It wasn't a happy laugh. It was the kind of laugh that carried weight, that teetered on the edge of exhaustion and something darker. "You have no idea," he muttered.

Kristina's brows furrowed. "Rusty..."

But before she could finish, Kent's voice rang out from the other side of the room. "Team, quick huddle before I head out for the night."

A collective groan rippled through the pit, but everyone dragged themselves toward Kent and Wally standing in front of the photocopier. Everyone except Rusty.

Wally cleared his throat. "Okay, listen. I know the last couple of weeks have been tough. The pressure's high, I get it. But you need to push through. You have ten days left in this renewal period, and you're behind. You need to make up ground."

Rusty crossed his arms, still seated in the pod. "So, what? Can there be any more pressure already put on us, Wally? Wait, I'm getting one more email about fucking muffins?" Rusty's voice carried through the sales pit.

A few people chuckled, but Kent's face remained stone-cold. "No, Rusty. More effort. This is our livelihood. If we don't deliver, the organization will make changes. We all know what that means." The laughter died immediately.

Rusty finally spoke again, his voice low but razor-sharp as he slowly stood. "What exactly are you saying, Kent?"

Kent exhaled, choosing his words carefully. "I'm saying that this isn't the time to slack off. Everyone needs to dig deep. Find another gear."

Rusty scoffed. "We've been grinding for weeks, Kent. If there were another gear, we'd be in it by now."

Kent ignored him. "Just stay focused. Get your renewals in. We can't afford to let this slip."

The huddle broke, but nobody felt any better.

As the team dispersed, Kristina lingered behind, waiting until the others were out of earshot before approaching Rusty. "Hey," she said softly. "You sure you're okay?"

Rusty hesitated. The answer was no. No, he was not okay. He was barely keeping his head above water. But despite all the advice he had dispensed to Shane or Max lately, admitting that he was struggling felt like a surrender. But Rusty was struggling and desperately trying not to wave the white flag.

"I'm fine," he said, forcing a smirk.

Kristina didn't believe him, but she nodded anyway. "Okay. Just... don't burn yourself out anymore."

Rusty didn't reply right away. "I'm just...tired. I'm fucking done, Krissy."

Kristina sat down in Jay's chair. She wanted to speak but couldn't find the right words. "You're not alone, Rusty. It's been a long day. Everyone's on edge from their interviews with Garry. I think we all feel like you do. But we all need you to take care of yourself. We need you to take care of your wife and your daughter. Frank needs to do the same. So does Salty. Everyone needs to. I'm here for you if you find your words, buddy."

Unresponsive, Rusty simply stared at the ceiling until Kristina stood up, shot him a soft smile and walked out of the pod.

As the office emptied, he continued staring at the ceiling, trying to find an answer to his frustrations, yet he continued seeing nothing. Then his phone buzzed again. Yet another call from Amy.

He closed his eyes, exhaling shakily. He knew he was hiding. He knew he had to face her, eventually. Had to face the inevitable.

But not yet. How could he?

So, he let the call ring out. His sixth missed call from his wife. Then he picked up his headset and dialled another client. Because as long as he was working, he wasn't thinking. And as long as he wasn't thinking, he could keep running.

CHAPTER 34

"The Next Day"

After furiously typing away at another email, Rusty stood up from his desk and started to pace. His shoulders were hunched, his eyes bloodshot, and his jaw clenched tight. He worked with a single-minded intensity as if stopping for even a moment would cause everything to unravel.

Shane and Jay found Rusty pacing near the photocopier, visibly agitated. "Can anyone generate an invoice here? Anyone?"

"The invoice server is down because of the concert on-sale," Salty explained without even looking up.

"Unbelievable," Rusty snapped. "I'm trying to close two renewals, and I can't even print the fucking invoice!" He continued to pace. His breathing short. His blood boiling. "This is fucking BRUTAL!"

Kent's door opened, his head poking out. "Settle down, Rusty."

Rusty whirled around. "Settle down? I'm tired of this! Nothing works, nothing changes, and we're just supposed to 'do what we can' like it's all on us!" Rusty's words now fast.

The white flag starting to rise inside him. "But hey, don't worry, none of us are slacking, KENT!"

Dan also emerged from his office, his expression firm as he pointed inside. "Rusty, get in here."

"Fuck you, Dan!" Rusty snapped.

"Get in here!" Dan yelled back, unfazed. He aggressively pointed to his open door. "Let's talk."

"Talk? We've talked, Dan. We've all aired our grievances. We all met with Garry. We've all sat in on meetings and impromptu pit chats, the only outcome of which is to have more meetings. Nothing happens. Nothing is ever good enough. What's the fucking point?" Invisible to everyone else, Rusty had raised the white flag, and it was now flapping wildly in the hurricane-force wind.

Rusty hadn't noticed Wally and Garry emerging from Garry's office, but Dan did. "Richard," Dan demanded, his voice now low but authoritative. "For your own good, get the fuck in here, man!"

Rusty hesitated, glaring at Dan, who quickly shifted his gaze to Garry's office before returning it to Rusty.

Rusty angrily shrugged and started following Dan into his office after slamming his pen and notebook to the ground.

Having witnessed the spectacle, Max ran over to pick up Rusty's items and returned them to his desk.

Jay noticed Max, lowered his eyes and nodded quietly. Then he stood and watched the door shut behind them, shaking his head. "Tensions are boiling over."

Salty sighed. "And they're only going to get worse."

Hours after Rusty's tipping point, the atmosphere in the pit and Wally's stern words forced everyone to put their heads down and get back to work. Conversations between colleagues were minimal. Each word weighed down by the tension that had consumed the room.

Rusty's frustration didn't just come out of nowhere but seemed to come out of nowhere that day. His frustrations were not unique. Everyone felt similar frustration. But they desperately tried to keep their own sanity together. Rusty's frustration had quickly spiralled out of control, but it had been building up for days. He hadn't slept for days, maybe even weeks. The lack of sleep was certainly a contributing factor to his erratic behaviour. His mind kept spiralling, and it was unrelenting.

Max sat at his desk, surrounded by piles of notes and spreadsheets. The unrelenting pressure to perform kept him in his seat well into the evening, mirroring the example set by the veterans around him.

But even through the haze of his own fatigue, Max couldn't help but notice that something about Rusty had really changed. Especially today.

The next morning, Rusty did not come into the office.

The office felt off. At least not in the way it had over the past few weeks or with Garry's scrutiny hanging over them like a storm cloud. The one-on-one meetings with Garry and the lack of direction made everyone uneasy.

Rusty's absence spoke volumes. Rusty was always there grinding through renewal calls, pacing by the photocopier, muttering about numbers, strategy, or how management was out of touch. If he wasn't at his desk, he was hovering by someone else's, half-working, half-letting his colleagues bitch about something and trying to calm their nerves and fears.

But today, his chair sat empty. His desk, untouched from the day before, just prior to him practically blowing up in front of everyone including Wally two days earlier, with Kent, and almost Garry, Wally the day before. His headset remained where he had left it, the cord coiled neatly in an unnatural way, like he had meant to pick it up but never got the chance.

No one said anything at first.

But Jay was the first to notice, his eyes flicking toward Rusty's desk before looking at Kristina. "Anyone hear from him?" he asked, keeping his voice low.

Frank shook his head, his fingers hovering over his keyboard from the other side of the pod wall. "Nope. Nothing. No texts, no emails."

"Maybe he just needed a day." Jay continued his conversation with Frank. "We've all wanted to disappear lately. Maybe he turned off his alarm and slept in."

Frank leaned back in his chair, chewing the inside of his cheek. "Nah. Rusty doesn't just not show up. Even when he's sick, he's here, hacking up a lung on the phones."

Shane, who had been scrolling through his phone, snorted. "Maybe he finally said 'fuck it' and just quit."

Nobody laughed.

Unbeknownst to anyone else in the pit, Rusty was grappling with a loss that had shattered his entire world.

Two days prior, Amy had called him several times. At first, it was just to say she wasn't feeling well. That something felt off, but she wasn't sure what it was. She told him she was cramping, that it felt different than anything she had experienced before with Emma. Rusty barely registered her words, nodding along as he skimmed through emails.

"Drink some water, babe. Try to relax and lie down. I'll be home later," he advised.

An hour later, the phone rang again. This time, her voice was shaking.

"Rusty, I need you to come home. Please. Something is wrong."

There was panic in her tone, a raw desperation that should have snapped him to attention. But instead, Rusty exhaled sharply, rubbing the bridge of his nose as he stared at the never-ending list of non-renewals. He was already behind. He could not afford to fall further behind.

"I'll be home soon," he said, fully intending to come. But then he got distracted when he was called into his one-on-one meeting with Garry. The worry for his wife's well-being likely contributed to how short he was answering Garry's questions. By the time his one-on-one was over, he forgot all about Amy's call. Forgot what she had called about and mistook all her other calls for Amy wanting to start a fight. Not today. Not at the office. This wasn't a good time.

But Amy called again. And again. Each time, he let it go to voicemail.

His racing thoughts added even more excuses in his head: 'She's just upset that I've been working late.' 'She wants me to drop everything again.' 'She's probably just overreacting.' 'She just doesn't understand how much pressure I'm under. She just doesn't care.'

By the time he finally walked out of the office, it was much later. The pit was empty, his teammates long gone. His inbox was clear. His numbers were steady.

Amy had stopped calling. Crisis averted.

But he still had five unread voicemails.

For the first time all day, unease settled in his chest. He pulled out his phone as he stepped into the parking lot, his stomach twisting as he scrolled through the missed calls.

There were seven in total. He swallowed hard and tapped her contact, pressing the phone to his ear. It rang once. Twice.

Three times. Then, for the first time in their entire relationship, his call went straight to voicemail.

His fingers tightened around the steering wheel the entire drive home, tension creeping into his shoulders. He told himself she was just mad. He prepared to eat shit as soon as he got home. He convinced himself that she was trying to make a point. That he'd walk through the front door, she'd yell at him for working late, and they'd argue like they always did.

But as soon as he stepped inside, he knew—

He was too late. The house was eerily quiet. He could smell something. What the fuck was that smell? Then he heard a soft noise coming from upstairs. The only sound was Amy's quiet, broken sobs from the bedroom.

He ran up the stairs two steps at a time and rushed into the bedroom. She didn't even look up even when he carefully walked towards her.

She was curled into herself, wrapped in the blankets they had bought for the nursery, her face blotchy and swollen from crying.

Rusty stood there, frozen.

Amy turned her face toward him then, her voice hoarse and raw.

"Where were you?"

He had no answer. He knew.

She had gone to the hospital earlier, alone and had been told there was nothing they could do. She birthed the baby and had to process the trauma that morning, alone.

He sat beside her, emptily staring straight ahead. His body felt heavy and numb. He was sitting next to her, but she didn't move either. She didn't reach for him. She just stared at the ceiling, empty. Still crying.

Rusty tried to hold her, but she was stiff, unresponsive. Eventually, he just lay beside her, helpless as she cried herself to sleep. He stayed awake, staring at the shadows on the walls, replaying every moment in his head. At least every moment he thought had happened. Everything Amy went through. Alone. Every call he ignored. Every excuse he made. Every second he could have been there but wasn't.

Even after he had fallen asleep, maybe for an hour between midnight and 4 a.m., his thoughts continued to haunt him. At 4 a.m., he was jarred awake by a terrifying nightmare—a baby crawling toward the edge of a cliff before slipping over the edge. In his dream, Rusty screamed and lunged forward. In his bedroom, Rusty screamed and lunged himself headfirst into the wall beside him. He woke up in a crumpled heap on the floor. How could he process something like this?

Amy barely spoke to him except to softly say his parents had come and took Emma indefinitely until they all could figure out what to do. Until they figure out how to move forward. But could the even?

Rusty did not speak at all. And when the silence became unbearable, when the guilt pressed so hard against his chest that he thought it might crush him—he did the only thing he knew how to do.

He ran.

He ran back to the office and buried himself in work the next day. He had arrived at the office before dawn because he believed that if he was working, he wasn't thinking. And if he wasn't thinking, he could pretend he wasn't drowning in grief. Then he tried to process an invoice, and everyone witnessed how quickly things escalated from there.

Rusty broke down, collapsing to the floor in a similar crumpled heap in his bedroom as soon as Dan's door closed behind him. He started to hyperventilate, desperately trying to catch his breath. Dan guided Rusty to his couch, where he lay down, and Dan got him a bottle of water from his mini fridge. Rusty explained everything to Dan. The guilt. The devastation. The loss. Everything he could think of. Dan lent an empathetic and sympathetic ear. They both cried. When Rusty was calm and ready, Dan walked over to Rusty's desk, grabbed his coat and quietly escorted his fallen colleague up the stairs to the parking lot, where they both got into Dan's car. Dan quietly drove Rusty home without anyone in the sales pit noticing either was gone.

CHAPTER 35

"Dan and Kara"

Now at Rusty's house, Dan watched from the driver's side with a heavy heart as Rusty walked into his home. He rested his head against the window, staring up at the sky. Like his gaze, his thoughts were far away. Rusty's grief had struck a chord—a painful reminder of his own demons: guilt, burnout, and anger. Demons he had worked hard to bury, but that still clawed at the edges of his mind.

It had been almost a year since the divorce was finalized, but the scars still felt fresh. Dan hadn't always been like this. Early in his career, he had been known for his calm, level-headed approach to the job. But the relentless pressure of professional life—late nights, missed family milestones, impossible targets—had chipped away at him over time. How could he not? The cracks in his carefully maintained façade were impossible to ignore.

Dan's breaking point had come two years earlier during a particularly gruelling renewal cycle. The pressure to hit targets was unrelenting, and the tension followed him home every night. His wife, Kara, tried to support him, but Dan's growing frustration with work left him distant, irritable, and volatile at the best of times.

One night, after another long day at the office, Dan came home to find Kara waiting for him in the kitchen. The kids were already in bed, their homework spread across the dining table like a reminder of everything he had missed. Kara's expression was strained, her arms crossed tightly over her chest.

"We need to talk," she said, trembling slightly.

"Not now," Dan replied, tossing his laptop bag onto the counter.

"Yes, now," Kara insisted. "You're never here, Dan. And when you are, you're... angry. Distant. I'm trying, but I can't do this alone."

Dan turned sharply, his frustration boiling over. "What do you want from me, Kara? I'm doing everything I can for this fucking family!"

"For this family?" she shot back, her voice rising. "You think throwing yourself into work and coming home like this is helping? Look around, Dan! The kids barely see you anymore; when they do, they're scared of you!"

The words hit him like a slap, but instead of calming him, they ignited something darker. In a blind rage, Dan swept his arm across the counter, sending their homework and a mug crashing to the floor. Kara flinched, and the look on her face— fear, hurt, disbelief—was enough to make him pause.

But the damage was already done.

He stormed into the living room with fists clenched. He hurled a throw pillow across the room. It knocked over a picture frame on the mantle, the glass shattering as it hit the hardwood floor. Terrified cries rang from upstairs, but Dan didn't notice, nor did he stop there. He kicked over a chair, sent a stack of books tumbling from a side table, and slammed his fist through the drywall, breaking the knuckles on his dominant hand. Thankfully, Dan had never raised his hand at Kara or the kids, but this was a little too close for comfort.

Kara stood frozen in the doorway, tears streaming down her face. "Dan... stop," she whispered. His chest heaved; his left fist trembled while his right fist now bled from the broken knuckles; it was damage his mind had yet to register. Whatever happened to him that day was all too much. However, whatever problem he processed miserably was now a much larger problem with severe complications. He looked around at the mess he had made—the broken glass, the scattered papers, the terrified expression on his wife's face—and felt a wave of shame crash over him.

"I..." he started, but the words caught in his throat as he collapsed to the floor in a crumpled heap, folding in on himself. His sobs were genuine and raw, and they were unrelenting. It was the kind of crying that came from a place so deep inside that the feelings they represented had not surfaced in years.

He gasped for air in short, shallow bursts. Sweat soaked his shirt, and his heavy breathing made it difficult to regulate his body. He clutched his shirt, his fingers clawing at the fabric as though trying to rip it away would relieve the pressure.

And yet, even as he lay there, curled into himself, Kara kept her distance. She stood frozen in the doorway, her arms wrapped tightly around her own torso, as though holding herself together was the only way to stay upright.

"Dan..." she whispered, but her voice cracked, and she didn't step closer.

He couldn't answer at first. He couldn't even lift his head to meet her gaze. His voice was lost somewhere in the category five hurricane spinning inside his mind. 'What have you done? What's wrong with you? You're losing everything! Kara... the kids... they're afraid of you,' he thought.

Kara shifted slightly, her hands trembling as she wiped at her face. "Dan... you need to breathe. You're... you're having a panic attack." Her words barely registered. The room felt impossibly small, the walls closing in around him. Every sound—including the muffled cries of his children upstairs—rang in his ears like a deafening roar.

"You're okay," Kara said, though her voice lacked the conviction, concern, or warmth she had shown the last time this happened, the last time Dan swore it wouldn't happen again. She took a hesitant step forward but stopped herself, her arms still wrapped protectively around her middle.

"You're okay, Dan."

But he wasn't okay. He wasn't even close to okay. The pain in his hand finally broke through the storm with a sharp, throbbing ache that pulsed in time with his racing heart. It was grounding in its own way, a physical reminder that he was still here, still real, even as everything else slipped away.

When he finally lifted his head, Kara had returned from running upstairs to calm the children. She stood in the doorway, her arms now dropped to her sides, but she hadn't moved any closer.

"I'm sorry," Dan croaked, his voice barely audible. "I'm so... sorry."

Kara's eyes glistened with fresh tears, but she didn't speak. She simply shook her head and turned away, leaving Dan alone amidst the wreckage of their home and their relationship.

That night, the police came to investigate after a neighbour called about the noise. No one was hurt, but the sight of uniformed officers standing in his doorway was enough to drive home the severity of his actions.

Dan pleaded guilty to a lesser charge of disturbing the peace. As part of his sentence, he was required to attend anger management classes and meet with a therapist to address his outbursts. He went through the motions, completing every requirement the court had handed down, but by the time he finished, Kara had already made up her mind.

"I can't do this anymore, Dan," she said, serving him a restraining order when he returned from his last therapy session. Her voice was calm but resolute. "The kids deserve stability. And so do I."

He begged her to reconsider, promising that he had changed this time, that he would continue to see a therapist and do better. But Kara had heard it all before. A month later, the divorce papers arrived.

Dan drove back to the office all while thinking about his past. Now, sitting in his usual chair, Dan stared blankly at the framed photo on his desk. It was old—taken years ago, back when he and Kara were still happy. The kids were younger then, their faces bright with laughter on one of their trips to their favourite resort in the Dominican Republic. He couldn't bring himself to replace it, even though it constantly reminded him of everything he had lost.

The sound of a chair scraping across the floor snapped him back to the present. He glanced out into the pit and saw Max and Jay deep in conversation next to Rusty's empty desk. Rusty's absence made the room feel quieter, heavier, and Dan couldn't help but wonder if his advice to take the day off would make any difference.

He leaned back in his chair, running a hand over his face. He had done the work—completed the classes, sat through therapy, and learned to manage his anger. But the scars of his past and his deformed knuckles kept vigil. Dan had seen this unfold with Rusty and couldn't shake the feeling that Rusty was one bad day away from unravelling again, or worse. He closed and locked his office door, retreated into the silence of his office, and lay on the couch. He knew both he and Rusty had long roads ahead.

CHAPTER 36

"New Ideas, Same Uphill Battles, aka You Can Put Lipstick on a Pig, But it's Still a Pig"

Dan was devastated for Rusty and his family. He advised him to take the rest of the week off, but they compromised on the next day if Rusty felt he could return. The goal of the mini-exile was so Rusty could take time to process everything without putting too much spotlight on his absence. Rusty was in no state to explain to anyone, and Dan needed to protect that privacy. Dan, however, came from a place of experience and was worried that the more Rusty ran from Amy and the tragedy, the more he would spiral downward.

Dan and Kristina sat in a quiet booth at a small Italian restaurant. The smell of garlic and marinara filled the air, but neither seemed particularly interested in their half-eaten plates of pasta. The conversation kept circling back to the meetings with Garry.

"I've never been grilled like that before," Dan said, pushing a meatball around the plate with his fork. "He had that look, you know? Like he already knew the answers and was just waiting to see if you'd show your hand—or worse, fuck up."

Kristina nodded, her brow furrowed. "Same. It was all about results, processes, and culture. He kept smiling, but it felt... off."

"Yeah," Dan agreed. "Like he was cataloguing everything we said, looking for a reason to use it later."

Kristina set her fork down and leaned forward slightly. "What do you think he's planning? I mean, this can't just be about feedback."

Dan shrugged, but his expression was grim. "Could be cuts. Restructuring. Hell, maybe he's just trying to figure out who's on his side. It could also be that the owner is setting up Garry because Wally is too loyal to us. Wally's been around too long, knows too much, and is incapable of making hard decisions."

"So they bring in an 'outside consultant' who has loads of industry experience, a track record of results, and no affinity to anyone here. No emotions. Just business. I can see that," Kristina whispered. "Where does that leave us?" Her tone was still soft but pointed.

Dan met her gaze. "You tell me. You're gunning for Manager, right? What's your next move?"

Kristina hesitated, her fingers tracing the edge of her glass. "If I get to be Manager, I want to make real changes. Support the team, not just hit numbers. But Garry... I don't think he sees me as more than a box to check for diversity."

Dan nodded. "I get it. He's got a 'big picture' thing going on, and we're just pieces on the board to him. That's why I've got to aim higher. Director of Sales—or, VP of Sales. That's where the decisions are made."

"Director? VP?" Kristina asked, raising an eyebrow. "You ready for that?"

"More than Kent ever was and more in tune with reality than Wally is, too," Dan said, his lips curving into a wry smile. "And if Garry's looking for someone to step up, I've got to make sure he sees me as the answer."

Kristina tilted her head, a faint smile playing at her lips. "So we're both playing chess now, huh?"

Dan chuckled. "Welcome to the game."

Max waited patiently for Kristina and Dan to return from lunch. Once they settled in, he approached Kristina's desk, his notebook clutched tightly in his hands. She was nursing a post-lunch cup of tea, looking as drained as the rest of the sales pit. Renewals had sapped the life out of the pit, leaving little energy for enthusiasm.

"Hey, Krissy, got a minute?" Max asked, his voice tinged with hesitation.

Kristina raised an eyebrow but gestured for him to continue. "Sure. What's up?"

"Group nights," Max said, flipping open his notebook. "Rusty and I have been brainstorming ethnic-themed nights—Indo-Canadian, Hellenic, Jewish—communities no one has really tapped into before. The idea is to sell group tickets, create cultural programming during the game, and host postgame receptions."

Kristina exhaled slowly, setting her mug down. "I like where your head's at, but planning something like this isn't as easy as it sounds. Concessions won't just change their menus for one night, and management? You'll need a crowbar to get them on board."

Max grinned. "We thought of that. What if we partner with community associations and offer sponsorship packages? They could bring in local businesses to cover costs, and we tie in a charitable donation angle. That way, it's not just about selling tickets—it's about engagement."

Kristina leaned back, considering. "Okay, I'll admit, this could work. But temper your expectations. Management's going to push back hard."

Max, Kristina, and Dan gathered in the conference room that afternoon, facing Wally, Garry, Kent and the game-day entertainment manager. The tension in the room was thick, a continuation of the unease that had plagued the team all week.

Max opened strongly. "The concept is simple: ethnic theme nights targeted at specific communities. We tie in group sales with cultural programming—music, dance, a post-game reception. It's a unique experience that appeals to untapped markets."

Wally was the first to scoff, leaning back in his chair. "Cultural programming? Like what, Bollywood dancers at intermission?" He let out a dismissive chuckle. "You're kidding me, right?"

"Yeah! Bollywood dancers! Exactly!" Max replied, unfazed. "Why not embrace it? It would make the game-day experience fresh and exciting."

Wally's expression darkened. "We don't mix politics or religion with sports."

Kristina's jaw tightened. "Being Indo-Canadian or Hellenic isn't political or religious—it's cultural. This isn't about making a statement; it's about connecting with communities that already live here."

Dan jumped in. "Connecting with communities who want to be involved but have never really had the chance to do so. Bottom line? We've got thousands of empty seats on nights like Tuesday against Buffalo. This could have helped us move those while building goodwill."

Wally and Garry exchanged looks before Wally sighed. "It's a logistical nightmare. Changing the music, adding programming—it's a lot of work for one night."

"It's a lot of work," Kent echoed, though his voice lacked conviction.

Max refused to back down. "It's worth the effort. If we do this right, we're not just selling tickets for one game but creating lifelong fans. And if it doesn't work? What's the real cost? Those seats would be empty anyway."

Wally drummed his fingers on the table. "All right. Show me a detailed proposal. No promises, but if the numbers work, we'll talk."

After the theme night pitch, Kristina went to Jay's desk and they dialled David, one of Jay's ticket brokers from Boston, who agreed to speak with her. The conversation took a sharp turn almost immediately.

"I know this is problematic, and I'll take responsibility," she admitted. "But I wasn't given much information—just that we need to renegotiate or retract some of the deals."

David's tone was measured but sharp. "Look, I'm not going to shoot the messenger, but this is a disgusting way to do business. Renewals shouldn't be subject to change after the fact. What you're doing? It's unethical, possibly illegal."

"I hear you," Kristina said, rubbing her temple. "I'm putting together a proposal incorporating feedback from brokers like you. I see you as a partner, not an adversary."

David sighed. "Kristina, at this point, I'm thinking of pulling my entire account. I'm sure you know how big my account is."

As David continued, Jay scribbled $145,000 on a sticky note in front of her.

"The hypocrisy is astounding—you take StubHub's money to participate in the secondary market, yet now you treat brokers like dirt? Do you know how much money I've lost this season because of low attendance?"

"I can only imagine," she said sincerely.

David wasn't finished. "Every team has some sort of policy that makes life difficult for brokers— limiting seats, forcing full payments, blocking trades. But yanking deals midway through renewal and after you've already processed my deposits? I thought I had seen it all, but that's a new low."

"I know," Kristina admitted. "Jay and I've spent years building relationships with brokers. This kind of stunt will undo all of that. We're working together to try to come up with a beneficial plan for all involved. That's why we are having this conversation. Because it's a conversation, and we respect your opinions."

David exhaled. "You can ask Jay. I was even willing to increase my commitment. I wanted to grow my business with your team. Now? I don't trust your front office at all."

Kristina tapped her pen against her desk. "I'm fighting to make sure we honour existing agreements. If we alienate brokers, we're screwed. Until this team is good enough to sell out every night, we need you guys."

David hesitated. "Look, I appreciate your honesty. But if this keeps up, word will spread fast, and your team will be in serious trouble."

Kristina closed her eyes for a moment. "I'll keep you posted. Thanks, David."

Kristina sat at her desk long after the office had emptied, staring at the final draft of her broker program proposal. She knew this was the team's best shot at salvaging relationships before everything imploded. Taking a deep breath, she printed a copy and marched toward Dan's office.

Dan looked up as she knocked on the doorframe. "Still here?" he asked, rubbing his eyes.

Kristina dropped the proposal onto his desk. "Yeah, because somebody has to fix this mess."

"Good luck with that, Krissy," he said with a crooked smile.

Kristina handed him the freshly printed proposal as he started flipping through it. "All right, walk me through it."

Kristina crossed her arms. "We need to secure at least five million in broker sales to take the pressure off the rest of the team. If we do that, we can focus on other areas instead of chasing every single empty seat."

Dan nodded. "Makes sense. But how do we prevent the brokers from gaming the system?"

Kristina leaned forward. "One dedicated account manager—Jay. No more brokers getting bounced from one rep to another. He'll handle renewals, set sales targets, and make sure we prioritize the brokers who actually move inventory."

Dan tapped his pen against the desk. "And the ones causing problems?"

"Jay and I talked about this. They're out," Kristina said bluntly. "No excessive payment issues, no constant swaps that disrupt inventory, and no brokers who take seats just to return them later."

Dan smirked. "So, you're cutting out the amateurs?"

"Exactly."

Dan leaned back, considering. "What's in it for them?"

Kristina flipped the page. "Better tools. Bulk e-ticket delivery. Maybe one single writable DVD package with all their tickets as PDFs. No hard tickets so they can't sell them and then resell them accidentally."

"Amateurs don't have a system. This could work."

"Then, for nights like next Tuesday, we will give them bulk ticket buying options for underperforming sections at a significant discount. We're not giving tickets away, just transferring the risk to them."

Dan sat up, flipping to the next page. "Nice. And for our top brokers?"

"Limited access to concerts and events."

Dan raised an eyebrow. "Concert tickets?"

"If we keep them happy, they'll stay loyal," she explained. "It's just enough to keep them engaged— no ridiculous perks. Nothing close to what I'm trying to come up with for our flexible benefits program."

Dan nodded. "And what about exchanges?" he said, yawning and rubbing his head. "Or did you mention that already?"

Kristina sighed. "We control them. No more free-for-all. We allow limited trades under strict conditions."

"This is solid. But Wally and Kent are going to push back."

"Let them. The alternative is pissing off every broker we have and dealing with even more empty seats next season. Jay and I talked to one of Jay's high-value brokers."

"How high-value?"

"About $145,000 and willing to invest more. And David isn't even one of our top five brokers."

Dan smirked. "You're always right, Krissy."

Kristina smirked back. "Yeah, good luck convincing them of that."

Max had his fight. Kristina had hers. They both knew they were right for trying to push the envelope. Dan believed in them. But history had proven one thing time and time again: just because something made sense didn't mean management would do it.

The next morning, Dan rubbed his temples as he listened to the league-wide conference call on fan retention strategies. Beside him, Max and Kristina sat with notebooks open, absorbing the flood of information. Every team in the league was involved, with some presenting new initiatives for next season.

Max scribbled furiously, muttering, "I've learned more in the last 40 minutes than I have in the last three weeks."

On the other hand, Kristina saw new opportunities—both to gather intel for the ticket broker program she was developing and gain visibility within the league.

"League-wide, a 1% improvement in renewals translates to approximately $8 million in additional revenue," a league rep announced.

That number hung in the air. The league saw a 12% increase in full-season renewals and a 2.2% increase in partial renewals. The trends were positive, yet Dan's team struggled to keep pace.

Some team reps even expressed shock at how aggressive Dan's team's renewal deadlines and targets were.

Kristina shook her head. "So, we're two weeks ahead of some teams in invoicing?"

"Some haven't even started yet," Max added, stunned.

"Jesus," Dan muttered, jotting down notes. "If renewal rates were climbing, why was this team still lagging?"

Another league rep spoke up. "The cost of acquiring a new customer is still five times higher than retaining an existing one."

Kristina glanced at Dan. "That's why we need the broker program," she whispered. "

Dan nodded. "That's why marketing should help us retain and not expend so much effort on net new."

Meanwhile, Max was intrigued by what teams were doing to increase engagement with ticket holders.

"Most clubs are ramping up their touchpoints," the rep continued. "In fact—48% have at least six unsolicited touchpoints per season with full-season ticket holders. Only 2% of teams have fewer than three."

Kristina exhaled sharply. "That's double what we do," she whispered.

Dan's face tightened. They were failing at touchpoints. Badly.

The conversation then shifted to the economic outlook.

"Only 32% of clubs are optimistic about their market," the rep reported. "Another 16% are somewhat optimistic. The rest? Neutral or worse."

Dan clenched his jaw. That included them.

The numbers kept coming—new full-season sales were up 298% league-wide.

"What the hell?" Max whispered.

"Boston and Washington skewed the data," the rep clarified. "Without them, the increase is actually 46.2%."

Dan sighed. "Still better than us."

As teams shared best practices, Kristina found herself taking note of everything.

"Dallas has a colour-coded renewal ranking system," a rep explained. "Red, yellow, green—based on tenure, attendance, and payment history."

"Buffalo hosts town hall meetings with fence-sitting season ticket holders."

"Philly's reps offer customized payment plans, including a 5% deposit option."

Kristina shut her notebook decisively. "I already have ideas."

As soon as the call ended, Kristina turned to Dan.

"Hey, did you read my broker proposal?" she asked.

Dan nodded. "What I saw was really in-depth. And the way you presented, it means you are very passionate about this. To say I'm proud of you would be an understatement. Good job, Krissy."

Kristina grinned. "Do you think Kent, Wally or Garry even opened the file?"

Dan smirked. "Not a chance."

Kristina sighed. "I'll start talking to brokers in the meantime—see where they stand at the potential of it all."

Later that day, Dan and Shane grabbed lunch at a nearby diner.

Shane scrolled through his phone, grinning. "Sales texts," he chuckled. "So much better than sexts."

Dan rolled his eyes. "Who's closing?"

"Capshaw Chemical. Quarter-season suite share. If he were here right now, I'd have the guy sign this napkin."

"So what's holding it up?"

"They want a suite in the visitor's end. Right now, I can only get them one in the home end."

Shane paused, suddenly staring at his plate.

Dan noticed immediately. "Something on your mind?"

"I got a call last night from Sam Carroll."

Dan leaned in. "The recruiter?"

"He says he has an opportunity. I didn't reach out to him, Dan. I wasn't even looking. I swear!"

Dan set his fork down. "Relax. What's the offer?"

"Territory manager."

Dan blinked. He said nothing.

"Territory manager at...Capshaw Chemical."

Dan's eyes opened wide. "You want to sell industrial paint?"

"When the base salary is $170K plus perks, you at least have the conversation."

Dan whistled. "Jesus. $170K?"

"Plus, plus," Shane replied.

Dan leaned back. "Plus, plus?"

"Car allowance. Expense account. Perks out the ass."

Dan sighed. "That's a big jump from what we could possibly offer."

"I know," Shane muttered. "And that's why I couldn't sleep last night."

Dan nodded thoughtfully. "Look, I'd be a lousy friend if I told you not to explore it. Just remember— you'd be slinging paint for a chemical company with a very shady past. You can ask Max all about that place."

Later that afternoon, Wally and Garry called another impromptu pit meeting, bringing two cases of beer and a large clear plastic bag full of leftover popcorn from the concession stands as another peace offering.

Garry opened bluntly. "Look, we know you're frustrated."

Dan nodded. "Between budget constraints, ridiculous client demands, and that fucking boy band concert torpedoing sales, it's been a nightmare."

Garry nodded while Wally handed out blank sheets of paper. "We need your help," he stated. "Write down every instance where one of your clients was contacted without your knowledge and sold suite nights, shares, packs, or groups."

Garry added, "Even if they were just pitched. And—your top three frustrations internally."

Rusty, who had returned to the office earlier that morning, folded his arms. "Only three?" he laughed louder than necessary. "So... you want us to prove how messed up the system is, but we only have three frustrations? Please tell me that's three frustrations each because at least twenty guys and girls here could easily give you three unique frustrations each!" Rusty rambled, pointing across the room in every direction.

"Rusty," Dan pleaded.

"No, no. Go on, Rusty," Garry encouraged, "please, let it all out. This is all-important context."

Rusty scoffed again. "You got it. We get paid ZERO percent on premium games. Half on group sales. And the first year of a five-year suite deal? 3%. It's robbery. Nothing new there either, but you wouldn't know because you're now the FNG, Garry!"

Some of the pit snickered, while others mostly gasped. Slightly amused, Garry turned to Dan and asked, "What's an FNG?"

"Uh, oof, well," Dan said, flustered, trying to find the definition without undermining the importance of Rusty's comment in front of everyone. Dan was caught in a very difficult position. Loyalty to his friend and colleague, or loyalty to his boss and job.

Realizing the tension, Frank also chimed in. "After the season we had, 0.5% on renewals is a joke, too. And don't get me started on suite sales cutting our grass."

"With our own fucking clients, Garry!" Rusty exclaimed. "I'm sure you will learn to appreciate the incestuous nature of sales in this organization."

There were more quiet conversations amongst the sales pit.

"Fascinating," Garry said, a mystified look on his face.

Steve finally spoke up. "Nobody up top gives a shit about us."

Dan exhaled deeply. He knew Garry had lost the room, and it wouldn't go over well. "That's what we need to fix."

But deep down, Dan and everyone knew the truth: this team was held together with Band-Aids, and the wounds were about to get deeper because Garry was about to rip the Band-Aids off.

CHAPTER 37

"Rusty's ~~Tipping~~ Breaking Point"

It was Tuesday the following week. The air in Captain's Club turned conference room felt even thicker than the pit. It was oppressive, heavy, like being trapped in a leaky submarine, with water slowly filling up the chamber, leaving no air and no way to escape from. The black-painted walls only amplified the sense of claustrophobia. Panic began to creep in, amplifying the tension that already hung in the air like a storm cloud ready to burst.

The long tables, hastily arranged into a U-shape by the operations department, were crammed with the entire sales force—inside sales, retention, suites, groups, and every layer of management. They sat shoulder to shoulder, their collective exhaustion evident on their faces and body language.

At the front of the room, Garry Breckenridge presided over them like a general addressing his troops before a battle they all knew they were going to lose. His calm voice carried an air of practiced authority, which sounded meaningful if you weren't listening. But most of the team was listening. And they didn't need to hear Rusty's frustrations days earlier to know that Garry Breckenridge was full of shit and a wolf in sheep's clothing.

Garry had been droning on for thirty minutes now, spewing corporate anecdotes about culture and accountability— about how 'change starts with us' and how 'we all had to be aligned for the greater good'. He told stories about other markets, teams, and sales floors that had turned things around under his leadership. At least, that's what he told them. But Garry's stories bore no resemblance to the dumpster fire of a situation they were all currently in.

Wally sat to Garry's left while Kent sat stiffly beside him, arms crossed, jaw clenched. Dan was motionless, hands folded in front of him. For the first time in a very long time, Dan was not asked to present during the meeting, and while both he, Kent and Wally knew what was coming, they knew this would not end well. Everyone in the room knew that, too.

Garry acknowledged that this conversation about the renewal campaigns and commission from renewals should have happened months ago, but with a modest chuckle, he shrugged it off. "Better late than never, right?"

His comment was met with silence. No one laughed. No one even exhaled. Just silent defeat. And then, Garry opened the latch and got ready to drop the bomb on Nagasaki. He turned to Kent. "Perhaps you can explain how the compensation plan has worked in the past for our retention and inside sales teams?"

Kent cleared his throat, his voice devoid of energy as he looked sadly at the sales team. "Uh, as most of you know, historically, retention reps were paid 0.5% commission up to 50% of their book value. It would then increase to 1% once 70% of the book was renewed, with another bump to 1.5% at

85%. If a rep hit 100% renewal, they'd receive a retroactive commission and a bonus."

Heads nodded. It was far from perfect, but it was the only option, so it worked when it worked. Garry smiled in that tight, calculated way. "Thank you, Kent. Well, I have the authority from the Owner today to roll out something new. Something we believe is even better."

The PowerPoint slide behind him changed. "Your new compensation plan will retroactively start when the first renewals went out a few weeks ago. We believe this works in your favour. We'd like you to consider it as...as a sign of good faith and of course, our appreciation. After all, most of you have now hit 70%, if not more, of your renewal targets." He clicked the mouse to advance to the next slide with a side-by-side comparison of the previous and today's comp plans. "Under our new system, you'll see that there will be $0 commission until 70% of your total book value is reached." Click.

Some of the group gasped as the slide changed.

"But, upon hitting 70% of your total book value, which will include renewals, new sales, and upgrades ...there will be a $2,000 bonus at 70%. You'll receive another $2,000 bonus when your total book value hits 75%." Click.

"Then at 85%, 95%, and 100%, additional payouts ranging from $2,000 to 5,000 for reaching 100% of your total book value."

That was it. The room went deathly silent. It took over thirty minutes to reach that point, but only seconds for the weight of what was being proposed to crush everyone in the room. This wasn't just a pay cut—this was a complete gutting of their earnings. For some of the veteran reps, it meant losing $30,000–$50,000 in commission, given the size of their book.

A hollow, sinking feeling settled in Rusty's chest. It felt like suffocating while murmurs broke out across the room. A few reps exchanged disbelieving glances. Kristina sat stone-faced, gripping her pen so tightly with disbelief that her knuckles were white. Frank muttered something under his breath; it may have been a prayer. No one was outright objecting yet. Nobody knew how. But the resentment was building.

And then Garry made his final mistake. He turned back to the group, smiling as if he had just handed them a gift from God Himself.

"Does anyone have any questions?" he asked.

Then Rusty raised his hand.

"Yes, thank you, Rusty," Garry acknowledged, pointing at him in the middle of the room. Rusty couldn't sit still, so he slowly pushed his chair away from the table and stood. He stood and surveyed the room first, taking in the long faces, the dejection, the quiet rage of his closest colleagues, who had become the closest thing to family he had at the moment. His body trembled—not with nerves, but with exhaustion. Dan uncomfortably shifted in his seat, his jaw tightening, his fists clenching underneath the table. He pretty much knew what was coming next, but he couldn't stop it. There was nothing he could do to stop it.

Rusty exhaled slowly, his voice hoarse. "Garry, I don't have a question. It's more of a comment," he said as Dan looked away.

Garry nodded, expecting compliance. Rusty's lips curled into a broken, bitter smile.

"This…" He gestured at the screen. "This compensation plan? It's fucking bullshit." The entire room stirred. A few reps gasped. Dan closed his eyes.

Garry remained still as Rusty continued. "You cannot do this to the hardworking men and women of the sales pit. You can't just rip the rug out from under people who have built their careers here, who have given everything to this team, everything to the fans. Who sacrificed their time, families, and mental health for what? To facilitate a positive relationship between our fans and this team?"

Max, seated beside Rusty, couldn't help but gaze at his colleague, who was resolutely standing there, embodying the spirit of sacrifice for the greater good. Just a few yards away, Garry, Kent, Wally, and Mark were lined up like marksmen, their gazes fixed and unwavering, preparing to pull the trigger on a monumental decision. The tension in the air was intense. Each second stretching out like an eternity as Garry aimed not only at a target but also at the uncertain fate of his mission. Max felt a mixture of admiration and apprehension churn within him—this was a moment of collective courage, a test of their resolve, and the stakes couldn't be higher.

Rusty's voice rose, filled with anger, frustration, and something even deeper. "This may have worked wherever the hell you came from, truthfully, I really don't give a shit. Because whatever fantasy market you pulled this from, is not this market. So it's about time you get with reality. You said 70% of our total book...not just renewals. Total. This entire retention team has worked day and night, tirelessly putting up with peace offerings of Baconators, donuts and stale sandwiches. We've called 96% of all season ticket holders. We've had meetings, in-seat visits.... everything we could possibly do to get our renewals up. To save season ticket holders who have stood above a raging river, ready to jump in headfirst because we fuck everything up. We are all to blame for this abomination because we are so compliant. But it's all we fucking know, Garry. We have no fucking choice but to be compliant and put our heads down like good little soldiers."

Garry scanned the crowd. He was losing them, and he knew it. Dan and Kent did nothing. What could they do? There was no saving Rusty now. There was no saving any of them, for that matter. This was a runaway train.

Rusty continued, "some of us have book values of $6,000,000. If we renew 70&, that's 4.2 Million dollars that we get a commission of zero point zero zero 5 % on. That's $21,000 in commission. But hey, thanks for the $2,000 bonus, Garry. That's a big delta!"

"It's clear you have very strong feelings for this, Rusty. I'm sorry you feel so strongly," Garry said, his tone infuriatingly calm. "Your insights are very much appreciated, and we'll certainly consider those as we finalize these plans."

But then, Garry made a calculated move that showed his true colours. He polled the crowd. "Does anyone else feel that we have missed the mark on this presentation?"

Frank immediately raised his hand. So did Steve, Scott, Bryan, and Brad. They held their hands up while Shane, Kristina, Jay, Salty, Max, and others looked on in horror, unable to process the chaotic scene unfolding before them.

Garry took note. A silent list of names. A list for the severe punishments to come. Rusty sat back down. He had nothing left to say. He had given everything he had left in him, but at this moment, he had barely anything left. Because now? Now Rusty just didn't care anymore. He remained silent as his heart pounded. Adrenaline flowing through his veins, carrying anger and rage like lightning through his veins.

The room continued to exchange quiet banter. Stunned, yet quiet banter. Garry pretended to remain composed, but the stiff set of his jaw and the way his fingers and toes curled out of sight under the table would have given him away. He had now lost the room, and he knew it.

But Rusty didn't give a shit. Because the truth was, he had nothing left to lose. 'When there's nothing left to burn, you have to set yourself on fire' he thought to himself, and boy, was he going to go out in flames.

He was past caring, past fighting for a system that had already failed him. And no one in this room except maybe Dan knew just how far gone he was. They didn't know that eight days ago, Rusty and Amy had lost their unborn son. Eight unforgiving days. One gut-wrenching moment, now two moments traded in for future considerations and a lifetime of pain.

The burden of it had torn him apart from the inside out, rotting him down to his very core until he couldn't contain it anymore. And now, here he was. Sitting in a room full of thankless, unrelenting upper management grin-fucking assholes, being force-fed some bullshit sermon about team culture from a clueless, corporate stooge who had never spent a single fucking day in the trenches with any of them.

Rusty clenched his fists under the table, his fingernails digging into his palms to feel something other than the ache inside his chest. Probably less than the ache Amy had felt just over a week ago.

He had tried to hold her as she sobbed into his chest, shaking with grief, unable to process the absolute cruelty of it all. But where was she to hold him now? He had lost that privilege when he wasn't there for her. This was poetic justice. He wasn't there for her, and now, where was anyone? No matter. This was a scene from a Hollywood movie as the noble hero sacrifices himself for the greater good of society. This was Rusty's Bruce Willis in Armageddon moment because the truth was—Rusty was already gone. Lost in space. Lost mentally. Lost emotionally.

He was a man running on fumes.

And now, this? This fucking meeting? This fucking week from hell.

Seconds continued to feel like hours. The meeting had still not resumed. So Rusty looked up, scanning the room for any familiarity. He saw Frank's blank face and his leg bouncing under the table, a nervous tell. Kristina's jaw was locked so tight, it was a miracle she hadn't shattered a tooth. Salty had his arms crossed, glaring at the table. Max was a dear in the headlights, stunned. They were all thinking the same thing: This is bullshit. This is wrong. But there's nothing we can do about it. And perhaps that was the part that broke Rusty the most about professional sports. That acceptance of defeat. Collectively throwing their hands up. Waving the white flag as he has raised the week before.

He had spent the last five years of his career bending over backwards for this organization. Grinding, sacrificing, breaking himself for a team that would never give a shit about him. His issues weren't just about the money. His issues were mostly about respect, or the lack thereof.

And Garry Breckenridge, that epic clown, Rusty thought, was brought in to do the dirty work. He was the boxer's cut man tasked to stop the bleeding. To trim the fat and make the hard, emotionless decisions that were best for the business. Not for corporate culture. Not for the hardworking heroes who worked in professional sports. Not for his found family in the sales pit. But for the organization's bottom line. This wasn't unique to professional sports.

And at that moment, Rusty remembered, clear as day, what selling your soul to the devil really meant. Because he had this thankless, 'I haven't been fucked like this since grade school' feeling before. A few seasons back, after the four-month lockout, when hockey finally crawled back from the grave, the sales team had been gutted—from twenty-five full-time staff to just eight part-timers, barely hanging on. Fans had been furious. They weren't just mad about the lockout—they were mad at the entire fucking system. The greedy owners. The overpaid players. The skyrocketing ticket prices. The fan experience. And who was left to pick up the pieces? Not the players. Not the executives. Not Garry fucking Breckenridge. No. It was them. The sales team. The ones who had to field the angry calls, who had to smooth things over, who had to convince people to stay loyal to a team that had just spat in their faces and cheer for players, some making thousands of dollars per game.

Rusty, Salty, Frank, Shane, Jay...they had worked themselves into the fucking ground, balancing outrage and diplomacy, trying to keep relationships intact with people who had every reason to walk away. But why didn't any of them walk away? Why did they keep that dream alive? Surely, if it was really that bad, they should have just walked away. But nobody could. Because they felt a camaraderie, a collective and mutual love and respect for one another. And for what?

Rusty remembered it too well—the moment Wally had stopped him in the hallway after a particularly brutal day, eerily like how he interacted with Jay. "Rusty, what's wrong with you?" Wally had asked, squinting at him like he was some kind of malfunctioning robot. Note, this was not the same as asking, "Are you ok?"

Rusty had blinked at him, dead inside. It wasn't Wally's fault. He probably didn't understand the severity of that moment because he came from an era when it wasn't okay to speak of your emotions.

"I'm not well, Wally," he had answered, his voice flat. "I'm mentally exhausted, and emotionally bankrupt, too."

In that moment, Wally reached out, placed a hand on Rusty's neck, and took his pulse. "You're still alive, Rusty," Wally said. Then, with a shrug— "And you still have a job. So get back to it." And then Wally walked away dismissively; like Rusty's suffering was just a minor inconvenience. Like it didn't matter. Like Rusty didn't matter.

Returning to the present, Rusty knew that Garry Breckenridge did not matter. He didn't respect anyone in that organization and certainly hadn't earned anyone's respect either. Rusty looked up at Garry, at Kent, some of the incompetent suits who had spent years sitting in cushy executive offices, collecting six-figure paycheques, while they bled the real workers dry.

CHAPTER 38

"The Fallout"

The boardroom was suffocatingly quiet that morning. A week had passed since Rusty's very public defiance. A fucking week of walking on eggshells. Coming into work, making renewal calls, and everyone acting like nothing had happened. The sales pit was different. Things had changed.

Now, Rusty sat across from Garry, Dan, and Lena, facing the inevitable. This was their first meeting of the day. Probably best to get it over with and just rip the Band-Aid.

The room was designed to impress outsiders – a polished mahogany table, high-backed leather chairs, and framed action shots from pivotal moments in the team's history—but all Rusty saw was a coffin. His coffin. The final resting place of his 5-year career with the team.

Garry sat at the head of the table. His usual chameleon-like façade of corporate charm stripped away. He didn't need to pretend anymore. Here, in the safety of his own cage, he could be the ruthless predator he truly was.

Lena sat beside him, silent but calculating, her presence more of a formality than a necessity. Dan, meanwhile, looked exhausted, a prisoner of this situation, his jaw clenched tight as he refused to meet Rusty's eyes. How could he?

There were no final rights. No last meal. Just lethal injection.

A single envelope lay on the table between them. Rusty didn't need to open it to know what it contained. "Richard," Garry began, his voice clipped, bitter. "I think we all knew this day was coming." He folded his hands together, his fingers tapping against each other methodically. "Your behaviour last week was unacceptable. Undermining leadership in a public forum, using inappropriate language, and actively sowing dissent among your colleagues—it's a miracle you're even being offered a severance package at all."

Rusty leaned back in his chair, crossing his arms. "Oh, I'm sorry, Garry. Were you expecting a 'thank you'?"

Garry smirked, but his eyes were ice. "Not at all. You've made it abundantly clear how you feel about this organization; frankly, the feeling is mutual. Your services are no longer required. Other members of the team will handle your renewals, and you'll be compensated for your work up to today."

Rusty exhaled through his nose, keeping himself steady. "K. Let's get on with it then."

Garry pushed the envelope forward. "Your severance. We believe this is more than fair given your years of service and the results from this renewal campaign."

Rusty didn't move to take it. "What's the number?"

Lena, all business, spoke up. "It's based on an 86% total book value."

Rusty let out a short, humourless laugh. "86%?" He shook his head at Dan, Garry and then Lena. "Try again, Lena. I hit 95% of renewals."

Garry's smile tightened. "These numbers are final."

Rusty finally picked up the envelope and slid the papers out. His eyes scanned quickly, and his stomach turned. They weren't just undercutting his renewal percentage—they weren't properly factoring in his years of service properly, either.

"You're not even including the one-month salary per year of service," he said coldly.

Garry didn't blink. "We've calculated what we believe to be fair compensation. Given the circumstances, that is."

"Fair? That's rich, coming from you." He dropped the severance package back onto the table. "Fix the numbers, Garry."

"These are accurate, Richard. I received them from accounting myself."

Rusty let the silence hang for a moment before leaning forward and planting his hands on the table. "Fix the numbers, Garry. This compensation plan you've used to determine my severance—it's based on the one you unceremoniously unveiled last week."

"That's correct," Garry said without hesitation.

Rusty cocked his head and sat up more confidently than he had in months. Dan, sensing his friend's certainty, shot him a subtle smile—a quiet gesture of respect and encouragement, yet he was careful not to get caught by Garry.

"Where's my signed contract with this new compensation plan?"

Garry blinked.

Rusty pressed. "I'll wait."

Garry glanced at Lena, who remained impassive. "Well, we never formally—"

"Sorry? You never formally, what?" Rusty cut him off, his voice now razor-sharp. "You never presented it. Is that right?"

"We did not," Lena said, no longer silent nor calculating.

"What do you think, Garry?" Rusty leaned in as Garry remained quiet. He had lost the room yet again.

He knew it.

"That's what I thought. So legally, and I'm happy to confirm this with my labour lawyer—who is one of, if not the best, labour lawyers in the city, but the previously signed compensation plan from last season's renewal campaign is still in force."

'Way to be a leader, kid!' Dan thought to himself, his face now beaming with pride.

For the first time in public, Garry's confidence faltered.

"We'll review your concerns and get back to you."

"Honestly, Lena, you're better than this. These aren't concerns. They are my legal rights. So, you'll fix the numbers," Rusty corrected. "I'll give you one week to figure this out. Or you'll absolutely be hearing from my lawyer." He tilted his head, letting the words settle. "And believe me, she would love taking a run at this entire place."

Rusty took his copy and pushed the empty papers back toward Garry. "See you in a week."

And with that, he stood, adjusting his jacket. He turned for the door, and Lena escorted him back to his desk.

Minutes later, Lena escorted Steve into the same board room and sat him in the same chair Rusty had occupied earlier. Unlike Rusty, Steve never took contract law in school and wasn't prepared for battle. He didn't really understand what was going on.

Garry studied him, his irritation barely masked. "Steve, we appreciate your time with the organization and are happy to provide this severance. We believe it's more than fair."

Steve nodded dumbly, flipping through the pages without understanding a word. "Uh, yeah. Looks good, I guess."

"You understand that the numbers are based on the new compensation model," Garry added, his voice devoid of any warmth.

Steve nodded again, unsure. "Sure, yeah."

Garry's lips curled slightly, amused at how easy this was. "You'll receive your severance cheque once you sign your release."

"So, I sign this today, then?"

Garry slid a pen across the table in anticipation, the same way the old witch kept encouraging Snow White to take a bite of the poison apple. Steve picked up the pen.

"I'd recommend taking some time to review the terms carefully and consider seeking legal advice," Dan advised as Garry and Lena both shot him glares. These were his first words of the day, and he used them well.

"Thank you, Dan," Garry said bitterly. "Yes, he should speak with...a career counsellor."

Steve walked out, unaware that he had almost accepted thousands less than he was entitled to.

Lena smirked. "Are you kidding me?"

Garry leaned against the high-back leather chair, keeping his position in place while he filled with tension. He had almost stumbled his way through the last meeting with Steve, that is, until Dan chimed in. If only he could have crossed an easy one off his list. No luck. He also hadn't fully recovered from the schooling he received from Rusty.

Losing the room's attention not once but twice was devastating, although he would never admit it.

Now, preparing to present Frank with his severance package felt like standing on the edge of a cliff.

With Lena and Dan stepping out, the silence felt almost suffocating.

He rubbed the back of his neck and sighed, wrestling with a surge of anxiety and trying to steady his thoughts. He looked around the empty room, the lingering echoes of conversation hanging in the air. "It's just business," he reminded himself, but a nagging doubt loomed large. Would Frank understand? Would he get angry? Garry shook his head, banishing those thoughts as he composed himself.

Moments later, Frank and Lena entered, his expression unreadable. Dan was not invited to this meeting.

"Garry. You wanted to see me?" Frank's voice was calm, but an edge lurked beneath.

"Yeah, Frank, thanks for coming in," Garry replied, forcing a smile that felt more like a grimace. He motioned for Frank to sit. "I'm sure you've heard some discussions about the changes happening in the company."

Frank crossed his arms. "I have, and I'm not too fond of how those discussions have been leading. What's next?"

Garry took a deep breath. "I want to be upfront with you. This isn't easy for us," he said, attempting to be diplomatic. He glanced down at the severance package in his hands. "We know that you've been a vital part of this team, and it's heart-wrenching to have to deliver this news."

"Just get to it, Garry." Frank's tone was clipped. "Rip off the Band-Aid."

Garry finally met his gaze, determination mixing with his apprehension. "Frank, the company is restructuring, and we've let you go. I have your severance package here." His voice trembled as he slid the papers across the table. "I know this represents a lot for you, and I want you to take the time to consider it. I recommend seeking legal advice or sitting down with someone you trust to go over it all."

Frank's eyes narrowed, the heat of disbelief washing over him. "So that's it? After everything, I just get... a packet? You think that's enough? You think you're doing me a solid, Garry?"

Garry shifted uncomfortably. "I wish I could change things, but—"

"But you won't," Frank interrupted, slamming his palm on the table. "You won't. You're just giving me numbers and hoping I'll Walk away quietly?"

Feeling cornered, Garry replied softly, "It's not that simple for any of us, Frank. I wish I had more to offer, but this is what we have come to."

Frank leaned back in his chair, "you call this a severance package? It's a slap in the face."

Lena's heart raced, but she remained steady. "We understand you're angry and have every right to be. Just... think about it. You've done incredible work here, and that deserves recognition. Don't let this define your worth."

There was a tense silence, the air thick with unspoken emotions. Finally, Frank's posture softened slightly. "And what if I decide I want to fight this? What then?"

Garry met his gaze, resolute. "This...this is...."

"This is bullshit, Garry," words spat out of his mouth. Frank slammed the envelope down without opening it.

Garry barely lifted an eyebrow. "I understand you're upset."

Frank leaned forward, his nostrils flaring. "You don't understand shit."

"We're not here to rehash the past, Frank."

"The past?" Frank barked out a laugh. "You mean the time I went at it with fans in this same fucking building? What was that, sixteen years ago?"

Garry's expression darkened. "I was simply testing…"

Frank's hands clenched into fists. "You don't fish for personal shit in one-on-ones, Garry. You don't get to pretend to be someone's friend just to use it against them later."

"And yet, here we are."

Frank stood abruptly, knocking his chair back. "I was right. Rusty was right. We all were right. You're a goddamn snake."

Lena sat still, but her eyes flicked to the door, wary of how close this was getting.

Garry leaned back, unfazed. "Take the severance, Frank. Or don't. I don't fucking care."

Frank took a breath, then two. And then he laughed.

"Fuck you, Garry. Fuck you and all your lies…actually…I take it back. You. Don't. Care…those are the truest words you have spoken your entire time here. You are a fucking coward."

And with that, he stormed out, leaving Garry alone in the boardroom as Lena ran after him.

And for the third time that day, Garry had lost the room. And he knew it.

Garry sat alone in the board room for over an hour, offering himself pep talks until he was ready for his next dismissal. With Rusty, Steve and Frank out of the way, Garry had three more on his initial hit list:

Brad. Bryan. Kent.

CHAPTER 39

"A Full Blown Rebuild"

It was Friday, March 31, 2017, ten days after the dismissals. The sales pit still smelled like burnt coffee, stale desperation, and broken dreams. The printer still jammed every third print job, and the shared fridge in the kitchen still held a graveyard of abandoned lunches from employees long gone. This still included Frank's long-forgotten Tupperware tomb, containing month-old leftover grilled cedar plank salmon. It remained permanently sealed with congealed mystery sauces or just dill and mayo gone bad. Everyone knew it was Frank's, but nobody had the heart to throw it out. So, there it remained, like flowers left at the scene of a car crash.

A Post-it note still stuck to Rusty's corkboard, serving as a reminder for a client call that would never happen. Hidden inside his top drawer lay a photo of Rusty, Amy, and Emma from their last summer vacation—a reminder of happier times, times that had somehow gotten lost in all the chaos. Lena must have missed it while cleaning out his desk; she was never very thorough.

It was a brand-new sales pit, even moments after the cuts came. Now, ten days later, something was missing. Scratch that—someone was missing. A lot of someones: Rusty. Frank. Brad. Bryan. Steve. Kent. Six desks no longer buzzed, and most of them were now empty. Six voices silenced. Six larger-than-life personalities in their own way, cut off at the legs.

But life in the pit moved on, of course. It always did.

Because they were still in the renewal period, phone calls still had to be made. Renewals and new sales still had to be secured, and the sales bell still needed to ring to keep the lights on, the players paid, and maybe, just maybe, their own salaries and commissions.

Tickets still had to be sold. Shane still sent out poorly addressed envelopes scrawled worse than Rusty's daughter Emma could. Clients still needed their hands held through their various crises— missing parking passes, promised concert tickets for sold-out shows that were never fulfilled, complaints about prices, feeling valued, feeling heard, complaints about the lack of vegetarian options at concessions. And so on, and so on.

But the soul of the pit had been gutted.

Rusty and Frank had been anchors—not just in leadership and tenure, but with their presence. Yes, they were loud, opinionated, and impossible to ignore. Rusty's flair for fashion and Frank's flair for the dramatic went well together. Their colleagues loved them because they called out bullshit when they saw it. They stood up for the new guys. They offered work, life, relationships, and all sorts of advice to anyone who asked for it, but they never preached. They never presented just one side of the story and never looked at life through a blurred lens. They were tactful and tasteful but fiercely protective.

They advocated for the fans. They sent memes at exactly the right time. Frank farted at exactly the wrong moment, but that was all part of his charm. That's what made life in the pit so bearable, even when it wasn't. They chirped at each other so viciously that if you didn't know better, you'd think they were mortal enemies rather than close friends. But for Frank and Rusty, if they chirped you or made fun of you in front of your face, it meant you were part of their tribe. It meant they could chirp at you about something, and it wasn't thinly veiled, nor because they wanted to break you down, but because they respected you, loved you, and expected the same brutal chirps in return. And that's what the pit had become: close friends who would go to battle for each other, and there were so many wars to fight.

While the pit also lost Kent, Brad, Bryan, and Steve, their presence was not really outliers like Frank and Rusty. The pit lost a lot of its personality that day. Sure, Shane was a personality, and Jay had his quirks, but without Rusty to selflessly let them pitch their social plans or attend a pyramid scheme meeting or offer fashion advice—and Frank offering life advice in the form of pop culture references and cooking tips—the place felt... muted.

Garry Breckenridge had preached for a culture shift. And he got one. It just wasn't in the way he had intended.

In sports, when a GM comes in and trades away the veterans, they hardly ever call it a rebuild—at least not to the public. They call it a retool. Just a small adjustment. A tweak. Something to freshen up the room and bring in a new wave of energy. Except everyone knows that's nonsense.

What Garry had done was a full-blown rebuild. He had come in and gutted the core. He shipped out the experienced guys and replaced them with unproven rookies, draft picks, future considerations, and players to be named later. He shed salary and got rid of some of the biggest voices in the room.

Gone were the guys who challenged him, who weren't afraid to call him out, who had been there long enough to know what worked and what didn't. The pit was now stocked full of new hires, FNGs, and rookies trying to find their footing. Some might thrive, but most would stumble their way and wouldn't make it.

But make no mistake, this was not a retool. It was a complete teardown.

Like so many sales teams, everyone feeds off everyone. You need the yings to the yangs. You need the loud and the quiet, the mentors and the rookies, the old guys who know every trick and the young guys who are willing to try anything. That balance had now been obliterated.

In its place? Silence.

Well done, Garry. Well done.

CHAPTER 40

"Transition Lenses"

-Rusty-

Nobody was immune to the difficult transition. Rusty had nothing left. Nothing. On the afternoon of his final meeting with Garry, he sat at his kitchen table, blankly staring at everything and nothing. He traced a finger over the ceramic handle of the personalized mug Amy had made for him on her Cricut machine years ago. He noticed a tiny crack running along its base for the first time. How long had it been there? Weeks? Months? Years?

Was this a birthday gift? An anniversary? He couldn't remember. His eyes drifted to the sink. Plates, a frying pan, one fork, and a few empty glasses. Not his. He hadn't eaten. Probably Amy's. But she hadn't been home much. He didn't even have the energy to tell her what had happened yet. She should know, but he didn't want to pile on yet another ambiguity about how they would move forward—another hurdle that would require enormous effort to overcome.

The faucet had a slow, rhythmic drip... drip... drip. He locked onto it, hypnotized by the tiny, perfect beads of water forming and falling into a glass, one after another, slowly filling it up. At least that glass is half full, he thought as he tried to count them, but his mind refused to keep the numbers in order. Seven... no, eight... wait, was that nine? He let it go. It didn't matter.

A single crumb sat on the counter near the edge of the sink. Probably from toast. Who ate toast? Was it Emma? Did she eat before going to daycare? The hood over the stove's light flickered. It was barely noticeable, but he caught it nonetheless. The refrigerator hummed a faint, subtle pulse like a dying heartbeat. Was it the motor? The wiring? Should he check the breaker? Maybe he should call an electrician or a repairman. His gaze snapped to the fridge door, where a faded magnet from some local HVAC company clung at a slight angle. Magnets from all their travels together—Mickey Mouse from Disneyworld, the famous Las Vegas sign from his buddy Tom's bachelor party, the Dave Matthews Band summer tour 2013—so many memories from his past. He reached out and adjusted the crooked magnet from Portugal so it sat perfectly straight. That felt... better.

His fingers drummed on the table. He was not used to this pace—slow and dazed. He had been constantly on the go for the past five years, or maybe more. Perhaps that was why he had never noticed every single detail he was noticing now. He had never noticed the uneven patterns of the floor tiles, and now they annoyed him. Emma's red crayon drawing, with "Daddy" missing. Maybe that was for the best, he thought.

His eyes fell to his phone on the table. The screen was dark. Had anyone texted? Had Amy? Dan? Anyone from the office? He should check. He should check. But he didn't. Had he not learned anything from Amy? It didn't matter anymore.

A small tear in the paper blinds above the kitchen sink caught his attention next. Just a frayed little piece, barely hanging on. He reached for it slowly, methodically, and pulled. The thread unravelled just a little more. His heart pounded. He wasn't sure why. He let go.

The faucet dripped. The light flickered. His son was gone. His job was gone. His marriage was gone.

He felt like he could go at any moment, too—floating away, untethered, in the silence of his own thoughts, like the Donald Duck balloon Emma had accidentally let go of almost immediately after he bought it for her at Disney. Ten dollars, American, just gone—floating away into the sky. He had been frustrated then. Amy had tried to remind him that Emma didn't know better. How could she? She was three at the time. But that didn't matter. Rusty's temper had been short back then. Oh, if things were different. If he didn't get so jaded with everything. If money didn't influence so much of his life. Maybe things could have changed. But how could things change if he didn't know they needed to change? Working with guys like Jay and Shane, who spent money like it was water, made it difficult to keep up with. As hard as he tried to differentiate himself from his younger colleagues—who had nowhere near the same life responsibilities as him—the more he realized he was like them. Amy was the voice of reason, the "no fun police," and if she weren't around, he could do whatever the heck he wanted, whenever he wanted, with whomever he wanted.

But if he hadn't met Amy, he would never have known the joy of being Emma's daddy—watching her grow, laughing and playing with her, falling asleep with her while she listened to his heartbeat on his chest as a tiny baby. Why didn't Amy think to capture that moment? That was so precious, and it was lost on her. But maybe if he wasn't around, Emma would be better off. Amy was a much better parent than he was. He was never home, for Christ's sake. His eyes caught the picture on the fridge again. It teased and mocked him. What was Amy telling Emma about her daddy? That he wasn't coming home? That he didn't love her? Why didn't Emma draw him in her picture of happiness?

He hyper-focused on the original severance package that lay unopened on the counter. Ninety-two percent renewals. Didn't matter. Five years of sacrifice. Didn't matter. Would that have changed anything if Garry knew the pain and horror he and Amy experienced? Could Garry even empathize with his situation? That didn't matter either.

Every moment felt like moving through wet cement. He didn't want to get up from the table. He didn't want to eat, even though his stomach told him otherwise. His phone buzzed, but he didn't want to answer it, even as messages poured in from old colleagues. Max checked in. Jay. Kristina. Even Dan.

But he ignored them all.

Then, hours later, the mudroom door swung open, and Emma's tiny feet stomped into the house. Amy followed immediately after, carrying Emma's Petunia Pickle Bottom diaper bag—the one with the pattern Rusty had picked out. Amy was still there. Physically. But emotionally? She was gone. He could see it in her eyes. One night, weeks before, he had mistakenly asked, "Are you okay?"

She had laughed. Not a real laugh. Something hollow. She hadn't answered immediately. She hadn't answered until he asked again.

-Frank-

For twenty-two years, Frank had woken up at the same time. He made the same Folgers coffee, showered at the same time, had a bowl of apple cinnamon oatmeal while watching reruns of shows from the '80s on the Kodi box Shane had suggested he buy. He grabbed the same keys off the counter and drove the same route to work. It was muscle memory—an automatic loop that required no thought.

It was a short trip; he could practically see the arena from his backyard, just a stone's throw away.

But now? Now, it felt like another planet.

He still followed the routine for the first two weeks after being let go. He got up, showered, got dressed, ate breakfast, watched an episode, grabbed his keys, and then he'd drive.

Not to Home Depot, where his wife had suggested he apply. No chance in hell, he thought.

Not to any job interviews, because who the heck was hiring a fifty-something-year-old sales guy?

Scratch that—former sales guy.

Just... nowhere.

It wasn't until he got halfway to the arena—sometimes at a red light, sometimes pulling into the gas station near the on-ramp—that reality would hit him: there was no work to go to.

So, he'd sit there, staring at his phone, endlessly and mindlessly scrolling through nothing. He pretended to check emails that no longer existed, opening old messages and work threads with funny memes, reading and re-reading them like some pathetic historian sifting through ancient artifacts from a life that felt like it had vanished. The memes made him smile and laugh.

Some mornings, instead of driving back home, he'd wander into the gas station, buy a black coffee he didn't want, and make it last. Sitting in his car, in the corner of the parking lot, just watching commuters rush in and out, all of them going somewhere. Somewhere that mattered to them.

But Frank? Nowhere. That was the part that scared him the most. At 52 years old, he thought he was in a horrific limbo—too old to start over, too young to retire. His mind swirled, sometimes out of control. Nobody was knocking down doors to hire an aging sales guy with zero digital marketing experience and a résumé full of ticket renewals. He wasn't some hotshot young hire with "new ideas."

He wasn't a rising star who could be moulded into something greater. He was just another guy in his 50s with great connections but only an English degree and years of what he thought was insufficient real-world experience. This made him a replaceable, disposable guy who had spent his entire adult life selling something nobody really needed.

His wife tried to be supportive, but he could see the concern in her eyes. She had started making subtle suggestions about applying at places "just for now" and "just to see how you like it." Grocery stores, banks—hell, even Home Depot. But is this what more than twenty years got you these days? "Maybe you could do something part-time," she had said carefully one night, choosing her words like a bomb technician defusing a live wire. Frank had been silent. Because the truth was, he'd already gone to Home Depot. Just to see. Just to scope it out. He had walked through the aisles, hands stuffed into his jacket pockets, watching a guy at least fifteen years younger than him trying to explain the difference between two types of lightbulbs by simply reading the packaging. That guy had a job.

A shitty job, sure. But a job.

And Frank? Frank didn't have shit. No disrespect, he thought, but the idea of standing there, wearing an orange apron, helping people find lawn care products, light bulbs, plywood planks or #8 screws made his stomach churn.

He wasn't some young kid taking a job while he figured out his next step. He kept reminding himself repeatedly, almost daily, that he was a 52-year-old former ticket salesman who had spent two decades believing his job meant something, but now it didn't.

One morning, his wife found him sitting on the couch, fully dressed for work, staring at the blank TV screen. "Frank," she said softly, standing in the doorway. "You don't work there anymore."

Frank didn't look at her. His hands were clasped together, thumbs tapping against each other, brain foggy with useless thoughts. "I know," he muttered. His voice flat, distant and defeated. "I don't know what else to do."

She exhaled, nodding, but didn't say anything else.

Because what could she say?

This wasn't just a job to Frank. It was his life.

For two decades, he had been Frank Washburn from Sales. Now? He was just... Frank Washedup.

And he fucking hated it.

-Brad-

Brad had a particularly difficult transition, even by Rusty's standards. He had always enjoyed drinking, but there was a significant difference between social drinking with friends or colleagues and needing to drink just to get through the night. Losing his job had flipped that switch.

The following weekend, after his final meeting with Garry, Brad had one too many drinks at a friend's place. He didn't feel intoxicated when he got into his car; his head was clear, and his vision was fine. He had done this plenty of times before. Then came the flashing red and blue lights in his rearview mirror.

His stomach dropped. Now he felt like throwing up—was it nerves or the alcohol? The officer barely glanced at him before asking a rhetorical question: "You been drinking tonight, sir?"

Brad's throat was dry. He wanted to lie and say, "No, just a beer with dinner, officer." But what was the point? He knew he wasn't going to get out of this one. The breathalyzer beeped: 0.11. Brad was not obliterated; he wasn't even that sloppy. But he was over the legal limit as he was placed in handcuffs and led to the back of the cruiser.

Sitting there with his wrists bound, his head tilted back against the seat, he stared at the roof and muttered, "Jesus Christ, I'm a fucking idiot."

A DUI was not just a slap on the wrist; it was a serious charge of driving under the influence. A month later, he found himself in court, listening to the judge list off his new reality as if it were nothing more than a grocery receipt. The penalties included a $1,500 fine, a one-year license suspension, mandatory driver rehabilitation program enrollment, and an interlock device installation in his car—assuming he ever wanted to drive again. Brad was in deep trouble.

But it wasn't just the fines. It was all the other consequences that nobody discussed until it was too late. His insurance rates skyrocketed. What had once been a manageable monthly bill would now be three or even four times what it was before. His job prospects? He hadn't even started looking for a new job, and now, with a fresh DUI on his record, they were virtually non-existent. Not that he would be applying for driving jobs, but who would want to hire someone with this kind of mark against them? How would he even get to and from work? The bus? Are you kidding?

His parents couldn't help either. He hadn't told them about his situation, and he wasn't even sure how to go about it. What was he supposed to say? "Hey Mom, hey Dad, I lost my job, got drunk, and got arrested. Hope you're proud! Send money!"

-Steve-

Steve hadn't wanted to go back to the casino. He knew it was a bad idea. He knew the house almost always won. But when he sat at home, staring at the deposit receipt from his severance cheque, his brain whispered: What if you could make it more?

It started small. A few hundred. He won some, he lost some; that was life. Even if he went back and lost, he was young, had just worked for one of the most famous organizations in town; surely that would give him some cachet. He wouldn't be unemployed for long. So he went back. Just one big bet, he thought. One bet, and I'm done.

A few hours later, Steve sat in his car, hands shaking, staring at multiple ATM receipts that confirmed what he already knew. He had lost almost everything. His stomach twisted as he thought about what came next: rent, bills, groceries — and nothing left to pay for them.

-Bryan-

Bryan didn't resist his transition. When the axe fell, the severance papers landed on the desk, and Garry delivered his smug little corporate send-off about "new opportunities," Bryan merely shrugged it off. He had already made up his mind when Garry first arrived. He had a sense of how things would unfold, and he was right. So, he decided he was going home.

The family farm had been dormant for years. His parents were gone now, and the land was his. For the first time, he had nothing tying him down.

No more quotas or cold calls. No more late nights at the arena. No more endless meetings about "synergy" and "maximizing revenue streams" with Garry, Kent, Wally, or even Dan.

Just dirt, air, and peace. He didn't know much about running a farm, but he figured it couldn't be harder than selling season tickets during a losing season. So, he began to learn. He read as many books as he could during his downtime, catching up on lost time and absorbing everything he could about anything. He studied crop rotations, hydroponics, and soil health. He learned how to repair old irrigation lines and spent hours down YouTube rabbit holes about vertical farming and maximizing yield.

"You actually did it, huh? The farm thing?" Kristina said, congratulating him. Bryan grinned through the video call, wearing a flannel shirt.

"I told you. You all laughed. But look at me now—fresh air, no bullshit renewal campaigns, and my biggest problem is whether my crops get enough rain."

Shane smirked. "Still got weed?"

"Got a whole goddamn green field!"

"Woooooo!" Shane cheered.

Kristina smiled. "Guess you won that bet, huh?"

Bryan chuckled. "Yeah. Guess I did."

For the first time in years, his stress wasn't about commission cheques or how quickly he responded to emails. It revolved around rainfall, seed germination, and whether he would attempt to raise chickens. If he did, he would need to figure out how to keep the wolves out of the barn. And for the first time in his life, he didn't have to buy his weed illegally. Because now? He could just grow it himself.

Bryan had always been the most laid-back guy in the pit—someone who never took things too seriously, rolled with the punches, and could feel just as comfortable in a suit at a corporate networking event as he did in a hoodie at a dive bar. Now, he was simply Farmer Bryan. Somehow, it felt like this was who he was meant to be all along.

-Kent-

For Kent, it was always about family. That was what he told himself, anyway. That was why he left the office early. That was why he didn't answer emails past 5:00 PM. That was why he prioritized weekends at the cottage over game nights at the arena.

And now? Now, he had all the time in the world to do exactly that. In a way, Kent's transition was the easiest of them all. He wasn't drowning in grief like Rusty, nor was he waking up lost like Frank. He wasn't making desperate, self-destructive choices like Brad or Steve. In fact, Kent's days were structured, predictable, and safe.

Mornings were spent at the hockey rink, watching his son's practices, sipping coffee while chatting with the other parents. Afternoons were for home projects—fixing things around the house that he had ignored for years. Summers were for the cottage, where he could sit on the dock with a beer, his feet dangling over the edge, watching the dog catch a frisbee while the sun set on the lake.

In many ways, this was the life he had always wanted. But make no mistake—Kent struggled. Kent had been a company man. Sure, he wasn't the hardest worker—but he had a role, a title, and a reason to get up in the morning. Now, he was just another guy at the rink. Just another weekend warrior at Home Depot with his life.

For someone who had spent his entire career avoiding real responsibility, Kent was suddenly confronted with a terrifying realization: he had nothing left to run from. At first, it felt liberating for Kent. No more sales meetings or pretending to be on calls when he wasn't. No more last minute "urgent" projects landing on his desk that he'd immediately pass off to Dan.

But freedom has a funny way of turning into emptiness. A few months in, Kent's routine began to unravel. He lingered too long in the mornings, found himself watching one too many YouTube videos on home repairs, and started walking slower in grocery stores, aimlessly wandering the aisles like a man with nowhere to be. He found himself checking LinkedIn, scrolling through updates from old colleagues still in the game, still grinding, still part of something. They had meetings. They had targets. They had purpose. Kent had another weekend at the cottage.

But Kent had learned to be very good at not talking about things. He wasn't about to sit down with his wife and say, "Hey, I kind of miss work." That would sound ridiculous.

Yet, the truth was, as much as he resented the grind of his old job, he missed the noise. Kent had spent years surviving corporate life by doing as little as possible. Now, without it, he realized something unsettling: he had spent so much time not investing in his work that he had never built an identity beyond it. He wasn't the guy who dominated the sales floor for the right reasons. He knew his reputation wasn't great, and in recent months, or maybe even recent years, he wasn't the guy people leaned on for advice. He wasn't the guy who made a difference in the pit, and now, more than ever, the reality hit him hard.

Because he also knew he was the guy who showed up just enough to stay relevant. The completely clueless manager who openly questioned whether the team really needed to upgrade the scoreboard to LED screens. He didn't understand the potential impact of new digital advertising streams and continued to fixate on the static outdoor walkway that hadn't been updated for years. Most of the advertisers were out of business or had undergone dramatic rebrands. Yet, perhaps that was how Kent and even Wally felt about their roles in the industry. They were old relics of the past, refusing to move forward meaningfully, and unable to make emotional connections with their staff. It wasn't their fault. After all, they came from a different generation. They felt they had earned their place through their instrumental roles in bringing the team into the league.

And now, at least for Kent, that was gone. But Kent was a master of adaptation. So he did what he had always done— he adapted. He leaned into family life with everything he had. He coached more. He volunteered more. He filled his days with activities to ensure he never had to sit in silence long enough to question anything. Because Kent was always good at making it look like everything was fine. And as long as he kept moving, kept busy enough, he wouldn't have to stop and ask himself: who the hell am I?

CHAPTER 41

"The Ascension?"

It was now Wednesday, April 5, 2017, and Dan was sitting in his brand-new office. It still felt strange not being right in the sales pit. His desk was spotless—no half-eaten Tim Hortons donuts precariously perched on the edge, and no Shane dramatically throwing stress balls at the ceiling. Just quiet. But his office lacked the warmth of Frank's heart, Rusty's drive and fans-first approach, Bryan's determination, Brad's culinary stories, and Steve's gambling tips and tricks. Dan even missed Kent because after Kent left, Dan realized that Kent knew one thing better than most. That family mattered. Work should be left at the office. His respect grew and he wished he could have seen that in Kent long before Dan lost his family.

A bottle of scotch sat on the corner of his desk with a note attached. "From one survivor to another. Try not to let it kill you." There was no name, but he had a good idea of which one of those recently departed sales mutts sent it. Dan exhaled, running a hand through his hair. Director of Sales.

Sure, it looked good on his door. It would look good on his LinkedIn when he updated it. Colleagues from other teams with whom he'd met on numerous video calls or at league meetings would be happy for him. But the job itself? That was a different story. More meetings, more budget approvals, more time dealing with the real higher-ups, and less time with the team.

A knock on the door startled him as Kristina walked in, dressed sharper than ever—tailored blazer, high heels, glowing confidence. "You know, Krissy, if I had any doubts about whether you'd step up, they're gone now. You belong in this role."

She grinned as she took a seat. "Did you ever think we'd actually make it?"

Dan smirked. "Honestly? No. And certainly not under any of these circumstances," he acknowledged, as there was a long, silent, and uncomfortable pause.

"It's... kind of... weird, don't you think?" she asked softly.

"Yes," he said, sliding a manila folder across the desk. The finalized fan and community development program she, Max, and Rusty had worked so hard on. Her name was at the top. "It's official," he said. "Your flexible benefits program? Approved. Your broker partnerships? Signed." He leaned back, giving a small, reluctant nod. "You did it, Kristina."

She just stared at the folder for a second, as if she couldn't believe it was real. Then, a slow smile spread across her face. She had worked twice as hard as everyone else to get here. She pitched ideas that were initially laughed out of the room. Yet she continued to take risks. She knew the job wasn't just about renewals and quotas but about evolving.

Kristina looked up at Dan. "You gonna be okay in here? Kinda lonely, isn't it?"

Dan chuckled, rubbing the back of his neck. "I miss having a team. I miss Rusty. I miss Frank. I miss the stories. I miss my family. I miss the pit."

Kristina smirked. "You used to be one of us."

Dan sighed, glancing at the arena outside. "I still am, Krissy. Deep down in my plums, I still am."

Back in the pit, Shane hated the new seating chart. Mostly because Kristina now sat where Dan used to, and he missed Rusty's presence. Jay was not the same either, and Shane barely went out after it all went down. It had been about a month since the culture shock and cuts and only a few weeks since the promotions. He had been half-expecting Kristina to fail, get overwhelmed, and realize she wasn't cut out for this. But she wasn't failing. She was thriving. And she was implementing things—not just discussing "next season" ideas that would die on a whiteboard. No, she was making changes. Making changes now.

And it was pissing him off. He watched her lead a morning huddle, joking easily with the team, answering questions, and walking through new strategies. She had tasked him with mentoring the new retention staff hired straight out of college, excited for their 'dream job' working in professional sports.

Shane now knew the opportunity had passed him long ago. She immersed herself in meetings, respected and trusted the process, and rarely faltered under pressure. She wasn't just his manager now; she was better at this job than he was.

Shane gritted his teeth, faking a smile as she made eye contact with him while returning from her meeting with Dan. The manila folder was pressed tightly against her chest and tucked under her armpit. He'd rather swallow a bag of glass than admit it, but deep down, it bothered him in a way he couldn't quite explain.

He tried to confide in Dan about it over lunch but to no avail. "You ever just feel... like this job is getting too political?" Shane asked, stabbing at his garden salad with tuna as if it had personally insulted him.

Dan, scrolling through emails on his phone, barely looked up. "What?"

Shane leaned in. "I mean, come on. Kristina? She's been here, what, five years? I've been here twelve. And now I have to report to her?"

Dan set his phone down. "She's the best person for the job, Shane. Deep down, I know you know this."

Shane scoffed. "You don't think it's a little... convenient? HR pushing the whole 'we need more women in leadership' thing? Like, great, whatever, but she's still got to earn it, you know?"

Dan stared at him. "She did earn it," he stated, as Shane felt something twist in his gut. For the first time in his twelve years with the team, Dan wasn't on his side. Dan wasn't one of them anymore.

Shane forced a laugh, shaking his head. "Man, you've changed."

Dan took a sip of his coffee, unfazed. "You haven't, Shane."

Shane didn't like the way that sounded.

CHAPTER 42

"Rubbing Salt in the Wound"

Salty had always been the glue guy. He wasn't the loudest. He wasn't the flashiest. He wasn't the type to make grand speeches or demand attention. But he was consistent. Dependable. Smart. So when Garry gutted the department and filled it with rookies, someone had to clean up the mess.

Kristina was focused on running the show. Shane was barely keeping it together. And the rookies? The rookies were floundering because they had no mentors. No direction as they were thrown into the burning fire without so much as a bucket of water. But somehow, Salty became the guy they turned to.

It was, and it wasn't part of his or Garry's plan. Until his post-mortem one-on-one with Kristina, Salty had never seen himself as a manager. He always thought of himself as a player, not a coach.

Someone who helped in the trenches but not from a larger office.

But in their 'how do we move forward' meeting, Kristina had asked, "What do you want, Sal?" And for the first time, he had an answer. Salty was offered the opportunity to make the Inside Sales Manager position his own. It didn't take much time for him to do things how he wanted to, and to Salty, Kristina, Dan, and the inside sales reps who desperately needed direction, it all made sense.

So Salty took it, and suddenly, he became the guy responsible for the next generation. He didn't bark orders like Garry. He didn't micromanage like some insecure exec trying to prove a point. He just helped. Salty taught the new generation how to engage and talk to clients, not just sell to them. In fact, he taught them how to handle rejection and ways to stay sane in a job designed to burn people out.

And to his surprise? He was damn good at it. Maybe he wasn't Rusty. Maybe he wasn't Frank. But he didn't need to be anything more than who he was; that was exactly what these kids needed. Salty realized he had built something that mattered.

Meanwhile, Jay had spent his whole career feeling like a rookie. He never took anything seriously. He never worried about the future. He never thought about settling down. In short, maybe he was more like Peter Pan than he liked to believe.

That is, until Jennifer. At first, he had no idea why she liked him. She was sharp, patient, and had her life together. And for some reason, she saw something in him. She even got him off the Vodka Cranberries.

"You're a grown man," she teased. "Drink something that doesn't taste like an air freshener."

So he switched to tequila. With a shot of salt and lemon.

Salty had found his place as a leader. Jay had found his place as a man. And in their own ways, they had both finally stopped being rookies.

Jay stayed with the team but took on a much more senior role managing the ticket broker program. He was instrumental in brokering new partnerships with ticketing platforms like TickPick, StubHub, and Vivid Seats. He travelled more, attended major events, and sat at negotiation tables with executives who, for the first time in his life, actually took him seriously.

He would often attend the international ticket broker conference, a gathering of the best and worst in the industry. It was here he found himself an unlikely bridge between brokerages and professional teams. Jay had an instinct for reading people, a skill he had honed from years of lighthearted banter and skirting responsibility. Now, that very skill made him valuable. He knew how to talk, listen, and more importantly, find the middle ground where deals got made.

Jennifer watched his growth with a mix of pride and amusement. "You know," she said one evening over drinks, "you're actually kind of impressive now."

Jay smirked. "Don't spread that around. I have a reputation to maintain."

Their relationship had evolved along with him. There were no grand ultimatums, no dramatic gestures. Just an understanding that whatever this was, it was real. He still had his moments—days when he wanted to throw responsibility out the window and let life happen. But those days were fewer and farther between.

For the first time in his life, Jay wasn't just skating by. He was building something. And maybe, just maybe, he was finally ready to stop being a rookie—for good.

CHAPTER 43

"The Rebuild that Never Was"

Now, back in 2021, the screen of the virtual pit beers flickered as Salty set down his drink and smirked. "Remember Jaxxyn? With two X's and a Y?"

Frank nearly choked on his beer. "Two X's and a Y? What was he, a biological experiment gone wrong? Sounds like someone's parents were trying too hard to be non-binary! What's next, a name with a Z just to really throw biology out the window?" He shook his head."

"Frank!" Salty scolded, a bemused grin spreading across his face. "That comment was acceptable and expected back in the day, but it's a different time and place now."

"In my day, we had names, not 60 point words in a Scrabble game. Wait, isn't the XXY gene also known as the serial killer gene?"

"You know, Frank, we also hired a Jaxon," Jay added. "J-A-X-O-N"

Frank threw his hands in the air in disgust. "Daniel-son, tell me you didn't have a role in hiring Jax-On, Jax-Off," Frank said before realizing what he had said.

Shane lost his shit. Jay too.

"Please tell me he got fired! Or arrested."

Jay shook his head, grinning. "Nope. He got promoted. Director of Strategy or some bullshit title."

"Are you kidding me?!" Frank was beside himself, turning a dark shade of plum.

"Of course he was." Dan laughed and rolled his eyes. "Garry would've loved him. No independent thoughts, corporate as hell. Probably took notes in a fucking Moleskine."

Kristina exhaled, swirling her glass. "Do you guys remember the day he sat at Rusty's desk?"

Shane groaned, pinching the bridge of his nose. "Oh my God. That was the moment I knew we were completely fucked."

Jay chuckled. "You had just come back from taking a shit, too."

"Listen." Shane pointed at him. "I was gone for five minutes. Five. Minutes. And in that time, this kid just waltzes in, pops in his fucking headphones, sips on his banana smoothie like he's some Silicon Valley startup CEO, and plops his ass down at Rusty's desk. Are you fucking kidding me?"

Frank was not laughing now. "If I had been there, I swear to God, I would have thrown him out the door like Uncle Phil tossing Jazz."

Salty grinned. "I was gonna say something, but what was the point?"

Kristina shrugged. "The kid wasn't breaking any rules. He was just... clueless. Like, aggressively clueless. And he felt entitled."

"No respect." Shane shook his head. "You don't just sit there. Not without knowing. Not without earning it."

Jay raised an eyebrow. "Didn't you sit at Rusty's desk once?"

"That was different!" Shane protested. "I was hungover and needed his comfy chair."

Kristina sipped her drink. "That whole year, we did everything we could to keep the pit's spirit alive."

Salty nodded. "But it faded. Pit Beers?" he asked rhetorically. "A distant memory."

Kristina sighed. "The first time I invited the rookies, a few showed up, but they were glued to their phones, talking about work like it was a networking event."

"A networking event." Frank scoffed. "I want to throw up. Classic mutts."

"They left early," Jay added, "to 'get some 'rest' before the next sales push.'"

"Pussies" Frank yelled. "No offence, uh, Krissy."

"They don't make sales guys like they used to. Uh...no offence again, Krissy."

Shane buried his face in his hands. "Pit Beers used to be wild. Unhinged. Full of chirps and well-timed roasts. That whole place used to be different."

"Now?" Kristina leaned back on her couch. "It felt like a forced company outing."

"Nobody chirped each other," Salty said. "Nobody told stories. Nobody got so drunk they did something embarrassing enough to be joked about for months."

"At least not like in the past," Jay smirked.

Shane sighed dramatically. "We're fucking old. What have we done with our lives?"

Brad grinned. "Not a damn thing, apparently."

Salty shook his head. "And don't even get me started with the group chat. That became a ghost town, too."

Kristina chuckled bitterly. "I even added the rookies. Tried to get some banter going."

Jay smirked. "You even sent a gif of some washed-up athlete making a comeback...Brett Favre?"

"No one responded." Kristina exhaled. "Actually, scratch that. Thirty minutes later, one of the rookies—Adam? Alex? Who even knows at this point?—finally replied:

'Hey Kristina, just checking—was this meant for the whole group? Or just managers?'"

Frank nearly fell out of his chair. "Snowflakes!"

Kristina rolled her eyes. "I closed the chat, put my phone face-down, and just stared at the ceiling."

Salty pointed at her. "I remember that. That was the moment we knew it was over."

"Then there was that email chain incident," Salty said, shaking his head.

"Oh, here we go." Bryan smirked.

"It was probably you, Shane," Salty continued. "Someone sent a meme about a bad sales month."

Shane shrugged innocently. "Couldn't've been me."

"No, he's right. Shane never had a bad sales month," Jay giggled.

"Ass kisser!" Frank yelled.

"HR was to say," Kristina deadpanned. Everyone groaned, but Kristina laughed. "I got an email from HR asking if it was 'appropriate workplace communication.'"

Salty grinned. "She walked right over to my desk, showed me the email, and I just closed my laptop and said—"

Kristina and Salty simultaneously: "Oh, for fuck's sake."

Frank was crying laughing. "You can't make this woke shit up!"

Jay just shook his head. "The culture was dead."

Shane sighed, swirling his drink. "Replaced by polite, corporate, small talk."

"Shane, You also got soft!" Frank criticized.

Shane leaned back on his expensive Italian leather sofa. "You guys realize... none of that sat right with me. Like, at all."

Dan smirked. "You really are old, Shane."

"No, I'm not!"

"You are, dude." Jay grinned. "You and I—well, mostly you—spent years being the guy who didn't take anything seriously. You lived for the chaos. The chirps. The unhinged energy of the pit. And now?" Jay shook his head, pointing at him. "Now you are sitting here, pissed off, reminiscing about the good old days, talking about 'respect' and 'culture.' Like some grizzled old coach. That's growth, my guy."

"I am NOT ready to be the old guard!" Shane groaned.

Salty chuckled. "Whether you like it or not, that's what we all are now."

Shane sighed dramatically. "This place used to be fun."

"Yeah. It did."

Frank sat up. "You know, from my perspective, Jaxxyn wasn't the problem. The rookies weren't the problem. The problem was that the pit was no longer yours. It was a different place now, run by a different kind of person. And it wasn't Kristina's leadership or Salty's mentoring that had changed things. It was just... time. The new hires didn't know. They never would."

"And that's what hurt the most," Shane said with a sombre look.

CHAPTER 44

"Quit While You're Ahead, Kid"

Max sat at his desk, staring at the glowing screen in front of him, the names of his 300 clients flickering like ghosts of the past. Once, these names meant something—a testament to his climb, hustle, validation, and rewards for his hustle and hard work. Now, they felt hollow, like cheap trophies collecting dust on a forgotten shelf.

Rusty was gone. Frank was gone. Others, too. People who had spent years grinding, sacrificing, believing. Their reward? A severance package, an empty office, and a silence that hung over the team like a funeral procession.

He thought he could stomach it—thought he understood how this business worked. But nothing could have prepared him for seeing Rusty, a man who had poured his heart and soul into this place, walking out with a cardboard box full of memories no one cared about but him. The worst part? The look on Rusty's face. It wasn't shock. It wasn't even anger. It was resignation. A man who had spent years fighting a system that, in the end, had already decided his fate.

It was a system that would eventually cost him dearly. And Max didn't want to fall victim to the same fate. Max walked and looked at the chair that Rusty formerly occupied. He glanced across the room at other pods before turning around to see that Jay was currently banging his head on his desk, trying to salvage a renewal call that had spiralled out of control. Shane, oblivious, strutted to the coffee machine, boasting to anyone who would listen about a four-club, full-season package he had closed—while on the toilet, no less.

"Big day already, and it's not even 9:30!" Shane chirped, flashing his grin.

Max didn't respond. He just watched, his stomach churning, a slow realization dawning. He had seen this before. The desperation masked as confidence. The transactional friendships. The relentless cycle of churn-and-burn.

Did he leave a bad, bad place and show up somewhere a whole lot worse?" he wondered aloud. He had left one corporate hamster wheel disguised as a career for another. At least at Capshaw Chemical, the toxicity was quiet and unspoken. Here, a place where every handshake was a transaction, every meeting a performance. It had drained him, dulled him, made him question everything.

Max exhaled sharply. He wasn't naïve. He knew professional sports were brutal. He had initially accepted the long hours, the thankless grind, the relentless pressure. But he had told himself it was different because it meant something. Meant something to him. Maybe he didn't think about it long enough. Maybe he got caught up in the dopamine hit of meeting Dan serendipitously that night on the concourse. But now, he wasn't so sure.

He walked back to his desk and glanced back at his screen, his fingers hovering over the keyboard. Then, almost without thinking, he started typing. A thought, or rather a similar flicker of an idea that solidified into something more with each new click. His heart thudded in his chest as he opened a new document, his mind moving faster than his fingers.

Maybe the sales pit wasn't it. Maybe it never was. As Rusty would say, he had enjoyed facilitating a positive relationship between the team and its fans, but he now knew that he could do so much more and still keep his soul for the next life.

The realization wasn't loud. It didn't crash into him like a wrecking ball. It was quiet. Subtle. A weight he hadn't realized he was carrying finally lifting, so without hesitation, he hit print.

In the distance, the printer whirred to life, spitting out the document that suddenly felt heavier than it should have. Max stood, his legs unsteady and walked over to grab the warm page. He barely registered Jay's muffled cursing from his desk as he passed, nor did he notice Shane mindless surfing the Harry Rosen website, his mind elsewhere.

He marched straight to Kristina's office and shut the door behind him.

"Max?" she asked, eyebrow raised.

He placed the document on her desk, exhaling as if he'd just dropped the weight of the world. This was a feeling he knew well. Déjà vu. "Hey, Krissy, I think we need to talk."

Company policy was that if a sales employee decides to quit, they are walked out of the office on the same day. After speaking with Max, she understood that someone as sensitive as Max was not a good fit in sales. She knew enough about him over the past two months to know that he had not stayed true to himself and did more than he was comfortable with doing, trying to fit into the sales pit. For those reasons, she didn't push back; not because she didn't want to, but because she knew it was for the best. It was now Kristina's responsibility to follow protocol and walk him to HR as a precautionary measure. She didn't worry about Max, but protecting sensitive information and company assets was a department-wide practice. This practice helped mitigate the risk of misusing confidential data, prevent workplace disruption, and maintain a secure environment for the organization and its remaining employees.

Kristina gave Max a hug before he walked out of the office. He walked to his Honda Civic with an odd sense of relief. The weight of deadlines, expectations, and the looming presence of Frank's infamous rules had finally lifted.

At first, Max thought leaving would be like leaping off a cliff. Instead, it felt more like stepping off a curb—disorienting but manageable. Within weeks, he landed a position at a creative agency firm across town, one with a modern, open-concept office and a culture that didn't feel like it had been frozen in the '90s...aside for their vintage Pac-Man arcade game. There were no Frank-style decrees, no rigid hierarchies. Just creative work. And Max was good at it. Business development? Check.

Client relations? Check. Max was happy and he didn't have to sell his soul to find happiness.

His new role came with a corner office—if you could call it that. The office was open-concept, and each of his teammates had a spot in front of a window overlooking the bustling street below. There were two long rows of desks with a collaborative space in the middle. Max lucked out and technically got to the corner office because he had a window on both sides of his computer monitor.

It was bliss which was more than he could say for his last job. The pay was better, too. The work was more stimulating, and he didn't dread Monday mornings for the first time in years. His reputation followed him, and soon enough, he was leading a team, making decisions instead of just carrying out someone else's. Clients respected him, colleagues sought his input, and Max found himself enjoying the challenge in a way he hadn't.

But his career wasn't the only thing that changed.

It started with a text. A simple, harmless message from Kelly, the receptionist. She had been a friend, a quiet confidante who saw everything that happened in the office and had encouraged him once while they were still colleagues to consider looking elsewhere. The text was casual, congratulatory even: 'Heard you landed on your feet. Drinks to celebrate?'

One drink turned into two, then dinner, then an unspoken understanding. They had danced around something, always keeping their conversations on the safer side of friendly. Max had never crossed the line—not with Frank's rule hanging over his head like an ever-present storm cloud. It wasn't written anywhere, but everyone knew it. Frank had enforced it like gospel. And for Max, it had stuck—part respect for Frank, part fear of complicating the one job he truly cared about. But now? Now, he wasn't an employee anymore. He was just Max. No more arena badge. No more extension number. No more pit.

And really, wasn't this just like Squints and Wendy Peffercorn all over again? Sure, Max might not have pulled an over-the-top, poolside stunt to steal a kiss, but he had swung out of his league. He wasn't about to call himself a legend in the making, but the sheer fact that Kelly had stuck around made him feel like he had just belted one into the cheap seats.

Their relationship unfolded naturally, steadily, without the secrecy or complications that office romances invited. It was definitely not the office scandal the rest of the sales pit would have clamoured over, and it was much better that way! Kelly, it turned out, had been planning to leave, too. She had ambitions that extended beyond answering phones and scheduling meetings. She enrolled in a business admin course, and Max admired her drive as much as her company.

A year after leaving, Max attended an industry gala—not as a last minute invitee but as a representative of his new company. It was one of those networking events where everyone pretended not to be sizing each other up. He spotted Frank across the room, deep in conversation with someone who looked just as exhausted as Max used to be. Frank didn't see him, but Max didn't mind. He didn't need closure, he just needed confirmation. Confirmation that he wasn't crazy for walking away. Max thought Frank looked to be in better health and spirits; he was right.

By the time Max and Kelly moved in together, he had stopped thinking of his old job as the defining chapter of his life. It had been a stepping stone, nothing more. And as he poured himself a drink in their new apartment, he smirked at the thought of Frank's golden rule—the one he had followed to the letter, only to break it the moment it no longer mattered.

Maybe Frank was right in the strictest sense, but Max had learned something else along the way: the best things in life don't come from rules. They come from knowing when to leave them behind— and occasionally, from swinging big and knocking one out of the park.

CHAPTER 45

"Sunday Bloody Sunday"

Dan arrived ten minutes early, which was rare for him. He had spent the entire drive across town wondering if this was a mistake: dinner with his ex-wife, Kara. It wasn't a date or even a friendly catchup. It was a necessity—a meeting between two people who once shared a life of love, now connected only by their teenage daughter, who barely spoke to him, and their eleven-year-old son, who had missed out on many childhood memories with his dad.

He spotted Kara the moment she walked in and waved her over. She looked... lighter, he thought. She appeared healthier—not just physically, though the stress lines he once recognized were softer—but there was something else. For the first time in fifteen years, Kara carried a looseness in her shoulders and an ease in her demeanour. She looked happy.

Dan already knew she was seeing someone—a lawyer. Someone stable, he thought. Or maybe just someone who could care for, support, and love her in ways Dan had stopped doing years before everything fell apart. He couldn't even be mad about it. Kara deserved it.

She slid into the booth across from him as they exchanged pleasantries.

"Hey," he said.

"Hey," she replied.

The conversation began like every email they exchanged— short, polite, and a little strained. It was just like old times. They talked about Morgan, their fourteen-year-old daughter, who had recently decided she was too old to say "I love you" to her father.

"She did well on her school project this week," Kara said.

"That's good," Dan replied.

"She's thinking about trying out for the soccer team next year, Dan. She's quite athletic."

Dan forced a smile. "She always loved playing in the backyard," he said as Kara looked at him, deciding whether to say something. Then she sighed just as the server arrived to take their orders.

She already knew what she wanted and didn't even look at the menu. On the other side of the table, Dan ordered whatever he saw first—a formality.

Once the server left, Kara rested her elbows on the table. "Dan... we need to talk about something," she said softly so as not to draw attention to their table. Dan felt a familiar weight settle in his chest.

She didn't even need to say it. He already knew.

"Morgan doesn't want to do the back-and-forth anymore," Kara said carefully.

Dan stared at her. "She says it's too much," Kara continued. "Packing a bag every week, splitting time.

She's getting older. She's got school, friends... a boyfriend. She just wants stability."

Dan's jaw tightened. "And by stability, you mean?"

"She wants to stay with me. Full-time," she said as she lowered her head.

There it was. The beginning of the end. Dan leaned back in his chair, running a hand over his face. He couldn't be surprised. He had barely been present, even when he was there.

Morgan had withdrawn. So, he withdrew. It was only a matter of time before their son, Ryan, would start doing the same. This was a moment Dan had feared since they split, and now Morgan was just making it official.

"She's still your daughter, Dan," Kara said gently. "She just... doesn't want to keep bouncing between houses," she assured as Dan let out a bitter laugh.

"She's still a child, Kara!" Dan whispered angrily. "Why are you alienating her from me?" he asked bitterly. "And how long before Ryan does the same?" he muttered.

Kara didn't answer. She didn't have to.

"I am not alienating her from you. She's fourteen, Dan. She can decide on her own. I've tried telling her to take her time because this is a big decision."

Dan swallowed. "So, what does this mean?"

Kara softened. "She said she's been thinking about this since she was twelve. And...it means you still get to see her. Just... not every week. Maybe Sundays. Maybe holidays. Whenever she wants."

"Jesus Christ, Kara. We both know what that means: less time, less connection, more distance," he said.

"That's a possibility, Dan. I'm sorry. Truly, I am."

Their lunches arrived moments later, which momentarily cut some of the tension.

"So. Work's still..." Kara started.

"Insane? Yeah," Dan interrupted, almost laughing. "Yeah. But hey, I got promoted. Director of Sales."

Kara's lips barely moved. "Wow," she said, her tone shallow and unimpressed.

Dan took a sip of his water, suddenly hating the way she looked at him.

"Kristina got promoted too—Manager of Sales. She's really turning things around. The flexible benefits program, broker partnerships—all of it got through."

Kara nodded. "Is she the one you fucked?"

"Excuse me?"

"You heard what I said, Dan. Is she. The one. You. Fucked?" she repeated.

Dan was flabbergasted and now on the defensive. "I have no idea where that came from, Kara. I never cheated on you. I couldn't even give you time. How could I have given it to anyone else?"

"You know what, it doesn't matter anymore, Dan," she said flatly.

"I promise. I know I let the job take over, and I wasn't good in the spouse department. I still haven't started dating anyone. But I get the sense you have. You have a new aura to you. A new... confidence. What does he do?"

"Sorry? I thought you knew I swore off toxic men like you," Kara snapped.

"What does that mean?" he asked.

"Jessica is a social worker. She works with at-risk youth."

"Wow, Jessica, eh?" Dan smirked. "I never thought you'd have requested a trade to another team, Kara."

"Hey, I know how much you just love sports metaphors, so how about this... you put me on the trading block and kept me in the press box out of the action. Then you offloaded me without a second thought. So, no, Dan, I didn't request a trade... I was traded for a box of pucks."

Dan spoke softly, and carefully to not engage further. "I'm sorry, Kara. You're not wrong."

Dan wasn't expecting Kara's frustration, but he didn't fight it. She needed to be heard, and he needed to just sit there, eat shit, and listen. Then he laughed.

"What's so funny?" she said aggressively.

"You said... box," Dan said smugly; so much for eating shit.

"You're so immature, Dan." Kara rolled her eyes before smiling with a little giggle. "You know, I've been thinking a lot about the paths you've both chosen, and it hit me just how different our worlds are now. You're wrapped up in a profession prioritizing profits over people, and Jessica invests time and energy into understanding individual needs. She's out there fostering genuine connections and promoting real healing in people's lives. But I can't help but notice that in the sales pit it often comes down to superficial tactics designed to close the deal, regardless of whether you've truly addressed your clients' concerns. Do you realize how that creates a cycle of inauthenticity?"

Dan paused, then nodded in agreement. "It's like we're at opposite ends of a spectrum—one of us striving to make a difference while the other simply plays the game."

"I just wish you could see the impact of that difference," Kara replied, her tone much softer.

The server came around to ask how the first few bites tasted. Dan hadn't even started.

"Just great," she said. Then, after a pause, she added, "Anyway, do you even like it, Dan?"

Dan exhaled. "Do I like what? The non-existent sex?"

"No, Dan. Is the new job worth all the hassle you barely survived to get? Do you like it?"

"It's what I've been working for."

"That's not what I asked," she said, which kicked off what felt like an eternity of uncomfortable silence before Kara picked up her glass, swirled the Pinot Grigio, and finally spoke.

"You know, Dan... you were never there."

His stomach clenched. "I know."

"No, you don't," she said softly. "Even when you were home, you weren't there."

"You're right. I have nothing to say to that. You're right. I was never there."

Kara sighed, tilted her head back, took a long gulp of her wine, and shook her head. "I kept telling myself it was just a phase," she continued. "That the hours would get better, that you'd find a way to balance everything. But you never did. Because there was always another season, another contract, another reason why work had to come first. And it almost always came first, Dan."

Dan swallowed, staring down at the table as Kara softened.

"I think the good thing about all this is that I'm not mad at you anymore," she said. "I was. For a long time. But I'm not anymore. You are who you are."

Dan forced a smirk, but it barely held. "And what's that?"

"You are a man who only knows how to love one thing at a time," Kara said, her words sharp like daggers into his heart. That one hit. That one hit hard.

"I'm sorry for what I said earlier," she added.

"What part?" Dan asked smugly.

"For asking if you slept with her and for letting my frustrations come out like that. I've tried to work on that."

"You're allowed to have emotions. You are allowed to speak your mind. I'm sorry for the insensitive, sexist comment. Ultimately, it's important that you are happy. You look happier, and you deserve that."

"We both do, Dan. If we are happier, then our kids will be happier too."

After lunch, Dan sat in his car, gripping the steering wheel. His phone buzzed with emails and texts; he ignored all of them. Kara was right: the back-and-forth was a grind. He was a child of divorce and felt it had messed him up, too. He wanted what was best for his kids, but he had now nearly lost everything outside of work. And for what? A title? A bigger paycheque? The respect of his boss? More responsibilities? More bullshit?

Suddenly, Dan realized that Kara was right. He had built his entire life around this job, and now there was no one left to share it with. Dan caught himself looking in the rearview mirror as Kent had always said. But there was no one behind him—nobody clamouring for his job because it wasn't the glitz and glamour gig he once thought it was.

CHAPTER 46

"When the World Ends"

It was April 15th, just shy of a month after his dismissal. Rusty was not the same. He had stopped checking his phone. The messages from colleagues, family, friends, and even Dan had dwindled. The flood of support and well-wishes had now become a slow drip. At first, it was the usual "How are you holding up, pal?" and "We're here if you need anything," and "Love you, buddy." But when he stopped replying, the messages mostly stopped, or there was radio silence altogether. It was probably easier that way for all parties. Now, nobody wanted to overstep boundaries or get involved if it was only going to be, as Shane called it, "a one-sided friendship."

That night, the house was quiet. Too quiet. Amy, still unable to comprehend the weight of their loss and growing increasingly more frustrated with Rusty's mood swings was gone for the night, choosing to stay at her sister's place, seeking shelter from the pain that had stolen her soul. She hadn't said much to Rusty before she left—just a simple "You should get some rest. Please try to do something positive for yourself."

Positivity. Rest. Rusty scoffed at the words. Rest and sleep had been a foreign concept to him for months leading up to everything and had transformed into an impossibility for weeks. Every time he closed his eyes, he saw blood on the bathroom floor. Blood down Amy's thighs and blood on his hands from his inability to help in that moment. He saw their obstetrician's face, carefully blank and sombre, as she delivered the words that shattered their world. He saw Amy curled up in bed, sobbing and clutching the baby blanket his sister had made them, a baby blanket they would never use. And perhaps most haunting of all, Rusty saw the same tiny white casket in his nightmares again, positioned in the middle of a large open space. Pushing through the thick fog, walking slowly and cautiously towards it, he faintly heard Amy's scream in the distance. The scream growing much louder as the lid of the casket swung open. Normally, this would be enough to shake Rusty awake in a cold sweat and panic. He'd ground himself by turning over and placing his hand on Amy's hip or walking to his daughter's room to see her sleeping peacefully.

Through even denser fog, another object appeared— a much larger mahogany casket directly behind and overshadowing the tiny ivory box he had seen too many times before. Both vessels were now inside the empty nursery—the one he and Amy had recently finished together. He built up the courage to open the larger one as he approached it. Oddly and unexpectedly, it was empty aside from the baby blanket, cloth diapers, and Rusty's blue hippopotamus stuffie from when he was a baby. The stuffie was the only comfort he felt this entire dream and what he desperately needed. So he crawled inside the casket and shut the lid above him.

A car with a loud muffler rattled the windows as it drove by in the middle of the night. He woke up again, but this time, Rusty felt more panic. He felt that he had truly failed this time, especially without his wife and daughter close for comfort. He had failed everyone. The thumbing bass of the techno music in the car outside was too much for him.

Rusty lay at the edge of the bed, staring at his hands. His knuckles were white, his fingers trembling, his shirt's collar soaked with sweat. The weight on his chest felt heavier than ever, like an unrelenting vice pressing him into the mattress. His legs were unable to move. He had lost feeling in his toes. He had lost everything.

The baby. The job. His sense of purpose. He had tried. God, had he tried.

He had tried throwing himself into work, burying himself in renewal calls and endless spreadsheets as a distraction he thought he needed. He tried pretending that if he just worked harder, just pushed through the pain, maybe he could outrun it. But it caught up to him anyway.

Rusty saw it. Dan saw it.

When Rusty had finally broken down in Dan's office, when he had finally said the words out loud— We lost the baby, Dan—he had expected something else. Pity, maybe. A pat on the shoulder, a meaningless "I'm so sorry." But Dan had just looked at him with tired eyes and said, "I know this feels impossible. But you're not alone."

The words stuck with him, but they didn't feel true. Because when he was alone—when the silence of the house wrapped around him like the suffocating fog from his dreams—it felt like there was no way out. There was nothing left to do but crawl into the casket and shut the lid.

Rusty exhaled shakily as the blood returned to his feet. He willed himself to stand up. Then he stood up. But the walls of the cold and quiet house felt too close. He needed air. He needed space. He grabbed his coat, barely registering its weight as he stepped outside into a late April night. The night air was sharp, crisp against his skin, and the humidity made everything feel heavier, too. It was the type of cold and wetness that soaked the marrow in his bones. But at this point, he didn't care. He didn't know where he was going. Maybe he'd just walk until he couldn't feel feelings anymore.

So he walked for what felt like hours. The neighbourhood's streets were empty; the world around him was mostly quiet except for the louder-than-normal distant hum of late-night or early morning traffic from the expressway kilometres away. The darkness stretched around him, vast and endless, like his dreams of late.

His thoughts spiralled and spiralled and spiralled, a relentless storm inside his skull.

"Amy deserves better than this. Emma deserves better than this," he quietly reminded himself. "She deserves someone who can take care of her. Someone who doesn't crumble the second things get hard."

He stopped walking, pressing the heels of his palms into his eyes. He failed to realize in that moment that there was nothing he could have done to prevent this tragedy. Nine out of ten times, he was able to take care of the situation—his fight or flight would always kick in, and he'd punch, claw, kick, and scratch his way to safety. Once, when he and Amy were driving home late at night, a deer suddenly bolted across the road. His instincts kicked in, and he gripped the wheel, avoided overcorrecting, and steered the car into the skid. Even though their hands were shaking and hearts were pounding like a drum, he didn't freeze; he approached the situation calmly, and after catching his breath and ensuring Amy was okay, he checked his mirrors and continued the drive home. Under normal circumstances, he could remind himself of his heroic efforts, but this one hit hard.

His mind conjured impossible scenarios where he could have swooped in and changed the outcome—like a car skidding. But this wasn't like those moments. There was nothing he could do but watch the world end. And that was the part he couldn't live with. It wasn't just the loss itself. It was the helplessness he felt. He hated feeling helpless and hopeless. The agonizing truth was that, for all his instincts to fight, protect, and take action, he had been powerless.

If there had been a way, any way, to stop the tragedy from happening, Rusty would have done it. Every fight response, every survival instinct, every ounce of his being would have been poured into saving Amy and their child. But the cruellest part of it all was that there was no fight to be had. No action to take. No villain to stop. Just an unrelenting, merciless reality that unfolded in front of them despite all his will and readiness to change it.

Now, outside in the cold air, his mind refused to accept any of that. Instead, it ran a relentless, vicious loop of what he should have done and what he could have done if he had known better. "If I had driven her to the hospital sooner... Maybe the doctors could have intervened. Maybe there was something they could have done. We should have noticed the signs earlier... Amy's fatigue, the discomfort—this wasn't like Emma's birth—what if I had paid more attention? What if I had known what to look for? I should have done more around the house; if I had just taken on more stress so she didn't have to... Maybe she wouldn't have pushed herself so hard. Maybe her body wouldn't have failed their child. Wait, you should have protected them better... YOU were supposed to keep them safe. That was your job. Your purpose. And you failed!"

The grief had settled into his bones, heavy and unshakeable. It wasn't just sadness. It was something darker. Something deeper. It felt permanent. He felt stuck. Trapped. The exhaustion was overwhelming. It wasn't just lack of sleep—it was something more.

He thought about calling someone. Dan, maybe. Frank. Hell, even Shane. But what would he even say? "Hey, I can't do this anymore?" No one wanted to hear that. He thought about going to the hospital. But that felt impossible, too. What would he even say when he walked through the doors into the emergency room? "Help me, I feel like I'm drowning?" They'd probably shrug, tell him to go sit in the waiting room for hours, give him a prescription, and tell him to go home and sleep.

As if sleep would fix this.

Rusty turned onto a quiet street and stopped in his tracks.

He was tired. More tired than he had ever been in his life. The wind picked up, cutting through his coat. He wasn't okay. And maybe... maybe that was the first step. Admitting it.

Saying it, even if just to himself. "I'm not okay," he said aloud.

He thought about Amy. About the way she looked at him lately, like she was scared he was slipping through her fingers. Because he was.

He thought about his daughter, who was still too young to understand why her dad wasn't himself anymore. He thought about Dan, who had seen him, arguably the moment his suit of armour had broken down to expose his heart and soul. Dan, a friend, colleague, and mentor who had told him— without judgment—that he wasn't alone.

Rusty reached into his pocket, fingers trembling as he pulled out his phone.

His contacts blurred together as he scrolled through tears from the howling wind on his face. He stopped on Dan. His thumb hovered over the call button. A lump formed in his throat. Surely, Dan would pick up. He knew Dan would pick up. And if he didn't... Rusty could call his sister. Maybe they wouldn't have the answers. Maybe they wouldn't know what to say. But maybe they would listen. And maybe... maybe that was enough.

He took a deep breath as his finger floated softly above the call button. All he had to do was lower his finger and let the call go through. But then he didn't press the call button.

The moment passed as quickly as it had come, fading like a dying ember swallowed by the cold. Dan didn't care.

His hands fell to his sides, the phone slipping back into his pocket like it had never left as the weight returned, pressing down on him harder than before. He was so close, yet further than ever. Because what was the point? What could he possibly say to fix this?

No one could take away the guilt and change the fact that he had failed.

The cold seeped deeper into his skin, but he barely noticed. He had thought he'd already reached the lowest point. He had thought he had already seen the worst of it. Rock bottom was supposed to be the foundation he built himself up from. But it didn't feel that was even possible because this was different. This wasn't just pain. This was...nothing. Just a hollow, all-consuming emptiness, like the vast room in his dream.

In that moment, something changed. He realized that his darkest moments had once been filled with fear. Would've, should've, and could've, or with anger and grief.

But now? Now, he felt nothing. And that was so much worse.

Rusty turned, his feet moving without thought, carrying him down the street, past flickering streetlights and shuttered storefronts. He didn't know where he was going. And for the first time in his life... he didn't care.

His feet carried him toward a bridge. The air felt even heavier here. The rapids from the river below him were calling his name. 'Funny the way it is,' he thought as he started to sing the lyrics from a Dave Matthews Band song: "Standing on a bridge, watch the water passing under, it must have been much harder when there was no bridge, just water, now the world is small, remember how it used to be, with mountains and oceans and rivers and stars..."

Rusty stopped at the railing, gripping the cold metal with trembling hands. He closed his eyes. Breathed in. Felt the weight settle deeper. It was all too much. The crushing guilt. The endless cycle of waking up and feeling like he couldn't breathe. The silence at home was thick with grief and words neither he nor Amy could say out loud. He thought about her face the night they lost the baby. The way she clutched at him, begging him to fix it. And he couldn't.

He thought of his job that had come to a crashing halt weeks earlier. He had sacrificed his precious time for the thought of losing his professional identity. Time away from his wife and daughter. Time struggling to make a sale. Time frustrated beyond comprehension at the unrelenting pressures of professional sports. Trying to kiss ass. Trying to put a square peg in a round hole and not feeling like he was his true, authentic self the entire time he worked there. The way it had made him jaded, dispassionate, and void of the emotions that had originally attracted him to the industry in the first place.

He had never felt more powerless in his life. He had never felt more like a failure, and it all came crashing down.

His mind was so loud now. A relentless chorus of self-loathing, of regret, of that sickening, gnawing nothingness. It would be so easy. "To change the world," he sang softly, "start with one step. However small, the first step is hardest of all." One moment. And he might die trying.

CHAPTER 47

"Playing Telephone"

Almost four years to the day before the virtual pit beers and long before COVID, social distancing and lockdowns, Amy's hands trembled as she pressed the phone to her ear, listening to the steady ringing on the other end. Dan picked up on the third ring, his voice groggy, unaware of the way the world had just shifted beneath their feet.

"Amy?" he asked, confused. She never called him, let alone this late.

"Dan," her voice cracked. "Have...have you heard from Rusty?"

Dan sat up immediately. "No... what? Why? What's going on?"

"He...he wasn't home when Emma and I got back from my sister's," she said, the panic rising in her throat. "His wallet, his keys—they're on his nightstand. Nothing seems out of place. But he's not here."

Dan swung his legs out of bed and sat up, his heart hammering in his chest. Rusty wasn't the type to just disappear. Sure, Rusty had been struggling—everyone had seen it in flashes—moments where he seemed to drift off just beyond reach, lost in thoughts that clouded his once-bright demeanour. Sometimes, he'd lose his temper unexpectedly, snapping at colleagues, Amy or Emma over trivial matters. His patience had worn thin, and his extreme mood swings became more frequent; one moment, he would laugh heartily, then another, he would be consumed by an unshakeable melancholy, leaving others to wonder what or how it shifted so dramatically.

This erratic behaviour only intensified after he and Amy lost the baby. The subtle signs evolved into more pronounced shifts. Shifts that ultimately cost him his job after he openly expressed his disgust with the newly proposed compensation plan.

But this was beyond erratic... this was something else. Dan had no idea of the deep-seated guilt and crushing grief Rusty had felt because he did not know all the details. He didn't realize the extent of Rusty's isolation, the way he had stopped answering text messages or how he misinterpreted Amy's constant attempts at contact as anger and disappointment instead of panic and fear. His laughter felt forced, and genuine smiles became a rarity, as if expressing joy had become an exhausting chore. Nobody knew that truth, and with each day, it was clear that Rusty was slipping further than he or others could comprehend.

Hours turned into a day. Then another. Calls went unanswered. Texts remained unread. Police were called. And all the while, Amy held their four-year-old daughter close, whispering reassurances she didn't believe.

How could she explain it? How could she one day sit her daughter down and tell her that her daddy just couldn't do it anymore? That the weight of the world finally got to him, dragging him down into the depths of the river below? That the man who had once been so full of life and fought so hard for everyone else had no fight left for himself? That her daddy made a selfish choice, or that her daddy had chosen to give up over her. Now was not the time for those thoughts.

But days stretched into a week. Dan kept this confidential information as long as he could, but rumours, gossip and quiet dread of the inevitable spread.

It was now April 21, 2017. In yet another simple twist of fate, news broke in the worst way possible—fragmented, hushed, passed from person to person like a secret too painful to say out loud. It wasn't an email from HR, not an official statement from the police or Amy, not even a whispered conversation from Dan. It was a text. A goddamn text. Skidooers found him. Alone. On the side of the river about two kilometres from his house. The skidooer had heard Rusty was reported missing. After calling the police, and without thinking, he sent a text to his friend even before the coroner had finished transporting Rusty to the morgue.

It started with Jay. His phone buzzed, and the smirk on his face evaporated. His fingers tightened around his blackberry as he read and reread the message, his brain refusing to process the words. The colour drained from his face, and suddenly, the pit felt suffocating again.

"No..." he whispered. "No..." he repeated over and over again.

He turned to Shane. Shane—always loud, always in motion—froze. His eyes flicked across the screen, once, twice, then a third time, as if reading it again might change the words in the text. For the first time in years, Shane was speechless.

Shane and Jay quietly made the difficult walk to Dan's office. They interrupted his department leadership strategy meeting with Salty and Kristina. They didn't care. It was also probably best that everyone was there because Dan, Salty and Kristina had to know. They closed the door and quietly shared the text Jay received. Once again, the bond of the sales pit challenged them in ways they never dreamed possible.

Amy told Dan she would call him the moment she heard from Rusty or the moment she heard from the police. Dan checked his phone. Nothing. He exhaled loudly, leaning back in his chair while looking at Shane and Jay, almost pleading with them for advice. Salty and Kristina offered little support either. How could anyone?

Was it Dan's responsibility to tell Amy or her responsibility to tell Dan. Did Amy even know the news? So, the five of them sat there, frozen in silence. Waiting.

Dan and the others didn't have to wait long. Dan startled as his phone buzzed. It was Amy calling. He struggled, trying to compose himself quickly. By the fourth ring—the ring before the call would go to voicemail—he finally had the courage to answer.

Amy was hysterical. Dan sat in silence, soul-crushing silence as Amy shared the details she had received from the police who knocked on her door. He calmly motioned for Jay and Shane to take a seat next to Kristina. They both sat on Dan's couch.

Dan rubbed his face hard as if trying to physically wipe away the moment like it was caked on dirt after a Tough Mudder race. Salty sat motionless, gripping the chair handles tight, staring at Dan, hoping the text Jay received was in error or just a sick joke. Jay's knee bounced violently, often hitting the bottom of Dan's desk.

Shane tried to rewind to happier times when he playfully chirped Rusty's ridiculously patterned shirts or when he and

Jay desperately tried to convince Rusty to 'live a little' and come with them on a poorly planned trip. He remembered that Rusty had told him that it was okay not to be okay. That he understood how Shane felt because he had a similar experience. Rusty had bridged the gap between them that day, and Shane now questioned whether he had ever told Rusty how much that conversation meant to him. Now, he didn't have a chance to.

Then his inner thought quickly turned into anger: "You knew he was fucking struggling, and what did you do about it? Nothing. You did nothing!"

Then Dan finally spoke. His voice hoarse and soft. Too soft for Amy to hear, so he repeated himself again. "I'm so sorry, Amy. What...what did they say happened?" Amy confirmed the information in Jay's text—a snowmobiler had found him by the river. Alone. Her devastating words echoed in their heads: that Rusty was gone. Toxicology reports would not be available for over a month, but there was no sign of foul play that day. No evidence of intentional damage or harm. Not cuts, or broken bones.

"Could it have been a tragic accident?" she pleaded with Dan. "Why would he do this?"

Deep down, Dan felt that Rusty was just a defeated soul that had lost the will to live. He asked Amy if there was anything he or the team could do for her. He offered to come by and encouraged her to call him if she needed anything. Even if she needed to talk. He hung up his phone and lowered his head to rest in the shape of a diamond his fingers had made as he put both elbows on his desk. He exhaled deeply. Then another, and another before he couldn't keep his composure together, and he began to cry. And for the first time in a long time, he cried. He cried at the impossible loss—

not just as a friend or colleague, but as a man, son, brother, husband and daddy.

Kristina, Salty, Shane and Jay quickly followed suit, and the four grown men and one woman shared a moment. They cried in Dan's office together. A long, aching silence filled the space before Dan exhaled deeply again.

"We have to tell Frank," he said, nodding his head, knowing that was the right thing to do. "I don't know how to break the news, though."

Shane wiped a tear with his sleeve. "I'll do it." He said as he bravely volunteered to be the one to deliver the news.

"Are you sure?" Salty asked.

"Absolutely not," Shane said. "But we can't tell him over a phone call or text."

Shane was right. This needed to be communicated to Frank in person. So, he quietly left the office and drove the short distance to Frank's house, gripping the wheel so tight his hands and knuckles hurt. He sat in Frank's driveway for what seemed like forever trying to muster up enough courage to be the bearer of bad news. Then he looked up and saw Frank in his living room, investigating why a car was in his driveway. They locked eyes, and when Frank opened the door, he knew something was wrong the second he saw Shane's face. Something was very wrong.

"Shane. What is it?" Frank asked softly, voice already shaking as Shane walked up the walkway.

Shane couldn't respond right away. Seeing his old friend for the first time since he was let go would have been hard enough but under these circumstances? Shane didn't know how to say it. He didn't know how to break it to a man like Frank, who had seen so much and endured so much. So, he just said it without sugarcoating anything.

"He's gone, Frank."

The words hit them both like a freight train.

"No!" was all Frank could muster. That one word. No sarcasm, humour, or exasperation—just a raw, guttural sound that cut through the silence like a surgeon's blade.

Frank's hands started to shake as Shane sadly nodded in confirmation. Shane couldn't contain his emotions and started to cry again. Frank initially stood in shock. His breath taken away from him. Until his legs backed him up on their own, carrying him deeper inside his house like his body had already decided for him. He slowly lowered himself and sat on the stairs, his hands clasped between his knees, shoulders hunched forward as if trying to physically brace against the weight of the words. Shane sat next to him, silent.

Neither of them spoke. Because what the hell was there to say? How did it get to this point?

It was two hours later, and the sales pit had never been this quiet. After Shane volunteered to inform Frank, he, Dan, Kristina, Salty and Jay agreed that Dan could not face telling the team alone. The team needed Dan's leadership and guidance like never before, and needed their colleagues' strength, love and support to show solidarity in this incredibly tragic and challenging situation, too.

People filled the space in front of the photocopier that had held countless impromptu meetings before. This was not just another impromptu meeting. Dan had asked everyone to join his mandatory meeting after they turned off their cell phone and put their desktop ringers on mute. Kelly from reception held all calls. The usual noises—ringing phones, nervous laughter, and deals being closed—was silent. Unnaturally silent.

Dan stood at the front of the room, staring and following Shane as he patrolled the sales pit, ensuring nobody was on phone calls or busy doing something that didn't matter in that moment. He gave Dan a nod after he finished his rounds and walked to take his place next to Dan.

Dan had delivered a lot of bad news in his life, let alone his career, but this was different. His knees felt weak, and his throat felt like he was swallowing molasses. On Dan's left side stood Kristina and Salty. On Dan's right stood Shane, Jay, and now Frank.

Frank, whose presence brought both nostalgia and pain had been unable to come closer to the arena than the gas station. He had returned to the arena and parked in his usual spot before walking down the same stairs he had for over twenty years. It was a painful reminder of his absence from the sales pit. He hadn't even attended a game since his dismissal, and the thought of returning at any other time felt paralyzing, even to pick up his severance cheque, which he asked to have mailed to him.

However, stepping into the office for the first time in over a month to support his colleagues and honour their longtime friend, colleague, and brother was a no-brainer. The moment felt heavy with meaning, as the found family understood the importance of him being there. Frank was a welcomed sight.

They stood together in unison; together was the only way they could share the weight of their collective grief and show that they would keep moving forward. No matter how difficult the journey ahead might be, they did it together.

"I don't..." Dan's voice wavered, and he hated it. He sucked in a breath and tried again. "I don't know how to say this. I don't even know if I can."

As familiar red and glassy eyes looked at him intently waiting, Dan exhaled slowly.

"Rusty's gone."

Guilt and sadness seeped into every corner of the office. A slow, creeping poison with the what-ifs, the should-haves, and the regrets they would carry in their hearts and minds forever.

Shane stood solemnly, staring at the floor. He had already broken down once, screaming into his hands in his car after telling Frank. Now, he just looked hollow. Jay leaned forward; his hands clasped together so tightly his knuckles were bloodless. He kept shaking his head as if denying it could somehow make it not true.

"He..." He hesitated. "They found him this morning. Near the shore of the river, about two kilometres from his house."

A sharp, involuntary inhale from somewhere in the room caught everyone off guard. Someone murmured no under their breath.

Dan didn't say the word. Suicide. He didn't have to. Everyone knew.

"I—" Jay's voice cracked as he tried to speak. His lips were dry, so he stopped himself, breathing hard through his nose. He resorted to simply running a hand through his hair.

"And I know what you're thinking. That we should've done more. That we should've known. But the truth is... sometimes, we don't get the chance." There were a few nods from around the room, but no one looked convinced.

"This isn't fair," Shane muttered, his voice thick with something between grief and anger. "It's not fucking fair."

"None of this is," Kritina said, her eyes shining.

"He should be here," Shane continued, pointing to the pod he shared with Rusty and Jay. "He should be in that chair, bitching about his clients, telling us about his life and showing us those goddamn ugly shoes."

A few half-hearted chuckles, broken and raw. Everyone appreciated what Shane tried to do, but then there was silence again.

Dan's throat tightened. "I don't have the right words. I don't think there are any. But I know one thing—Rusty mattered," Dan said with the most energy he had all day as he pointed to the ground. Then, his energy grew. "He mattered to his wife, Amy. He mattered to his 4-year-old daughter, Emma. He mattered to this team. To the sales pit. To every single one of us and to every single one of his clients. And I don't want any of you to think, for even a fucking second, that you don't matter, or that you have to go through any of your battles alone. Because you all matter. The sales pit is a family!"

Dan continued to gain emotional strength as he made eye contact with everyone around the room. "This has been an absolute grind. It has easily been the most difficult period of the past ten years. Frank, Salty, Shane and I can attest to that. But none of that matters right now. Your family matters. Your mental health...matters." His words rang through the entire office. "Don't be a Goddamn hero by pretending everything is fine when it's not."

Heads nodded slowly. There were more sobs. Like Dan had crawled into everyone's brains and spoke the words they had been thinking about.

"We're gonna figure out how to get through this together. We're going to celebrate and honour him and all his contributions to this entire organization," Dan continued. "I don't know what that looks like yet. It's too early to know. But you can be sure there will be a toast, a gathering, maybe something bigger. But whatever it is, we will do it together.

Because that's what this place is. That's what it's supposed to be. I..." He scanned the room, searching for the right thing to say—something that could make this easier for everyone. But there was nothing. So he just said the only thing that felt true. "I wish he knew how much we fucking loved him."

Jay let out a shuddering breath. Shane wiped his face roughly with his sleeve. Someone in the back started quietly crying again.

That night, Dan, Shane, Frank, Salty, Kristina, and Jay collectively visited Amy, sharing their heartfelt condolences and offering whatever they could to support her in this incredibly difficult time. They understood the weight of her loss and wanted to ensure that she felt surrounded by love and community. After their visit, they gathered at a bar where they had spent countless nights laughing, engaging in spirited debates, and raising a glass to whatever challenges the sales pit had thrown at them that day. As they reminisced about the good times, a sense of purpose began to form among them.

They planned a true celebration of life as a group, acknowledging how precious and fragile life can be. They discussed the importance of honouring their lost friend and supporting those he had left behind.

Frank had one more cardinal rule: that they would commit to getting together every year on the same date to honour their friend.

CHAPTER 48

"Shane Sanders: The Rebuild that Was"

One night, a few weeks after Rusty's suicide, Shane went out alone—not for the chase but just to feel something... different. The enormity and sobering consequences of losing a friend, and the tragic circumstances leading up to it, haunted him. He couldn't stay in that headspace for long, so he thought about work.

Even work had negative connotations. Salty was now leading the inside sales reps, and Kristina sniping him for the Sales Manager role still lingered as well. It wasn't jealousy exactly, but something adjacent to it. Regardless, it was a reminder that life was moving for everyone else. At least that's what it seemed. He thought he could get over it by getting under someone else.

It didn't happen that night.

After about twenty minutes, Shane realized the bar just wasn't his scene. So, by 12:47 a.m., he stepped back into his condo the same way he left—alone. He threw his keys and they clinked and slid onto and off his granite countertop. The place looked like a showroom—engineered hardwood, clean lines, curated lighting, a very expensive Italian leather sofa. Everything in its place.

He opened the fridge. Expired milk. A half-eaten sub from four nights ago. A jar of Grey Poupon that had been more useful as a prop for his ball hockey tournament audition tape than it ever was on a sandwich.

He leaned against the fridge door, phone in hand. Scrolling. Photos of old nights out, birthdays, road trips, office parties, clients who turned into friends, and friends who turned into ghosts. Somewhere between the nostalgia and the silence, he found himself searching again—Capshaw Chemicals – Careers. The same job posting. The recruiter had reached out over a month ago. $170,000 base, big upside, less drama? How was that still available?

Dan had casually talked him out of it at the time, mocking the idea of selling paint for a chemical company with a reputation more toxic than its products. "You'd have to sell your soul," Dan had said. "Then again, you already sold yours twelve years ago."

He smirked at the memory, but it didn't stick.

He moved to his contacts. Tried calling his brother. Hmm...straight to voicemail. Then he tried an old booty call. No answer either. He wasn't expecting one and it wasn't about rekindling anything—it was just... a need to connect.

The truth was, Shane had spent years being the guy who could walk into any room and own it. But lately, it felt more like a character. The bravado, the flirtations, the office antics—they used to be fun. Now, they just felt like muscle memory, and he wasn't sure if he liked that.

He sat down on the edge of the sofa. The same expensive Italian leather that had seen more high-stakes sales calls than genuine conversations. He rubbed his face and sighed.

To Shane, sales still made sense. He liked that there were rules and clear expectations. You play to win the game, and you either win, or you don't. Everything else in life—the feelings, the relationships, the what-ifs—that was the part he never quite figured out. So, he leaned on what he survived on all his life. Results and control.

He grabbed a warm beer from the cupboard. The late-night sports replays were on, but he kept the volume muted. It was just Shane. Just him. The flicker of the screen. And a question he wasn't quite ready to ask himself out loud: What now?

But that night was Shane's 'TSN Turning Point', a feature on TSN hockey broadcasts that highlighted the most significant play or moment in changing the outcome of a game. This time, it was for the better.

In the mornings that followed, he didn't spring into action like he used to. There was no Rocky-style montage, and he tried to stop chasing shiny objects. Unlike before, when he needed immediate gratification, he started to realize that greatness took time. So, Shane started with the only thing he could control: his body.

He went back to the gym in the condo—not to get jacked, not to impress anyone, but to clear his head. His workouts became less about the aesthetics or colour coordinated outfits, and more about repetition. Routine. New muscle memory. Something that didn't lie. He firmly believed 'if you showed up and put in the work, you got stronger. If you didn't, you didn't.'

He also stopped ghosting Jay. The random "yo, you up?" texts were replaced with actual phone calls. They started talking outside of work—not just about fantasy football or work drama—but about life. About aging. About the strange disconnection they both felt between who they were and who they thought they'd be by now.

Neither he nor Jay knew it, but those conversations were slowly helping Shane rewire the way he thought about connection—what it really meant to show up for someone.

Life in the sales pit continued for Shane and with his new lease on lifestyle, he was even better at his job than before. A few weeks later, Shane messaged Kristina.

'Coffee sometime? Just to catch up. Promise no dumb jokes. Well… maybe one or two.'

Her reply came an hour later. 'Saturday. 3 p.m. You're buying.'

They met at a little Italian bistro, whose owner, Antonio made the best double shot Americanos in the city. Kristina wore a charcoal blazer, hair slicked back in a bun. Shane showed up in jeans and a plain black hoodie.

He didn't try to charm her. There was no need to rewrite their history, only learn and move forward. He just sat there. Listened. And somewhere between her sips of a flat white and the awkward silence, he said it out loud for the first time in years.

"I've been struggling." He didn't say it dramatically. Didn't try to dress it up. He just named it. Kristina nodded. She didn't rescue him with sympathy, and he didn't expect her to. But she stayed. And that was enough. She encouraged him to continue to work on himself. To continue being a leader in the organization and to seek professional help. That same night, Shane sat at his computer and Googled therapists. It felt weird at first. Like he was shopping for a mechanic, but for his brain. He looked for clinics with private entrances. No shared waiting rooms. No nosy receptionists asking, "First time?"

He booked a session. He told himself it was just for one hour, to talk through some things. At least that's how he rationalized it. Soon, he was talking about his mother. About how love in his house came on a contingency plan—be good, perform well, don't embarrass anyone. How he'd learned early that vulnerability wasn't safe, and mistakes were liabilities.

He cried once. Not in some big, dramatic movie-scene way. Just quietly. During session three. When the therapist asked him a simple question: "When's the last time you felt like someone really knew you?" He couldn't answer.

But he kept going back. Kept showing up. His benefits only covered the first two and a half sessions, but he didn't care. For the first time in his life, he felt like he was truly investing in himself.

Eventually, the recruiter from Capshaw followed up and told him the job was still his if he wanted it. It definitely was bigger pay and a chance to start fresh. But he didn't take it.

Not because he was scared. Not because of pride. He just knew that reinvention without reflection is a loop, not a ladder. He didn't need a fresh start—he needed to finally finish something without running. So, he stayed. And for the first time in over a decade, Shane changed how he did the job.

He became a mentor. Not because anyone asked him to, but because he saw himself in the new hires—their posture, their overeager pitches, their fear of failure disguised as swagger. So he started hosting short "lunch and learns". Topics like "How to sell without sounding like a tool" and "Why you should probably stop sending 8-paragraph follow-up emails." He learned that last one from he and Jay's experience with Rusty trying to convince his wife to go on the ultimate 'road trip' that somehow involved flying to San Francisco via Las Vegas.

Kristina became a regular part of his life again. Not like before. Something more grounded. More mutual. There were no grand reconciliations. Just check-ins. Moments in time to ask one another 'how are you doing?' and 'I'm here if you need me.'

One night, after wrapping up a brutal renewal stretch, Shane, Jay and Dan sat in the office with takeout and whisky. And for the first time ever, they talked about everything— burnout, shame, identity. No jokes. No filters. Just three men, trying to figure it all out.

By the next season, Shane was leading the charge for change in the office. He and Kristina founded the DEI committee—brought in speakers, pushed for inclusive hiring, and made sure the token posters weren't the only thing changing.

He started attending a local men's group, too. Quietly.

It was awkward at first. Folding chairs. Fluorescent lights. Grown men admitting they didn't have it all figured out. But it worked. Because no one was trying to win. No one was "on."

Just honesty. Messy, raw honesty. He learned how to listen. Really listen. And how to sit in discomfort without needing to crack a joke.

Back at the office, his sharp wit stayed intact. But the cruelty? That slowly disappeared.

He still chirped. Still pushed the occasional buttons but he stayed behind the line now. And if he crossed it, he owned up to it. Apologized. Not with flowers or grand gestures, but with words. "I was out of line. That's on me."

People noticed. The new reps didn't fear him. They sought him out. The women in the office didn't avoid the elevator if they saw him inside. They invited him to meetings.

Jay once said, "It's like someone took Shane and upgraded him to Shane 2.0—but kept the sarcastic software."

And honestly? That felt right.

When COVID hit, the office went dark. Everyone went remote. Slack and Zoom became the new pit. Sales slowed to a crawl. Everyone was spiraling in their own ways. But Shane stayed consistent.

Jay texted him often. Random GIFs. Rants about toilet paper shortages or having to Lysol his bags of chips and cans of Chef Boyardee Ravioli before loading up the car. Shane always replied—even if it was just a thumbs-up, or a meme, or a "still here." Sometimes, that was enough.

At night, after Zoom calls and silent replays and whatever was left of his takeout, Shane opened a notebook. He wrote down the stuff that didn't make it into meetings. The regrets. The little victories. The memories. The things he was learning and unlearning; at least trying to unlearn. It wasn't profound nor was it pretty due his poor penmanship that could compete with a four-year-old's. But it was his thoughts and Shane finally understood something he never had before: You have to stop pretending you're invincible. Sometimes change isn't loud. Sometimes the most powerful thing a person can do is start again—quietly, honestly, and without making a scene.

CHAPTER 49

"The End is the Beginning is the End"

Back to April 21, 2021

Frank looked at Dan in the top centre of his virtual pit beer call. "Hey, Big Boss Man, how does it feel to be back here with all us peasants?"

Dan smirked, lifting his scotch, finding Frank in the bottom left corner, with the beach video playing in the background. "Feeling good, Frank. Feeling pretty good."

"Tell us, Dan-o," Brad cut in. "How's life as a corporate stiff? Did Kent give you any tips on getting out?"

Dan hesitated. "None whatsoever" he said as the call erupted in laughter. "Actually, I take that back. I think Kent knew his priorities better than anyone else in the sales pit. He knew that family was the most important thing, and that you cannot work yourself to death. I respect that more now than ever before. I was too far into it all to realize, but look at my life; actually, look at so many of our lives...we've burnt so many bridges with our spouses, and our kids...was it really worth it? They're the innocent bystanders in all of this."

"That's pretty powerful stuff, Dan. I couldn't agree more," Frank assured.

But Dan remained paused and did not say anything else then because the truth was that he missed how things were. He missed being on the front lines with the sales team. He missed the grind. He missed listening to them bitching about quotas, donut peace offerings, Baconators, and he missed pit beers in real life. Sure, he still participated in the occasional threatening and condescending "what have you done for me lately" sales meeting, but it certainly wasn't the same as when Kent ran the show.

Dan opened his mouth to respond—but a flashback sent him to his old sales manager's office, sitting with Frank, Shane, Kristina, Jay, Salty, Max, and finally, Rusty. He really felt like he let Rusty down. If only he hadn't asked Rusty to join the meeting with him and Kristina. If only he had stopped Rusty from letting his justifiably negative thoughts out to Garry, Wally, and others. Rusty didn't have the same level of cache as the higher-ups, at least not in the same way Dan did.

Milliseconds later, he found himself alone in his office, an empty chair in front of him with Rusty's lanyard draped over it, thinking about the last conversation he had with him.

Rusty sighed, shaking his head. "I don't know if I'm happy, Dan. I'm really struggling. I've been having dark thoughts. Scary thoughts. I don't know if I'll be able to handle them."

Then the chat went silent as Dan saw Rusty still in the pit. Still fighting the fight. Dan just watched him.

Frank leaned back, stretching. "Well, I'll tell you this, boys—life has never been better."

Bryan nodded. "Same here. Sleeping better. No stress. No anxiety attacks at two in the morning. I've stopped drinking too! And I took up farming, if you can believe it! I have my own miniature donkey, and I sell honey from my beehives at the local farmer's market... outdoors and socially distanced, of course. Next time I see you, I'll bring you some!"

Brad sipped his drink. "I still can't actually enjoy a fucking hockey game now. You know how shitty that is? To sit there like a normal fan while still mentally calculating which sections need a push? I haven't even been back to a game. I just can't do it."

"Christ, Brad, that was two years ago!" Salty said. "The team could use your support!"

"I don't owe the team shit!"

"I was back at least..." Frank started counting on his fingers, then his other hand. "At least four games this season, before the COVID lockdown. Last season? Found a way to get to maybe ten?"

Steve grinned. "I can bet on the games now. Legally. But I don't..."

Brad rolled his eyes. "Yeah, we all remember how that went. You and your parlays!"

"Big ol' Frank loves me some of 'dos parfaits!" Frank said, licking his lips.

Steve smirked. "Hey, I made a shit-ton of money on GameStop stock too!"

Jay nearly spit out his drink. "Holy shit, Steve, you were right about that!"

"I told you, man. You laughed at me, said it was a meme stock, but when that thing hit three hundred a share—see ya!"

"Okay, okay! I cashed out at the top, didn't I?"

Brad snorted. "Yeah and then dumped it all into fucking Dogecoin—see ya!" he mocked.

Frank shook his head, laughing into his beer. "That's why I stuck to Bitcoin, boys. Started mining right after they shut down Disney in March 2020."

Dan raised an eyebrow. "You? Mining Bitcoin? Wait, what's significant about Disney shutting down in March?"

Frank smirked. "I really don't know. It was the first time Disney shut down since World War two, and that was a big deal. Disney is kind of my barometer, I guess. If she's going down, I just ask, 'What would Mickey do?' But yeah, I ordered a couple of graphics cards off a guy on Kijiji and built a rig in my garage. Thing sounded like a fucking jet engine, but it made me some monnnnnnneeeeey."

Brad cracked up. "That's why you were bitching about your hydro bill, isn't it?"

Frank nodded. "Hydro bill tripled and then tripled again. But whatever, I paid for it in crypto, baby!"

Shane leaned back. "Frank, tell me how you managed to get into Bitcoin, yet you didn't know how to turn on your camera?"

Frank winced. "Learn proper penmanship, Shane! Besides, let's just say I had a LOT more time on my hands back then, no thanks to Garry fucking Breckenridge."

Brad groaned, shaking his head. "I know, right?"

Frank held up a hand. "Look, boys, I will admit, if Garry didn't swoop in..." he started before pausing. "Let me start over... Garry fucking Breckenridge," Frank muttered. "That guy did more damage in six months than a goddamn wrecking ball or... my first marriage."

The Virtual Pit Beers call erupted in laughter.

"Seriously, I have more fond memories of a fart than I do of that guy," Frank continued, taking a final sip of his beer. "And not even a good fart. Like, one of those deeply concerning ones that make you stop what you're doing and re-evaluate your life choices. I bet you get those all the time, Shane!"

Bryan choked on his drink. "Jesus Christ, Frank."

Dan chuckled, but it was hollow.

Garry Breckenridge arrived like a cold front in February—sudden, ruthless, and impossible to ignore.

He slashed ticket sales reps like they were nothing more than line items on a spreadsheet. He gutted fan development initiatives that had taken years to build. He cut sponsorship activation staff because, in his infinite wisdom, "We'll just make the ticket guys sell it."

It was a massacre. A bloody, fucking massacre.

Garry's goal had been simple: reshape the department in his own image. It had worked before, so why wouldn't it work here? He wanted control and obedience. A yes-man culture. No resistance, no questions—just good soldiers marching to his tune.

And for a while, it looked like he had succeeded.

"Without you and Rusty, Frank, the pit was quiet," Jay started.

Frank exhaled, shaking his head. "That's never a good sign."

"Sure, the new sales mutts followed their orders," Jay continued. "And Garry was happy because they were a bit more... impressionable?"

"The old guard was gone." Frank nodded.

"Exactly," Dan said, leaning forward. "But what Garry didn't understand about professional sports was that culture isn't built overnight. You don't just trade out the veterans and expect rookies to take their spots."

Salty, arms crossed, added: "Each time he made a decision, client trust eroded even more. The longtime fans, the ones who had Rusty and Frank's numbers saved in their phones? They didn't want to deal with some 23-year-old kid reading off a script."

Kristina shook her head. "And within a few months, the cracks were showing. Sales plummeted. The rookies didn't have the experience or relationships to sell at the same level. Not even Salty's leadership could save them." She turned to him. "There really wasn't anything you could have done, Sal."

Frank smirked. "I'm sure within a few months, Garry had lost the room, even with the new mutts."

Jay raised his glass. "Totally."

Dan chuckled. "Because even ownership was starting to notice. They had brought Garry in to fix things." He then paused. "Instead, he burnt the house down."

Frank sighed, swirling his beer. "Oh, to be a fly on the wall, to watch Garry struggling, fighting to keep his job."

"Would've been a hell of a sight," Jay agreed.

Because then, just when the dust settled—when everyone thought they might finally get used to the new, shittier reality with fewer opportunities, less thank-yous, and more hassle—as Rusty had predicted, both he and Garry were gone.

"The sales team was left in capable hands," Frank admitted, tipping his bottle toward Kristina, Salty, and Dan. "When these COVID restrictions are over, God willing, this team's turnaround will be your legacy. No thanks to Garry."

Jay snorted. "Dude, he didn't even bother saying goodbye."

Shane, who had been quiet, suddenly piped up. "Who didn't? I didn't need a goodbye from Garry!"

"No shit," Jay shot back.

Frank chuckled, shaking his head. "Would you say goodbye if you'd just burnt an entire department to the ground? A crop duster doesn't stick around to see if the crops are okay." He took a sip of his beer. "Garry Breckenridge— epic clown and crop duster extraordinaire."

Shane laughed. "Good ol' Frank, always able to insert a little subtle humour in every conversation."

Kristina sighed. "I still can't believe he bailed for Croatia."

Dan smirked. "Fewer COVID restrictions."

"Croatia doesn't extradite to Canada, either!" Frank joked.

Kristina raised an eyebrow. "Rules didn't apply to Garry."

Dan sighed, tapping his fingers against his glass. "Let this be a lesson to us all. Trust your gut. If something smells like shit, looks like shit, chances are—"

"As Rusty said, it's fucking bullshit," Jay finished, nodding.

Dan exhaled sharply. "Breckenridge was never going to stick around. We were just a stepping stone. Another glossy photo on his wall of flames... I mean, wall of fame." He smirked. "His words, not mine."

There was a pause before Frank took a long sip of his new beer, exhaled, and muttered, "...But you know what?" Frank sighed. "I'd have probably died in that pit of a massive heart attack if Garry hadn't done his best job of getting me the fuck out of there."

Kristina grinned. "So what you're saying is... Garry saved your life?"

Frank scowled. "Don't put that evil on me, Krissy!"

The call erupted in laughter.

Dan interjected. "I think it's safe to say that everyone, regardless of whether you still work here or not, has all had, and all will have a 'Garry'."

Frank nodded. "I have three Garry's right now!"

But Dan just sat there, thinking. Because as much as they all hated Garry, as much as they all cursed his name, maybe Frank was right. Maybe Garry getting rid of them had saved them all.

"You know what?" Frank continued, "I miss all our little inside jokes. I could totally write about the trials and tribulations of working in professional sports. Actually, scratch that...Rusty would have written one hell of a book about this place."

"He always had a way with words" Kristina acknowledged.

"He absolutely did. And besides, we know that all of us would be in it. Because, as we've already established, you're all characters!"

"Including you, Frank?" Dan chuckled.

"Dut dut dut dut....especially me, Daniel! And I'm sure some of his portrayals or stories would seem logical to the people who read it, and chances are, if you..."

He paused, then smirked. "If you knew what to look for, you'd find the real gems. Little Easter eggs he would have hidden throughout the story. Inside jokes. Random throwaway lines or snippets that only we would understand. It would be like...like a secret code." Frank grinned, his eyes now the size of toonies. "He'd obviously take tremendous liberties, and I can only imagine how he'd portray Garry...but I know he would have a lot of fun...poking fun at how absolutely ass-backwards some things were....because they were," Frank said, pointing at them all.

"Like the infamous 'Tiny Dancer moment—you know the one." Dan winked.

Everyone laughed, even Kristina, who nearly accidentally snorted her drink.

"Or random references," Shane continued. "Like that time we all wore matching polos to the staff party without realizing it, and someone's wife said we looked like the worst boy band of all time."

"You mean The Sales Hits?" Jay grinned.

"Exactly!"

"Or in your case, The Sales Shits!" Frank corrected. "But yes, stuff like that!"

"You'd read a chapter and think, 'Wait... was that line about me?'" Dan added.

"And you'd be right" Frank nodded. "Or at least...half right... or maybe you'd be wrong, who knows, there'd really be no way of knowing, ya know?"

"But would the book be a memoir or just an observation?" Kristina asked, raising an eyebrow.

"It would be tactfully done, but it would have to be one tiny window into the world of professional sports. Because writing about everything to do with sales...that would be an impossible task, Krissy. Some things just can't be written. Some things are better off being experienced. And some things are just...better left unsaid," Frank said, his tone shifting as the grin faded into something softer. "I wouldn't touch the politics. God knows there's already enough of that bullshit going on in the world. Knowing Rusty, I know it wouldn't be about throwing anyone under the bus."

"It'd be about the people," Dan added. "The relationships. The laughs. The heartbreak. The weird little moments that somehow meant everything."

He paused, letting the weight of his words settle. "Fuck, we could all write a book one day. Maybe one day I will. But it wouldn't be my place to out anyone, or to make fun of someone who couldn't handle it. It wouldn't be about mocking. If someone struggled, or broke down, or walked away—that's not a punchline. That's life, and I think it would be very important to talk about how important it is to be vulnerable."

Shane looked down, then back up again, his voice steady. "I know it would come from a place of love. Of respect. I bet you his portrayal of me would be off the charts. People would read about me...or...or you Franky, or whoever, and would think, 'do these people really exist?' and 'wow, his character development is strong.' That...man, that would be totally epic."

"The ultimate tribute," Jay added.

Shane continued. "If you worked in the Sales Pit, he'd want you to know how much it meant to him to have worked alongside me...I mean, all of us—even if we only shared a few months, or a few shifts, or even just one really bad game night. It mattered. That experience mattered."

Frank leaned in.

"And if you didn't work in this Sales Pit, or never worked in sales at all, I think the book would still want you to understand that it's not all about going to games, meeting players, or wearing team gear like it's some shiny dream job. This shit is hard. It's real. It's thankless most days. It's not for the faint of heart. But damn, it teaches you a lot."

"It couldn't be written about the sales pit today," Salty started. "It would have to be written about back in the day. Long before cancel culture started calling bullshit on toxic behaviour. So much has changed, arguably for the better. It took some time, but I'm still proud to work here."

"Hey, having experienced our sales pit, and currently, a slightly different sales pit, I can honestly say that it's the same shit, different pile. But what's not the same, and what makes this place, totally different, is the people."

Dan looked around his screen, letting his eyes linger on each familiar face.

"I'd want someone reading it to feel like they were right there with us—sitting in that dusty old pit, eating donuts off a filing cabinet, chirping each other between calls, wondering how we got here and how we'd survive another season. It wouldn't be a tell-all. It would absolutely be a tribute."

He smiled, raising his drink toward the camera. "A tribute to the ones who sold the dream..."

"But lived the nightmare?" Bryan interrupted.

"I wouldn't necessarily say that, Bry," Frank corrected. "Those who sold the dream, and somehow, didn't lose themselves completely in the process."

As the conversation flowed around him, Dan sat still, listening, just taking it all in.

Frank interrupted the chatter, raising his bottle one final time. "Hey, hey! Shut up! Everyone!" His voice was much softer now. "It's great to see how everyone has moved on and how each of Garry's casualties found a new, happier lease on life." He exhaled. "That is... everyone except Rusty. Can we all just acknowledge...we didn't get to say goodbye to Rusty?"

The call fell silent. There was an even longer pause. Frank lifted his beer slightly. "Miss you, pal. See you on the other side, man."

And one by one, like they had done on the same day for the past four years, they all raised their glasses.

Jay swirled his tequila in his glass, throat tight, memories flashing through his mind. These people had been more than colleagues, more than just friends. They had all been a piece of their shared history, a brother and sister from another mister in arms. For some, that chapter had closed, for others, that chapter continued to define who they were, for the better.

No one said much after that. They didn't need to. Because they all knew the same thing: Rusty should have been there, laughing along with them. And no matter how much time passed, there would always be an empty seat at the table where he once sat.

On Mental Health

The Sales Pit is a story about men's mental health. For generations, men have been taught that emotions are a liability—that strength lies in silence and self-sufficiency. But unaddressed pain lingers and ultimately takes its toll. Suppressing emotions isolates individuals rather than building resilience, making it harder to connect and increasing the risk of self-destruction. This book challenges that outdated mindset. This book uncovers the demons that come with high-stakes environments, the burnout no one warns you about, and the silent battles fought behind closed doors.

Like hockey and sales, and as Bessel van der Kolk coined, 'the body keeps score'—often in ways we fail to notice, and the cost of ignoring it is greater than we've been led to believe. Unresolved trauma doesn't just linger in the mind; it embeds itself in the body, showing up as chronic stress, tension, and illness. It follows you into your next job, the next chapter of your life, even your relationships—whispering that you're never truly safe and that the rug could be pulled out from under you at any moment. Some people get so sick that they can't even move on to the next job. They remain stuck, drained, and unable to break free from the damage left behind because it's often just too much to handle without proper support.

But hockey and sales are two male-dominated industries that have long been built on competition, excess, and the relentless pursuit of success. In both worlds, toughness isn't just valued; it's expected. You must push through pain, shake off setbacks, and, whenever possible, never show weakness.

For many men, professional sports is the ultimate dream— the glory, the brotherhood, the rewards. But no one talks about what happens when that dream fades into a nightmare. The same goes for sales. The high-pressure grind, the "always be closing" mentality, and the belief that your worth is measured by your numbers or status—until one day, you realize you're running on empty, still chasing that dream.

To survive in the sales and sports industries, one often needs to exude dominance, resilience, and bravado. Sensitive and emotional men like Rusty and Max don't just struggle—they're often chewed up and spit out. Sensitivity is often punished in industries that reward this level of bravado, forcing men to either adapt to the system and fit in or risk being left out and left behind. In professional sports, drinks after work aren't optional; they're expected. Deals are scaled in lavishly hosted suites, and the biggest closers like Shane aren't just good at sales—they're masters of the game, the ones who work hard, party harder, and wake up to do it all over again. It's a culture of excess—money, power, sex, and status—all dangled like a prize for those who can keep up.

But beneath the surface, the cracks start to show. The pressure to perform, to be "on" at all times, to suppress anything that looks like weakness—it grinds people down. At some point, the drinking stops being fun. The competition stops being healthy. The persona becomes a mask, and before you know it, the game is playing you instead of the other way around.

It's the dark side of success, the part no one wants to talk about. But it's real. And for many men, it's a trap they don't escape until it's too late.

Mental health is at the core of this story because it comes from learned experiences. I lived it. The dream and the nightmare. I did everything I could possibly do in professional sports aside from winning a championship. Even though I am no longer in that industry, I still live it.

Anxiety, depression, and PTSD didn't fade when my time in professional sports ended. They followed me, lingering long after, shaping my days and disrupting my nights. But were my struggles caused by my time in pro sports? Hardly. I was battling long before that. If anything, the relentless grind of the sales pit only poured gasoline on the fire.

For years, I told myself to push through. To grind. To tough it out. Because that's what we were taught. In the sales pit, struggling wasn't an option. You hit your numbers, kept your head down, and didn't complain. If you did, there was always someone waiting to take your spot—and your sexy business card.

The weight of it all is crushing, and survival isn't guaranteed without support. Thankfully I had and continue to have a support system. Family, friends and therapists who pulled me back to land when I thought I was drowning. Who offered me a safe space to speak my mind, a friendly, empathetic ear and made sure my concerns and struggles were important. Not everyone has that. Not everyone is so lucky.

Even today, I struggle. Even though I have everything I need—family, friends, an exciting career, opportunities to travel and do the things I love doing, I still struggle. I don't think a day goes by that negative, spiralling thoughts haven't crept in, quietly whispering that my kids are better off without me, or that I don't matter, or that I am not good enough. Thoughts of hanging myself or jumping off a bridge. My therapist introduced me to Dr. Dan Siegal, whose science-backed technique to calm spiralling thoughts is to actually put your feelings into words, or as he called it, 'name it to tame it.' This book has been a therapeutic process of naming my emotions and attempting to tame over thirteen years of racing thoughts. The technique has helped. My racing, spiralling thoughts haven't broken me yet. But it still might.

Because that's the scariest thing about mental health—the unknown. Trauma lingers. It doesn't take much for thoughts to spiral, either. Even relatively trivial or small things like a triggering commercial, a vague email, a car driving by in the middle of the night with a loud muffler or just a messy kitchen may not be enough to push someone over the edge, but as we learned in The Sales Pit, even when you thought you had things relatively under control, 'things got out of control.' It's never just one thing. It's often death by a thousand cuts.

It's time we acknowledge that given all the pressures of everyday life and today's social and political climate, it's very easy to feel overwhelmed. For me, it's being a dad, a son, a partner, an employee, a leader, a homeowner, a co-parent, an ordinary decent human being. Fuck, it takes a lot of work, strength and endurance, doesn't it? And society doesn't help our cause either because society often glorifies a different type of endurance and strength—athletes playing through injuries, first responders carrying trauma, professionals sacrificing everything for success. That needs to change. Fuck bravado. Fuck silence. Fuck outdated definitions of weakness.

Throughout The Sales Pit, real strength isn't suffering in silence; it's knowing when to ask for help and when to ask if someone you care about needs help. We may find ourselves, or see others struggling so deep that it's difficult to see the light at the end of the tunnel. There are so many thoughts and feelings living under the surface. We need to find ways to bring them to the surface and turn thoughts into words. Words of humility. "Help. Words of encouragement. "I'm here for you. I believe in you." Words seeking a friendly ear or empathy. "I hear what you are saying."

And that's why this book matters. Too many people often suffer in silence, believing they have to endure it alone. But they don't. The conversation around mental health has grown louder, but awareness isn't enough. Access to real support remains a privilege, not a given.

Today, a heightened awareness of mental health has exposed the urgent need for better funding and support for vulnerable populations—at-risk youth, the homeless, LGBTQ+ individuals, low-income families, and survivors of domestic violence. The mental health crisis in our society is deeply intertwined with issues of access and equity, revealing how vast swathes of the population remain underserved.

The stigma and perception discourage many, especially men from reaching out, further perpetuating cycles of suffering that could be alleviated with proper support. Even for those fortunate enough to have health benefits that include mental health treatment, the reality often falls painfully short.

Many insurance plans provide only a meagre $500 in annual coverage for mental health services—a sum that barely scratches the surface of what individuals require for effective treatment. As a result, many are limited to just a handful of therapy sessions before being forced to cope alone, suffering in silent isolation without the critical support they desperately need.

For too many, this leads to self-medication—whether through prescription drugs, alcohol, gambling, food, sex, or social media. Temporary fixes that numb the pain rather than heal it. The cycle continues, the crisis deepens, and real solutions remain out of reach.

A significant theme of this book revolves around talking about feelings and that discussion and vulnerability isn't weakness—it's survival. When men suppress their emotions, they isolate themselves, making it harder to seek help when they need it most.

Open conversations about mental health create space for real connections. Candid discussions become healthier coping mechanisms, and together with proper support systems, opening up shows that we are not suffering alone.

Through some of my discussions with friends, family, and colleagues who lived this way, a few said it was like I crawled into their heads and spoke words they had been meaning to say or express for years. I hope this book inspires everyone to speak what's on their mind. To live their authentic self and be ok to not be ok.

Beyond men battling the expectations of toughness, The Sales Pit also addresses how women like Kristina face a different kind of fight—the struggle to be taken seriously in arenas built to exclude them. Her meteoric rise shattered glass ceilings in an industry that often resists change, proving that success doesn't have to fit the mould. But breaking barriers doesn't mean breaking free from pressure. While women fight to prove they belong, men fight the silent war of proving they're enough. Different battles, same cost.

This book aims to illuminate those hidden battles, giving voice to neglected emotions. It redefines strength—not as mere endurance but as the courage to acknowledge feelings, share burdens, and seek help.

Because no one should have to fight alone.

Chris Mustakas is a Canadian author, storyteller, and proud father of two. Born in Waterloo, Ontario and now living in Ottawa, he balances family life, endless creative projects, and a career rooted in marketing, communication, and leadership.

Professionally, Chris is the Chief Marketing Officer for Ferrari & Associates Insurance and Financial Services, a boutique brokerage known for bespoke solutions and high-touch service. He holds an Honours Arts degree in Speech Communication with a minor in Human Resources from the University of Waterloo, as well as an MBA and a Master of Recreation Administration from the University of New Brunswick.

After grad school, Chris spent over five years working for a professional hockey team—doing everything except hoisting a Stanley Cup. His time there was both formative and bittersweet, laying the groundwork for many of the themes explored in his writing.

Though this novel marks his official debut, Chris is no stranger to the written word. He's contributed to newspapers, ghostwritten speeches, and helped others find their voice through storytelling. His work often explores resilience, mental health, identity, and the humour found in unexpected places.

Outside of work and writing, Chris is an avid collector of vinyl records, sports memorabilia, port wine, and whiskey. He's a longtime fan of live music and can frequently be found in the crowd at concerts—especially when Dave Matthews Band is on tour.

Chris wears his heart on his sleeve (often under a bold shirt) and believes in the power of words to connect, challenge, and heal. He's also a fierce advocate for mental health, drawing on his own experiences to help reduce stigma and encourage honest conversations.

He prefers his orange juice unpasteurized, his records analog, and his stories deeply human.